SILENCED

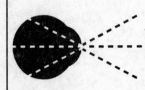

This Large Print Book carries the
Seal of Approval of N.A.V.H.

SILENCED

KRISTINA OHLSSON

THORNDIKE PRESS
A part of Gale, Cengage Learning

GALE
CENGAGE Learning®

Detroit • New York • San Francisco • New Haven, Conn • Waterville, Maine • London

GALE
CENGAGE Learning

Copyright © 2010 by Kristina Ohlsson.
English language translation © 2013 by Simon & Schuster, Inc., and Simon & Schuster UK.
Originally published in Swedish as *Tusenskönor.*
Thorndike Press, a part of Gale, Cengage Learning.

Thorndike Press® Large Print Core.
The text of this Large Print edition is unabridged.
Other aspects of the book may vary from the original edition.
Set in 16 pt. Plantin.

LIBRARY OF CONGRESS CATALOGING-IN-PUBLICATION DATA

Ohlsson, Kristina, 1979–
  [Tusenskönor. English]
  Silenced / by Kristina Ohlsson.
    pages ; cm. — (Thorndike Press large print core)
  ISBN-13: 978-1-4104-5876-6 (hardcover)
  ISBN-10: 1-4104-5876-8 (hardcover)
  1. Large type books. I. Title.
PT9877.25.H57T8713 2013b
839.73'8—dc23   2013006610

Published in 2013 by arrangement with Atria Books, a division of Simon & Schuster, Inc.

SILENCED

■ ■ ■ ■

IN THE BEGINNING

■ ■ ■ ■

Such a refuge ne'er was given.

The meadow with its grassy greenness and wildflowers had always been hers. It had not been particularly hard to make a deal with her sister; all she had to do was agree that she could have the attic room in the summerhouse. She would never understand how her sister could accept a swap like that — a boring old attic room for a meadow. But she kept quiet. After all, her sister might decide to impose further demands on her.

The meadow, overgrown and left to run wild, was beyond the boundary of their garden. When she was younger, the tallest plants had reached right up to her chin. Now she was older, they only came up to her waist. She strode through the grass with light, easy movements and searching eyes, felt the flowers and stalks grazing her bare legs. The flowers had to be picked in silence, otherwise it would not work. There had to be seven different kinds and they had to be picked on midsummer's eve and put under her pillow. Then she would see him, the man she was going to marry.

At least that's what she had thought when she was little and picked midsummer flowers for the very first time. Her sister had teased her.

"It's Viktor you want to see," she said with a laugh.

She had clearly been naïve and stupid, even back then. It was not Viktor at all, but someone else. Someone secret.

After that first time she had repeated the same ritual every year. She was too big now to believe in that superstitious old stuff anymore, of course, but it still felt like an important thing to do. After all, there wasn't exactly much else to keep her occupied, she noted cynically. Year after year her parents insisted that they come and celebrate midsummer out here in the country, and every time it felt more of a trial. This year it was even worse, because she had been invited to her friend Anna's party. Anna's parents were having a big midsummer celebration and their children's friends were invited, too.

But her dad wouldn't let her go.

"We'll celebrate midsummer the way we always do," he said. "Together. That's the way it's going to be, as long as you're still at home."

Panic swept over her. Couldn't he see how unreasonable he was being? It would be years before she could even begin to think about leaving home. Her sister's disloyal behavior didn't help, either. She was never invited to parties, anyway, and thought being on their own with their parents in the country was fine. She even seemed to like the peculiar guests who emerged from the basement at dusk and were made welcome on the glazed veranda, where Mum let the venetian blinds down to make it difficult to see in.

She hated them. Unlike the rest of the family, she found it impossible to feel any sympathy or pity for them. Scruffy, smelly people who didn't take responsibility for their own lives. Who couldn't think of anything more sensible to do than lurk in a basement out in the sticks. Who were satisfied with so pathetically little. She was never satisfied. Never.

"You must love your neighbor," her dad would say.

"We must be grateful for what we've got," said her mum.

She had stopped listening to them a long time ago.

She caught sight of him just as she was picking the fourth flower. He must have made some sort of sound, otherwise she would never have noticed him there. She swiftly raised her focused gaze from the meadow and flowers, and her eyes were dazzled by the sun. Against the light he was no more than a dark silhouette, and it was impossible to see his age or identity.

She screwed up her eyes and shaded them with her hand. Oh yes, she knew who he was. She had seen him from the kitchen window a couple of evenings ago, when Dad came home late with the latest batch of guests. He was taller than most of them. Not older, but taller. Sturdier. He had a very distinct jawline that made him look the way American soldiers used to in films. Square-jawed.

They both stood stock-still, eyeing each other.

"You're not allowed out," she said with a haughty look, although she knew there was no point.

None of that lot in the basement ever spoke any Swedish.

Since he did not move or say anything, she sighed and went back to picking her flowers.

Harebell.

Oxeye daisy.

Behind her, he was on the move, slowly. She glanced furtively back, and wondered where he could be going. Saw that he had come closer.

She and her family had only ever been abroad on one occasion. Just once they went on a normal package holiday, sunbathing and swimming in the Canaries. The streets were teeming with stray dogs that ran after the tourists. Their dad got very good at chasing them away.

"Shoo," he would roar, throwing a stone in some other direction.

It worked every time. The dog left them and went chasing after the stone he had thrown.

The man in the meadow reminded her of the stray dogs. There was something unpredictable in his eyes, something indecipherable. Maybe anger, too. She was suddenly unsure what he would do next. Throwing a stone did not seem an option. One glance toward the house confirmed what she already knew, that her parents and sister had taken the car into town to get some fresh fish for the celebration dinner. Another ludicrous so-called tradition her parents had invented to preserve their image of a normal family. As always, she said she didn't want to go with them, preferring to pick her flowers in peace and quiet.

"What do you want?" she asked irritably.

Irritably and with a growing sense of alarm. There was nothing wrong with her instincts, she recognized the scent of real danger. And this time, all her senses were telling her she'd got to take control of the situation.

The flower stalks felt rough in her hand as she clasped them tight. She only had one left to pick. A humble daisy. A weed with pretensions, her dad liked to call it.

The man took a few more steps toward her. Then he just stood there, a few meters from her. A broad, sneering grin spread slowly across his face. And at that moment she knew what he had come for.

Her legs were quicker than her thoughts. Her spinal reflex signaled menace and at the same instant she broke into a run. The edge of the garden was less than a hundred meters away; she shouted for help again and again. Her piercing cries soaked into the silence of the meadow. The dry earth muffled the sound of her springing steps and the heavy thud as he brought her down after only twenty meters' flight. Almost as if he had known from the outset that she wouldn't get away and had just let her run for the thrill of the chase.

She fought like an animal as he tossed her over onto her back and wrenched at her clothes, so forceful and methodical that her overheated brain registered that this was something he must have done before.

And when it was all over and she lay there weeping in the hollow their bodies had made in the green depths, she knew this was something to which she could never reconcile herself. In her clenched fist, every knuckle raw from her hopeless fight, she was still clutching the summer nosegay. She dropped it as if it were burning her fingers. The flowers were entirely redundant now. She already knew whose face she would see in her dreams.

When her parents' car pulled up outside the house, she was still lying in the meadow, unable to get up. The clouds looked as though they were playing a clumsy game in the blue sky. The world seemed unchanged, though her own was shattered forever. She lay there in the meadow until they realized she was missing and came out to look for her. And by the time they found her, she had already become another person.

■ ■ ■ ■

THE PRESENT

■ ■ ■ ■

Though He giveth or He taketh,
Our Father His children ne'er forsaketh;
His the loving purpose solely
To preserve them pure and holy.

■ ■ ■ ■

FRIDAY,
FEBRUARY 22, 2008

■ ■ ■ ■

STOCKHOLM

Unaware that he would soon be dead, he delivered his final lecture with great enthusiasm and commitment. Friday had been a long day, but the hours had passed quickly. His audience was attentive, and it warmed Jakob Ahlbin's heart that so many people besides himself were interested in the subject.

When he realized just a few days later that all was lost, he would briefly wonder if it had been his last lecture that did it. Whether he had been too open in the question-and-answer session, revealed that he was in possession of knowledge nobody wanted him to have. But he did not really think so. Up until the very moment of his death he was convinced it would have been impossible to ward off disaster. When he felt the pressure of the hard hunting pistol against his temple, everything was already over. But it did not stop him from feeling great regret that his life had to end there. He still had so much to give.

Over the years, Jakob had given more lectures than he could remember, and he knew he had put his talent as a fine speaker to good use. The content of his speech was usually much the same, as were the questions that followed it. The audience varied. Sometimes its members had been instructed to attend, sometimes they sought him out of their own accord. It made no difference to Jakob. He was at ease on the podium no matter what.

He generally began by showing the pictures of the boats. Perhaps it was a mean trick, but he knew that it always hit the spot. A dozen people in a boat that was far too small, week after week, increasingly exhausted and desperate. And like a faint mirage on the horizon there was Europe, like a dream or a flight of the imagination, something they were never meant to experience in real life.

"We think this is an unknown phenomenon for us," he would start. "We think it belongs to another part of the world, something which has never happened to us and never will."

The picture behind him quietly changed and a map of Europe came up on the screen.

"Memories are short sometimes," he sighed. "We choose not to remember that not so many decades ago, Europe was in flames and people were fleeing in panic from one country to another. And we forget that barely a century ago, more than a million Swedes decided to leave this country for a new start in America."

He ran his hand through his hair, stopped for a moment, and checked that his audience was listening. The picture behind him changed again, now showing Max von Sydow and Liv Ullmann, a still from the film of Vilhelm Moberg's Emigrants series.

"A million people," he repeated loudly. "Don't for one minute be fooled into thinking Karl-Oskar and Kristina saw their trip to America as anything but a punishment. Don't imagine they wouldn't have stayed in Sweden if they could. Just think what it would take to force you to make a break like that, to leave your old life behind and start all over again in another continent without a krona in your pocket and with no more of your possessions than you could cram into one pitiful bloody suitcase."

The expletive was deliberate. A clergyman swearing was always highly shocking.

He knew very well where he could expect to run into opposition. Sometimes it came when he showed the Karl-Oskar and Kristina picture. Sometimes it was later. This afternoon it happened straight after the first time he swore. A youth sitting in a row near the front clearly found it provocative and raised his hand before Jakob could go on.

"Excuse me interrupting," he said in a shrill voice, "but how the hell can you draw a parallel like that?"

Jakob knew what was coming next, but still frowned, playing along for the good of the cause.

"Karl-Oskar and Kristina and all the other Swedes who went to America worked themselves into the ground when they got there. They *built* that damn country. They learned the language and adopted the culture. Got jobs straightaway and kept their heads down. This lot who come over to Sweden nowadays don't do any of that. They live in their own little ghettos, don't give a shit about learning Swedish, live on benefits, and don't bother to get jobs."

The hall went quiet. A sense of unease swept through the audience like an unquiet soul. Unease that there might be trouble, but also the fear of being exposed as someone who shared the young man's opinions. Quiet muttering spread through the hall and Jakob waited a few moments longer. He had

24

often tried to explain this to any politicians who would still listen: staying silent did nothing to defuse thoughts and frustrations like those just expressed.

The young man shifted in his seat, folded his arms, squared his chin, and waited for the clergyman to answer. Jakob let him wait, assuming an expression to indicate that the comment had come as news to him. He looked at the picture behind him, and then back at his audience.

"Do you think that's what they thought when they made the journey here? Take the ones who paid up to fifteen thousand dollars to get from burning Iraq to Sweden. Did they dream of a life in a crummy sixties complex from the *Homes for a Million* program, on some sink estate way out on the edge of the city? Of being stuck there with ten other adults in a three-room flat, day after day, with nothing to do, separated from their family? Alone? Because fifteen thousand is how much it costs for *one* person to make the trip."

He held one long finger straight up in the air.

"Do you think they ever, in their wildest imagination, could have thought that they would be met with the sort of exclusion we're giving them? Offering a trained doctor a job as a taxi driver if he's lucky, and someone less educated not even that."

Being careful not to look reproachful, Jakob turned his eye on the young man who had spoken.

"I believe they thought like Karl-Oskar and Kristina. I think they expected it would be like getting to America a hundred years ago. Where the sky was the limit for anyone prepared to put their back into it, where hard work paid off."

A young woman caught Jakob's gaze. Her eyes were shining and she had a crumpled paper tissue in her hand.

"I believe," he said gently, "there are very few people who would *choose* to sit staring at the wall of a flat on an estate if they felt there was any alternative. That's the conclusion my work has brought me to, anyway," he added.

And that was about where the mood changed. Exactly as it always did. The audience sat quietly, listening with growing interest. The pictures kept on changing, keeping pace as his tale of the immigrants who had come to Sweden over recent decades unfolded. Painfully sharp photographs documented men and women shut in a lorry, driving across Turkey and on to Europe.

"For fifteen thousand dollars an Iraqi today gets a passport, the trip, and a story. The networks, the people smugglers, extend all over Europe and reach right down to the conflict zones that force people to flee."

"What do you mean by a story?" asked a woman in the audience.

"An asylum seeker's narrative," explained Jakob. "The smuggler tells them what they need to say to have a chance of being allowed to stay in Sweden."

"But fifteen thousand dollars?" a man asked dubiously. "That's a huge amount of money. Does it really cost that much?"

"Of course not," Jakob replied patiently. "The people behind these networks are earning incredible sums. It's a ruthless market, and totally unjust. But it's also — in spite of its brutality — to some degree understandable. Europe is closed to people in need. The only ways in are illegal ones. And they are controlled by criminals."

More hands were waving and Jakob answered question after question. Finally there was only one hand left, a young girl's. The one clutching the crumpled tissue. She was red-haired, with an overgrown fringe hanging down like a curtain over her eyes, giving her an anonymous look. The sort of person you can't describe afterward.

"Are there people who get involved in all this out of sheer solidarity?" she asked.

It was a new question, one Jakob had never had at any of his lectures before.

"After all, there are plenty of organizations in Sweden and the rest of Europe working with refugees, so isn't there anyone there who helps asylum seekers get to Sweden?" she went on. "In a better and more humane way than the smugglers?"

The question sank in and took hold. He hesitated for quite a while before he replied. Not quite knowing how much he ought to say.

"Helping people enter Europe illegally is a criminal act. Regardless of what we think about it, that's a fact. And it also means anyone doing that would be committing a punishable offense, which is enough to deter even the most noble of benefactors."

He hesitated again.

"But I have heard that things might be starting to change. That there are people who empathize strongly enough with the refugees to want to give them the chance of getting to Europe for a considerably lower sum. But as I said, that's only hearsay, nothing I know for certain."

He paused, felt his pulse start to race as he prayed a silent prayer.

He wound things up the way he always did.

"As I've told you, I don't think we need to worry that there are vast numbers of people in the world wishing they lived on a sink estate in Stockholm with no work or permanent housing. What we really must think about, on the other hand, is this: Is there anything a father will not do to make secure provision for his children's future? Is there any act a human being will not commit to create a better life for him- or herself?"

At the same time as Jakob Ahlbin was bringing his final lecture to a close and receiving loud applause, a Boeing 737 that had left Istanbul a few hours before touched down at Stockholm's Arlanda Airport. The captain who had flown the plane to the capital was informing the passengers that it was minus three outside and that snow was forecast for the evening. He said he hoped to welcome them back on board soon and then an air steward asked all passengers to keep their safety belts fastened until the sign was switched off.

Ali listened nervously to the voices making the announcements but understood neither the English nor the other language they spoke, which he took to be Swedish. Sweat was trickling down his back, making the shirt he had bought for the journey stick to his skin. He tried not to lean back against his seat, but did not want to attract attention by leaning forward as he had done on the flight from Baghdad to Istanbul. He had been asked several times by air stewards if everything was all right and whether he needed anything to drink or eat. He shook his head, wiped the sweat from his top lip with the back of his hand, and closed his eyes. He hoped that they would be there soon, that it would all be over and he would know he had reached safety.

He was tingling all over with anxiety. He squeezed the armrests with both hands and clenched his jaw. For what must have been the hundredth time he looked around the plane, trying to work out who his escort might be. Who was the secret person sitting among all the other passengers just to make sure he behaved himself and followed his instructions? A shadow, sent by his liberator. For his own good. For everybody else's good. So there would be no problem for others, like him, who would be given the chance to come to Sweden on such generous terms as himself.

The false passport was tucked into the

breast pocket of his shirt. He had put it in his hand luggage to start with, but had to take it out when the stewardess came and pointed at the sign saying his seat was next to an emergency exit. That meant you were not allowed to have your bags under the seat in front of you but had to stow them in the overhead compartments. Ali, almost giving way to panic, could not bear to be separated from his passport. With trembling hands he opened the zip of his bag and rummaged for the passport, which had slipped down to the bottom. He gripped its hard covers, thrust it into his shirt pocket, and handed the bag to the stewardess.

The instructions once he was in Sweden were crystal clear. On no account was he to ask for asylum while he was still at the airport. Nor was he to leave his documentation behind or hand it over to the escort on the plane before he got off. The passport contained a visa that said he was a business traveler from one of the Gulf states and entitled to enter the country. The fact that he spoke no English should not be a problem.

The plane taxied in, gliding surprisingly softly over the hard frost-covered tarmac and approached Gate 37, where the passengers were to disembark.

"What happens if I fail?" Ali had asked his contact in Damascus who had first made him the offer.

"Don't worry so much," the contact replied with a thin-lipped smile.

"I've got to know," said Ali. "What happens if I fail in any of these tasks I've got to do? I've spoken to other people going to the same place. This isn't the way it usually happens."

The contact's look had darkened.

"I thought you were grateful, Ali."

"Oh, I am," he said quickly. "It's just that I wonder —"

"Stop wondering so much," the contact broke in. "And you are not, under any circumstances, to say anything about this to anyone else. Not ever. You've got to focus on just one thing, and that's getting into this country the way we've arranged, and then you must carry out the task we shall be giving you. After that you can be reunited with your family. That's what you want, isn't it?"

"More than anything else."

"Good, so worry less and focus more. If you don't, the risk is that you could be more unhappy than you have ever been in your life."

"I can't be any more unhappy than I am

now," whispered Ali, head bowed.

"Oh, yes you can," answered his contact in a voice so cold that Ali stopped breathing from sheer terror. "Imagine if you lost your whole family, Ali. Or they lost you. Being alone is the only true unhappiness. Remember that, for your family's sake."

Ali closed his eyes and knew he would never forget. He recognized a threat when he heard one.

As he passed through passport control ten minutes later and knew he had got into the country, the thought came back to him again. From this point on, there was only one way forward: the path taking him away from the life he was now more certain than ever he had left behind him forever.

■ ■ ■ ■

WEDNESDAY, FEBRUARY 27, 2008

■ ■ ■ ■

The homemade croissants on offer in the Criminal Investigation Department staff room looked like something else entirely. Peder Rydh took two at once and grinned as he nudged his new colleague, Joar Sahlin, who gave him a blank look and made do with one.

"Cocks," clarified Peder in a word, holding up one of the croissants.

"Pardon?" said his colleague, looking him straight in the eye.

Peder stuffed half a croissant into his mouth and answered as he was chewing it.

"They look like limp prickth."

Then he sat himself down beside the female police probationer who had started work on the same floor a few weeks earlier.

It had been a tough autumn and winter for Peder. He had celebrated his twin sons' first birthday by leaving their mother, and since then he had screwed up pretty much everything else as well. Not at work, but privately. The woman who had wanted to be his girlfriend, Pia Nordh, suddenly turned her back on him, saying she had found someone else.

"It's the real thing this time, Peder," she had said. "I don't want to sabotage anything that feels so right."

Peder gave a snort and wondered how serious it could really be for a good lay like Pia Nordh, but had the sense not to voice his opinion out loud. Not just then, anyway.

The really frustrating thing after Pia dumped him was that it had been so hard to find any new talent for a bit of fun. Until now. The probationer couldn't be more than twenty-five, but she seemed more mature somehow. The main point about her was that she was too new to have heard all the stories about how Peder had behaved. About the way he had left his wife, and been unfaithful even while they were still together. About his boys, so little and doubly abandoned by their daddy, who in the middle of his paternity leave decided he could not stand being cooped up at home with the babies and handed them back to their mother. Who had just managed to start working part time after a postnatal year of serious depression.

Peder sat as close to the probationer as he could without seeming weird, still well aware that it was too close anyway. But she did not move away, which Peder took as a good sign.

"Nice croissants," she said, putting her head on one side.

She had her hair cut short, with wayward curls sticking out in all directions. If she hadn't had such a pretty face, she would have looked like a troll. Peder decided to chance it and grinned his cheekiest grin.

"They look almost like cocks, don't they?" he said with a wink.

The probationer gave him a long look, then got to her feet and walked out. His colleagues on the next sofa pulled mocking faces.

"Only you, Peder," one of them said, shaking his head.

Peder said nothing but went on with his morning coffee and croissant in silence, his cheeks flushing.

Then Detective Superintendent Alex Recht stuck his head round the staff room door.

"Peder and Joar, meeting in the Lions' Den in ten minutes."

Peder looked around him surreptitiously and noted to his satisfaction that normal

39

order had been restored. He could not get away from his reputation as the randiest male on the whole floor, but he was also the only one who had been promoted to DI when he was only thirty-two, and definitely the only one with a permanent place in Alex Recht's special investigation team.

He rose from the sofa in a leisurely fashion, carrying his coffee cup. He left it on the draining board, despite the fact that the dishwasher was wide open and a bright red sign saying YOUR MUM DOESN'T WORK HERE told him where everything should go.

In something that seemed as distant as another life, Fredrika Bergman had always been relieved when night came, when fatigue claimed her and she could finally get to bed. But that was then. Now she felt only anxiety as ten o'clock passed and the need for sleep made itself felt. Like a guerrilla she crouched before her enemy, ready to fight to the last drop of blood. She usually had little trouble emerging victorious. Her body and soul were so tightly strung that she lay awake well into the small hours. The exhaustion was almost like physical pain and the baby kicked impatiently to try to make its mother settle down. But it hardly ever succeeded.

The maternity clinic had referred her to a doctor, who thought he was reassuring her when he said she was not the only pregnant woman afflicted by terrible nightmares.

"It's the hormones," he explained. "And we often find it in women who are experiencing problems with loosening of the joints and getting a lot of pain, like you."

Then he said he would like to sign her off sick, but at that point she got up, walked out, and went to work. If she was not allowed to work, she was sure it would destroy her. And that would hardly keep the nightmares at bay.

A week later she was back at the doctor's, sheepishly admitting she would like a certificate to reduce her working hours by 25 percent. The doctor did as she asked, without further discussion.

Fredrika moved slowly through the short section of corridor in the plainclothes division that was the territory of Alex's team. Her stomach looked as though a basketball had accidentally found its way under her clothes. Her breasts had nearly doubled in size.

"Like the beautiful hills of southern France where they grow all that lovely wine," as Spencer Lagergren, the baby's father, had said when they saw each other a few evenings earlier.

As if the painful joints and the nightmares were not enough, Spencer was a problem in himself. Fredrika's parents, entirely unaware of the existence of their daughter's lover even though they had been together for over ten years, had been dismayed when she told them just in time for Advent Sunday that she was pregnant. And that the father of the baby was a professor at Uppsala University, and married.

"But, Fredrika!" her mother exclaimed. "How old *is* this man?"

"He's twenty-five years older than me and he'll take his full share of the responsibility," said Fredrika, and almost believed it as she said it.

"I see," her father said wearily. "And what does that mean, in the twenty-first century?"

That was a good question, thought Fredrika, suddenly feeling as tired as her father sounded.

What it meant in essence was simply that Spencer intended to acknowledge voluntarily that he was the father and to pay maintenance. And to see the baby as often as possible, but without leaving his wife, who had now also been let in on the secret that had hardly been a secret.

"What did she say when you told her?"

Fredrika asked cautiously.

"She said it would be nice to have children about the house," replied Spencer.

"She said *that*?" said Fredrika, hardly knowing if he was joking or not.

Spencer gave her a wry look.

"What do you think?"

Then he had to go, and they had said no more on the subject.

At work, Fredrika's pregnancy aroused more curiosity than she had hoped, and since nobody actually came out with any direct questions, there was inevitably a good deal of gossip and speculation. Who could be father to the baby of single, career-minded Fredrika Bergman? The only employee in the Criminal Investigation Division without police training behind her, who since her recruitment had managed to annoy every single one of her male colleagues, either by paying them too little attention or by questioning their competence.

It was a surprise, thought Fredrika as she stopped outside Alex's closed door. That she, initially so skeptical about staying in her police job, seemed to have found her niche there in the end and stayed on beyond her probationary period.

I was on my way out from the very start, she thought, putting one hand on her belly for a moment. I wasn't going to come back. Yet here I am.

She rapped hard on Alex's door. She had noticed his hearing did not seem that good these days.

"Come in," muttered her boss from the other side of the door.

He beamed when he saw who it was. He did that a lot these days, and certainly much more often than anyone else in the division.

Fredrika smiled back. Her smile lasted until she saw that his expression had changed and he was looking concerned again.

"Are you getting much sleep?"

"Oh, I get by," she replied evasively.

Alex nodded, almost to himself.

"I've got a fairly simple case here that . . ." he began, but stopped himself and tried again. "We've been asked to take a look at a hit-and-run incident out at the university. A foreign man was found dead in the middle of Frescativägen. He'd been run over and they haven't been able to identify him. We need to put his prints through the system and see if it comes up with anything."

"And otherwise wait for someone to report him missing?"

"Yes, and go over what's been done already, so to speak. He had a few personal items on him; ask to see them. Go through the report, check that there doesn't seem to be anything suspicious about the case. If there isn't, close the file, and report back to me."

A thought flashed through Fredrika's mind so fast that she had no time to register it. She squeezed her eyes shut, trying to retrieve it.

"Okay, I think that's all," Alex said slowly, looking at her contorted face. "We've got a group meeting in the Den about another case in a minute or two."

"See you there, then," said Fredrika, getting up.

She was back in the corridor before she realized she had forgotten to bring up the matter she went to see Alex about in the first place.

The curtains were closed in the meeting room known as the Lions' Den, and the place was like an overheated sauna. Alex Recht threw back the curtains to see light flakes of snow falling from the dark sky. The TV weather girl had promised that morning that the bad weather would move away by evening. Alex had his own views on that subject. The weather had been capricious ever since the start of the new year: days of snow and temperatures below zero alternating with rain and gales, fit to make anyone curse.

"Bloody weather," said Peder as he came into the Den.

"Dreadful," Alex said curtly. "Is Joar on his way?"

Peder nodded but said nothing, and Joar came into the room. The group's assistant, Ellen Lind, was right behind him, along with Fredrika.

The newly installed projector up on the ceiling whirred away quietly in the background and all Alex's attention was focused on the computer as he tried to coax it into action. The group waited patiently; they knew better than to point out that any one of them would be better at the technical stuff than their boss.

"There's something I've got to tell you," a gruff Alex said in the end, pushing the laptop aside. "As you may have noticed, this group hasn't really been working as initially planned. We were brought together so we could be called on for particularly difficult cases, above all missing persons and particularly brutal violent crimes. And when Fredrika went down to part time, we were given Joar as backup, for which we're extremely grateful."

46

Here, Alex looked at Joar, who met his eye without comment. There was something reserved and reticent about the young man that Alex found surprising. The contrast with the skillful but sometimes wayward Peder was striking. At first he had seen this as a positive thing, but within a couple of weeks he began to have his doubts. It was obvious Joar found Peder's way of talking annoying and offensive, while Peder seemed frustrated by his new colleague's calmness and flexibility. Pairing Joar with Fredrika Bergman would probably have been a better idea. But she was on reduced hours on doctor's orders now, and hampered by this pregnancy that was taking so much out of her. Certificates referring to severe pain, sleep problems, and nightmares crossed Alex's desk, and when Fredrika did manage to come into the office, she looked so pale and weak that her colleagues were quite shocked.

"It turns out, perhaps not surprisingly, that when it comes to the crunch, there aren't enough of us and we need reinforcements, and in between times we're often on loan to the Stockholm police homicide department to help out with their cases. So the question has been asked: do we need to be a permanent group, or should we be dispersed among the Stockholm police or the county CID instead?"

Peder was the one who looked most dismayed.

"But, but —"

Alex held up a hand.

"There's been no formal decision yet," he said, "but I just wanted to let you all know that it's on the cards."

No one said a word, and the projector stopped whirring.

Alex fiddled with the papers he had in front of him on the desk.

"Anyway, we've now got a case — well, two actually — that our friends in the Norrmalm police need a hand with. A couple in their sixties, Jakob and Marja Ahlbin, found dead yesterday evening in their flat by another couple who had been invited round for dinner. When nobody answered the door, and the other couple couldn't get through on any of the phones either, they opened the door with their own key and found the pair dead in the bedroom. According to the preliminary police report, which is based mainly on a suicide note written by the dead husband, he shot his wife and then himself."

The computer belatedly began to cooperate, and crime-scene pictures flashed up on the white screen behind Alex. Ellen and Joar each gave a start at the sight of the enlarged pictures of bodies with gunshot wounds, but Peder was spellbound.

He's changed, Alex thought to himself. He wasn't like that before.

"According to the note, he had found out two days earlier that their elder daughter, Karolina, had died from a heroin overdose, and he saw no reason to carry on living. He himself was treated for serious and recurring bouts of depression all his adult life. Only this January he underwent ECT treatment, and he was on antidepressants. A chronic sufferer, in fact."

"What's ETC?" asked Peder.

"ECT," Alex corrected him. "Electroconvulsive therapy, it's used in particularly difficult cases of depression. As a way of kickstarting the brain."

"Electric shocks," said Peder. "Isn't that illegal?"

"As Alex said, in controlled form it has had very positive benefits for severely ill patients," Joar interjected in a matter-of-fact tone. "The patient is under anesthetic during the actual treatment and the vast majority show striking improvement."

Peder stared at Joar but said nothing. He turned to Alex.

"Why have we been saddled with this case? It's already solved, isn't it?"

"It might not be," replied Alex. "The two people who found the couple say it's impossible to believe that the man murdered his wife and then shot himself. They did recognize the weapon, a .22-caliber hunting pistol, because the two men would often go hunting together, but they were adamant when questioned that it would be entirely out of character for him to be so crazed by grief as to act like that."

"So what do these friends think did happen, then?" asked Fredrika, making her first contribution to the meeting.

"They think they must have been murdered," said Alex, giving her a look. "Both of them apparently held positions in the Swedish Church: he was a vicar and she was a cantor. Jakob Ahlbin has been quite prominent in recent years in debates about immigration. These friends of the couple claim they were such fervent believers that suicide simply wouldn't have been in the cards. And it seems incomprehensible to them for Jakob to have received the news of his daughter's death and not passed it on to his wife."

"So what do we do?" asked Peder, still not convinced the case was worthy of their attention.

"We'll interview the two who found the couple again," Alex said firmly. "And we need to get hold of the Ahlbins' younger daughter, Johanna, who has probably not been informed of her sister's and parents' deaths. That may prove tricky; no one's managed to locate her yet. I dread the thought of the media releasing the names and pictures of the deceased before we find her."

He looked at Joar and then at Peder.

"I want you two as a team to interview the friends, once you've been to the scene of the crime. See if there seems any good reason to pursue this any further. Then divide your forces and interview other people if you need to. Find more people who knew them in the church."

As they were getting to their feet, Peder asked: "And what about the other case? You said there were two."

Alex frowned.

"The other one I've already allocated to Fredrika," he said. "Just a routine thing, an unidentified man found dead near the university this morning. He seems to have been in the middle of the road after dark and was run over by someone who didn't dare to stop and hand himself over to the

51

police. And don't forget what I said."

Peder and Joar waited.

"Make sure you find the daughter double quick. Nobody should have to get the news that their parents have died from the tabloid press."

BANGKOK, THAILAND

The sun was just disappearing behind the skyscrapers when she realized she had a problem. It had been an incredibly hot day with temperatures way above normal, and she had been feeling hot and sticky since early that morning. She had had a long succession of meetings in stuffy rooms with no air-conditioning and a picture had started to emerge. Or perhaps it was more of a suspicion. She could not decide which, but the follow-up work when she got home would undoubtedly answer all her questions.

Her return to Sweden was not many days away. In fact it was approaching all too quickly. It had been her original intention to round off the long trip with a few days of holiday sunshine down in Cha-Am, but circumstances beyond her control had put paid to the plan, and she realized the most practical thing now was to stay in Bangkok

53

until it was time to go home.

What's more, her father's latest email had made her uneasy:

"You must be careful. Don't extend your stay. Be discreet in your investigations. Dad."

Once the last meeting of the day was over, she asked to borrow a phone.

"I have to ring the airline to confirm my flight home," she explained to the man she had just interviewed, taking out the plastic wallet with the electronic tickets she had printed out.

The phone rang several times before the operator answered at the other end.

"I'd like to confirm my flight back with you on Friday," she said, fiddling with a Buddha figurine on the desk in front of here.

"Booking number?"

She gave her booking reference and waited as the operator put her on hold. Tinny music began to play in her ear, and she looked idly out of the window. Outside, Bangkok was boiling, getting ready for the evening and night ahead. An unlimited choice of discotheques and nightclubs, bars and restaurants. A constant din and a never-ending stream of people going in all directions. Dirt and dust mixed with the strangest sights and scents. Hordes of shopkeepers and street vendors, and the occasional huge elephant in the heart of the city, although they were prohibited. And between the maze of buildings, the river cutting the city in two.

I must come back here, she told herself. As a proper tourist, not for work.

The tinny music stopped and the operator was back on the line.

"I'm sorry, miss, but we can't find your booking. Could you give me the number again?"

She sighed and repeated the number. The man who had lent her his office was clearly losing patience, too. A discreet knock at the door indicated his wish to reclaim it.

"Won't be a minute," she called.

The knocking stopped as the endless loop of music resumed. She was kept waiting longer this time and was deep in reverie, imagining future tourist trips to Thailand, when the operator's voice broke in.

"I'm really sorry, miss, but we can't find your booking. Are you sure it was with Thai Airways?"

"I've got my e-ticket right here in front of me," she said irritably, looking at the computer printout in her hand. "I'm flying from Bangkok to Stockholm with your airline this Friday. I paid 4,567 Swedish kronor. The money was taken from my account on the nth of January this year."

She could hear the operator working away at the other end; he had not bothered to put her on hold this time.

"May I ask how you traveled to Thailand, miss?" he asked. "Did you fly with us?"

She hesitated, recalling the earlier stages of her trip, which she did not want to refer to.

"No," she replied. "No, I didn't come with you. And I was not traveling from Stockholm when I entered Thailand."

The names of a string of cities flashed on and off in her mind. Athens, Istanbul, Amman, and Damascus. No, it wasn't information anyone else needed to know.

The line went quiet for several minutes, and the man knocked on the office door again.

"Will you be much longer?"

"There's a bit of a problem with my airline ticket," she called back. "It won't take long to sort out."

The operator came back on the line.

"I've made a really thorough check and spoken to my line manager," he said firmly. "You have no booking with our company, and as far as I can see, you never did have."

She took a breath, ready to protest. But he preempted her.

"I am very sorry, miss. If you would like to make another booking, we can help you with that, of course. Not for Friday, I'm afraid, but we can fly you home on Sunday. A single ticket will cost you 1,255 dollars."

"But this is ridiculous," she said indignantly. "I don't want another ticket, I want to fly on the one I've already bought. I demand that you —"

"We've done everything we can, miss. The only thing I can suggest is that you check your email account to make sure it really was our airline you booked with and not someone else. There are sometimes false tickets on sale, though it's extremely rare for that to happen. But as I say, check that and then contact us again. I've reserved a seat for you for Sunday. Okay?"

"Okay," she answered in a weak voice.

But it was not okay. Not at all.

She felt weary as she hung up. This was the last thing she needed just now. The whole trip had been dogged by administrative hitches. But it had never occurred to her to worry about the flight home.

She strode out of the room into the corridor.

"I'm sorry to have taken so long, but there seems to be a problem with my flight home."

He looked concerned.

57

"Is there anything I can do to help?"

"Is there a computer with Internet access I could borrow? Then I could get into my email and double-check my booking."

He shook his head.

"Sorry, miss, I'm afraid we haven't got one here. Our Internet connection was so bad that we decided we'd be better off popping to the Internet café round the corner when we needed to go online."

She took her leave, thanking him for his help and all the important information he had been brave enough to entrust to her with, and went to the café he recommended.

There was a spring in her long-legged step as she went into the café and asked to use a computer for fifteen minutes. The proprietor showed her to computer number three and asked if she wanted coffee. She declined the offer, hoping she would be on the way back to her hotel very shortly.

The fan inside the computer whirred as the processor tried to upload her inbox onto the screen. She drummed her fingers impatiently on the table, sending up a silent prayer for the system not to crash so she had to start all over again. She knew from experience that the Internet abroad was not what it was in Sweden.

The café's air-conditioning was as noisy

as a small tank rumbling along, reminding her of the region she had visited before her trip to Thailand. Her hand went automatically to the chain she wore round her neck, under her blouse. Her fingers closed round the USB memory stick that hung on it, resting against her chest. There, encased in that one little bit of plastic, were all the facts she had collected. She would soon be home and all the pieces of the puzzle would fall into place.

"Sure you'll be all right?" her father had asked with an anxious note in his voice, the evening before she left.

" 'Course I will."

He stroked her cheek, and they said no more about it. They both knew she was more than able to look after herself, and anyway, the trip had been her own idea, but the question still needed asking.

"Just ring if you need any help," her father said as they parted at Stockholm's main airport.

But she had only rung once and the rest of their communication had been by email. She had deleted the emails as she went along without really knowing why.

The computer had finally accessed the site and something came up on the screen.

> You have entered the wrong password.
> Please try again.

She shook her head. This was clearly not going to be a good day. She tried again. The computer growled as it labored away. And again:

> You have entered the wrong password.
> Please try again.

She tried three more times. Each time the same message. She swallowed hard.

Something's going wrong. Really wrong.

And another part of her mind threw up the thought: ought she, in fact, to be scared?

STOCKHOLM

Peder and Joar drove in silence through Kungsholmen, over St. Erik's Bridge and on toward Odenplan, where the elderly couple had been found dead. Peder was at the wheel, racing to every red light. A suspicion had planted itself in the back of his mind after the croissant incident in the staff room. Joar had not even cracked a smile when Peder came out with his funny cock joke. That was bad. Clearly a sign. Peder had got better at observing those over the years. Signs. Signs that a colleague was of the other persuasion. Batting for the other side. Gay.

Not that he had anything against it. Absolutely not. Just as long as he didn't try it on with him. Then he'd see him in hell.

He squinted sideways at Joar's profile. His colleague's face was remarkably finely drawn, almost like a painting. A face like a mask. The eyes were ice blue, the pupils ver dilated. The lips were a little too red, ne eyelashes implausibly long. Peder screwed up his eyes to get a better look. If Joar wore makeup, he could take his own car in future.

The traffic lights turned from green to red and Peder had to put his foot down to get through. He did not need to look at Joar to know his colleague disapproved.

"Hard to know whether to stop or speed up when it's like that," said Peder, mainly to have something to say.

"Mmm," responded Joar, looking the other way. "What was the name of the street?"

"Dalagatan. They lived on the top floor. Big flat, apparently."

"Are the bodies still there?"

"No, and forensics are supposed to be finished now, so we can go in."

They said nothing as Peder parked the car. He fished out the parking permit and slunk after his colleague into the building. Joar ignored the lift and set off up the five flights of stairs to the couple's flat. Peder followed, wondering why the hell they weren't taking the lift when it was so many floors up.

The stairwell was freshly decorated, the walls white and shiny. The steps were marble, the window frames painted brown.

The lift shaft in the middle was an old-fashioned, wrought-iron affair. Peder's thoughts went to the woman from whom he had separated, Ylva. She hated confined spaces. Peder had once tried to seduce her in his parents' guest cloakroom during a boring family dinner, but Ylva found making love in such a small space so stressful that her skin came up in bumps and she couldn't breathe properly.

They had laughed over that story countless times.

But not these past eighteen months, Peder observed bitterly. There hadn't been much bloody laughing at all.

There was no sign of forced entry to the couple's front door. The label on the letter box simply said AHLBIN. Joar rang the bell and a uniformed police officer opened the door. He and a crime-scene technician were the only ones there.

"All right if we come in?" asked Peder.

The officer nodded.

"They're just doing the windows, then they'll be finished on the forensic side."

Peder and Joar advanced into the flat.

"Was it rented?" asked Joar.

The officer shook his head.

"Owner-occupied. They'd lived here since 1999."

Peder gave a whistle as he went round the flat. It was spacious and had high ceilings. All the rooms had beautiful stuccowork and the expanses of white wall were sparingly hung with paintings and photographs.

Peder thought Fredrika would have loved this flat, though he had not the least idea how her own home was decorated.

Why was that? Why didn't people go round to each other's places nowadays? The fact that he had never been to Fredrika's was not very surprising, but with other colleagues it was harder to understand. He hated the lonely evenings in the flat where he had moved the previous autumn. Although he was buying rather than renting, he hadn't done any work on it. His mother made curtains and bought cushions and tablecloths, but when he showed no sign of wanting to help, she lost interest. He could hardly blame her.

The couple's flat had windows looking out in three directions and there were four main rooms. The kitchen and living room area was open plan. A sliding wall divided the living room and library. Then there was a guest bedroom and the bedroom where the two bodies had been found.

Peder and Joar stopped at the door and surveyed the room. They had both seen the crime-scene report written by the officers who were first to arrive. The initial assessment would presumably hold good even once forensics had finished their job. Jakob Ahlbin had shot his wife in the back of the head. She must have been standing with her back to the doorway, where Jakob had presumably been. So she had first fallen headlong onto the bed but subsequently slipped onto the floor. Then her husband had walked round the bed, lain down on it, and shot himself in the temple. The farewell letter had been on the bedside table.

There was nothing in the room to indicate any sort of struggle before either of them died. No furniture seemed to have been moved; nothing was broken or smashed. The woman was in her dressing gown when they found her. The indications were that she had started getting ready for the guests they were expecting about an hour later.

"Do we have a more exact time of death?" asked Peder.

"Their friends found them at seven and the pathologist estimated they'd been dead scarcely two hours. So they must have died at about five."

"Has anyone interviewed the neighbors?" asked Joar. "The shots must have echoed through the building."

The officer standing just behind them nodded.

"Yes, we've talked to everyone who was at home, and they heard the shots. But it all happened so fast and the residents here are all fairly elderly and couldn't be sure exactly where the sound was coming from. One of them even rang the police, but when the patrol car turned up, no one could say for sure which flat the shots had come from, and there was no other disturbance. Nobody had noticed anyone coming or going just afterward. So the patrol car moved on."

"So sound travels in the building? Since people were confident enough to say fairly definitely that nobody came or went?" Joar asked tentatively.

"Yes, that must be right," replied the uniformed officer.

Just then there was the sound of furniture scraping the floor in the flat below.

"There, what did I say, sound travels here," said the officer, rather more self-assured now.

"Were they in the whole time?" Peder asked.

"Who?"

"The neighbors you interviewed, the ones who live below here."

The officer took a surreptitious look at his

notebook.

"No," he said. "They didn't get back until eight last night, unfortunately. And there's only one other flat on this floor, and the people who live there weren't at home either."

"So none of the nearest neighbors were in when the shots were fired?" Peder observed.

"No, that more or less sums it up."

Joar said nothing, just walked around the room, frowning. He glanced occasionally at Peder and the uniformed officer, but held his tongue.

There's something shady about him, thought Peder. Apart from the fact that he's gay, he's got something else to hide.

"This mark," Joar said suddenly, breaking into Peder's thoughts. "Do we know anything about that?"

He indicated a streak of pale gray arcing across the wall at the head of the bed, just behind the lamp on the bedside table.

"No," said the officer. "But it could have been there for ages, couldn't it?"

"Of course," said Joar. "Or it could have been caused by the lamp being knocked sideways off the table onto the floor. If that's what happened."

"You mean there could have been a violent tussle in here after all, and the lamp went flying?" asked Peder.

"Exactly so, and when it was all over, someone put the lamp back in its original place. We can ask forensics to check it out, if they haven't already."

He crouched down.

"It's not plugged into the wall," he added. "Maybe it was pulled out of the socket when it fell off the table."

"Hmm," said Peder, and went over to the window to look out.

"All the windows in the flat were shut when we got here," reported the policeman. "And the front door was locked."

"From the inside?"

"Erm, there was no way of telling. That's to say, it could have been either. But we think the door was locked from the inside."

"But it could have been locked from outside? Do we know who had keys to this place?"

"According to the friends who found the bodies, they were the only ones with keys to the flat. And the daughter who'd just died had a set. That was something they found extremely upsetting, by the way."

"The fact that she had keys to the flat, too?" Peder asked, baffled.

"No, the fact that she's supposed to have taken an overdose," the officer clarified.

"Admittedly they hadn't seen her for a few weeks, but as far as they were aware, she had a very good relationship with her parents. And it was news to them that she was on drugs."

Joar and Peder exchanged glances.

"We need to talk to those friends of theirs as soon as possible," said Joar. "Do they live near here?"

"Down on Vanadisplan. They're in."

"Let's get down there right away," said Peder, already on his way to the front door.

"Give me a minute," said Joar. "I just want one more good look round before we go."

Peder planted himself in the middle of the living room and waited impatiently for Joar to finish whatever it was he was doing.

"Going round the flat, what sort of sense do you get of the people who lived here?" Joar asked him.

Peder looked about him at a loss, caught off guard by the question.

"That they're not short of money," he said eventually.

Joar, who had come to a stop a few meters away, facing him, put his head on one side.

"True," he said. "But anything else?"

Joar's tone of voice made him feel uneasy, though he could not work out why. As if the questions triggered some complex within him of which he had been unaware until now.

"I don't really know."

"Try."

Provoked, Peder tramped demonstratively round the living room and into the kitchen area. He carried on through the hall, into the library and guest room, and then back to his starting point. "They're well off," he reiterated. "They've had money for a long time. Maybe inherited some. It almost looks as if they don't live here. Not properly."

Joar waited.

"Explain."

"There are almost no pictures of their children. Only a few from when they were little. The photos on the walls aren't of people, they're landscapes. I don't know enough about art to say much about their pictures, but they look expensive."

"Is there any exception to what you've just said? About it looking as though nobody really lives here?"

"The bedroom, maybe. They've got photos of themselves in there that look quite recent."

The parquet flooring creaked as Joar moved across the room.

"I thought exactly the same as you," he said, his tone indicating he was pleased about it. "And I wonder what that tells us, because down at Vanadisplan we've got another couple who claim they knew this family extremely well. Whereas I get the impression that the people who lived in this flat are pretty cool and impersonal people who don't let anybody get particularly close. I think we need to bear that in mind when we go and see them in a minute. That, and the fact that the impression we've got might well mean something else as well."

"Like what?" asked Peder, interested in Joar's analysis in spite of himself.

"That they had a second home where they felt more themselves, and where we can presumably get to know them better."

It was a strange world she worked in. It was hardly the first time the thought had occurred to her, but every time it did, it caught her slightly off guard. Fredrika Bergman was generally very careful to point out to herself and others that she had chosen her current position as part of a longer-term career strategy and did not see it as anything she would be doing for very long. The reason she took such care to point this out was as simple as it was depressing: she did not like the job very much.

As a civilian appointee in a sea of police officers, uniformed or otherwise, she was constantly being reminded how different she was and how odd her colleagues found her. She had thought on numerous occasions how peculiar this was, because she was rarely seen as odd or different in other contexts. But things had undeniably improved. Particularly as far as Alex and Peder were concerned; they seemed to view her in a different light since that case they had worked on together the previous summer. A baptism of fire for them all.

Fredrika was also aware that she herself had changed since then, too. She tried to pick her battles. Initially she had flared up at everything, but the unexpected tribulations of pregnancy had made her increasingly reluctant to rise to the bait. But there were still times when conflicts proved unavoidable. Take her recent little visit to the CID fingerprint unit. She had asked one simple question: Had they by any chance found a match for the fingerprints of the unidentified man found dead in the road at the university, either in their own records or in those of the Migration Agency?

The question produced an extremely defensive response from the woman she had found to ask. Didn't Fredrika know what the workload round here was like since it all got too much for Gudrun last month? Didn't she realize the big biker gang investigation the CID had launched the previous week took precedence?

Fredrika had not been particularly sympathetic, knowing nothing of Gudrun or her sick leave, or the biker investigation, for that matter. What's more, she was pretty sure there was no specific reason for the delay; the woman had simply forgotten to check the dead man's prints.

"You can't come charging in here making all sorts of demands," the woman snapped from behind her computer. "Absolutely typical of someone like you with no police experience, no sense of priorities."

Fredrika merely replied that she was sorry to hear her colleague had so much on her plate, and of course she could wait a few more days for the result, which the woman could pass through when it was ready. She thanked her and withdrew in the direction of the lifts as fast as she could.

Fredrika sat down heavily in her office chair. Her mother thought she was still unusually slim for someone at such an advanced stage of pregnancy, but Fredrika found it hard to take that seriously. The baby was kicking frantically, its angry little feet pounding against the inside of her belly.

"Getting a bit impatient, aren't you?" murmured Fredrika, putting one hand on her stomach. "Me too."

Her parents asked her if the pregnancy was planned, and she told them it was. But she had avoided going into much detail. It was last summer, that summer of never-ending rain, when the plans assumed concrete form. Fredrika was coming up to thirty-five and had to reach a decision on how to deal with her lack of children. Or rather — what steps she should take. There were not that many options. Either she adopted a child as a single parent, or she went to Copenhagen and solved the problem by insemination. Or she found someone to live with and had children the natural way.

But this last option did not feel entirely uncomplicated. The years had gone by and Fredrika had not yet been able to make a relationship really work. And after every failed attempt she had gone back to Spencer, who seemed eternally chained to a marriage neither he nor his wife was happy with.

It was not until they were on holiday together at Skagen that Fredrika felt able to bring up the subject.

"I'm thinking of adopting," she said. "I want to be a mother, Spencer. And I understand that you can't be, and don't want to be, part of that, but I still needed to tell you how I feel."

Spencer's reaction had taken Fredrika completely by surprise. He was dismayed, and went on at great length about how reprehensible it was to uproot children from other parts of the globe simply to send them to love-starved people in Sweden.

"Are you really going to subscribe to a system like that?" he asked.

Fredrika burst into tears, sobbing: "What alternative have I got? Tell me that, Spencer, what the hell am I supposed to do?"

So they had talked about it instead. For a long time.

Fredrika smiled. It was childish of her to think that way, but it did amuse her how much the project had provoked her parents.

"But, Fredrika, whatever's got into you?" her mother asked skeptically. "And who is this Spencer, anyway? How long have you known him?"

"Over ten years," said Fredrika, looking her mother firmly in the eye.

Fredrika swallowed. Pregnancy and all those hormones had triggered extreme mood swings. One minute she would be laughing out loud, the next minute crying. Perhaps she ought to reevaluate her self-image. It clearly wasn't only police colleagues who considered her abnormal; her own family was starting to wonder, too.

Frustrated, she reached for the report drawn up at the scene of the unidentified man's death. No identity documents. He still had not been reported missing. Hardly any personal possessions on him. The doctor who examined the body when it reached the hospital said in his preliminary report that he had found nothing on the body to indicate the man had been subjected to any physical violence before the impact. Fredrika noted that a full autopsy had been requested.

She went through the plastic wallet on the desk in front of her, which contained the things found on the man's person. A pamphlet in Arabic script. A gold necklace. A ring with a black stone, wrapped in a slip of paper. Another scrap of paper, rolled into a hard little ball that took ages to unwind. More Arabic characters, on both bits of paper. And then a map. It looked as though someone had torn one of the map pages out of an old telephone directory and crumpled it into a ball. Fredrika frowned. It was a map of Uppsala city center. On the edge of the map, someone had scribbled something; this, too, seemed to be in Arabic.

The fatigue that sporadically paralyzed her brain briefly gave way to a suspicion. She wondered what to do with it. It probably wouldn't lead anywhere, but it was just as well to check. She went into the next room to consult Ellen.

"Where can I find someone to read and translate Arabic text?" she asked.

■ ■ ■ ■

It was Alex Recht himself who took the call from the vicar of Bromma Parish. They exchanged a few polite phrases before the vicar got to the point.

"It's about Jakob Ahlbin, who was found dead yesterday."

Alex waited.

"I just wanted to assure you on behalf of the church that we will help you with everything you need. Everything. This is a terribly sad day for us. What happened is simply unfathomable."

"We do understand that," said Alex. "Did you see each other socially, as well?"

"No, we didn't," said the vicar. "But he was a highly valued member of our parish team. As was Marja. They've left a gaping hole behind them."

"Would it be convenient for us to come and see you sometime today?" asked Alex. "We want to talk to as many of the people who knew them as we can."

"I'm at your disposal whenever you want," the vicar replied.

When the call was over, Alex briefly considered ringing his father. It was an impulse he felt increasingly rarely these days, and the only reason he had it now was that the case was so clearly linked to the church. Alex's father was a Church of Sweden clergyman, as was his younger brother. Alex had had to fight hard once upon a time to justify his choice of career to his parents. All firstborn sons in the family had taken holy orders, going back generations.

Finally his father had given in. A career in the police was a kind of calling, after all.

"I've chosen this because I can't see myself making a better job of anything else," Alex had said.

And with these words he had finally won the battle.

The telephone on his desk rang. It made him feel warm inside to hear his wife Lena's voice, even though it had also been making him feel a bit uneasy of late, as well. There was something worrying her, but she was not saying what.

"Are you going to be late tonight?" she asked.

"Probably not."

"You won't forget your physio appointment?"

"Of course not," he said peevishly.

They talked about what to have for dinner and what they really thought of their daughter's new boyfriend, who looked like a hard rocker and talked like a politician. "A bloody disaster," was Alex's succinct verdict, and that made Lena laugh.

Her laugh was still echoing in his head even after they had hung up.

Alex looked down at his scarred hands. They had got badly burned in that insane case of the missing girl the previous summer. Little children were abducted from around the capital and later found murdered. The hunt for the perpetrator had taken less than a week, all told, but it had been more intense than anything else in his whole career. The fire in the murderer's flat was like a bizarre grand finale to an equally bizarre case.

Alex flexed his fingers. The doctors had promised him full mobility if he just gave it time, and they had been right. Alex remembered nothing of the fire itself, and he was glad of it. He had never been on sick leave for so long before, and just a few weeks after his return to work, he and Lena had gone to South America to visit their son.

He chuckled, as he always did when he thought about the trip. Good grief, what a mess the police force was over there.

The phone rang again. To his great surprise it was Margareta Berlin, head of HR.

"Alex, we've got to talk about Peder Rydh," she said flatly.

"Oh yes?" said Alex hesitantly. "What's up?"

"Croissants."

Although he had been in Sweden for a number of days, he hadn't yet seen the country at all. He had taken the airport bus from Arlanda into the center of Stockholm as instructed, and waited in the bus station on a seat outside a newsagent's shop.

He had had to wait half an hour before the woman came. She did not look at all as he had expected. She was much shorter and darker than he had imagined Swedish women to be, and she was wearing a man's suit, with trousers instead of a skirt. He was suddenly unsure of what to say.

"Ali?" asked the woman.

He nodded.

The woman glanced over her shoulder, then took a mobile phone from her bag and gave it to him. Such relief washed over him that it almost made him cry. Handing over the phone was the signal he had been waiting for, the receipt for having found the right place.

He stuffed the phone into his pocket with clumsy fingers, feeling for his passport in his shirt pocket with his other hand. The woman gave a distinct nod as he passed it to her, and leafed quickly though it.

Then she gestured to him to go with her.

She took him through the bus station, which was called the City Terminal, out onto a street full of cars. Just to the left of the entrance, alongside the pavement, were more bicycles than Ali had ever seen at a bus station. Swedish people must cycle all the time.

The woman urged him to keep up and when they reached her car she directed him to get into the passenger seat. He watched with fascination as she took her place at the wheel and started the car. It was much colder than he had expected, but the car was still warm.

They drove through the city in silence. Ali assumed she spoke no Arabic, and he had no English. He stared out of the window, taking in everything he saw. All these bridges and stretches of water everywhere. Low buildings and much less noise than he was used to in cities. He wondered where all the street vendors plied their trade.

Fifteen minutes later, the woman parked

in an empty street and indicated that he was to get out of the car. They went into one of the low-rise buildings and up the stairs to the second floor. It took three keys and a succession of locks before she got the door open. She went into the flat first; he followed, head bowed.

The place smelled of cleaning products with an underlying hint of stale cigarette smoke. Ali could smell fresh paint, too. The flat was not large, and he assumed he would get a larger flat later on, when his family came to join him. He felt a pang at the thought of his wife and children. He hoped they were all right and would be able to manage until he got his residence permit. His contact had promised it would not take long; he would get the permit as soon as he had fulfilled his side of the bargain with those who had financed his escape.

The woman showed him the small bedroom and living room. The fridge was fully stocked with food and there were plates, saucepans, and other utensils in the kitchen cupboards. Ali had scarcely ever cooked a meal before, but that was the least of his problems. The woman gave him a folded sheet of paper and then turned on her heel and left the flat. He had not seen her since.

Three days had now passed.

Anxiety was making his skin crawl. For what must have been the hundredth time he took out the piece of paper the woman had left him and read the short text in Arabic.

Ali, this is your home for your first weeks in Sweden. Hope you had a good journey and will soon settle into the flat. We have tried to make sure you have everything you need. Please stay indoors until we contact you again.

Ali sighed and shut his eyes. Of course he would not leave the flat — he was locked in, after all. Tears burned the insides of his eyelids, though he had not cried since he was a little boy. The flat had no telephone and the mobile phone the woman had given him did not seem to work. The TV set only showed channels he did not understand; Al Jazeera was not on offer. Nor did there seem to be a computer. The windows would not open and the fan in the kitchen did not work. He had smoked quite a few packets of cigarettes and did not really know what he would do when they ran out.

Other things were running out, too. He had drunk all the milk, and the juice. He had eaten nearly all the bread in the freezer because he had not felt like doing any proper cooking. The plastic-wrapped burgers in the fridge had acquired a gray coating, and when he started peeling some potatoes to cook, he found they were green.

Ali rested his head against the window, drumming on the glass with his long fingers.

It's got to be over soon, he thought. They've got to come back so I can keep my side of the agreement.

The call from Alex took Fredrika by surprise. He explained in a few succinct phrases that Peder had been recalled to HQ and he, Alex, wanted her to go with Joar to interview the elderly couple who had found the Reverend Ahlbin and his wife.

They were sitting in a sort of circle. Four large armchairs round a little wooden octagonal table. Fredrika, Joar, and the man and woman who had found their friends shot dead the evening before: Elsie and Sven Ljung, both children of the mid-1940s and retired for several years. Fredrika reflected on how different people's appearances could be. Elsie and Sven really did look like pensioners, even though they had barely reached state pension age. Maybe that was what happened when you stopped working and stayed at home all day?

"Have you always lived this close to each other?" asked Fredrika, referring to the proximity of the dead couple's home to their own.

Elsie and Sven exchanged glances.

"Well, yes," said Sven. "We have, actually. Our houses were near each other back in the days when we all lived out in Bromma, and then we all moved into town within a few years of each other. Once the children had left home. But it wasn't something we planned, living this close to each other again. We laughed at the way fate takes a hand in things sometimes."

The corner of his mouth twitched, but the smile did not reach his dark eyes. It struck Fredrika that Sven must have been quite good-looking in his youth. Craggy features, a bit like Alex Recht, and gray hair that must once have been dark brown. He was tall and rather stately, his wife quite diminutive by comparison.

"How did you and they get to know each other?" asked Joar.

Fredrika was finding that Joar's voice often startled her. He had the knack of sounding so genuinely interested in everything. Yet so correct. Tedious bugger, she had heard Peder mutter on occasions. It was not a view she shared.

"Through the church," Elsie said firmly. "Jakob was an assistant vicar in the local parish, you know, just like Sven, and Marja was in charge of church music. I was a lay reader myself."

"So you all worked in the same parish? How long for?"

"Almost twenty years," said Sven with a hint of pride in his voice. "Elsie and I worked in Karlstad before that, but we moved to the Stockholm area when the children started senior school."

"So your children were friends, too?" asked Fredrika.

"No," Elsie said hesitantly, looking away from her husband for some reason, "not really. Marja and Jakob's two girls were a bit younger than our boys, so they didn't go to school together. Of course we met on social occasions as families, and sometimes at church. But no, I wouldn't say they were good friends."

Why not? thought Fredrika. The boys can't have been that much older.

She left it for the time being, but thought she could detect Elsie blushing.

"What can you tell us about Jakob and Marja?" asked Joar with a slight smile. "I know all this is terribly hard for you, and I know you've already had to tell other officers all this, before we were put on the case, but Fredrika and I would be very grateful if you had time to answer a few questions."

Elsie and Sven slowly nodded their assent. There was something about their body language that Fredrika found disturbing. Something awkward. Fredrika could not in her wildest dreams imagine the couple to be involved in what had happened, but they had been behaving as if they had something to hide even before she and Joar began their questioning.

"Jakob and Marja's relationship was a very solid one," Elsie declared. "A really good marriage. And they had two lovely girls. Both of them good at what they did, in their different ways."

Fredrika caught herself wanting to roll her eyes. "A really good marriage." What did that actually mean?

"Were they very young when they met each other?" asked Joar.

"Yes, they were," said Elsie. "He was seventeen and she was sixteen. It was considered a bit scandalous, back then. But once they got married and had children, everyone forgot about how it all started."

"But as I said, that was before we knew them," put in Sven. "We only know what Jakob and Marja told us."

"Were you close friends?" Fredrika asked delicately.

And she saw she'd scored a bull's-eye. Sven and Elsie fidgeted and looked uncomfortable.

"We were close friends, of course we were," said Sven. "I mean, we had keys to each other's flats, for example. For practical reasons, mainly, and because we always have done, what with living so near each other."

But, observed Fredrika. There was a *but* trying to get out.

She waited.

It was Elsie who came out with it.

"But we were closer before," she said in an undertone.

"Any particular reason for that?" Joar asked lightly.

Elsie appeared to droop.

"Not really, but, well, how shall I put it, I suppose we grew apart. It doesn't just happen when you're young, it can happen in later life, too."

Sven nodded eagerly, almost too eagerly, as though Elsie had said something really brilliant, though not necessarily true.

"We've found ourselves in different circles these last few years," he said, looking almost cheerful as he spoke, as if the words were coming much more easily than he had thought they might. "And after Elsie and I gave up work, the church wasn't quite such a hub for us any longer."

"But they'd invited you to dinner yester-day?" Fredrika inquired.

"Oh yes. We still saw each other socially sometimes."

This steered the conversation naturally round to what had actually happened the evening before. They had rung the doorbell repeatedly, knocked and then hammered on the door. Waited and then knocked again. Tried ringing the house phone and then Jakob and Marja's mobiles. And got no answer anywhere.

"I started to have this feeling," Elsie said, her voice trembling. "A sort of premonition that something awful had happened. I can't explain why I had that feeling and insisted we let ourselves into the flat with our key. Sven thought I was being silly and we ought to just go back home and wait. But I wouldn't, and said if he went home I'd go in and look by myself."

Elsie had won the debate on the landing and unlocked the front door with the key she had in her handbag.

"Why did you have their spare key with you?" asked Fredrika.

Sven sighed.

"Because I think keys are valuables you should always keep with you," Elsie replied almost angrily, glaring at Sven.

"So you always carry all your keys with you?" asked Joar with a disarming laugh.

"Yes, of course," said Elsie.

"Our house keys, our younger son's house keys, the boat keys," muttered Sven, shaking his head.

Joar leaned forward in his armchair and said: "What did you think when you found them?"

It went very quiet.

"We thought somebody had shot them," whispered Elsie. "We ran out of the flat and rang the police straightaway."

"But now you know the police found a farewell note," ventured Fredrika.

For the first time in the interview, Elsie looked on the verge of tears.

"Jakob's been struggling with his condition as long as we've known him," she said in a high-pitched voice. "But he'd never have done anything as crazy as shooting himself and Marja. *Never.*"

Sven nodded in agreement.

"Jacob was a man of the church and would never have betrayed his God like that."

Joar stroked his coffee cup.

"We all like to think we know our friends inside and out," he said in a controlled tone.

"But there are a few basic facts in this particular case that can't be ignored."

To Fredrika's surprise, Joar got up and started walking slowly round the room.

"One. Jakob Ahlbin suffered from chronic depression. He'd had electric shock therapy for it, several times. Two. Jakob was on medication. We found pills and prescriptions in the flat. Three. A few days ago he was told that his elder daughter had died of an overdose."

Joar paused.

"Is it really out of the question for him to have gone mad with grief and shot his wife and himself to end their suffering?"

Elsie shook her head vigorously.

"That's not right!' she cried. "None of it. For Lina, of all people, to have taken an overdose. I've known that girl since she was tiny and I can swear on the Bible she's never been anywhere near any kind of addiction."

Sven nodded again.

"For people like us, who've known the family for decades, this all sounds so odd," he said.

"But then all families have their problems and secrets, don't they?" Fredrika said.

"Not that sort of secret," Elsie said with conviction. "If either of the girls had been on drugs, we would have known about it."

Fredrika and Joar looked at each other, silently agreeing to change tack. The daughter was dead; there was no point discussing it further. And Jakob's state of health would be better assessed by a doctor than an elderly couple who happened to be his acquaintances.

"All right," said Fredrika. "If we disregard the most obvious line in this inquiry, namely that Jakob was the perpetrator, who else could have done it?"

There was silence.

"Did Marja and Jakob have any enemies?"

Elsie and Sven looked at each other in surprise, as if the question had caught them unawares.

"We're all agreed that they're dead," Joar said mildly. "But if it wasn't Jakob, who was it? Were they involved in any kind of dispute, as far as you could tell?"

Elsie and Sven both shook their heads and looked down at the floor.

"Not as far as we could tell," Elsie said wanly.

"Jakob's work with refugees made him quite a prominent figure, of course," said Fredrika. "Did that ever create problems for him?"

Sven straightened up instantly. Elsie tucked back a lock of gray hair that was hanging down over her pale cheek.

"No, not that we ever heard," said Sven.

"But it was an issue he felt very strongly about?"

"Yes indeed. His own mother came from Finland, and then stayed here. I'm sure he saw himself as being of immigrant stock."

"And what did his work comprise, exactly?" Joar asked with a frown, sitting back down in the armchair.

Elsie looked shifty, as though she did not know what to say.

"Well, he was involved with all sorts of organizations and so on," she replied. "He gave lectures to lots of groups. Was very good at it, at getting his message across, just like when he was preaching."

"Men and women of the church sometimes hide illegal migrants," Joar went on, with a lack of subtlety that surprised Fredrika. "Was he one of those?"

Sven took a gulp of coffee before he answered and Elsie said nothing.

"Not as far as we were aware," came Sven's reply at last. "But yes, there were rumors of that kind."

Fredrika glanced at her watch and then at Joar. He gave a nod.

"Well, thank you for letting us take up your time," he said, and put his visiting card on the table. "We shall probably need to come back and speak to you again, I'm afraid."

"You're welcome to come whenever you need to," Elsie said quickly. "It's important to us, being able to help."

"Thank you for that," said Fredrika, and followed Joar into the hall.

"By the way, do you know where we can get hold of the couple's other daughter, Johanna? We've done all we can to contact her, so she doesn't hear about her parents' death from the media," said Joar.

Elsie blinked, hesitated.

"Johanna? She'll be on one of her trips abroad, I imagine."

"You don't happen to have her mobile phone number?"

Elsie pursed her lips and shook her head.

They had put on their coats and were on their way out when Elsie said: "Why didn't they cancel?"

Fredrika stopped, half a meter from the door.

"Pardon?"

"If the girl had died of an overdose," Elsie said, her voice tense, "why didn't they cancel the dinner party? I talked to Marja yesterday, and she sounded her usual calm, cheerful self. And Jakob was playing his clarinet in the background, the way he often did. Why were they behaving like that if they knew their own deaths were only hours away?"

BANGKOK, THAILAND

The darkness had wrapped Bangkok in a blanket of night by the time she gave up. She had been to no fewer than three Internet cafés in the naïve hope that one of her two email addresses would work, but in vain. The system just kept telling her she had typed in either the wrong user name or the wrong password, and should try again.

She was dripping with sweat as she moved through the Bangkok streets. It was a coincidence, of course. Thai Airways' failure to locate her booking must just have been caused by some internal blip in the airline's system. The same applied to her email accounts, she told herself. There must be some major server problem. When she tried tomorrow, it would all be fine.

But she felt her stomach knotting, the pain radiating in all directions. She could not shake off her sense of unease. She had taken all the precautions the project demanded.

Only a handful of people knew about her trip, and fewer still knew the real reason for it. Her father was one of them, of course. She did a mental calculation and concluded it must be about one in the afternoon in Sweden. Her hand was slippery with sweat as she felt in her pocket for the mobile phone she had equipped with a Thai SIM card the day she arrived.

The phone crackled, cars tooted, and voices shouted to be heard above all the noise with which Bangkok city was vibrating. She pressed the phone to one ear and put her finger in the other to try to hear. The phone rang once and then an unknown woman's voice informed her that the number no longer existed and there was no forwarding option.

She stopped abruptly in the middle of the pavement, heedless of people walking into her from in front and behind. Her heart was pounding and the sweat was pouring off her. She rang again. And again.

She glared distrustfully at the phone and tried ringing her mother instead. She was transferred straight to voicemail, but decided there was no point leaving a message because her mother virtually never used her mobile. She tried ringing her parents' landline instead. She closed her eyes and imagined the telephone ringing in the library and hall simultaneously and her parents each leaping to a phone as usual. Her father generally got there first.

The phone echoed into emptiness. One ring, two, three rings. Then an anonymous female voice told her this number, too, no longer existed, and no forwarding number was available.

What on earth was going on?

She could not honestly remember an occasion on which she had felt truly afraid. But this time it was impossible to ward off the anxiety that was creeping over her. She racked her brain in vain for a rational explanation for her failure to get hold of her parents. It was not just that they were out, it was more than that. They were no longer subscribers. Why ever would her parents do that without telling her? She told herself to stay calm. She ought to get herself something to eat and drink, perhaps sleep for a while. It had been a long day and she had to decide what she was going to do about the trip home.

She gripped the mobile phone hard. Who else could she ring? If she restricted herself to people who already knew where she was, the list would not be very long. And anyway, she had not got their numbers; they were her father's friends. As far as she knew, most of them were ex-directory to make sure they were not disturbed outside work. She felt tears prick her eyes. Her rucksack was heavy and her back was starting to ache. Worn out with worry, she set off back to the hotel.

There was in fact one more person she ought to be able to ring. Just to make sure everything was all right, just for some help to reach her parents. Yet she still hesitated. They had not been close for several years now, and from what she had heard, he was in considerably worse shape than he had been then. On the other hand, she did not have many options left. She made up her mind just as she stopped to buy something to eat from a stall selling chicken kebabs.

"Hi, it's me," she said, relieved to hear the familiar voice answer. "I need a bit of help."

To herself she added:

"I'm being cut off from the world."

STOCKHOLM

Alex Recht assembled his team in the Den straight after lunch. Fredrika slipped in just as he was starting the meeting. Alex noted that she looked a bit brighter. He avoided catching Peder's eye. He had still not told him why he had been summoned back to HQ, only sent a message via Ellen that he was to take a look at anything on the Ahlbin case that the public had rung in with. Since the couple's identities had not yet been released in the media, the number of calls had been pretty sparse.

"Right," Alex said briskly. "Where do we stand?"

Fredrika and Joar looked at each other, then Joar looked at Peder, who nodded mutely to Joar to present what they had found out in the course of the day. Joar rounded off with a report of the conversation with Sven and Elsie Ljung, who were convinced their friends had been murdered.

"So they stuck to that when they talked to you, too?" asked Alex, leaning back in his chair.

"Yes," said Fredrika. "And they raised quite an important point, actually."

Alex waited.

"They went round to their friends' place because they'd been invited to dinner. Why wasn't the dinner called off if the couple had just heard their daughter had died?"

Alex sat up straight.

"Very good objection," he said, but furrowed his brow. "Though according to the farewell note, only Jakob knew the terrible news. So in that case it wasn't surprising that Marja sounded normal on the phone."

"But the Ljungs also questioned the whole story of the daughter's death," Joar elaborated. "And as regards whether Marja knew about her daughter or not, we can't be sure."

"But it can't be that difficult to check, can it?" said Alex dubiously. "Whether the daughter's dead, I mean."

"No, not at all," said Fredrika. "We've got copies of the doctor's forms, confirmation of death and cause of death, from Danderyd Hospital. She apparently died from a drug overdose, and it was clear from the paperwork that she'd been an addict for some years. The hospital called the police but there were no indications that the death was anything other than self-inflicted. So no further steps were taken. But we don't know who actually broke the news to her parents. Their friends didn't seem to know she was a drug addict."

"That bit about the Ljungs and Ahlbins not being so close anymore is interesting," said Alex, changing tack. "Did they say why?"

Fredrika hesitated.

"Not exactly," she said slowly. "There was something they didn't really want to tell us, but I didn't get a sense of it being particularly relevant to the case."

Silence fell. Fredrika gave a discreet cough and their assistant, Ellen Lind, jotted something on her pad.

"Okay, then," said Alex. "Where shall we go from here? Speaking for myself, I shan't be happy until we've interviewed more of the Ahlbins' friends and acquaintances. It would be a shame if we couldn't find anyone taking a contradictory view to the Ljungs on whether Jakob Ahlbin fired the gun and whether the daughter was on drugs."

He shook his head irritably.

"What more do we know about the daughter's death?" he said, frowning. "Anything

105

strange there?"

"We haven't had time to go into it in detail," Joar put in. "But I was planning — sorry, *we* were planning to take a closer look this afternoon. If it seems worth our while."

Alex tapped his pen gently on the table.

"I'd like to suggest something else. Fredrika, how's your afternoon looking?"

Fredrika blinked several times, almost as though she had been sleeping through the meeting.

"I'm going to try to get some scraps of paper translated," she replied. "That thing I rang you about. I've nothing else on."

"Scraps of paper," echoed Peder suspiciously, mainly to have something to say.

"The hit-and-run victim outside the university had various scraps of paper on him, scrunched into little balls. They've got things written on them in Arabic."

"Since we're talking about that case," said Alex, his eyes on Fredrika, "is there anything at this stage to indicate it could have been a deliberate criminal act?"

"No," said Fredrika. "At least, not according to the doctor who did the preliminary report, but there'll be a full autopsy later."

Alex nodded.

"But that's hardly going to take all afternoon, knowing you. How about going into the Ahlbin daughter's death a bit more and trying to write a summary of what happened so we're all clear on the sequence of events? Not because I think we'll unearth anything revolutionary, but it would be good to know we'd checked it out thoroughly."

Fredrika gave a cautious smile, hardly daring to look at Joar. Maybe he was like Peder, one of those who hated to be passed over. She had not had time to form any proper opinion of him, but her first impression had been a good one. Really good. A quick glance in his direction reassured her. He looked completely unperturbed. Yes, she was impressed.

"I'll be glad to follow up the daughter's death," she said, "but I'm afraid I won't be able to stay very long this afternoon."

"It doesn't matter. You can carry on tomorrow morning," Alex added quickly.

Peder tried to catch his eye across the table, wondering what was going on.

Alex felt anger bubbling up inside him, and swallowed several times.

"Joar and I are going to pay a visit to the parish where the Ahlbins worked," he went on. "I had a call from the vicar there, earlier on today, and he was very keen to sound cooperative. We'll interview him before we decide how to take it from there — see if there's any reason to think anyone else was involved, or if we can assume Jakob was the sole perpetrator. And we'll all offer up a prayer that we find their other daughter, Johanna, by the end of the day."

Peder was staring at Alex.

"And what am I going to do?" he asked, trying not to sound as if he was whining.

He failed.

"You are going to see the head of HR at two o'clock," Alex said flatly. "And if I were you, I wouldn't be late."

Peder's heart leaped with anxiety.

"Was there anything else?" said Alex.

Joar hesitated, but then went ahead.

"We got the feeling the flat wasn't their proper home," he said.

"How do you mean?" asked Alex.

Joar looked sideways at Peder, but found his colleague was sitting staring at the wall, his face immobile.

"As I say, it was just a feeling," said Joar. "But it seemed so impersonal, almost as though the whole place was designed just for entertaining."

"We ought to investigate that angle," said Alex. "Summer cottages and the like won't necessarily be in the parents' names; one of the daughters could just as well be the registered owner. Fredrika, can you look into that, too, while you're at it?"

Then Alex declared the meeting closed.

Peder, full of foreboding, went to see the head of HR, Margareta Berlin, at exactly two o'clock. He could not get Alex's stern look out of his mind. He had to wait outside her door for a few minutes before she asked him in. *What the hell was this about?*

"Come in and shut the door," said Ms. Berlin in her inimitable husky voice, very probably the result of high whiskey consumption and lots of shouting at subordinates as she climbed her way to the top.

Peder did as he was told. He had enormous respect for the tall, powerfully built woman behind the desk. She wore her hair cut short, but still looked very feminine. Her large hand waved to indicate he was to take a seat on the other side of the desk.

"Does the name Anna-Karin Larsson say anything to you?" she asked, so brusquely that Peder jumped.

He shook his head and swallowed.

"No," he said, embarrassed to find he had to clear his throat.

"No?" said Margareta, suddenly less abrasive, though her eyes were still dark with anger. "Hmm, that's rather what I thought."

She paused before going on.

"But maybe you do know whether you like a croissant with your coffee?"

Peder almost sighed with relief. If this was about nothing worse than that stupid remark, the meeting would soon be behind him. But he still had no idea who Anna-Karin Larsson was.

"So," said Peder, with the lopsided smile he used for disarming women of all ages. "If it's yesterday's croissant incident you want to talk about, let me start by saying I meant no harm."

"Well, that's reassuring, at any rate," Margareta said drily.

"No, I really didn't," he said magnanimously, holding up his hands. "If anybody in the staff room took offense at my, er . . . how shall I put it, slightly crude way of expressing myself, I apologize. Of course."

Margareta observed him across the desk. He stared back stubbornly.

"Slightly crude?" she said.

Peder hesitated.

"Very crude, maybe?"

"Yes, actually," she said, "extremely crude, even. And it's a matter of deep regret that Anna-Karin was confronted with that sort of behavior in only her third week with us."

Peder gave a start. Anna-Karin Larsson.

Was that her name, the luscious new trainee he'd made such a fool of himself with?

"I shall go and see her and apologize in person, naturally," he said, talking so fast he almost started stuttering. "I —"

Margareta held up one hand to stop him.

"Naturally you'll apologize to her," she said forcefully. "That's so self-evident as not to count as any kind of redress here."

Bollocks. Some third-rate bit of skirt who couldn't cope with the pressure except by running off to HR at the first opportunity. As if she could read his thoughts, Margareta said: "It wasn't Anna-Karin who told us about this."

"Wasn't it?" Peder said mistrustfully.

"No, it was someone else who found your behavior offensive," said Margareta, who was now leaning across the table with a concerned look. "How are you, Peder, really?"

The question nonplussed him so much that he could not summon a reply. Margareta shook her head.

"This has got to stop, Peder," she said loud and clear, in the sort of voice normally only used for addressing children. "Alex and I have been aware of what you've been going through these past eighteen months, and how it's affected you. But that's not enough,

I'm afraid. To be blunt, you've put your foot in it once too often now, and this morning's croissant episode was the final straw."

Peder almost started to laugh, and raised his arms in a gesture of appeal.

"Now, hang on —"

"No," roared Margareta, bringing the palm of her hand down on the desk with such force that Peder thought he could feel the floor shake. "No, I've hung on long enough. I wondered whether to intervene when you got drunk at the Christmas party and pinched Elin's bottom, but I heard the two of you had worked it out between you and assumed you realized you'd gone too far. But clearly you hadn't."

You could have heard a pin drop, and Peder felt his objections to her verdict piling up and turning into a shout, which he only kept inside him with a huge effort. This wasn't fair in any way and Peder was going to bloody well throttle the bastard who'd squealed about the croissants.

"I've booked you a place on a workplace equality course which I think might be an eye-opener for you, Peder," she said frankly.

Seeing his reaction, she went on quickly:

"My decision isn't negotiable. You attend the course, or I take this problem to a higher level. I also want you to agree to an appointment with a psychologist through the healthcare provider we have a contract with."

Peder opened his mouth and then closed it again, his face flaming.

"We as employers cannot accept this sort of conduct, it simply won't do," she said in the same firm tone, pushing a sheet of paper over the desk toward him. "The police force is no place for office fornication. Here, these are the dates and times of your appointments."

For a moment he contemplated refusing to take the sheet of paper and telling her to shove it up her fat arse, and making a run for it. But then he remembered that Alex knew the story and even seemed to be in on the conspiracy. Peder clenched one fist so hard that the knuckles went white, and snatched the paper with the other hand.

"Was there anything else?" he said with effort.

Margareta shook her head.

"Not for now," she said. "But I shall be keeping a close eye on how you deal with your colleagues from now on. Try to see it as a fresh start, a second chance. Take the opportunity of getting something out of this, especially out of your talk to the psychologist."

Peder nodded and left the room, convinced he would fucking well kill the woman if he stayed a second longer.

Neither Alex Recht nor Joar Sahlin said a word as they drove the short stretch from HQ in Kungsholmen to Bromma Church, where Jakob and Marja Ahlbin had worked. Ragnar Vinterman, the vicar, had promised to meet them at the parish rooms at two thirty.

Alex's thoughts went to Peder. He knew he had been hard on him at the meeting in the Den, but he did not really know what else he could have done. The croissant episode was as odd as it was unacceptable, and revealed poor judgment in a colleague whose employer had placed a good deal of trust in him. Alex knew well enough that the boy had been having a hard time in his private life over quite a long period. It was only natural for that sort of thing to affect one's judgment, and if Peder had ever commented on his own conduct in a way that showed he knew he was behaving badly, people might have been more tolerant. But Peder had not. He got himself into awkward situations more and more often, embarrassing his employer in front of other employees.

In front of other *female* employees.

Alex suppressed a sigh. And then there was Peder's peculiarly lousy sense of timing. The last thing they needed at the moment was any negative publicity, with the special investigation group's continued existence currently under discussion. It was enough that their only civilian appointment and only female investigator had been forced to go part time by a more than hellish pregnancy which Alex's bosses had initially construed as symptoms of stress and exhaustion. He had been more than thankful the day Fredrika finally gave in and followed the rules for a proper reduction in hours backed up by a convincing doctor's note.

Meanwhile, the group had acquired new blood in the shape of Joar. Admittedly only for a limited period, but still. The decision was in itself an indication that the group had not been written off. It had not taken Alex long to appreciate Joar as an exceptionally talented detective. By contrast with both Peder and Fredrika, he also seemed mentally stable. He never flared up like Peder, and never seemed to misconstrue things the way Fredrika tended to. He always stayed calm and his integrity appeared boundless. For the first time in many months, Alex felt as though he had someone he could talk to at work.

"Mind if I ask about your surname?" Joar suddenly said. "Is it German?"

Alex gave a laugh; it was a question he was often asked.

"If we go back far enough in our family tree, it apparently is," he replied. "Jewish."

He glanced sideways at Joar, keen to see if he reacted. He did not.

"But that was a long time ago," Alex added. "The men whose surname it was married Christian women, and the Jewish blood ties between mother and child were broken."

They were approaching the church. Alex parked outside the parish rooms as arranged. A tall, dignified-looking man was on the front steps in his shirtsleeves and dog collar, waiting for them. He was silhouetted like a dark statue against the white building and pale gray sky. Commands respect, was Alex's assessment before he was even out of the car.

"Ragnar Vinterman," said the clergyman,

taking Alex's hand and then Joar's.

Alex noted that he could not have been on the steps for long, because his hand was still warm. And large. Alex had never seen such large hands before.

"Let's go in," said Ragnar Vinterman in a deep voice. "Alice, our parish assistant, has provided some refreshments."

There were coffee cups and a generous plate of buns set out on one of the big tables in the parish rooms. Other than that, the whole place looked deserted, and Alex could feel how chilly the place was even before he took off his coat. Joar kept his on.

"I'm sorry it's so cold," said Ragnar with a sigh. "We've been trying to sort out the heating here for years; we almost despair of ever getting it to work. Coffee?"

They accepted the hot drinks gladly.

"I should probably start by expressing condolences," Alex said cautiously as he put down his cup.

Ragnar nodded slowly, head bowed.

"It's a huge loss to the parish," he said quietly. "It's going to take us a very long time to get over it. The grieving process is going to be hard work for us all."

The man's bearing and voice filled Alex with instinctive trust in him. Alex's daughter would have said that the vicar had the body of a senior athlete.

The vicar ran a hand through his thick, dark brown hair.

"Here in the church we always follow the saying "Hope for the best but prepare for the worst," but to do that you need to form a clear view of what the worst conceivable thing would be."

He stopped abruptly and fiddled with his coffee cup.

"I fear we who work and worship here had not really done that on this occasion."

Alex frowned.

"I don't think I quite understand."

"Everybody here knew about Jakob's health problems," he said, meeting Alex's gaze. "But only a few of us knew how bad things sometimes got for him. Only a handful of colleagues and parishioners knew he had had electric shock treatment several times, for example. When he was in the clinic we would generally say he was at a health resort or away on holiday. He preferred it that way."

"Was he afraid of being seen as weak?" asked Joar.

Ragnar turned his gaze to the younger man.

"I don't think so," he answered, leaning back in his chair slightly. "But he knew, just as we did, that there are so many preconceptions about the condition he suffered from."

"We gather he's been living with it for a long time," said Alex, kicking himself for not yet having got hold of Jakob's doctor.

"For decades," sighed the vicar. "Ever since his teens, really. Thank goodness treatment in that area has made such strides as time has gone on. From what I can understand, those early years were pretty ghastly for him. His mother was apparently diagnosed with the same thing."

"Is she still alive?" asked Joar.

"No," said the vicar, and drank some coffee. "She took her own life when Jakob was fourteen. That was when he decided to take holy orders."

Alex gave a shudder. Some problems seemed to pass from generation to generation like a relay baton.

"What's your view on what happened yesterday evening?" he said tentatively, seeking eye contact.

"You mean do I think Jakob did it? Did he shoot Marja and then himself?"

Alex nodded.

Ragnar swallowed several times, looking past Alex and Joar and out of the window at the snow covering the trees and ground.

"I'm afraid I think that is exactly what

happened."

As if he had just realized that he was sitting very uncomfortably, he shifted position on his chair and put one knee over the other. His big hands rested on his lap.

The only other sound was that of Joar's pen at work, adding to the half page of notes he already had.

"He was in such a wretched state those last two days," Ragnar said, his voice strained. "And I regret, yes, I regret with all my heart that I didn't sound the alarm and at least tell Marja everything."

"Such as what?" asked Alex.

"About Karolina," said Ragnar, leaning forward over the table and resting his face in his hands for a few moments. "Little Lina, whose life had gone so far off course."

Alex registered that Joar had stopped writing.

"Did you know her well?" he asked.

"Not as an adult, better when she was younger," said Ragnar. "But I heard reports from Jakob every so often on how she was living. On her addiction and her attempts to get free of it."

He shook his head.

"Jakob didn't realize what her problem was until a few years ago," he went on. "I mean, she'd always demanded so much of herself, and when she couldn't really reach that standard in her student years, she started taking various kinds of drugs. At first to enhance her performance, but later on the addiction was yet another problem she had to deal with."

"But her mother, Marja, she must have been aware of the problem, too?" Alex said dubiously.

"Of course," said Ragnar. "But the girl was much closer to her father, so he was the only one with the full picture. And since they had other problems in their life, he chose not to pass on to his wife all the details of what was happening to their daughter."

"But she must have noticed something," said Joar. "As I understand it, the girl had been severely addicted for a number of years."

"That's right," said Ragnar, a sharpness coming into his voice. "But with a bit of determination, things can be glossed over well enough, especially if the mother can't cope with the truth, even if she chose to see it."

"You mean she chose to shut her eyes to aspects of her daughter's state?" said Alex.

"Yes, I do," Ragnar said firmly. "And I don't know if it's all that surprising really.

They had had problems for many years with Jakob's condition, and suddenly their daughter was another problem. I suppose it was all too much for Marja. That's how it is sometimes."

Alex, himself the father of two children, was not sure that he agreed with the clergyman, but then he had no experience of what it was like to live with someone suffering from severe depression. There certainly was a natural limit to how much misery any one person could bear. Ragnar Vinterman was right in that respect.

"He got the news on Sunday evening," Ragnar went on. "He rang me just afterward and sounded shocked, desperate."

"Who broke it to him?" asked Alex.

Ragnar looked momentarily confused.

"I don't actually know. Does it matter?"

"Probably not," said Alex, but he still wanted to know.

Joar shifted uneasily.

"But he said nothing to his wife?" he asked.

Ragnar bit his lower lip and shook his head.

"Not a word. And he begged me not to say anything, either. He said he needed to try to understand the implications himself before he told Marja. I saw no reason not to do as he asked, and gave him until Wednesday, until today."

"Until today?" echoed Alex.

The vicar inclined his head in assent.

"Marja was coming to a parish meeting here today, and if Jakob still hadn't told her, I was going to do it myself. I mean, she had to know."

The thoughts went round and round in Alex's head. A picture was slowly taking shape.

"Did you speak to him again later, or was that the last time you were in touch?"

"We spoke once more after that," said Ragnar, sounding strained again. "Yesterday. He sounded oddly relieved on the phone, said he was going to tell Marja all about it in the evening. Said everything would be all right."

The vicar took a deep breath. Alex did not expect him to start crying, nor did he.

"Everything would be all right," repeated the vicar, his voice thick. "I should have realized, should have done something. But I didn't. I didn't do a thing."

"That's very common," Joar said in such a matter-of-fact voice that both Alex and the vicar stared at him.

Joar put down his pen and pushed away his notepad.

"We think we're going to be rational and understanding in all situations, but unfortunately human beings don't work like that. We aren't mind readers; in fact the only thing we *are* good at is "realizing" afterward, when all the facts are at hand, what we should have done. And then we hold ourselves responsible. When there's no need."

He shook his head.

"Believe me, you lacked vital information that, with hindsight, you've convinced yourself you had all along."

Alex looked at his younger colleague in astonishment.

There's so much we don't know about each other, he thought.

"Some of Marja and Jakob's other friends say it's out of the question for Jakob to have shot his wife and himself," he said, moving the conversation on.

Ragnar Vinterman appeared to hesitate.

"You mean Elsie and Sven?" he said gently. "It's a long time since they were really good friends with Marja and Jakob, and there was a lot they didn't know."

Like the daughter's drug habit, Alex thought to himself.

"Why was that?" asked Joar. "Why weren't they such good friends anymore?"

"Oh, they were still good friends," said

125

Ragnar. "Just not as close, from what Jakob said. Why? Well, I hardly know. They fell out over something a few years ago, and it was never quite the same after that. Then Elsie and Sven retired early, and when they left the parish they had even less contact with Jakob and Marja."

Joar was making notes again.

"And what about their other daughter, Johanna? Did she have problems as well?" asked Alex.

The vicar shook his head.

"No, not at all," he said. "I only ever heard good things about her. On the other hand," he added uncertainly, "I suppose I did hear rather less about her. She made it clear at quite an early stage that she wasn't as interested in the church as the rest of the family, wasn't a believer, and that created a certain distance."

"Do you know what she's doing now?" Alex asked curiously.

"She's a lawyer," replied Ragnar. "I'm afraid I don't know any more than that."

"So you don't know where we can get hold of her?" asked Joar.

"No, unfortunately not."

They sat in silence for a while. Alex drank some coffee and mulled over what they had discovered. Most of it now seemed quite logical. Jakob had not canceled the dinner date because it might have made Marja wonder what was going on. And the reason he had sounded so relieved on the phone was in all likelihood the classic one: he had decided to end their lives and thus found peace.

The only question mark was the daughter Johanna. Had she really drifted so far apart from her family that Jakob felt it legitimate to rob her of her parents? They really did need to get hold of her, and fast.

He decided to ask one last question.

"Say we pretend we don't think Jakob was disturbed enough to take his own life and his wife's, who else could it have been? Can you think of any possible alternative perpetrator?"

Ragnar frowned.

"You mean someone Jakob and Marja had such a violent disagreement with that they were murdered?"

Alex nodded.

"No idea. None at all."

"Jakob did a lot of campaigning on refugee issues . . ." began Joar.

"Yes, that might have landed him in trouble, of course," said Ragnar. "I don't know anything about it, though."

With that, the meeting was over. The men

ate the last of the buns and drank up their coffee, chatting about the snow, which was causing various disruptions. Then they shook hands and parted.

"I'm afraid his assessment may be correct," Alex said thoughtfully in the car on the way back to Kungsholmen. "But we must get hold of the daughter first and check that story against hers. And we must talk to the doctor in charge of Jakob's treatment."

But by the time Alex and Joar left work some hours later, they still had not located either of them. And although Alex had thought he had everything under control, a sneaking suspicion was beginning to grow that this might not be the case.

Fredrika Bergman was running for her life. With a protective hand round her belly, she was running faster than she had ever run before through the dark forest. The long tree branches clawed at her face and body, her feet sank into damp moss, and hot summer rain plastered her hair to her head.

They were close now, her pursuers. And she knew she was going to lose. They were calling to her.

"Fredrika, give up! You know you can never escape us! Stop! For the sake of the baby!"

The words lashed her onward. It was the baby they wanted, it was the baby they were trying to get at. She had seen that one of the men had a knife. Long and glinting. When they caught her, they would cut the baby out of her stomach and leave her to die in the forest. Just as they had all the other women she could see lying on their backs among the trees.

She could not go on much longer and her desperation grew. She would die in the forest, unable to save her unborn child. The tears pulled and tugged at her, slowing strides that had been so long and swift at first.

She finally tripped over a tree root and fell hard. Landed awkwardly, on her stomach, and the baby froze to ice and stopped moving.

Within a few seconds they were in a ring around her. Tall and dark. Each with a knife. One of them squatted down beside her.

"Now come on, Fredrika," he whispered. "Why are you making it so hard when it could be simple?" They crowded round her exhausted body, forced her onto her back, held her down.

"Breathe, Fredrika, breathe," said the voice, and she saw one of the knives being raised.

She screamed with the full force of her lungs, fought to get free.

"Fredrika, for Christ's sake, you're frightening the life out of me," boomed a familiar voice.

She forced her eyes open, looking around in confusion. Spencer's hard arms were holding her firmly; her legs were tangled in the duvet. She was sweating all over and tears were running down her face.

Spencer felt her relax, and sat down on the edge of the bed. He held her in silence.

"Good God, what's wrong with me?" whispered Fredrika, sobbing into his neck.

Spencer said nothing, just hugged her tightly.

"I'm sorry I didn't get here sooner," he said quietly. "I'm sorry."

Fredrika, not even able to recall that they had arranged to meet, was just glad he was there and said nothing for a long while.

"What time is it?" she finally asked.

"Half past eleven," sighed Spencer. "The plane from Madrid was delayed."

A memory forced its way to the surface. Madrid. He had been at a conference in Madrid. He was meant to land at half past six, they were going to have dinner together. But in the event he had only got there just before midnight, letting himself in with his own key. Before she got pregnant they had always met at Spencer's father's old flat, but now, with the baby, and Fredrika having such a hard time, they more often met at her flat instead. New challenges meant new routines.

Tears of disappointment welled in her eyes.

"I'm so bloody fed up with all this. I thought you were supposed to be happy when you were pregnant; placid. Bovine, almost."

Spencer gave that wry smile that had made her want to have him more than she had ever wanted any other man.

"Bovine, you?" He grinned, taking off his outdoor things.

"You didn't even hang your coat up?" Fredrika asked foolishly.

"No, you were making such a racket when I came in that I thought I'd better see to you first."

He padded swiftly back. Tousle-haired, with tired eyes. He was no youngster, Spencer. And he would soon be a father for the first time in his life.

"Good Lord, Fredrika, is this how it is every night?"

"Almost," she replied evasively. "But you've seen me like that before."

"Yes, but I thought it only happened now and again. It's awful to think of this going on when I'm not here."

Be here then, Fredrika wanted to say. Leave your boring wife and marry me instead.

The words froze inside her, swallowed up by an ocean of habit. Her relationship with

Spencer was as crystal clear as it had always been: they were a couple, certainly, but only within certain limits. He had never led her to believe things would be different just because he accepted his role as father of her child.

Fredrika got out of bed and went to the bathroom. Spencer had vanished into the kitchen to make a quick sandwich. She threw her sweat-drenched nightdress into the washing basket and took a shower. The warm, gentle jets of water felt desperately welcome on her skin. She twisted and turned under the flow, too tired to register that she was crying. Afterward she wrapped herself in a big towel.

At least she had had a good day at work. Short, but good. It had been hard to find anyone to translate the Arabic on her scraps of paper because all the translators were tied up on a big immigrant-smuggling case, with lots of material to work on for the national CID. Finally one of them had taken on her small inquiry and agreed to report back the next day.

Fredrika suppressed a sigh. There certainly would be plenty to do tomorrow. The translator's feedback, to go over, of course; and the doctor who had been responsible for Karolina Ahlbin when she was admitted to the hospital and then died of the overdose was also due to get back to her. The only concrete result of Fredrika's day was a memo about a big property out at Ekerö, a house and some land, that was registered in the names of the Ahlbin sisters and had previously been under their parents' names. Maybe that was the house where the family spent time together?

Fredrika felt a lump in her throat at the thought of Johanna Ahlbin, left all alone now. Fredrika had not been able to resist looking her up in the national register, while she was at it. Johanna Maria Ahlbin, born 1978, one year after her sister. Unmarried, no children. No one but her registered at that address, so it was a single-person household.

Was there anything worse? The child moved, as if worried it might get forgotten. Fredrika tried to soothe it by stroking her stomach. The baby was unborn. It was there, and yet it was not. If anyone had rung at her door and told her that her parents and brother were dead, she would fall apart. She would miss her brother above all. Fresh tears pricked her eyes. Apart from Spencer, there was really no one she thought of more highly.

She wiped away the tears that were running down her cheeks like lost beings. Her own child was hardly likely to have any siblings.

"You'll just have to manage," she whispered.

Then she raised her head and met her own red-rimmed eyes in the bathroom mirror. And felt ashamed. What had she got to be so upset about, when it came down to it? She was living a good life with friends and family, and expecting her first baby with a man she had loved for many years.

Grow up, she thought angrily. And stop feeling so sorry for yourself. It's only in fairy stories that people get any happier than this.

With the towel wrapped round her head, she left the bathroom and went out to Spencer in the kitchen.

"Can you make me a sandwich, too?"

The ring of the telephone cut through the flat just before midnight. He went to answer as quickly as he could, before it woke his wife as well. He moved cautiously past her closed door, grateful for once that they no longer shared a bedroom. His bare feet sounded loud on the parquet floor. With one smooth movement he silently pulled the study door shut behind him.

"Yes?" he said as he lifted the receiver.

"She's rung," said the voice at the other end. "She rang earlier today."

He did not respond immediately. He had been expecting the call, but it churned him up, even so. He decided it was a healthy re-action. No human being could be part of a project like this without feeling something.

"All according to plan, then," he said.

"Everything's going according to plan," confirmed the voice at the other end. "And tomorrow we go on to the next stage."

"Did she seem to suspect anything? Has she realized the all-encompassing nature of her predicament, so to speak?"

"Not yet. But she will tomorrow."

"And by then it's too late for her," he concluded with a sigh.

"Yes, by then it'll all be over."

He played with a pristine notepad on the oak desk. The gleam of a streetlight colored the flowers on the windowsill yellow.

"And our friend who came from Arlanda the other day?"

"He's in the flat where his contact left him. He should be ready for his task tomorrow."

Cars were passing in the road outside. Their wheels crunched over the snow. The exhaust fumes were white in the cold. How strange. Out there, everything seemed to be carrying on exactly as before.

"Perhaps we ought to have a break in operations when we've finished this?" he said softly. "Until all the fuss dies down, I mean."

He could hear the breathing at the other end of the line.

"You're not getting cold feet?" said the voice.

He moved his head from side to side.

"Of course not," he said in a quiet, emphatic voice. "But a bit of caution does no harm at the moment, with everyone's eyes on us."

The caller gave a low laugh.

"You're the only one they can see, my friend. The rest of us are invisible."

"Exactly," he said huskily. "And that's what we want, isn't it? It would be a shame if they found reason to take a closer look at me. Then it would only be a matter of time before they saw you, too, *my friend.*"

He put particular stress on the last words, and the laughter at the other end stopped.

"We're both on the same side in this," the voice said in a muted tone.

"Just so," he persisted. "And it would be as well if I wasn't the only person to remember that."

He hung up. Lit a cigarette, even though he knew his wife hated him smoking indoors. And outside the snow fell as if the weather gods were desperately trying to bury all the evil in the world beneath frozen rain.

■ ■ ■ ■

THURSDAY,
FEBRUARY 28, 2008

■ ■ ■ ■

STOCKHOLM

She had lots of red hair, a shapeless mauve dress, and very irritating body language. Her voice was shrill, her words harsh and angry. Peder Rydh was pretty sure she had BO and unshaven armpits, too.

Peder was sitting right at the back, at the end of the row of chairs, wondering what he was doing there. On a course about equality in the workplace. When there were so many more important things to do. If Margareta Berlin had been there, too, she would have been feeling shamefaced about her decision. Of all the equality courses in the world, this must be the worst. Pity. For Ms. Berlin.

He fidgeted. Restlessness tingled in his legs, bubbled up, and made his blood boil. It fucking well wasn't fair. It just wasn't.

He turned red at the recollection of Margareta Berlin's scolding. She had looked so goddamn sure of herself, imposing the sentence from behind her desk. As if *she* was the right person to be teaching *him* how to behave in the force.

And she'd had the nerve to bring up that little misunderstanding at the Christmas party, too.

Peder swallowed hard. He felt shame and apprehension, but also fury, pure fury. It hadn't been his fault. Anybody could see that. And what was more, Margareta Berlin had her facts wrong. The police force was no different from any other workplace; you could go to bed with anybody you liked.

More pictures came in his mind's eye, this time from the Christmas party.

Hot bodies on a cramped, improvised dance floor in the staff room. Far more alcohol than had been intended, dancing to some music that was not part of the main program. As his colleague Hasse put it the day after the party, things had got quite heavy. Peder had made the most of it. Lots of partying, lots of dancing. His feet had done the moves by themselves as he went whirling round with one female workmate after another.

Then he danced with Elin Bredberg. Shiny face, dark hair, and bright eyes. Peder had seen eyes like that before, oh yes. Hungry, come-hither eyes. On the pull.

Gagging for it.

And Peder was never backward in coming forward. If the door was open, he stepped inside. That was just the way he was. First he pulled Elin closer to him. Her eyes narrowed but were still smiling. Tempting, inviting. So Peder moved his hand from her back down to her bottom. Squeezed it and kissed her cheek.

Before he knew it, her hand came flying through the air and smacked him round the face. And the party was over.

Peder thought there were certain unwritten rules in life. Elin Bredberg must have known what messages he was receiving. He told her so, and demanded she take her share of the blame, if not all of it, which was what she really ought to do. In the end he had accepted that the fault was on his side. Not until the next day, when they were both a bit more sober and capable of normal conversation, but they had sorted it out between them, at least.

Though Peder still thought she was the one in the wrong.

And now look where it had got him. In a school hall in working hours, being lectured on equality by a woman who looked like a scarecrow and probably hadn't had any decent sex since Jesus was walking about in sandals.

Peder gave an inward groan. It was always so unfair. There was always some bad experience to shatter the least hint of happiness whenever it came along. That bastard who had squealed about the croissants had better mind his bloody back, because he had made himself an enemy in the force. A suspicion had dawned on him during the night, and the more he thought about it, the more likely it seemed.

"Gender is power," the lecturer boomed. "And women are, in a way, second-class citizens in this country. Even though Sweden is one of the leading democracies in the world."

She took a breath, her hair swinging all over the place.

"We're going to do a little exercise," she said crisply, surveying the hall. "I need a volunteer, a nice young man from the audience."

Nobody moved.

"Oh, come on now," she cooed. "It's not difficult. Just an exercise that's been around since time immemorial. And it's fun, as well."

Peder sighed. Sighed and let his thoughts drift to Ylva, from whom he had separated

144

six months before. Months of lonely evenings in his flat in the suburbs, and the boys coming to stay every other weekend. The odd evening or week of meaningless dates that never led to anything except sex that was hot the first time and then rapidly cooled.

His chest tightened, his eyes smarted, and he slumped a little in his seat. He wondered if it was the same for Ylva. He wondered if she felt empty, too.

Because that was how he felt.

Empty. So bloody empty.

The doctor's voice made Fredrika feel she was being watched, even though she knew it was ridiculous. The doctor was on the telephone and not there in front of her. If she were to guess what he looked like, she would say he had glasses and thinning hair. And maybe narrow, green eyes.

"Karolina Ahlbin was brought to the hospital in an ambulance last Thursday," said the doctor, whose name was Göran Ahlgren. "She was diagnosed with what would popularly be called an overdose, in this case an overdose of heroin injected into the crook of her arm. We did what we could to save her, but her internal organs had already taken such a battering that it was impossible to bring her back. She died less than an hour after she was admitted."

Fredrika jotted down what he had told her.

"I can send over copies of the confirmation-of-death and cause-of-death forms," he added.

"We've already had those," said Fredrika, "but I would be grateful for a complete copy of the patient's notes, if you wouldn't mind."

She could hear the hesitation in Göran Ahlgren's voice as he went on.

"Are there any suspicious circumstances?" he asked.

"No, not in her case," said Fredrika. "But her death is linked to another case, so . . ."

"I shall make sure you have the paperwork you need by this afternoon," said the doctor.

Fredrika got the feeling he was rather keen to hang up.

"Had she been a patient at the hospital before?" she asked.

"No," said Ahlgren. "Never."

There was a knock at Fredrika's door and Ellen Lind came in with some papers, which she put on the desk. They gave each other a nod and Ellen departed.

We should see more of each other outside

work, thought Fredrika, and felt tired at the very prospect.

She hardly had the energy to socialize with her existing friends.

Ahlgren cleared his throat to remind her he was still on the line.

"Sorry," Fredrika said quickly. "I just had a couple more questions about how Karolina was identified. Did she have any ID documents on her?"

"Yes, she did. She had a wallet in her back pocket with a driving license in it. Identification was made using the picture on the driving license and confirmed by her sister, who came with her in the ambulance."

Fredrika was struck almost dumb.

"Sorry?"

"Her sister. Just a moment, I've got the name here," said the doctor, leafing through some papers. "Yes, here we are. Her name was Johanna, Johanna Ahlbin. She was here to identify her sister."

The thoughts were whirling round inside Fredrika's head.

"We haven't been able to contact her sister," she said. "Do you know where she is?"

"I didn't speak to her for long," said Ahlgren wearily. "But I remember she mentioned an imminent trip abroad. I believe she left over the weekend."

Fredrika felt a growing sense of frustration. There had been no reference to the sister's presence in any of the documentation she had received from the hospital or the police.

"Did the police officers who were sent to the hospital speak to the sister?"

"Only briefly," said the doctor. "There weren't any obvious irregularities that needed looking into. I mean, the deceased came in with her sister, who filled us in on the background. And the identification was a straightforward matter, too."

The fatigue that normally slowed Fredrika's brain suddenly cleared away. She gripped her pen hard and stared straight ahead. So Johanna Ahlbin had been present when Karolina died. Then she had gone abroad and was not contactable. And two days ago her father's grief had made him take his own life.

"Who informed Karolina Ahlbin's parents of her death?" she asked, her voice unnecessarily stern.

If she had not known better, she would have said the doctor was smiling as he replied.

"I can't say for certain," he said. "But Johanna Ahlbin said she would do it."

"Do we know if she told anyone else about the death? Did she ring anyone while she was at the hospital?"

"No," replied Ahlgren, "not that I saw."

Bewildered, Fredrika tried to get to grips with the story that was emerging.

"What sort of mood did Johanna Ahlbin seem to be in while she was with you?"

The doctor paused, as if he did not understand the question.

"She was upset, of course," he said. "But not in a particularly dramatic way."

"Meaning what?"

"Well, she wasn't as distraught as a lot of relatives are when someone dies unexpectedly. I got the impression Karolina Ahlbin's drug abuse was known to the family and had been a problem for a long time. That doesn't necessarily mean the death was expected, of course, but it did mean the relatives were to some extent prepared for the possibility that this was how it might end."

Not her father, Fredrika thought dully. He was entirely unprepared. He shot his wife and then himself.

She ended the call to the doctor, not at all clear about what she had discovered.

An odd family. Very odd, in fact.

A glance at the clock showed it would

soon be time for the morning meeting in the Den. She reached for the papers Ellen had left on her desk. A copy of the follow-up report on the unidentified hit-and-run victim. She leafed through it quickly and saw there was nothing new in it. The pathologist performing the autopsy would send in a report later in the day.

Her thoughts went to the crumpled scraps of paper and the Arabic script she was having translated. They probably meant nothing, but still needed checking out.

The translator answered after the third ring.

"It wasn't the easiest handwriting to decipher," he said.

"But you could make it out?" Fredrika asked urgently.

"Yes, of course," said the translator, sounding almost offended.

Fredrika suppressed a sigh. It was always so easy to tread on people's toes, to cross lines that were never evident from the outset.

"We'll take the straightforward part first," began the translator. "The pamphlet. It's a prayer book. A collection of verses from the Koran, nothing strange about it at all. And there was nothing written in it, either. But then there are these bits of paper."

Fredrika could hear rustling at the other end.

"The first one has the names of two locations in Stockholm: the Globe and Enskede. Two Swedish words, but written down phonetically, in Arabic. That must be it, otherwise I've no idea what it means. And I'm an Arab myself, so I ought to know."

He gave a laugh and Fredrika had to smile. The translator's laugh died away.

"The other one, the one you told me had a ring wrapped in it, says: "Farah Hajib, Sadr City, Baghdad, Iraq.' "

"What does it mean?" asked Fredrika.

"No idea," said the translator. "And it may mean nothing beyond the most obvious thing, namely that in Sadr City in Baghdad there lives a woman called Farah Hajib. Perhaps the ring's hers?"

"What sort of place is Sadr City?"

"It's a lesser-known district of Baghdad which is, or at any rate used to be, controlled wholly or in part by the Shiite grouping known as the Mehdi Army," explained the translator in a matter-of-fact way. "A real trouble spot, you could say. Many people had to flee from there because of the conflict between the Shiite and Sunni Muslims after the fall of Saddam's regime."

Pictures from the news reports of the

inferno of internal antagonisms and clashes that was post-2003 Iraq resurfaced in Fredrika's mind. Millions of people moving into the interior of the country and into neighboring states. And added to those the very few, all things considered, who had made it all the way to Europe and to Sweden.

"Maybe she's here?" said Fredrika. "As an asylum seeker?"

"I'll send up my translation in the internal post," said the translator, "so you can check with the Migration Agency. Though I suspect it will be hard to locate her with just a name. You can't even be sure she has given the authorities here the same name."

"I know," said Fredrika, "but I still want to check. And how did you get on with the map? Could you decipher anything?"

"Ah yes, the map. I'd forgotten that."

There was more rustling.

"The writing says '8 Fyristorg.' "

"An address in Uppsala, then?"

"It seems to be, yes. That's all there was. But as I said, I'll send this up and you can get back to me if you've got any questions."

Fredrika thanked him for his help and decided her immediate priority was to check out the address in Uppsala, the city where she and Spencer had first met.

It was nearly ten and she only had a few minutes before the meeting. Time to banish Spencer from her thoughts so she could concentrate. She raised her eyebrows when she discovered what was at 8 Fyristorg.

It was the address of a Forex foreign exchange bureau.

Fredrika frowned and tried hard to think what had made her react so strongly to seeing the name Forex. Nothing came to mind, so she logged on to Vilma, the Migration Agency's system, to see if she could find a Farah Hajib in their database. Maybe the woman was in Sweden. And maybe she was missing a ring.

When he heard the key in the lock, he felt such a surge of relief that he almost burst into tears. The night had felt interminable and the flat was very cold. The lovely frost patterns on the outsides of the windows were the only aesthetically appealing things in this drab, temporary home.

Ali was not feeling good. He had had a stomachache and diarrhea for several days. The air in the flat was thick with cigarette smoke because none of the windows opened, and he sometimes found himself trying not to breathe in too often. He was also feeling the effects of prolonged insomnia. It had only taken a couple of sleepless nights for his senses to start feeling distorted by fatigue. Now he forgot a thought before he had even finished thinking it, and sometimes felt he was asleep even though he was awake.

This was not the life he had paid for. Even if he had paid a good deal less than many other people.

He met them in the hall, wanting to show that he was glad to see them, even so.

It was early in the day, not much after 9:30.

It was the same woman who had met him at the bus station. She had a man with her. He was short and very blond. It was hard to assess his age, but he looked about sixty. Ali's spirits fell. He had hoped for someone who spoke Arabic. To his surprise, the man opened his mouth and greeted him in his own language.

"*Salaam aleikum,* Ali," he said softly. "How have you been getting on in this flat?"

Ali swallowed and cleared his throat several times. It was so long since he had had anyone to talk to.

"It's fine," he said, his voice scratchy.

He swallowed again and hoped they could not tell that he was lying. It would be a disaster if they thought he was being insolent. The very worst thing would be if they sent him home. That would put him and his family back to square one.

The man and woman went farther into the flat and Ali trailed after them. They sat down in the living room. The woman put a few unopened packets of cigarettes on the coffee table and nodded to Ali. He smiled and tried to express his gratitude. He had had nothing to smoke all night, which had only increased the stress levels in his body.

"Thank you," he whispered in Arabic. "Thank you."

The fair-haired man said something to the woman and she laughed.

"We hope you didn't think we had deserted you," said the man, leaning back on the sofa with a troubled look. "It's just that we have to leave a few days between visits, as I'm sure you understand."

When Ali did not reply at once, the man added: "It was for your own sake, too, you know."

Ali took the first drag at a cigarette, feeling the nicotine start to soothe him.

"It was no problem at all," he said quickly, putting the cigarette to his mouth again. "I've been fine."

The man nodded and looked reassured. The woman picked up the briefcase she had

155

with her and put it on her knee. The lock flew open with a quiet click and she opened it.

"We've come to discuss the final part of your payment for setting you up here in Sweden," the man said with authority. "So you can get your residence permit and bring your family over, start a new life. And so you can move to your new home, learn Swedish, and look for a job."

Ali nodded eagerly. He had been waiting for this ever since he got off the plane.

The woman passed him a plastic wallet with some papers in it.

"This is the house in Enskede we thought you and your family could have," said the man, encouraging Ali to take out the papers. "We thought you might like to see it."

The pictures showed an anonymous little house joined to some others. The house was white and the lawn in front was very green. There were curtains at the windows. Ali could not help smiling. His family would love living there.

"Do you like it?"

Ali nodded. The man spoke Arabic well, better than many other foreigners Ali had encountered since the outbreak of the Iraq War. He wondered if he would be able to speak Swedish that well one day. The feeling of hope warmed his chest. Only those who did not make an effort risked losing everything.

The woman reached for the document wallet and Ali handed it back quickly.

"What do you want me to do?" he asked, shifting impatiently in the armchair.

His eyes were stinging with fatigue and hunger was making the pains in his stomach even worse.

The man smiled his warm smile again.

"How much did you tell them, back home in Iraq?"

Ali sighed.

"Not much. Just that you had a different sort of payment system from the other networks. That we paid less money and the rest was based on . . ."

He groped for the right words.

". . . favors on both sides."

The man's smile got even broader.

"Exactly," he said in the most approving of tones, as if Ali had done something first rate. "Favors on both sides, that's exactly it."

He gave a little cough and his troubled look returned.

"As I hope you realize, we're doing this because we wish you and your countrymen well. But everything costs money. The house costs money, the false passport that got you here cost money. And remember, in our system, on no account must you apply for your residence permit yourself. We have contacts who see to all that for you."

That was the very part of their arrangement that sounded so amazing and made Ali accept their very unusual terms: he was not to tell a single person, even his family, where he was going. Nor was he to say who his contacts were, prior to his departure. And he must swear on his honor that he had never been in Sweden before and did not know anyone there.

The first of these conditions was the only one that had really given Ali any trouble: not being able to tell his family anything. He had had to slip away from his marital home like a thief in the night and set out on his trip to Europe and Sweden all alone. He had, however, broken the third condition. He did in fact have a friend in Sweden, in a town called Uppsala, and he had alerted that friend in the most unobtrusive of ways to his arrival. The friend was no doubt already waiting for him to get in touch, though he had explained it would be a while before they were free to meet.

The other refugee smugglers seemed to hold the men in their charge in contempt.

They cost between five and ten times more, and their terms were downright miserable. There was no question of a residence permit with them, and Ali was very well aware of the prospects. The Swedish Migration Agency had initially granted permits to just about every asylum seeker from Iraq, but was now turning down 70 percent of all applications. If you were turned down, then you could appeal, but it could take years before you got a final decision. And if you lost, you had to go underground to stop the authorities throwing you out.

He could imagine nothing worse. The very thought of being separated from his wife, Nadia, for that long made it difficult for him to breathe.

So he nodded eagerly to this man who spoke of favors on both sides and the need to finance his residence permit.

"What is it you want me to do?" he asked again.

The man observed Ali in silence for a long time. Then he leaned forward and told him.

Once upon a time, everything had all been very different. Alex Recht had been a new, young member of the police force and had soon established himself as one of the promising names. After just a few years in uniform he had been brought into the CID, and there he had stayed. He was usually pretty sure he was happy there.

The idea of putting him at the head of a special investigation group with a hand-picked team from the Stockholm police had not been his. He had in fact been rather skeptical about the whole thing. He pictured a future in which huge, unwieldy investigations would land on his desk and there would never be enough people to deal with them, while between cases they would be twiddling their thumbs. He had been proved right, and that was still the position. After the summer's wide-ranging investigation of Lillian Sebastiansson's disappearance and murder, the flow of cases had been very uneven. The opening line was always the same: "Alex, could your group take a look at this?"

Sometimes the case proved to be as aberrant as it first appeared, but often there turned out to be no logical reason for Alex and his special team to take it on.

Alex currently had two cases on his plate: the case of the shooting of the Ahlbins, and the case of the unidentified hit-and-run victim in Frescativägen, up at the university. By the time he opened the meeting in the Den, Alex had already made up his mind.

160

Unless Fredrika had come up with anything persuasive on the latter, they would hand it over to their colleagues in the Norrmalm police.

Alex gave a bitter sigh. He was convinced that the furrow across his brow would soon be a permanent fixture. And he was not so sure he enjoyed his job anymore.

"Right, we're all here," he said loudly, so everyone would sit down.

They were few in number, as usual. Fredrika, Joar, and Ellen. Peder was missing, but Alex passed no comment.

"But, Peder . . ." began Ellen.

"He'll be in later," Alex said, with evident irritation.

Then he and Joar listened attentively while Fredrika told them what her call to the hospital had yielded.

"So it was Karolina's sister who identified her?" Joar said in surprise.

"Not just identified," said Fredrika. "She came with her in the ambulance and was there while they tried to resuscitate her. I've spoken to the officers who talked to her at the hospital. She seemed quite in control and told them very matter-of-factly about all her sister's problems. She told the officers it was a relief that her sister had found peace."

161

Alex stroked his chin. His fingers ached a bit, but the physiotherapy was gradually achieving the desired effect.

"So what does all this tell us?" he said slowly, leaning back in his chair. "Karolina dies in the hospital on Thursday. Her father doesn't get the news until Sunday, possibly from the other daughter, Johanna, according to the hospital doctor. But the mother is told nothing. And Johanna goes underground."

He shook his head.

"What have we managed to find out from Johanna Ahlbin's workplace? Where *is* the woman?"

"She's on leave of absence at the moment," replied Joar. "I finally managed to track down the company where she worked and spoke to somebody in authority, who told me she was on a period of leave. She's been gone a fortnight and isn't expected back for another three weeks."

"So she was already on leave of absence when her sister died?" said Fredrika.

"Yes," said Joar. "But the employer couldn't tell me why she'd been granted it. Private reasons, it sounded like. They weren't even sure if she was in the country."

"What employer grants five weeks' leave of absence without going into the whys and wherefores?" asked Fredrika.

"This one obviously does," said Joar with a dubious expression. "I explained to her boss why we were looking for her, and that it was urgent. But he still couldn't tell me any more."

"We haven't got an email address, have we?" Ellen put in.

"We can't break bad news like this by *email*," Alex said in dismay.

"No, but we could tell her we needed to speak to her," said Ellen.

"I was given her work email address," said Joar. "But there's no guarantee she'll be checking that while she's on leave. Her work mobile's switched off."

No one said anything. Alex turned over in his mind what he had heard, wanting his thoughts to fall into place so a clearer picture emerged.

"There's still something not right here," he said emphatically. "Why on earth would she break news as dramatic as her sister's death to her father and then leave the country? Without exchanging a word on the subject with her mum?"

Joar nodded, mainly to himself.

"It sounds odd, even when we take into account that the family knew about her sister's drug abuse so the death was not entirely unexpected."

"Which leads us to another strange thing," Fredrika went on. "How could anyone in their circle of acquaintances still have been oblivious to Karolina's addiction? She'd been heavily into drugs for a long time."

"I think Ragnar Vinterman gave us a clue to that," said Alex. "Karolina's addiction was something they chose not to talk about out loud."

"But if they'd had time to get used to the fact that she might die, that makes her father's reaction very strange," said Joar, steering the discussion back to the same old track. "According to Ragnar Vinterman, Karolina's drug habit had been wearing her parents down for a long time, and we've also learned that Johanna wasn't exactly distraught when her sister died."

"Perhaps they weren't that close?" suggested Fredrika. "Do we know anything about their relationship?"

"Or Johanna's relationship with her parents, for that matter," Alex added. "Why did she go off directly after breaking the news? She knew how unstable her father could be. Just because you keep your distance from your family, as we've heard that she did, it doesn't mean you behave completely irresponsibly toward them."

They were all absorbed in their thoughts. Alex drummed his fingers impatiently on the desk.

"But we mustn't confuse one thing with another," he said sternly. "The fact that their family relationships were rather odd is neither here nor there in this case, really. I don't see that any of the points we've been discussing change anything crucial."

The others nodded in agreement. Out of the corner of his eye, Alex could see Fredrika fiddling with some other sheets of paper she had in front of her. He had almost overlooked the unidentified man.

"We'll email Johanna Ahlbin at the address we've got," he said. "And we'll ask her employer to approach some of her colleagues, see if she was friendly with any of them outside work, in case they know where she is at the moment. And Joar and I will go to that other house, the one registered in the sisters' names, and see if we can turn up anything useful there. What do we know about the place, Fredrika?"

Fredrika put aside the sheaf of papers she was holding and shuffled through another one.

"The house is out at Ekerö," she told them. "It's been in Marja Ahlbin's family for a long time: it was originally bought by her maternal grandparents in the 1930s. Ownership was transferred to Marja in 1967, and then to Karolina and Johanna four years ago."

"Have they got equal shares in it?" asked Joar.

Fredrika nodded.

"Yes, according to the registry Johanna and Karolina Ahlbin own half each."

"And Marja's parents?" said Alex. "They're no longer with us, I hope, because otherwise we've forgotten to let them know that their daughter's been shot in the head by her own husband."

Fredrika's vigorous nodding confirmed this.

"Yes, Jakob's and Marja's parents have all been dead for some years," she said. "Jakob had a brother, too, but he emigrated to America. Marja had no brothers or sisters."

"Is this house out at Ekerö a big place?" asked Joar, looking thoughtful.

"I printed out a map," said Fredrika, showing them. "The house is at the far end of a little road. It's got a lot of ground with it and the property as a whole is valued at two and a half million kronor."

Alex whistled.

"So I assume the house goes to Johanna now Karolina's dead?"

"I suppose so," said Fredrika. "But I don't know if it could be called a windfall. There's still a big mortgage to pay off."

"Why was it transferred to their names so soon?" asked Joar. "Why would you put assets like that in the hands of a drug addict?"

"We'd better take a closer look at the conveyancing," said Fredrika.

"Let's look at the actual house first," declared Alex. "Then we can go into the paperwork."

He glanced over at Fredrika to check she had not taken exception to his rather authoritarian tone. They had had a few communication problems of that nature when she first joined the group.

But Fredrika did not look in the least bit ruffled.

Alex went on.

"How are you getting on with our unidentified man?"

Fredrika briefly summarized her results. The fact that the man had written various place-names and addresses on scraps of paper, and wrapped a ring in another bit of paper with a woman's name on it. The woman did not seem to be in Sweden, or at least, there was no asylum seeker from Sadr City in Baghdad registered under that name in the database.

"There isn't necessarily anything strange about it being a Forex bureau," Alex said tentatively. "He may just have had money to change, or something like that."

"But why do it in Uppsala?" wondered Fredrika.

"Because he lived there?" suggested Joar with a smile.

A faint smile crept across Fredrika's otherwise somber, earnest face. It had struck Alex on numerous occasions that she was actually rather beautiful.

"So what was he doing on the main road outside Stockholm University in the middle of the night?" she went on. "I get the feeling our man lived here, not in Uppsala."

Alex pulled himself upright.

"Is there anything at all to underline suspicions that he was killed deliberately?" he asked, not beating about the bush.

"No," said Fredrika. "Not as things stand. But I'm still waiting for the CID to get back to me about the fingerprint check, and I haven't had the autopsy report yet, either."

"All right," said Alex, "wait for those two reports, and then we'll decide how we're going to continue the investigation. *If* we're going to continue the investigation," he added.

Whether it was the effect of her pregnancy

or for some other reason, Fredrika did not seem to have any objections to that arrangement, either.

She's not herself, thought Alex, and started to brood. She generally advanced her ideas more tenaciously.

A knock at the door interrupted the meeting, and Peder came in. He did not look anyone in the eye, merely sank into a spare seat at the table.

"Hi," he said.

One step behind him came a man whom Alex knew was from the technical division.

"Sorry to disturb you," he drawled, standing in the doorway. "I thought you might like to see this," he went on, passing Alex some sheets of paper.

"What are these?" asked Alex.

"Printouts of emails sent to Jakob Ahlbin's church email account," said the technician. "We were given access today. He seems to have been receiving threats for a while now. He'd saved the emails in a separate folder."

Alex raised his eyebrows.

"Really?" he said.

The technician nodded.

"See for yourself," he said. "They were threatening to do some really nasty things, if Jakob didn't stop his activities. He seems to have got involved in some dispute he ought to have kept out of."

Joar got quickly to his feet and moved so he could read over Alex's shoulder.

"Look at the dates," he said, pointing. "The last one came less than a week ago."

Alex felt his pulse racing as he read the printouts.

"So he was receiving threats, after all," he declared.

And with that, the case of the late Jakob and Marja Ahlbin took a new turn.

BANGKOK, THAILAND

Her friend had told her to wait until he got back to her with instructions. He had promised to be in touch by two o'clock the next day. She looked uneasily at the time; it was just after three. Back home in Sweden it was nine in the morning.

For the hundredth time she took her mobile out of her bag and checked it. Still no missed calls. But then, timekeeping had never been his strong point.

The proprietor of the Internet café offered her another cup of coffee. He recognized her now, and looked sorry when she declined.

"Can I help?" he asked.

She tried to smile and shook her head.

"No, but thanks anyway."

Her eyes went back to the computer screen. She instinctively wished that her problems were the kind that could be solved by the intervention of a Thai café owner.

She had carried on ringing her parents, but to no avail. The only thing that had changed since yesterday was that her mother's mobile was now cut off, too. Her email was still not working and Thai Airways still maintained they had never heard of her booking.

"Don't worry," her contact said. "I'll get this mess sorted out for you. If you can just hang on till tomorrow, you'll see, it'll all be okay."

She wondered if she should ring him again, ask why he had not rung back.

Her stomach was rumbling and her head felt heavy. She ought to eat and drink something, top up her energy levels. She decided on the spot to go back to the hotel and try to find something to eat on the way.

The heat hit her as she came out onto the pavement. She went along Sukhumvit, the great artery through Bangkok city, relieved to know that her hotel was only two blocks away. Her handbag was rubbing her shoulder and she upped her pace. She slipped into a side street to get out of the sun. Her head turned from side to side as her eyes looked out for the first suitable place to eat.

Her mind on food, she was not concentrating and did not see him until it was too late. Suddenly he was there on the pavement with his knife drawn and his lips compressed. The cacophony of cars and people was less than thirty meters away, but in the side street it was just the two of them.

I'm not going to get out of this, she thought, and did not initially feel any fear.

The fear only came when he started to speak.

"Your bag," he spat, threatening her with the knife. "Your bag."

Standing there, she felt like crying. Not so much because she was being robbed for the first time in her life, but because she would now face even greater problems. Everything was in her bag. Her purse, her Visa card, her mobile. That had been her decision for the whole trip; she had judged it more risky to leave anything of value in the hotel than to carry it with her. The only exception was the computer, which she could not face lugging round with her. But that had been emptied of all information.

Her breath came in gasps. The bag reluctantly dislodged itself from her shoulder and slid down to her elbow.

"Quick, quick," the man with the knife exhorted, gesturing to her with his free hand to let go of the bag.

When she did not immediately do so, he launched himself forward and forced her to take two rapid steps back to avoid a stab wound to her arm. She tripped on an uneven bit of tarmac and fell over. The bag slipped to the ground and in a second the man was standing over her, grabbing it.

But he did not go. He unzipped the bag and started going through the contents.

"USB," he demanded.

She stared at him uncomprehendingly.

"USB," he shouted. "Where is it?"

She swallowed several times, shaking her head frantically.

"I haven't got one," she answered in English, trying to shuffle backward along the pavement, still on her back.

The man leaned forward and yanked her to her feet. She struggled to get free, twisting like a snake. Then the knife lunged at her again, very close this time. He pressed it to her face and she gave an involuntary jerk as she felt the cool metal against her skin.

Stressing every syllable, he said again: "Where is it?"

In silent panic she weighed up the alternatives. There were none, she realized as she saw the man's expression. It was angry and aggressive, but very controlled. He knew all too well what he was looking for.

She fumbled for the memory stick on the chain round her neck. He was still gripping her, far too hard. When he saw what she was doing, he wrenched at the chain and it broke. The memory stick fell onto the tarmac and he dived after it.

There would be no better chance of escape than this.

She ran faster than she had ever run before, her sandals slapping on the tarmac. If she could just get out onto Sukhumvit, she'd be safe.

"Stop!' shouted the man from behind her. "Stop!"

But naturally she did not stop, convinced as she was that it would be the most dangerous thing she could possibly do. This man had been employed by someone, and his assignment was not just to rob her. She had realized almost at once what was strange about his behavior. Muggers do not usually go through a handbag hunting for a USB stick. And how could he have known? How did he even know there was a USB stick to look for?

She ran all the way back to the hotel, taking a route that meant she could keep to the bigger streets all the way. She did not know exactly when he had given up the chase, but he stopped shouting after she put on a spurt along Sukhumvit. She did not turn round until she was in the hotel lobby, almost fainting and drenched in sweat. He was not there.

She sank to the lobby floor in despair.

A security guard and one of the receptionists came dashing over. Was she all right? Could they help her?

She wished with all her heart she could have laid the whole story in their open arms. She was tired now, incapable of summoning up the inner resources to see her project through. Coming on this trip alone suddenly seemed like a really stupid idea. What had she been thinking? Hadn't she understood the risks, sensed imminent danger?

"I've been robbed."

The hotel staff were dismayed. Robbed? In broad daylight in Bangkok? A white woman? They looked shocked, said they had never heard of such a thing before. The female receptionist went to get some water and the guard to ring the police.

As she drank, the receptionist inquired kindly whether she needed anything else.

"No," she replied, trying to smile. "I'd just like my key so I can go up to my room and wash."

The receptionist disappeared off to the desk and the guard paced impatiently up and down the lobby.

"The police will be here within half an hour," he assured her.

She tried to look grateful, well aware that the police could hardly help her in any significant way.

The receptionist returned. She looked worried.

"Pardon me, but what room number did you say it was?"

"214," she said wearily.

She gulped some more water, picked herself up and went over to the desk.

"I'm sorry, miss," said the receptionist. "In 214, we have a man who booked in the day before yesterday. Are you sure you have the right number?"

Suddenly she could not breathe. She stared at the hotel logo, which was all over the reception area to remind guests where they were.

Manhattan Hotel. The hotel where she had been staying for the past five nights.

Panic rose inside her. The hotel staff were now observing her with watchful eyes. She tried to keep her voice steady as she spoke:

"Sorry," she said with an effort. "I must have got mixed up. You're right, I don't remember my room number."

"Miss, we want to help you, but your name is not on our computer. Not for any room."

She swallowed hard.

"Okay, then perhaps you've registered me as having checked out, by mistake."

The receptionist gave an unhappy sigh.

"According to the computer, you have not been staying here at all."

A few seconds passed. She blinked to hold back the tears.

She looked the receptionist entreatingly in the eye.

"But you must recognize me. I've been going in and out of this hotel for several days now."

The receptionist exchanged glances with the guard, looked as though she wanted to ask something. Then she shook her head.

"Sorry, miss," she said, appearing genuinely sorry. "I have never seen you before. And no one else here has, either. Would you like me to help you ring for a taxi?"

STOCKHOLM

Peder Rydh tried to keep his anger in check as Joar and Alex set off for the Ahlbin sisters' house at Ekerö. Alex had left him the job of going through the emails that had come to light and working with the technical section to try to establish who had sent them. Fredrika had been entrusted with finding out as much as possible about Jakob's activities with refugee organizations. Even that seemed more exciting than poring over lousy emails.

Peder took out his mobile and tried ringing his brother, Jimmy. There was no answer and Peder threw the phone onto his desk. Of course he hadn't answered; everything else was going down the pan, so why not that, too?

A sense of guilt set in almost immediately. He should be glad Jimmy was not answering his phone, because it meant he was too busy doing something he enjoyed more.

"Jimmy's lucky having a big brother who cares about him so much," said the carers at the assisted living unit whenever Peder went there.

It sometimes seemed as if the unit was the only place on earth where Peder still made a good impression and felt welcome. Jimmy had lived there since he turned twenty, and seemed happy. It made his world the size he could handle and he was surrounded by people like himself who could not manage on their own.

"You have to remember that in spite of any setbacks, you're still living an enormously privileged life," his mother would say.

Peder knew what she meant, but it still bothered him to hear her say it. Fredrika Bergman, for example, hadn't got a sibling who had suffered brain damage at the age of five in a stupid game that went wrong; did that mean she was less duty bound than Peder to make the most of herself and her life?

Sometimes when he was sitting with one of his little boys on his lap, he would think about how incredibly fragile life was. Indelible images from childhood reminded him of the accident with the swing that had destroyed his brother's life and underlined how easily something could be irrevocably lost if you were not careful.

Careful. Trustworthy. Aware.

God knew when he had last been any of those things.

His mother, who functioned more or less as a nanny to the twins, had started watching him with a worried look when he got home late smelling of beer or went for drinks after work three evenings in a row. Something had happened to him to make him less considerate and more neglectful. It had happened when the boys were born and Ylva was sucked into that goddamn postnatal depression that went on and on.

But now it was as if he was the one who couldn't get his health back on track, not her. When they first separated he had felt strong and responsible. He had broken out of an impossible situation and done something radical to improve his life.

But it all gone to hell in a handcart.

As usual he just gritted his teeth. At least at work he had other things to think about.

He went through the checklist he had put together of all the threats sent to Jakob Ahlbin's church email account in the past two weeks. The tone grew more hostile as time went on, and the threats seemed to have started after the clergyman intervened in

181

some dispute that the sender felt was none of his business. The emails were not signed with a name, but with the initials *SP.* The initials also featured in the email address used to issue the threats.

Peder frowned. He was not sure what SP stood for.

He read the emails again. The first was dated January 20.

Dear Reverend Scumbag, we advise you to back off while you still can. SP

Back off from what? wondered Peder.

The next email had come a few days later, January 24:

We damn well mean it, Vicar. Keep away from our people, now and forever. SP

So SP was some kind of group, Peder could work out that much. But what else? The rest of the threatening emails did not offer any more contextual clues, but Peder saw that the tone had hardened. An email from the last day of January read:

If you don't give a toss about our friends, we don't give a toss about yours. We're going to make it hell for you. An eye for an eye, you fucking priest. SP

Hardly well written. But the message was clear. Peder wondered what Jakob Ahlbin himself had thought. He had not reported any of the threats as far as Peder could see.

Did that mean he had not taken them seriously? Or that he had other reasons for keeping the messages from the police?

The last two emails had arrived in the final week of Jakob's life. On February 20, the person had written:

You ought to listen to us, Vicar. You've got the trials of Job ahead of you if you don't stop your activities right away.

And then the last one, on February 22:

Don't forget how it all ended for Job; there's always time to change your mind and do the right thing. Stop looking.

Peder pondered. Stop looking for what? The name Job sounded familiar, but he could not place it. He was assuming it must be biblical. A quick Internet search confirmed it.

Job was apparently the man God tested more than any other to show the devil how far he could push those who lived righteously.

Job lost everyone, Peder noted grimly. But he himself survived.

He reached for the telephone receiver and rang the technical division to see if they had come up with any names for the sender of the anonymous emails.

It took no more than half an hour to drive

out of Stockholm to Ekerö. The roads were clear in the middle of the day, not clogged with rush-hour traffic.

"What do you think?" asked Joar, noncommittally.

"I don't think anything," Alex said firmly. "I prefer to know. And I know too little in this case to be able to say anything. But it's a cause for concern that Jakob received such serious threats just before he was found dead."

Alex did not need to spell out why it was a cause for concern. The problem was clear. If it turned out that there was proof Jakob had not been the perpetrator, they were in deep trouble with the investigation. Forensics had been through the flat with a fine-tooth comb without finding a shred of evidence that anyone else had been there at the time of the shootings. In his heart of hearts, Alex hoped Jakob would turn out to have done it. Otherwise things were going to get hellishly complicated.

They parked in the driveway and got out of the car. The sky was cloudless and the snow frozen hard. The best kind of winter weather and not the sort of conditions you spontaneously linked with death and misfortune.

The snow lay pristine in front of the house

and all round it.

"No one's been here for a while," said Joar.

Alex said nothing. For no particular reason, his thoughts went to Peder. Maybe he had been too hard on him; the case had been his from the start. But colleagues in this business had to expect a severe reprimand to result from improper behavior. It was irrelevant that he was having a rotten time at home; you could not bring private problems to work with you. Especially if you were a police officer.

"We'll go in as soon as the technicians get here," Alex said out loud, to stop the thoughts chasing round in his head. "I think they were just behind us on the road."

They had been granted a search warrant by the prosecutor because a criminal act was suspected. Finding a key to the house had been harder. Elsie and Sven Ljung may have had a spare key to Jakob and Maria's flat at Odenplan, but they did not have one to the house, and the daughters obviously could not be asked. In the end they had asked permission to go into the Ahlbins' and Karolina's town flats to look for the key, but could not find anything. So the technicians were coming to help them force entry through the front door with minimal damage.

"What did Karolina's place look like?" Alex asked Joar, who had been in on the search.

Joar initially did not seem to know quite how to answer.

"I certainly wouldn't say it looked like the home of a drug addict," he said finally. "We took some pictures; you can see them later."

"Did it look as if someone had gone in and cleaned it up afterward?" he asked, thinking of Johanna, who might have done something of the kind after her sister's demise.

"Hard to tell," Joar said honestly. "It looked more as though nobody had been there for a while. As if somebody had done a thorough tidy-up and then gone away."

"Hmm," said Alex thoughtfully.

The snow crunched under the wheels of the technicians' vehicle as they pulled up alongside the other car. Ten minutes later, they were in the house.

The first thing Alex noted was that the house was warm. The second was that it was furnished in a pleasant, homely fashion not at all like the way Joar and Peder had described Mr. and Mrs. Ahlbin's flat. It was clean and neat. The walls were hung with photographs of the family at various ages.

186

There were home-woven runners on the tables and the windows had curtains of a fairly modern style.

They went round in silence, unsure what they were looking for. Alex went out into the kitchen, opened cupboards and drawers. There was a liter of milk in the fridge; the carton was unopened and two weeks beyond its use-by date. That meant it could not be all that long since someone had been there.

The house had two stories. The two bedrooms upstairs each had a set of bunk beds in them. The landing between them was used as a TV room. On the ground floor were a kitchen and dining room, and a largish living room. There were bathrooms on each floor.

"Two lots of bunk beds," Alex remarked. "That's odd, isn't it? Before the sisters took over the house, you would have thought they were here as a family. It seems odd that Mr. and Mrs. Ahlbin slept in separate beds."

Joar considered this.

"Maybe it hasn't always been like this?" he said.

Alex heaved a sigh.

"Well, let's hope so," he said, heading back downstairs.

He wandered round the rooms, studying

the photos. Something was disturbing him but he was not sure what. He looked again. Mum, Dad, and two daughters sitting in the garden. It must be an old photograph, because the girls were little. More garden pictures, the girls older. Karolina and her parents, and one of Karolina on horseback.

Alex realized what it was that had disconcerted him.

"Joar, come here," he called.

Joar's feet thudded down the stairs.

"Look at these pictures," said Alex, sweeping a hand over the living room wall. "Look at them and tell me what you think."

Joar studied the photos in silence, walking up and down in front of them.

"Were you thinking of anything in particular?" he asked uncertainly.

"Johanna," Alex said resolutely. "Don't you see? She suddenly disappears from the shots and only Karolina's left. Looking the picture of health, I might add."

"But these photos go back a long time, surely?" said Joar doubtfully.

"They do," said Alex. "But the more recent ones look about five years old at most."

They did another tour of the house. Karolina was in several of the pictures upstairs, including an enlargement of one with her parents that had pride of place on the TV set. Johanna was conspicuous by her absence.

"Maybe they didn't like her," said Alex, mostly to himself. "Maybe they had a major falling-out over something."

But that theory did not seem to fit, either. Johanna was part owner of the house, after all. Why was she not in the photographs in her own home?

A technician stuck his head round the open front door.

"There seems to be a way into a basement round the back," he said. "Do you want me to open that door, too?"

The lock turned out to be frozen solid and not at all as cooperative as the first one. The technician had to work at it for nearly twenty minutes before the door finally creaked open. Alex looked down and saw a short, steep set of steps leading down to a basement. He was about to ask for a torch when he saw the light switch on the wall and turned on the light as he went down the steps. A lightbulb flickered into life.

What it revealed was a fully furnished basement that had probably not been used for a very long time. The kitchen had clearly been fitted in the early 1980s and the air was thick with dust, but they could see all they needed to. A bed settee in one corner, with some armchairs and a coffee table. Three sets of bunk beds along the walls. A very basic bathroom with a smell of mold. Another small room, windowless, with a further set of bunk beds. There was no bed linen on the beds, but they all had blankets and pillows.

Alex gave a laugh.

"Well, I'll be damned," he muttered. "It seems as though the rumors were right. If Jakob Ahlbin wasn't hiding illegal migrants here, then I'd very much like to know what he *did* use this basement for."

Joar looked about him.

"Confirmation classes, maybe," he said drily.

Alex had to smile, but was soon grave again.

"Gun cabinet," he said, nodding over to a tall metal cabinet standing in one corner of the room.

They went over and tried the doors. They were unlocked.

"We need to check whether any of the family had firearms licenses apart from Jakob," said Alex.

The siting of the gun cabinet gave Alex pause for thought. Why was it in the base-ment and not the main house, if the basement was used for concealing fugitives? Alex concluded it must have been moved at some stage, perhaps when the basement fell into disuse.

"Is this where he got it?" Joar said quietly.

"Got what?"

"The murder weapon," Joar clarified. "Was this where he got the hunting pistol for killing his wife and himself?"

"Or where somebody else did?" Alex said thoughtfully.

About an hour after the policemen left the house in Ekerö, another car turned into the driveway. It parked in the tire tracks of the police cars. Two men climbed out into the snow.

"Damn nuisance," said one of them, "them finding their way here before we did."

The other one, a younger man, was more relaxed.

"No damage done, I'm sure," he said gruffly.

"No, but it was a bloody close call," hissed his companion, kicking the snow.

The younger man put a hand on his shoulder.

"Everything's going to plan," he insisted.

The other man gave a snort.

"That's not the impression I'm getting,"

he said. "Some of us have even left the country, you know. When will she be back, anyway?"

"Soon," said the other man. "And then this will all be over."

Fredrika Bergman was hard at work assembling information about Jakob Ahlbin's work with refugee groups, and it was proving quite a task. Much of the material was not available electronically and she was obliged to go into the old paper archives in the library.

Jakob's commitment to the refugee cause went back decades and had occasionally been a matter of dispute even within the church. There had been particular trouble when Jakob actively championed a very sensitive asylum case, allowing the family to live in the church to avoid deportation.

"The day the police cross the threshold of my church with weapons drawn is the day I lose my country," he was quoted as saying in one of the many newspaper articles the story generated.

The family stayed in the church for

months and was finally given a residence permit.

It wasn't so much Jakob Ahlbin's views that courted controversy, more his actions. Jakob had not contented himself with writing articles and opinion pieces but had also campaigned for his cause in the streets and squares of various towns. He had even debated publicly with neo-Nazis and other right-wing extremists.

Jakob Ahlbin was in fact one of the few who had dared to engage in debate with the xenophobic groups that existed in Sweden, and unconfirmed sources also said he was part of a support group for young men in Stockholm — because the problem of right-wing extremists was an almost exclusively male one — who wanted to find a way out of whatever group or network they had joined. That fitted with the e-mail messages telling Jakob to keep out of things that were none of his business, thought Fredrika. She printed out the material on that subject, too. Peder would be glad to see what she had come up with.

Just after lunch she had the call from the pathologist who had completed the autopsy on the hit-and-run victim. The pathologist was quite curt, and as usual launched into phrases Fredrika did not understand. She hoped he was not going to go into too much detail; now she was pregnant she seemed much more sensitive to anything too specific about injuries and mangled bodies.

I've turned into a wimp, thought Fredrika, and had no idea what she could do about it.

"He died as a direct result of extreme external violence that must have been caused by the impact of the vehicle, a car," said the pathologist. "The injuries are consistent with a very violent impact which threw him a distance of several meters."

"Was he run into from in front or behind?" asked Fredrika.

"In front," replied the pathologist. "But it could be that he heard the car coming and turned round. What ought to interest you more is that they didn't just ram into him but also drove over him."

Fredrika held her breath.

"First we have the injuries that caused his death — the initial impact. On top of that he has injuries to his back, stomach, and neck, which must have been inflicted directly afterward, crush injuries. My guess would be that whoever it was simply backed over him as he lay there in the middle of the road."

Queasiness came flooding over Fredrika

and she had to steel herself to go on. That was just the sort of thing she did not want to hear.

She took a deep breath.

"So what you mean in plain language is that it couldn't possibly have been an accident."

"That's exactly what I mean," said the pathologist.

All of a sudden Fredrika felt very tense. Now there was another murder inquiry for them to deal with. Damn.

Alex and Joar were back at HQ by early afternoon. To Peder's irritation, Joar went straight to his office and did not offer him even the slightest update on the way. Peder rose resolutely from his desk chair and went in to see him.

"How did it go at Ekerö?" he asked, not bothering with any niceties.

He had his arms tightly folded across his chest and tried to look casual.

"It went fine," said Joar after he had observed Peder in the doorway for a few seconds.

"Did you find anything?"

"Well, yes and no," replied Joar, starting to sort through some papers. "I don't know that we were looking for anything in particular. But we found something, all right."

Cheeks flushing bright red, Peder persisted: "Like what?"

"Like a basement that seemed to fit the story of Jakob Ahlbin hiding illegal migrants."

Peder nodded, suddenly unsure what to do next.

"Fredrika and I dug up some important things, too," he said.

Joar smiled but did not look at Peder, and nor did he ask what they had found.

"Good," was all he said. "I hope you'll tell the rest of us all about it at the next session in the Den."

Peder said nothing and left. He had never come across such a goddamn stuck-up workmate in all his life. He was more high-and-mighty than even Fredrika used to be. Peder still had vivid memories of the heavy weather he and Fredrika had made of working together at first. If only she could be a bit more relaxed, a bit less pretentious. No. She'd always been good-looking, but that was about all you could say in her favor.

Peder could not make any sense of it. After all, unlike Fredrika, Joar was a regular police officer and a proper detective. The two of them should have worked well as a team. It was inexplicable to him why the powers that be had decided a few years back to recruit civilian investigators into the police. It was an affront to the collective competence of the force, as Peder saw it, and he was taken aback on his transfer to Alex's group to find one of those civilians in it. Time had passed since then, and Fredrika no longer made such a fuss about details. To start with, she had questioned everything, and taken a disproportionately major role in some of the investigations. Peder felt pushed to the point where he needed to bring up Fredrika's inadequacy in certain areas with Alex. But then she had got pregnant and that had turned her into another person.

He could not help a little grin as he thought of that pregnancy; there were plenty of rumors going round as to who the father was. An older, married man. Peder had laughed his head off the first time he heard it, and said he'd put money on it not being true. You would never catch Little Miss Prim making herself available to someone who belonged to someone else. Never. After a while he had started having second thoughts. It did not sound quite so out of the question as he had first thought. And it would explain why Fredrika was saying so little about the baby and the pregnancy. He couldn't stop chuckling to himself. There was a whore in every Madonna, as his granddad used to say.

"Have you got a minute?" he asked as he knocked on the open door of Fredrika's room.

She was sitting at her desk and gave a start, but smiled when she saw who it was.

"Come in," she said.

Her unusual smile and long, dark hair often set Peder off on smutty flights of fancy, and it made no difference that she was expecting.

He came in and sat down opposite her.

"Found anything?" he asked nonchalantly.

"Oh yes," said Fredrika, looking rather pleased with herself as she took a pile of photocopies out of a plastic folder. "I found out quite a lot about Jakob Ahlbin's refugee activities. And some important stuff about him belonging to a support network for former right-wing extremists. The group's still active, and is made up of police officers, social workers, and people from various immigrant associations."

She pushed the papers across to Peder.

"Perfect," he said flatly, wondering why he had never heard of the support group. He would have liked to work on that sort of thing.

"I've already been in touch with them,"

Fredrika went on, "and they've confirmed that Jakob Ahlbin was a member. He was among those who took the initiative in setting up the group, in fact. It's been going a couple of years."

Peder gave a whistle.

"And it upset a certain Mr. Tony Svensson so much that he started firing off threatening letters. Or emails."

"Tony Svensson?" asked Fredrika, confused. "Is that his name, the one who sent the emails?"

Peder nodded with satisfaction.

"Yes, it is, according to the technical boys and Comhem, the broadband service provider. We were able to trace the IP address most of the emails came from and he's the registered owner of that."

"Weren't there several people involved?" asked Fredrika. "You said the emails had come from different IP addresses."

"The others were at a library out in Farsta and a 7-Eleven shop in the Söder district. So there's no specified owner as such for those. But it seems logical for this Tony Svensson to have sneaked out and sent emails from different places. The content of all the emails was the same, which seems to point to them all being sent by the same person."

Fredrika gave a thoughtful nod.

"I haven't read them all yet. Could you let me have copies?"

"Sure," said Peder.

"What do we know about Tony Svensson? Is he known to the police?"

Peder's face split into a broad grin.

"Thought you'd never ask," he said triumphantly, settling into his seat to tell her all about what he had discovered. "Have you heard of an organization called SP?"

Alex convened a meeting in the Den when he and Joar got back from Ekerö. He felt a warm glow as he listened to Peder's account of the man who had issued the threats to Jakob Ahlbin. When Peder put his stupid behavior on hold, he was a very skillful detective.

"Tony Svensson was born and raised in Farsta," he reported. "He's twenty-seven now, and had his first brush with the police when he was twelve. Shoplifting and vandalism. The Söder police and social services worked pretty closely together on his case until he turned eighteen. He's had a couple of custodial sentences, the first one when he was seventeen and beat up his stepfather. Nearly killed him."

"Ah," said Alex with a resigned air. "Let

me guess — the stepdad was beating up his mum?"

"No," said Peder. "The stepdad refused to lend Tony three thousand kronor for a holiday in Ibiza."

"Damn," Alex said, taken aback. "So he's a right roughneck?"

"Yep," said Peder. "The other assault was gang-related. He kicked another guy black and blue and rounded it off by smashing an empty wine bottle over his head. Then he used a bit of the broken glass to slash —"

"Please," said Fredrika, whose face had drained of all color, "can we leave the details for later?"

She looked self-conscious and put a protective hand on her stomach. Almost as if she expected someone to come rushing through the door and assault her or the baby with a broken bottle.

Peder moved on, a bit put out that he had not been able to give every gory detail.

"Okay," he said. "He was going to be done for aggravated rape, too, but the prosecutor had to drop it for lack of evidence because the girl refused to cooperate. As usual," he added.

"Possibly frightened into keeping her mouth shut," Joar put in quietly, almost as if trying not to disturb anyone but still aware that he was doing so.

Peder clenched his fist under the table and went on as if Joar had not spoken.

"What's more, Tony Svensson's been implicated in a series of thefts and break-ins and he's also under suspicion of committing armed robbery. And to top it all, he's a known right-wing extremist and long-term member of a neo-Nazi organization called Sons of the People, the same lot who signed the emails to Jakob Ahlbin."

He indicated that his lecture was over by putting down the pen he had been holding throughout.

"Well done, Peder," Alex said automatically. "We've clearly got a good deal to go on here. Have we anything more concrete on the conflict between Jakob Ahlbin and this group?"

"We're looking at it now," Peder answered. "Maybe Fredrika can tell us where we stand?"

Fredrika sat up at the mention of her name and began as usual by opening her notebook. Alex had to suppress a smile that could have been misinterpreted as mocking. She was always so well prepared.

"Jakob Ahlbin has drawn attention to himself in two particular contexts," she began, and went on to tell them about the refugee family allowed to take refuge in his church while the migration agency ruled on their case. "And then there's the support group," she went on. "I've contacted the person who runs it, Agne Nilsson. He seemed very distressed by Jakob's death and wanted to come here and talk to us tomorrow morning. I said that would be fine."

"Did you say anything about the threats Jakob had been sent? Was he aware of those?" asked Alex.

"Yes, he was," answered Fredrika. "But no one had taken them seriously. I mean, they knew their work antagonized various people. And anyway, Agne thought the emails had stopped."

Alex looked surprised.

"Why did he think that?" asked Peder.

"Because they talked about it last week, and Jakob said he hadn't had any for over a week."

Peder leafed through the sheets of paper in front of him.

"That's not right," he said. "He got another three emails in the last fortnight he was alive."

"Strange," said Alex. "We'd better ask Agne about that tomorrow."

He made a note on his pad.

"And there's another strange thing," he

said. "Namely that no one else seemed to know about the threats. Not Sven Ljung, who found the bodies, and not Ragnar Vinterman, either. Why hadn't Jakob confided in anyone?"

Joar put his head on one side.

"It might not be that odd," he said softly. "Not if Jakob wasn't taking the emails seriously. Maybe it had happened before when he was working on other cases."

"Are there any other threatening messages in his inbox?" Alex asked Peder.

Peder shook his head.

"No, but that doesn't mean he hadn't had any. Just that he hadn't saved them."

Alex glanced at the time and decided to wind things up.

"Okay," he summed up. "We still don't know whether the threats are relevant for our purposes, but we definitely can't discount this information until we've talked to the support group and, of course, Tony Svensson himself. I want a printout of all telephone traffic to and from all the numbers Jakob Ahlbin used; see if we can find out if this Tony called him as well as emailing. Then we'll go to the prosecutor and ask if we can bring him in for unlawful menace to start with. Is there anything else in this case we need to discuss just now?"

Peder hesitated but then raised his hand.

"The fact that Job was mentioned in one of the last emails," he said, and told them his own thoughts on the matter.

He suddenly felt very stupid.

But Alex was paying attention.

"Interesting," he said. "What do the rest of you think?"

Joar shifted in his seat.

"Might be interesting, but not all that startling. It clearly hasn't passed Tony Svensson by that he was emailing a clergyman," he said, making Peder feel hot and uncomfortable.

"Assuming we can expect someone with Tony Svensson's background to know who Job was," said Fredrika. "Isn't that the most important thing to consider?"

"How do you mean?" asked Alex.

"I mean exactly what I say, that the odds of someone like Tony Svensson casually throwing biblical names into his correspondence and making them fit his purposes so well don't seem all that high."

Alex looked faintly embarrassed.

"I have to admit I didn't know exactly who Job was until Peder gave us his story just now."

Fredrika smiled and said nothing.

"By the way, has anybody got anything

new on Johanna, the daughter?" Alex asked, to change the subject. "It seems more and more vital for us to find her ASAP. Especially in the light of our visit to the Ekerö house today."

Nobody answered. None of them had anything new to impart.

Alex ran his eyes round the assembled company.

"Anything else?" he inquired.

Fredrika put her hand up.

"Yes?"

"Well, I've got more on that hit-and-run victim," she said.

"Ah," said Alex. "Do tell us!"

"It seems he was murdered," said Fredrika. "He wasn't just run over, you see — the car was also backed over him."

Alex groaned aloud with frustration.

"Damn," he said. "Just what we need, another murder inquiry."

His sense of the huge amount of work in front of him intensified. This was clearly a mess he was not going to untangle anytime soon.

As she was leaving work, Fredrika tried to phone Spencer. He did not answer, which unsettled her. Her need to hear his voice more regularly was growing daily, especially as evening approached and the time left to her before the terrors of the night was short.

How did I end up here? she wondered, for what must be the thousandth time. How could all my dreams and plans lead me to this miserable crossroads in my life?

The answer was always the same, as it was this evening, too. It was decades since she had been guided by her innermost dreams. She had been navigating by makeshift solutions and setting her sights on second-rate choices.

I am what you turn into when you are robbed of freedom of choice, she thought wearily. I am a residual product, marked by that wretched bloody Accident.

So there it was in her mind again, the Accident. The most tangible cutoff point.

Early in life she had set herself the goal of becoming a violinist. Music was her family's natural setting; Fredrika and her brother had practically grown up in the wings of a succession of major stages where they had waited with their father for the end of their mother's latest concert or recital.

"Can you see Mummy playing?" their father would whisper, his eyes suffused with pride. "Can you see the way she lives for what she does?"

Then, Fredrika had been too young to

reflect on what her father was saying, but later on in life she had started to question that phrase. Living for what you did, could that really be right?

And what dreams and visions did her father have? She was horrified to realize she had no concept of that at all. Perhaps he had had no greater wish than to follow his wife around the world and watch her dazzle one audience after another? Things had changed when the children started school, of course. Her mother accepted fewer engagements abroad, and for the first time the children had a clearer idea of their father's professional identity. He had a job that meant having to wear a suit, and he sold things. Successfully, it seemed. Because they were certainly well off.

Fredrika started violin lessons when she was just six. It was perhaps her first experience of what is described as love at first sight. She loved both the violin and her teacher, who must have thought her a good pupil, because he remained her teacher right up until the accursed Accident. And he had been at her side throughout her convalescence, offering encouragement and assuring her that it would still be possible to play as she had before.

But he was wrong, thought Fredrika, closing her eyes for a moment.

Many years had passed, but it was still so easy to conjure up the images in her mind. The car as it skidded, somersaulted, and went flying. The hard ground, the skis tumbling out of the roof box. Her friend's endless screaming when she saw her mother's face smashed against the side window of the car. And the firemen's desperate struggle: "The car could explode at any minute. We've got to get them out of there, and fast!"

Fredrika sometimes thought it would have been just as well if they had left her there in the car, since the life that came afterward was not worth living. Her left arm had been badly injured and would never be the same again. They made so many attempts that her whole life came to revolve round the battle to restore her arm.

"It won't be up to the strain," said the doctor who finally delivered a verdict. "You'll be able to play for a few hours a week, but several hours a day? Out of the question. You would be in the sort of pain that would be intolerable in the long term. And the wear and tear on your arm could easily make it entirely unusable."

He had not understood what he was saying, of course. He lived under the illusion that she was grateful, and glad to have survived. That she was glad she had not died, as her friend's brother had died. But she had no feelings of that kind.

Not then and not now, Fredrika thought dully, sitting on the sofa in the quiet of her flat.

She had never played the violin only for enjoyment, but as a way of life, a way of earning a living. And since the Accident she had not played at all. At the very top of a cupboard, right at the back, the violin lay untuned in its case, waiting.

Fredrika stroked her stomach, where the baby lay resting.

"If you ask me really nicely, maybe I'll play a little something for you one day," she whispered. "Maybe."

It was six o'clock by the time Alex got home. His wife met him at the door. There was a strong aroma of garlic.

"Italian tonight." She smiled as he kissed her. "I've got out a bottle of wine."

"Are we celebrating something?" Alex asked in surprise.

They seldom had wine during the week.

"No, I just thought we deserved a little treat," Lena replied. "And I got home from work a bit early today."

"I see. Why was that?"

"Oh, no special reason, but I had the chance, so I thought I'd come home and make something nice for dinner."

She gave a slightly shrill laugh from the kitchen, where she was making a salad.

Alex went though the day's post. They had a card from their son in South America.

"Great postcard," he called out.

"Yes, I saw it," Lena responded. "It's so nice to hear from him, isn't it?"

And she laughed that laugh again.

Alex went out to the kitchen and observed her as she stood with her back turned. She had always been the more openhearted and attractive of the two of them. She could have had whomever she wanted, but she had chosen Alex. Even though he had gray streaks in his dark hair from an early age and deep lines on his face. For some reason he had always found it a bit unsettling that he was somehow more of a chosen one in the relationship than she was. Over the years he had at times felt incredibly jealous when other men got too close to her or he felt inadequate in some way. This jealousy had been a problem for both of them and a source of shame for him. What was wrong with him, not trusting Lena, who had given him such a fantastic home and two wonderful children?

As time passed he felt more secure. That was partly thanks to his job. His profession helped him develop a good sense of intuition, and that almost always helped him get the better of the demons that taunted him with fancies that his wife was deceiving him behind his back.

His intuition brought him certainty. Certainty when everything was all right, and also when it was not. And this time it was not.

The feeling had been creeping over him for several weeks now. She was talking differently, waving her arms about in a way he could not recall seeing earlier. She would go on at length about subjects that were unfamiliar to both of them. About places she wanted to visit and people she wished she had stayed in touch with. And then there was that laugh, which had changed so rapidly from deep and intense to shrill and superficial.

Watching her from the back, he even thought her posture had changed. She seemed stiffer somehow. And she gave a little shudder when he took hold of her, laughed her new laugh, and pulled away. Sometimes her mobile rang and she went into another room to answer it.

"Can I help with anything?" he asked her back.

"You can open the wine," she answered, trying to sound happy and relaxed.

Trying. That was the thing. She was trying to be herself, as if playing some strange theatrical role that had unexpectedly landed in her lap. Alex's stomach hurt as fear clutched his insides and the demons awoke once more.

We ought to be able to talk about this, he thought. Why aren't we doing it?

"Did you have a good day at work?" she asked him when they had been sitting in silence for a while.

"Yes," Alex said gently. "It was fine. Lots on."

Normally she would have picked up the thread and asked more. But not anymore. Now she only seemed to ask things she didn't really seem to care about.

"How was yours?" he asked.

"That was fine, too," she said, opening the oven to check whatever it was she had cooked.

The smell was amazing, but Alex did not feel hungry. He asked her a few more questions about work, as always, and she gave him brief answers, her head turned away.

When they sat down to eat the delicious

dinner and drink the good wine, he had to force himself to swallow as he chewed.

"*Skål*," she said.

"*Skål*."

When he raised his head to catch her eye, he could have sworn it looked as though she was starting to cry.

■ ■ ■ ■

Friday,
February 29, 2008

■ ■ ■ ■

STOCKHOLM

It was morning and the flat was freezing cold. The smell of cigarette smoke was not as overpowering as before because they had mended the fan for him and given him the key to one of the little windows. It was almost lunchtime, but Ali did not feel like getting up. The bag stood on the floor at the foot of the bed, a grim and blatant reminder of his new reality.

He still did not know whom to curse for his misfortune. Perhaps his parents for bringing him into the world in a country like Iraq. Perhaps the American president who everybody loved to hate and who had toppled the great leader Saddam and then abandoned the people when the country collapsed. Or perhaps Europe, which refused to let him in on any terms other than those with which he was now faced.

Whichever way he looked at it, he could not see that it was his fault. He had neither started the damn war nor made himself unemployed and defenseless. All he had done was shoulder his responsibility like a decent husband and father.

His wife must be wondering where he was. And his friend, who had still not heard from him, must be wondering, too. He turned his eyes toward the cold window. His friend must be out there somewhere. In a city he did not know, in a land where he was a complete stranger. They would make a new start there, he and his family. It was for their sakes he was going to carry out his task on Sunday. He would never do anything like that ever again. For as long as he lived.

"There are some basic rules, my lad," his father had said when he was a child. "You don't fight and you don't steal. Simple, eh?"

His father had died by the time Iraq collapsed as a state and a nation, and everyday life turned to chaos. Perhaps even he would have understood that it had now become impossible to stick to the rules. Not because things were better before, but because things had been calmer and ostensibly safer. But only ostensibly. Many people knew how it felt to hear the cars pull up in front of your house early in the morning and have your private home violated and invaded by unknown armed men sent by the government to bring in a citizen for interrogation. Some of them were never heard of again. Others were returned to their families in a state that bore witness to such appalling atrocities that even their closest family had no words for them.

Iraq was different now. The unforeseen violence came from another direction and created even greater insecurity. Money had grown important in a way it had not been before, and suddenly kidnapping was part of daily life, along with theft and arson and armed robbery.

Was that the sort of person he, too, had become? With a bag containing a gun and a balaclava beside his bed, there was every justification for the comparison.

We couldn't go on, thought Ali. Forgive me, Father, for what I'm going to do, but we couldn't go on.

Then he reached out a trembling hand for his eighth cigarette of the day. Soon it would all be over and a better future would be secured.

Bangkok, Thailand

The Swedish embassy opened at ten and she was there waiting. It had been a long and wretched night. In the end she had had to check into a cheap youth hostel on the outskirts of Bangkok and had spent the night anxiously awake. The money she had with her, what little the mugger had not taken, was not enough to pay her bill. She asked the man at reception where the nearest Cashpoint machine was and implied she would soon be back with a handful of notes. He told her it was three blocks away, and she was able to leave the hostel without creating a scene.

The embassy was housed in a tall building just next to the Landmark Hotel on Sukhumvit, occupying two whole floors. Her relief at seeing the Swedish flag on the door was so great that tears came to her eyes.

She had planned her story carefully. She

must not on any account say why she had come to Thailand, but that was a minor problem as she saw it. She was a tourist, plain and simple. Like all the other hundreds of thousands of Swedes who came here every year. And the fact that she had been robbed of all her means could not be unheard of, either. In her trouser pocket she had the copy of the police report to substantiate her story. The rest of what had happened to her — the fact that someone had canceled her flight home, closed her email accounts, and checked her out of the hotel — was something she had decided not to tell them. It would provoke far too many questions that she was not prepared to answer.

The loss of all her work material was hard to bear. The full weight of it had hit home in the night. Even her camera with all the pictures was gone. She swallowed to keep the tears at bay. Soon she would be home and then she could start to sort out this mess. At least she hoped so, with all her heart.

Maybe she should have foreseen that it would never work. That whoever had already taken such pains to take apart her life bit by bit naturally had not overlooked the possibility that she would turn to the embassy.

But she had not thought that far ahead, and did not notice the hard stare of the receptionist which followed her as she was shown in to see a member of the diplomatic staff.

First Secretary Andreas Blom greeted her with a cool handshake. His face was impassive as he asked her to sit down. When an assistant came by to ask if his guest wanted coffee, he waved her away and asked her to leave the door open. Out of the corner of her eye she saw a security guard patrolling the corridor, never far from the room where she was sitting.

"I'm not sure what you think I can help you with," said Andreas Blom, leaning back in his seat.

He kept his hand clasped in his lap and looked at her through half-closed eyes. As if he was highly practiced in not expending too much energy.

She cleared her throat several times, wished he would offer her a glass of water. But all he gave her was silence.

"As I say, I'm in serious trouble," she began cautiously.

And she told him the story she had decided on. Of the mugging, and what she referred to as "a mistake" at the hotel, which meant all her luggage had disappeared.

"I've got to get home," she said, starting

224

to cry. "I can't get in touch with my parents and a friend who was going to help me hasn't rung back either. I need a new passport and to borrow a bit of money. I'll repay it as soon as I get home — if only you'll help me."

She let her tears flow freely, incapable of maintaining any façade. Only after a long silence did she raise her head and look at Andreas Blom. His face was immobile and he was still just sitting there.

"Is that your version of events?" he asked. She stared at him.

"Pardon?"

"I asked if that's the story you intend to tell the Thai authorities when they're dealing with your case?"

"I don't understand," she said.

"What did you say your name was?" he interrupted.

She automatically repeated her forename and surname.

"You're really not making it easy for yourself," he said.

His words were greeted with silence; she had no idea what he expected her to say.

"What I can help you with, Therese, is the following: legal representation, and a named contact here at the embassy. But if you don't immediately hand yourself over to the Thai police, your situation will automatically get considerably worse. You have already made things bad enough for yourself by giving a false identity to a person in a position of authority."

She said nothing when he had finished. Thoughts were flapping round in her head like wild birds.

"I don't understand, I'm afraid," she whispered, though she was beginning to suspect the full extent of her problems. "And my name's not Therese . . ."

Andreas Blom took a piece of paper out of his desk and put it in front of her.

"Is this a copy of a report you made to the police yesterday?"

She quickly took out her own copy and compared them. It was the same document.

"But that's not your name," he said, pointing.

"Yes, it is," she said.

"No," said Andreas Blom, "it isn't. Because this is your name."

He passed over another sheet of paper.

She stared at it without properly taking in what she was seeing. A copy of a passport with her photograph but a different personal identity number and another person's name. Therese Björk, the passport holder was called.

The room began to spin.

"No, no, no," she said. "That's not me. Please, there has to be a way to sort this out . . ."

"It can be sorted out very easily," said Andreas Blom firmly. "This is your passport and your identity. I've rung the Swedish police and the Swedish tax authorities to check. This is you, Therese. And this passport was found with all your other things in the hotel you were *actually* staying at, Hotel Nana. In the room you had left when the drug squad raided the hotel and found half a kilo of cocaine among your possessions."

She suddenly felt sick and was afraid she would throw up on the floor. What Andreas Blom said after that only got through to her intermittently. She had the greatest difficulty in joining the fragments together to make a whole.

"Between you and me, you've got a good chance at the trial if you do the following. One: hand yourself in right away. Two: tell them who it was that tipped you off about the raid so you could get out of the hotel in time. Two very simple things."

He held two fingers up in the air to underline how simple it was.

She shifted uneasily and could not stop her tears from flowing.

"Why would I come here to you and not leave the country if I was guilty of everything you've told me?" she said, looking him in the eye.

He leaned back in his chair again and gave a supercilious smile.

"Because this is Thailand," he said, "and you know as well as I do that for you there's no way out."

STOCKHOLM

The night had brought new nightmares, variations on a theme. In these dreams she was no longer being hunted but was tied to a tree, surrounded by men in hoods who wanted to harm her. Fredrika Bergman had no idea at all where these absurd scenarios had come from. They did not remind her of anything she had experienced or heard mentioned. And she hated being woken by her own screams, night after night, dripping with sweat and on the verge of tears. And tired. So horribly tired.

But she still went to work. She simply could not sit at home.

"How are you?" asked Ellen Lind gravely when they ran into each other in the staff room.

Fredrika did not even try to lie.

"Pretty bad, I have to say," she admitted. "I'm sleeping terribly badly."

"Should you be here, then?" asked Ellen.

"Shouldn't you be at home, resting?"

Fredrika shook her head stubbornly.

"No more than I already am," she said wearily. "I'd rather be here."

Ellen didn't ask any more questions. She, like everyone else, wondered what Fredrika had thought it was going to be like. Expecting a baby, largely on your own, and then giving birth without the father there.

Fredrika felt guilty because Ellen was always the one asking the questions and she never reciprocated. She never asked Ellen how she was, or about her children, or how things were going with the love of her life. They had met on a package holiday the previous year, and Ellen had fallen head over heels in love.

In love.

Until she fell pregnant, she had always been more or less content with the arrangement she and Spencer had. His coming and going in her life did not worry her; after all, she sometimes behaved the same way. Finding one lover and leaving another. Losing that lover and going back to Spencer. The problem was only becoming obvious now that she wasn't her former self anymore, and always felt better when she was closer to him. Of course he came as often as he could, and these days he always answered

230

the phone when she rang. But he still was not a permanent fixture in her daily life.

"I simply don't understand a thing about this whole situation," her friend Julia said one day.

The same friend who had often asked how Fredrika could bear to have sex with a man so much older.

"There are a lot of things we don't understand in life," Fredrika retorted with a sharp note in her voice, and they said no more about it.

There were lots of emails in her inbox. She could hardly bring herself to look at them; most of them were of no interest, anyway.

Time for the firearms refresher course, one of them said. *Anyone interested in sharing lifts?*

Some of the emails were from the union rep, asking her to get involved in improving conditions for the civilian employees. The police union seemed on occasions to be running a virtual campaign to stop civilian employees feeling at home in the force, and Jusek thought now was the time to hit back. Fredrika could not summon up the energy to care, though she would have liked to.

I've made my journey, she thought lethargically. I've chosen to stay here. For now.

And at the moment I'm not up to worrying about how other people feel.

She shuffled aimlessly though the paperwork in front of her. She must at least summon the energy to do what was necessary. Alex had said the dead vicar and his wife at Odenplan were to take priority over the case of the man in the road at the university. He had, in fact, decided they would try to get the latter off their plate. It was simply not possible for them to deal with two murder inquiries at once with their limited resources.

But all the findings were still being sent through to Fredrika rather than anywhere else. She read a report from the forensics lab which confirmed that material on the man's clothes showed the car had driven over him as well as running into him. There were traces of car paint on his jacket. They were working to identify the type of paint so they would be able to match it against a suspect vehicle, if one turned up.

She clicked on through her new emails. Still not a peep out of the national CID about the fingerprints. Frustrated, she picked up the phone.

"I was just going to ring you," the woman at the other end said eagerly.

Fredrika was taken aback by her chirpy

tone, so unlike two days before.

"Oh yes," she said, trying not to sound equally excited.

She failed, but the woman did not seem to notice.

"I ran the prints through our database, and this came up."

The woman's voice, carried with piercing clarity along the line, hit Fredrika with great force.

"Really?" she said in astonishment.

"Yes, it did," the woman said triumphantly. "Do you remember the armed robbery of the security van outside Forex in Uppsala last week?"

Fredrika's heart gave a jolt. *Forex.*

"Of course," she said quickly.

"A weapon suspected of being used in the holdup was found over the weekend by a man out walking his dog. That's very peculiar, given how minutely everything else was planned. Anyway, they were able to get a set of prints off the gun."

"The unidentified man's," Fredrika said tensely.

"Exactly."

She thanked the woman and hung up. The Forex robbery was the latest in a series of major armed holdups in and around Stockholm. She felt quite elated, as if she had achieved something important herself, just by making a phone call. This cleared up the confusion as to whom the case belonged; it would be entirely reasonable for it to go to the national CID, which was handling the robberies.

Fredrika was smiling as she knocked on Alex's door.

When he heard how easily he could be rid of the hit-and-run case, Alex moved with unusual speed. And as soon as the case had been transferred to the national CID, Fredrika was able to focus more wholeheartedly on the Ahlbin case. It was nearly eleven, and she and Joar were due to see Agne Nilsson from the support group for former right-wing extremists. It felt strange to have Joar at her side. Not wrong, not at all, but different.

He knocked on her door just in time for them to go down and receive their visitor.

"Ready?" he asked.

He gave a polite smile, stiff and correct.

It gave nothing away, reflected Fredrika. It just sat there in the middle of his face, as if drawn on a mask.

She wondered what was behind the mask. He did not wear a ring, but maybe he had a partner? Did he have children? Did he live in a house or a flat? Did he have a car or come in by bus?

Fredrika did not feel curious, but that was largely because she was so good at reading other people. She did not need to wonder about things because they were generally written all over people, even if they were not aware of it or did not want to admit it.

"Read and you'll know," her mother used to say.

And that was so true, in Fredrika's view.

Agne was at reception, looking lost. His appearance was not at all what Fredrika expected. He was short and stocky, pale with thinning hair. But his eyes — she caught herself staring at him intently — his eyes were hard and searching, bright and full of fiery energy.

Like a stubborn, unruly child, she thought as she shook his hand and introduced herself.

She saw that his eyes were automatically drawn to her stomach, but he made no comment. She was grateful. People seemed to assume, wrongly, that it was okay to touch a women expecting a baby in a way you would never think of touching her nonpregnant counterpart. A tender stroking of her stomach, with one hand or both. Fredrika felt a sense of panic on running into certain male colleagues in the corridor because she could feel their eyes boring into her. She had even considered raising the matter at a staff meeting, but could not find the right words.

They took Agne Nilsson to one of the visitor rooms with windows. The windowless interview rooms did not invite reasonable discussions. Nor was there any reason to treat members of the public not suspected of a crime the same way as criminals. So Joar went off to fetch coffee and Fredrika stood chatting to Nilsson.

"Perhaps you could tell us more about your group?" said Joar when they were all seated with their coffee.

Nilsson shifted in his chair, looking as though he did not really know where to begin.

"It started two years ago," he said. "Jakob and I were good friends going back a lot longer than that. Grew up on the same block."

He gave a sad smile and went on. The project had been Jakob Ahlbin's idea, as these things so often were. It all started when he was confronted by a young man who stayed behind after one of his lectures. He was dressed like most other young men, but his hair — or lack of it — and a number of tattoos revealed his ideological home.

"Don't go thinking it's that effing simple," he had told Jakob. "You stand there going on about what it's like for those immigrants and how the rest of us should behave, but not all of us have a goddamn choice. You can be effing sure of that."

It was the beginning of a long conversation. The lad was scared and unhappy. He had got into warped, right-wing circles at the tender age of fourteen, through his elder brother. Now he was nineteen, and about to leave school. His brother had left the movement some years before, moved away and found a job. He himself was stuck in Stockholm with useless school grades and nowhere to go, trapped in a circle of acquaintances he no longer felt he had anything in common with. And he had just met this girl. Nadima, from Syria.

"It should be her family, not my mates, who've got problems with us being together," the boy had told Jakob. "But her dad's as cool as anything about her meeting a Swedish guy. My mates, though, they'd kill us both if they knew."

The boy had taken about as much as any young person could bear. Jakob could see it, and that was what made him want to act.

"Give me a few days," Jakob said. "I know some people. I'll ask round about what someone in your situation could do."

But it turned out he had not had a few days. The gang had got wind that one of its members was thinking of leaving and taking up with an immigrant girl, and one day when the two were coming back from a walk, they were waiting for them.

Nilsson's eyes were glinting with moisture.

"It really shook Jakob," he said huskily. "The fact that he hadn't appreciated the urgency."

"What happened?" asked Joar, making Fredrika nervous.

She did not want any grisly details, fearing they would be too much for her.

"They raped her, one after another, and made the boy watch. Then they beat him pretty much to a pulp. He's in a wheelchair now, and brain-damaged, too."

Fredrika felt like crying.

"And the girl?" she asked, trying to keep things professional.

Nilsson gave a smile for the first time since his arrival. It was thin but heartfelt.

"She's part of our network," he said. "Quite openly. Works her socks off. She's the only one the local council has appointed to a full-time position. I think it's been a way for her to move on."

His words came as a relief to both Joar

and Fredrika.

"What was Jakob's function in more concrete terms?" asked Joar. "You said something about money from the council."

Nilsson nodded, to show he knew what Joar was driving at.

"As I say, Nadima's the only one employed full-time. And paid by the council, but apart from that they prefer to work with more established groups. We others have found various other ways of getting involved, with some support from our employers. Jakob was the only one who didn't, in fact; his work was almost entirely voluntary. Don't ask me why, but that's the way it was. His primary contribution was as our spokesman and our main 'ear to the ground,' as the police like to say. Did you ever see Jakob giving a talk?"

Fredrika and Joar shook their heads.

Nilsson blinked a few times. "It was fantastic," he said, beaming. "He could get anybody at all to start thinking along new lines. His thing was to present things his audiences had heard a hundred times before, but in a different way. And the energy he injected into it. He really got through to people."

He fiddled with one of his shirt buttons.

"He should have been a politician," he

239

said. "He was making his mark in that world, too."

I would have liked Jakob, Fredrika thought to herself.

"And what about his condition?" she asked. "Did that seem to affect him in any noticeable way?"

"No . . . I don't quite know how to put it," said Agne, pulling a face. "Of course there were times when it got the better of him, and he was quite frank in telling us about them. From what I understood, it was worse when he was younger."

"But you never talked about it in greater detail?" Joar asked with surprise in his voice. "Even though you'd known each other so long."

"No," conceded Nilsson. "We didn't. Jakob used to say that dwelling on his condition didn't make it any better, and I'm sure he was right to some extent. So he only referred to it in a very general way."

He cleared his throat.

"We mostly talked about work when we met. That felt right for us both."

"But the threats Jakob received, did you know about those?"

"Oh yes," said Agne. "Several of us had them around the same time."

Fredrika stopped dead in the middle of

her note taking.

"Sorry?"

Nilsson gave a firm nod.

"Oh yes," he said, "that was what happened. And it wasn't just that recent clutch of them, it had happened before as well."

"From the same sender?" asked Joar.

"No, but with the same aim, so to speak. Other times when people thought we'd interfered with things that were none of our business."

Joar took out the copies of the emails sent to Jakob.

"Do you recognize these?"

"I certainly do," said Agne. "I had some almost the same, as I told you. But mine didn't say 'fucking priest,' they said 'sodding socialist.' "

He gave a wan smile.

"Weren't you ever frightened?" put in Fredrika.

"No, why should I be?" said Nilsson as if it was not a question he had anticipated. "Nothing ever came of those threats. And they weren't exactly unexpected. We always knew that our activities would be bound to annoy and upset some people."

"But whoever wrote these sounds more than just annoyed," said Joar, indicating the sheaf of papers in his hand.

"Yes, but this was in the context of the latest case we'd been working on. A young man looking for a way out of the Sons of the People. We knew it was going to be damned difficult. And if the emails hadn't dried up, we were planning to go to the police. That's to say, there are police officers in our group who we can talk to, but I mean making a formal report — that was what we hadn't got round to."

Fredrika suppressed a sigh. She hoped they wouldn't take so long over it the next time.

"What do you mean when you say the emails dried up?" asked Joar, frowning. "Jakob was getting them virtually right up to the day he died."

Agne held up his hands.

"I really can't explain it," he said. "I spoke to Jakob last week and at that point none of us had had any more emails. I didn't get any after that, so I didn't raise the matter with him. And he didn't say anything, either."

He looked uncomfortable.

"Though I have to say we hadn't exchanged that many words over the past ten days. He had lots of lecturing commitments and I was pretty busy, too."

"Can we have copies of the emails you

received?" asked Joar.

"Yes, of course," said Nilsson.

"Do you know a Tony Svensson?" was Joar's next question.

Nilsson's face darkened.

"Yes, of course," he said again. "So does every social worker and police officer on the estate where he lives."

"Did you know he was the one sending your group members the emails? Well, sending Jakob's, at any rate?"

Nilsson shook his head mutely.

"What I mean is, we knew he was part of their organization. But I didn't know he was the actual one sending the threats. They were only signed SP, you know."

Joar seemed to be thinking.

"So what happened?" he asked after a while. "About the boy who was trying to leave the Sons of the People, I mean?"

"It was one hell of a mess, to put it bluntly," said Agne. "His name's Ronny Berg, by the way. But I wasn't in on the end of the case; Jakob took charge of it himself in the latter stages. And he hadn't had time to tell us how it all turned out before he died. But I gathered there was a question mark over the boy's real reasons for trying to get out."

Fredrika leaned forward with interest and

knew she must look ridiculous as she found her bump was in the way and had to straighten up again.

"How do you mean?"

"It seemed he wasn't trying to leave the organization for ideological reasons but because he had fallen out with one of the other members. But as I say, I don't know all that much about it. One of my fellow group members might know more; I could ask around."

Joar nodded.

"Yes, please do," he said.

And as he was gathering up his papers, Fredrika suggested tentatively: "You might need protection, Agne. Until we know how all this fits together. *If* it fits together."

Nilsson did not immediately respond, but then he said quietly: "So you think it might not be suicide after all?"

"Yes," said Joar. "But we can't be sure."

"Good," said Nilsson, looking straight at them. "Because not a single bloody one of us believes Jakob could have done it: shot his wife and himself."

Joar put his head on one side.

"Sometimes people aren't at all what they claim to be," he said mildly.

Just after 1:00 PM the news burst onto the website of one of the evening papers: GUN-SHOT VICAR AND WIFE: POLICE SUSPECT LINK TO RIGHTWING EXTREMISTS.

"Damn and blast!" roared Alex Recht, thumping his fist on the desk. "How the hell did that get out?"

In actual fact, there was no need to ask — things always leaked out at the preliminary inquiry stage. But Alex felt he had tried extra hard to stop it happening this time. And the truth was, very few people knew about their new line of inquiry.

"The media are besieging us with calls," Ellen popped her head round the door to say. "What can we give them?"

"Nothing," bellowed Alex. "Nothing at the moment. Have we managed to get hold of Johanna Ahlbin yet?"

Ellen shook her head.

"No."

"And why not?" groaned Alex. "Where the heck has the wretched girl got to?"

He hardly dared look at the computer screen from which pictures of Jakob Ahlbin were now staring back at him. It was all out there now, and there was no way of breaking the news to his younger daughter in person. The only things the journalists had missed out on were the names and pictures of the two daughters.

At least we tried, Alex thought wearily.

Ellen had been putting all her effort into trying to locate Johanna. The girl's employer and colleagues had provided them with the names and numbers of friends who might know her whereabouts, but no one could tell them where she was, how she was, or how much she already knew.

"It's too bloody awful," Alex said under his breath. "Having to hear news like that from the media."

"But we did try," said Ellen, looking unhappy.

"Yes, I suppose we did," said Alex, turning away from the computer.

"Oh, by the way, here's something the assistant in the technical section sent over," said Ellen, putting a plastic folder on his desk. "Printouts of lecture material they found on Jakob's hard drive."

"Anything useful?"

"No, I don't think so. But the name on the notepad could be of interest. Though I don't really know, of course."

"Notepad?" muttered Alex, looking through the sheets of paper from the folder.

He found it right at the back. An unobtrusive little fawn jotter with just one word on it, *Muhammed,* and then a mobile number.

"Where was this found?" asked Alex.

"In a locked drawer in his desk. It was underneath a pen tray."

Something he had hidden away, concluded Alex.

Perhaps Muhammed was an illegal migrant he knew personally, or someone who had sought him out for some other reason.

"Have we checked the phone number against our database?"

"I just did," she said, looking pleased with herself. "And something came up, in fact, related to a passport reported missing. The man's complete name and address were there."

She handed him another slip of paper. Alex gave her a smile in return.

"No criminal record," Ellen added, and then had to go because her mobile was ringing.

Alex wondered what he ought to do next.

He looked at the name and number on the slip, and then at the plastic folder with all the other material. And then he looked at the report of the lost passport, which Ellen had printed out. All these passports that "vanished." Without them, the stream of illegal migrants would have a hard time, Alex knew that.

We've turned Europe into a fortress as impregnable as Fort Knox, he thought grimly. At the price of losing control of the people who are going in and out of our country. Shameful for all concerned.

He gazed out of the window. Clear blue sky and brilliant sunshine, and the weekend only a few hours away. He blinked. There was no way he could face a whole weekend at home with Lena behaving like a stranger. She had become so inaccessible. For reasons he couldn't put into words, he felt he could not talk to her about what had happened or the way the whole situation was affecting him.

Why not? wondered Alex. We've always been able to talk about everything.

Perhaps he ought to give it a try. Perhaps. But either way, he was definitely going to try to put in a few hours' work over the weekend.

■ ■ ■ ■

At first it looked as though the week was going to end as badly as it had begun. Peder Rydh was instructed to go though all the phone lists the police had had from the phone company Telia and from Jakob Ahlbin's mobile supplier, while Joar got to go down with Fredrika to talk to Agne Nilsson. Peder felt as though he was going to blow sky-high with frustration, but then he heard he was to be one of those interviewing Tony Svensson that afternoon, and calmed down. As he went though the lists, he even felt a bit exhilarated.

Every time he had to deal with material from phone tapping or surveillance, he was amazed at the vast number of calls people made every day. Often you could work out some sort of pattern, of course, like married couples who sometimes rang each other twice a day and sometimes not at all. But there were lots of other numbers and contacts to analyze. Contacts that could seem highly interesting in terms of timing, but which on closer examination turned out to be the local pizzeria, for example.

In the case of Jakob Ahlbin's phone and any contact he might have had with Tony

Svensson, it proved quite simple. Peder grinned and punched the air as he found a match.

Svensson had rung Jakob Ahlbin on three occasions, and each time it was a very short call, making Peder assume he had got through to Jakob's answering machine. They would never be able to re-create the actual content, but the very fact that Svensson had rung Ahlbin was proof enough.

He hurried out of his office and over to Alex's. But he hovered uncertainly in the doorway; his boss looked even grumpier than usual. Peder gave a discreet cough.

"Yes?" said Alex severely, but softened when he saw who it was. "Oh, come on in."

Somewhat heartened, Peder went in and showed Alex the telephone lists.

"Good," said Alex, "good. Draw up an application to the prosecutor double quick; I want this bloke brought in for unlawful menace before the end of the day. Particularly now this crap's all over the media."

A warm feeling spread through Peder's body. So he wasn't being left entirely out in the cold. But with the warmth came the stress. Who had leaked the right-wing angle to the media?

He was heading for the door when Alex

said: "Er, you haven't got a minute, have you?"

It had been too good to be true, of course. Even before he sat down, he knew what Alex had on his mind. But the way he chose to express it came as a complete surprise.

"In this workplace, as long as I'm in charge," he said, "a croissant is a croissant. And nothing else," he said, emphasizing every syllable.

I'm gonna die, thought Peder. I'm gonna die of shame and I damn well deserve it, too.

He scarcely dared look at Alex, who went on relentlessly:

"And when one of my staff — for private or other reasons — is in such a state that he can't tell the difference between a pastry and something else, then I expect the person in question to get to grips with it and sort himself out."

He stopped and fixed Peder with a look.

"Understood?"

"Understood," whispered Peder.

And wondered how on earth he could carry on doing his job.

They met in the living room of the older man. It was their third meeting in swift succession, and neither of them felt particularly comfortable in the company of the other. But there was no way round it, in view of recent events.

"We knew it would generate a lot of attention," said the younger man. "It was hardly a surprise to any of us that a vicar committing suicide would be big news."

There was no point contradicting him. Planning and setting the stage for an operation like that was one thing. Carrying it through was something else entirely. Holding your nerve and staying calm was vital.

The older man spoke.

"There are a number of unfortunate circumstances that we need to be wary of," he said firmly. "The media reporting, for one thing. I wasn't expecting to see articles with names and photos of the deceased until tomorrow morning at the earliest."

"No, I don't think any of us were."

"Damn the police. Every investigation leaks like a blessed sieve."

There was a pause.

"This makes rather a mess of the timetable," sighed the older man. "Particularly for our friend abroad. When do we expect her back?"

"Monday, we thought."

"Does that seem credible? I mean, if the news is already out?"

"Most of it can be explained away," the younger man said in a matter-of-fact tone.

He looked awful when he attempted a smile. A series of operations to correct his injury had only achieved half of what had been hoped for. And now he had decided to settle for looking this way. The crooked smile had become his trademark.

The older man got up and went over to the window.

"I'm not very happy about the defection we had before all this happened. It disturbs me, I have to say. The fact that there's someone out there who knows too much. I hope you're right — that we can still consider him our friend. Things look bad for us otherwise."

"You know he hasn't had his share yet," said the younger one. "That should keep him in line. And he was deep in the shit himself when he backed out. He could never shop us and keep in the clear himself."

It was an argument that seemed to re-assure the older man, who briskly moved on to the next point on the agenda.

"I understand there was a problem with our latest daisy," he said, taking a seat in the wing-back chair by the bookshelf full of dictionaries and encyclopedias.

The younger man's face hardened. For

the first time since his arrival he looked visibly worried, and his words confirmed the fact:

"That's more of a problem. Unfortunately we weren't able to pick our flower before he spread the good news, as it were, to some of his friends. Or one, at any rate. Who then got in touch with the vicar."

The older man knitted his brow.

"Have we any way of assessing the scale of the damage?" he asked.

"Yes, we're pretty sure we can. And as I say, he didn't let on to many people. Unfortunately, we haven't got his friend's name. But I'm on the case."

The men fell silent. It was almost as if the sound had been absorbed by the bookshelves covering almost the full length of the walls and the expensive rugs on the floor. It was the older man who found his voice first:

"And the next daisy?"

The younger man's deformed smile appeared again.

"He's paying on Sunday."

"Good," said the older one. "Good."

And he added:

"Will this one live?"

Silence again.

"Probably not. He seems to have blabbed,

too, broken the rules."

The other man paled.

"This wasn't the way we envisaged things going. We can't have any more failures like this. Maybe we need to suspend the operation for the time being?"

The younger man did not seem capable of seeing that disaster could be imminent.

"Let's wait and see how our friend on the other side of the law plays his cards during the day today."

The older man pursed his lips.

"It shouldn't be a problem. He knows what will happen if he makes the mistake of betraying us."

His stomach hurt as he said the words, almost as if they made him afraid of himself.

Tony Svensson was a creature of habit. His world basically revolved round three places: network HQ, the repair shop, and his home. They opted for the repair shop.

It was all achieved without too much fuss. He spat and swore as the police cars screeched to a halt outside where he worked, but once he appreciated the seriousness of the situation, he stopped resisting. The officers who were there to pick him up said he even smiled as the cold metal of the cuffs closed round his wrists. As if the feeling rekindled memories from a time he had almost forgotten.

The prosecutor agreed that there was sufficient proof for suspecting Svensson of unlawful menace. The emails and phone lists were more than enough. It remained to be seen whether they could get a prosecution out of it; it depended on how cooperative Agne Nilsson was. Unlike Jakob

Ahlbin, he was still alive and able to testify about the threats. If he was willing. Not many people dared to testify against groups like Svensson's.

Peder and Joar were to conduct the interview. The energy which interviewing normally injected into Peder failed to materialize when he had to work with Joar. He glanced sideways at his colleague as they stood in silence in the lift. A pink shirt under his jacket. As if that was the sort of thing you could wear in the force. Another of those signs.

There's something weird about that guy, thought Peder. And I shall damn well find out what it is, even if I have to drag it out of him.

Svensson was waiting for them in the interview room where they had taken him after his formal admission to custody.

"You know what crime you are suspected of?" asked Joar.

Svensson smiled and nodded. It was obvious he had been through all this before and he was taking the whole thing phlegmatically. As if you simply had to reckon on things sometimes going wrong, and then you had to take the consequences.

Had he not been so unkempt, he might even have passed for good-looking. But his shaven head, tattooed arms, and oil-rimmed nails made him look like the gangster he was. His eyes were dark. Like two pistol bullets aimed at Peder and Joar.

He's sharp, Peder judged instinctively. That's why he's so cool. And because he's managed to get his solicitor here already.

"It would be helpful if you answered in words, so it can be heard on the tape," Joar pointed out in a friendly way.

Rather too friendly.

Peder went cold. There was something spooky about the role Joar was adopting. Too balanced to be true. As if he might suddenly fly off the handle, throw himself across the table, and kill the person on the other side.

Psychopath; that was the word that flashed into Peder's mind.

"Jakob Ahlbin," he said in a steady voice. "Does that name ring a bell?"

Svensson hesitated. His solicitor tried to catch his eye, but Svensson avoided his look.

"I may have heard the name sometime," he answered.

"In what context?" asked Joar.

Tony Svensson brightened up again.

"He interfered in the private affairs of me and my friends; that was how we got to know each other."

"In what way did he interfere?" asked Peder.

A sigh escaped the shaven-headed man on the other side of the table.

"He tried to come between us, make trouble."

"How?"

"By poking his nose into in a conflict that had nothing to do with him."

"What conflict?"

"Nothing I want to go into."

Silence.

"Maybe a conflict that concerned someone who didn't want to stay in your group?" said Joar, leaning back with his arms folded on his chest.

Just the way Tony Svensson himself was sitting.

"Yes, maybe it was," replied Tony.

"So what did you do?" asked Peder.

"When?"

"When Jakob Ahlbin took an interest in things that were no business of his."

"Ah, you mean then."

Tony shifted his position and the solicitor leafed unobtrusively though his papers. In his thoughts he was clearly already on the way to the meeting with his next client.

"I tried to make him see that he should stick to his own affairs and leave other people's out of it," Svensson said.

"How did you make him see that?"

"I rang him and told him to go to hell. And sent a few emails as well."

Joar and Peder automatically started flicking through the printouts they had in front of them.

"Did you say anything else in the emails?" asked Peder.

"You've got them right in front of you, for fuck's sake," hissed Svensson, his patience suddenly at an end. "Why don't you read them out?"

Joar cleared his throat and read out loud: " 'Things are looking bad for you, Ahlbin. Back off from this shit while you still can.' "

"Did you write that?"

"Yes," replied Tony Svensson. "But I don't fucking well see how anyone could call it a threat."

"Wait," said Peder gently, "there's more."

He read out: " 'Pity you can't stop fucking us about, scumbag vicar. Pity you can't see that the one in the sorriest state after all this will be you.' "

Svensson started to laugh.

"Still not a real threat."

"I'm not so sure about that," said Joar. "The expression 'sorry state' isn't usually used in a positive sense."

"But it's bloody hard to tell, isn't it?" said Tony with a wink.

The wink was a step too far for Joar and Peder sensed an instant change to the atmosphere in the room.

"All right, then," he said, hoping to take command of the interview for a while. "Let's try something a bit more colorful: 'You ought to listen to us, Vicar. You've got the trials of Job ahead of you if you don't stop your activities right away.' "

Svensson said nothing and his face froze.

Then he leaned across the table and raised a finger.

"I fucking well never wrote that," he hissed, underlining every syllable.

Peder raised an eyebrow.

"You didn't?" he said, feigning surprise. "So you mean someone else suddenly started emailing Jakob Ahlbin from your computer and signing themselves 'SP'?"

"Are you saying that email came from my computer?" demanded Svensson loudly.

"Yes," said Peder, looking down at his paperwork.

Only to discover that he was wrong. The email he had just quoted was one of the ones that had not come from the suspect's own computer.

Svensson saw Peder's expression change

261

and he relaxed, leaning back again.

"Thought not," he said.

"So you're claiming someone else was sending emails to Jakob on the same subject? Someone other than you?"

"That's exactly what I'm claiming," Svensson snapped. "I didn't email the vicar from any computer except the one I've got at home."

"You mean the one we've just brought in?" Joar corrected him with sarcasm. "We've just searched your place and taken a few things for examination."

The man's dark eyes grew even darker and Peder saw him swallow several times. But he said nothing.

He's clever, thought Peder. He knows when to leave it.

"Okay, is there anything else you want?" Tony said testily. "I'm in a hurry now."

"But we're not," Joar said firmly. "What did you say when you phoned Jakob Ahlbin?"

Tony gave a loud and exaggerated sigh.

"I left a total of three messages on the old man's answering machine," he said. "And they were almost identical to the emails. Which I sent from my own computer and nobody else's."

"Did you have any other kind of contact

with Jakob Ahlbin?" asked Joar.

"No."

"You never went to his flat?"

"No."

"So how come we found your fingerprints on his front door?" asked Joar.

Peder stiffened. *What in hell's name?* He had not seen any report of that.

Svensson seemed to have been caught equally off guard.

"I went there and rang the doorbell, all right? Banged on the door. But nobody opened it, and I shoved off again."

"When was that?"

"Um," said Svensson, and appeared to be thinking. "It must've been a week ago. Like, last Saturday."

"Why?" asked Joar. "If you didn't feel the need to send any more emails, then . . ."

"I was scared I'd judged it wrong," Svensson said angrily. "I sent the emails to calm the old geezer down, to get him to keep his nose out of our internal affairs. And then it, like, resolved itself, the difference of opinion we had in our group. At least that was the way we saw it. The guy we fell out with — well, we sorted it out between us. But then there was another round of trouble and I was sure the vicar was behind it again. So I went over to his place. But that was the only time."

Joar nodded slowly.

"That was the only time?" he repeated.

"I swear it," said Svensson. "And if you tell me you found my fingerprints inside the flat, you're lying. Because I've never been in there."

Joar sat mute and Peder seethed with fury. How the hell did Joar dare to go down to an interrogation without giving his colleague all the facts in advance?

Joar looked amused.

"Can we have the names of all the others who can confirm your version?" he said.

"Yep, sure," said Svensson, sounding exaggeratedly positive. "You can start by asking Ronny Berg."

Berg. The name Agne Nilsson had already given them. Tony went on: "That's if he wants to talk to you. Then you can hear what the vicar was demanding in return."

The last word ricocheted around the interview room. *In return?*

Just as Peder and Joar went off to interview Tony Svensson, Alex knocked on Fredrika Bergman's door and asked if she wanted to come with him to see someone.

"Where are we going?" she asked when she had gathered up her things.

Alex explained about the scribbled name and telephone number they had found in a locked drawer in Jakob Ahlbin's desk.

"I took a chance, you might say," he went on. "Rang the fellow up, told him what had happened, and asked how he knew Jakob Ahlbin. At first he refused to answer, didn't want anything to do with the police. Then he said Ahlbin had rung him about something; that was how they had come into contact with each other. But he wouldn't say what about."

"He didn't want to talk on the phone or he didn't want to talk at all?"

"He didn't want to talk at all, but I

265

thought if we went out there unannounced, maybe he'd want to talk after all."

They took the lift down to the garage. Fredrika thought how tired Alex looked. Tired, and worried, too. In another time, and another workplace, she would have asked him how he was, indicated she'd be happy to listen if he wanted to talk. But just now she could not summon the energy.

They drove across Kungsholmen in silence, took the E4 south to Skärholmen. Alex put the radio on.

"Have the media been beating a path to your door?" Fredrika asked, knowing what the answer would be.

"You can say that again," Alex said crossly. "And they simply can't accept that we have no bloody comment to make. We've got to raise our game here and at least come up with a line or two to keep the news crews happy, with the evening bulletins coming up."

Fredrika sat quietly, mulling things over.

"That's the thing I can't make any sense of," she said eventually.

"What?"

"The idea that Tony Svensson and his mates could get into a flat in the middle of town at five in the afternoon, shoot two people, and get away without anyone seeing them, and without leaving a single trace behind them. And on top of all that, get it to look like suicide."

Alex looked at her.

"The same thought had occurred to me," he said. "But I have to admit I'm having more and more trouble convincing myself it was suicide."

"Me too," Fredrika replied.

"How the hell could you be so irresponsible?" demanded Peder as soon as they were back upstairs in the department.

Joar looked restrained.

"The fingerprint report came in at the last minute and I didn't have time to tell you," he said with a slight shrug. "I'm sorry about that, but these things happen."

Peder believed neither of those things.

"I could have made a real fool of myself," he went on indignantly. "It was sheer luck I didn't put my foot in it."

He stood there, waiting for Joar's counter-move. When it came, it was as much of a shock as Alex's sortie earlier in the day.

"Luck?" said Joar, his eyes so dark that Peder's mouth went dry. "Luck?"

The tension in the air was as thick as smoke. Joar took a step closer.

"That seems to be what we have to hope

for all the time, working with you. I have to say I've no idea how you came to be promoted this far in the force, given how insensitive and unprofessional you are."

Peder clenched his fists, bounced on the balls of his feet, and wondered if he would make it out of the room without beating the hell out of his colleague first.

"Watch yourself," he said quietly. "I'm the one in the group on the permanent staff; nobody knows how long Alex will put up with your stirring."

Joar gave him a contemptuous look.

"Think we both know you'd be wasting your time, Peder. Alex is more than happy with my performance. How he assesses yours is a bit more doubtful. You and your croissants."

By the time Joar reached the end of his sentence, Peder was convinced this would be the first time in his life he assaulted another man in anger.

I'll take him down another time, the fucking madman, he vowed to himself as he turned on his heel and left the room.

In his office he wondered what he really knew about his colleague. Not much at all, he realized. He had worked on cases for the Environmental Crime Agency, and for the past year he had been with the Södermalm police. Just as Peder had been the year before that. He frowned. He often met up with the lads he had worked with there for a beer, but strangely enough they had never even mentioned Joar.

Thoughts were coming to him thick and fast now, and he could not stop them.

Pia Nordh was still working in Söder.

The name brought back so many memories that it almost hurt. Initially a sexual dalliance with an attractive colleague, to escape an everyday life that increasingly resembled a desert trek with no water or mirages. Then a habit. And then nothing. Until he was bored again. In the course of that bloody intense missing girl case last summer.

His fingers fumbled as he found her number. He was breathing heavily as it rang. And then her voice: "Hi, Pia here."

He felt warmth spreading through his chest. She was someone else's now, someone serious. The word made him feel quite sick — *serious*. What was that?

"Er, hi. It's me, Peder."

His voice sounded pathetic. Feebler than he had intended. There was no response.

"Hello, Peder," she said in the end.

"How're things?"

He coughed and tried to brace himself.

Somewhere inside he knew he had behaved badly toward her, but he would hardly improve matters by pretending to be her poodle now.

"Fine thanks," she said.

Still on her guard.

"Um, I was wondering if you could help me with something," he said, lowering his voice, unaccountably nervous that Joar was deranged enough to be out in the corridor eavesdropping. The blood was surging round his body and there was no quelling his agitation. How the hell had he managed to balls things up like this?

Out in the corridor, Joar laughed. Peder was wrenched back to real life and his thoughts were again on the colleague who had given him such a bitter pill to swallow.

"All right, I'm listening," Pia said in a soft voice.

"Joar Sahlin," said Peder, "do you know him?"

Silence.

"He's pretty new here," Peder went on, "and apparently he worked with your lot before that. I've had a few problems with him and I just wanted someone to check him out. See if there are any skeletons in his cupboard."

He heard a sharp intake of breath from Pia.

"For God's sake, Peder."

"No need to spend a lot of time on it," he added quickly.

She gave a dry laugh, and he could visualize her shaking her head. Her blond hair swinging to and fro.

"No need to spend a lot of time on it?" she repeated gruffly. "Well, that's very decent of you."

"I didn't mean . . ." began Peder, rather surprised by her reaction.

"Leave it," she hissed.

He blinked in consternation, but had no time to reply before she went on.

"Do you think I don't know what you're up to?"

All at once she sounded on the verge of tears.

"Leave it, Peder," she said again. "Just leave it."

And then — the words that made time stand still:

"Joar's the first guy for several years I've had a really good relationship with. We're looking for a flat so we can move in together. He's an extremely good man and human being. And then you do this."

There. Fury exploded, boiled over and

drove him almost out of his mind. He'd been working with that bloody psychopath for weeks. And the whole time — *the whole time* — he'd been in the weaker position. Joar going to the head of HR and squealing about the croissants. Joar having it off with his ex.

"You've got to let it go, and move on," she sighed as he said nothing. "For your own sake."

Shame came washing over him. She would never believe him if he said he hadn't had the slightest idea that Joar was her new boyfriend.

"Forget I rang," he hissed, and cut her off.

Then he sat at his desk and waited for his fury to drain away.

Muhammed Abdullah had come to Sweden more than twenty years ago. Saddam Hussein's regime had made it impossible for him to stay in Iraq, he told Fredrika and Alex once they had persuaded him to invite them into his flat.

There was plenty of room for Muhammed and his wife. The children had already moved out.

"But they both live nearby," he said, sounding happy about it.

His wife served coffee and biscuits. Alex looked around. Someone had put a lot of effort into matching curtains to tablecloths and pictures. There was a sweetish smell that Alex could not quite put his finger on.

As the man appeared to be relaxing a bit, Alex seized his chance.

"We're only really interested in what Jakob Ahlbin wanted when he got in touch with you," he said in a friendly tone.

Muhammed's face went white.

"I know nothing," he said, shaking his head. "Nothing."

"I don't believe that," Alex said gently. "But nobody in the whole police force thinks you are involved in the awful thing that happened."

He drank some of his coffee.

"Did you and Jakob Ahlbin have a lot of contact?" Fredrika asked genially.

"No," said the man. "Just that once. He called me. And then we met. That was the only time."

Alex could smell important information. And what was more, he could see that Muhammed thought it important, too. But he was scared, really scared.

Then he decided he had no choice. Leaned back a little on the sofa, his eyes flickering around the room.

"It was only a rumor," he said in a low voice.

"What was?" asked Fredrika.

"That there was a new way of getting to Sweden if you needed help."

His wife came back to hand round more biscuits. Nothing was said until she had finished.

"You know how it is nowadays," he said tentatively. "It can cost up to fifteen thousand dollars to get to Sweden. Lots of the people who need to get away haven't got that sort of money. When I first came it was different. *Europe* was different, and the routes weren't the same. I heard from the son of a good friend of mine in Iraq that he was coming to Sweden on different terms."

Alex frowned.

"And what were they?"

"Other terms," Muhammed said again. "It was going to cost less and it would be much easier to get a residence permit."

He took a deep breath and reached out for his coffee cup.

"But they were very demanding."

"Who?"

"The smugglers. They had strict rules and it would be the worse for you if you didn't stick to them. Or if you told anyone. That's why I didn't want to tell you, really. Not until my son's friend was here."

"Hasn't he got here yet?" Fredrika asked cautiously.

Muhammed shook his head.

"One morning he was just gone, his father told me. But he never got here. Or if he did, he must be in hiding."

"But shouldn't he have gone to the Migration Agency?" Alex wondered.

"Maybe he did," suggested Muhammed. "But he hasn't been in touch, anyway."

"Did he have family at home in Iraq?" asked Alex.

"A fiancée," said Muhammed. "They were going to get married, but he must have had to go in a hurry. And he didn't say anything to her before he left, either."

"Are you sure he even left his own country?" Fredrika asked. "Couldn't something have happened to him in Iraq?"

"Perhaps," Muhammed said evasively. "But I don't think so. It's not like it used to be, news gets around if anything happens to anyone. We would have heard if he'd been kidnapped or anything like that."

Alex digested this.

"What made Jakob choose to phone you? Did he know that you had this information?"

Muhammed's face closed.

"I've got a few contacts," he said carefully, and Alex knew he had hit the bull's-eye. "It was them Jakob Ahlbin was ringing about. And then we got onto the other thing; it was me that brought it up."

"Jakob wasn't already aware of it?"

"No, he got the information from me. After he rang me, we arranged to meet somewhere, and I gave it to him."

Muhammed looked almost proud.

"And these contacts of yours, who are they?" said Alex, trying to keep it casual.

"For other people who want to come to Sweden," said Muhammed quietly, looking down at his hands. "I'm not involved in that work myself, I just know who they can phone."

Alex had colleagues in the national CID who would have sold their own parents for names like those, but he decided not to give them Muhammed. They would have to find him for themselves.

"Do you think this has anything to do with Jakob Ahlbin's death?" Muhammed asked curiously.

Alex's answer was short and to the point.

"Maybe, we don't know. It would be as well for you not to tell anybody we've been here."

Muhammed assured them he would not.

And served them more coffee.

"Hope your friend turns up," said Fredrika at the doorway as they were leaving.

Muhammed looked uneasy.

"Yes, I hope so, too," he said. "For Farah's sake, if nothing else."

Fredrika stopped short.

"For whose sake?"

"Farah, his fiancée. She'll be beside herself with worry back home in Baghdad, I'm sure."

He gave a dejected sigh.

"You wonder how it can be possible. How someone can just disappear off the face of the earth."

They had a final meeting in the Den before the weekend started. Peder and Joar were still busy writing up the interview when Alex called them in. It was very plain to him that if looks could kill, then Joar would be a dead man. Peder's look had more hatred in it than any Alex had ever seen. What the hell had happened?

"Well, the whole bloody lot's out in the media now," Alex said indignantly. "And they've already made their minds up: the vicar didn't commit suicide but was murdered by right-wing extremists for taking a stand on the migrant question, which is such a hot potato at the moment."

He stopped.

"Is that right? Is Tony Svensson our man?"

"It's clearly a lead worth evaluating," Joar said thoughtfully, "but I don't think Svensson necessarily did it himself. There are plenty of other interesting characters around him."

"Such as?" asked Alex.

"I put together a few things after the interview," he said. "A contact of mine in the national CID gave me a hand; they've been watching these guys for a long time because they suspect them of some rather advanced varieties of organized crime. Svensson's the leader of the group, but under him — or alongside him, really — there are various other known criminals. One of them's a professional burglar, for example. He'd be more than capable of getting into the Ahlbins' flat in the middle of the day without being noticed. And another one seems pretty good at getting hold of guns."

"But the couple were shot with Jakob Ahlbin's own hunting pistol," objected Alex.

"True," said Joar. "But maybe they needed other weapons to threaten their way into the apartment?"

Alex considered this, and glanced toward Peder. The content of Joar's presentation was clearly new to him. Alex therefore turned to him.

"Peder, you were interviewing, too. What's your spontaneous reaction?"

"I suppose that could all fit," he said

tersely, and Alex could see the veins protruding tensely in his neck.

Peder got to his feet and nodded to Joar.

"Have you finished, then? I've got something I want to show everybody, too."

A picture appeared on the white screen behind him as he started a slide show he had prepared.

"This is Ronny Berg," Peder announced loudly. "He's the defector that Jakob Ahlbin had a row with Sons of the People about."

He fixed the impassive Joar with a triumphant look.

"I decided to have a chat with him this afternoon," he went on. "And he gave me some information."

"Did you go on your own?" asked Alex.

Peder breathed in.

"Yes," he said. "I didn't think it would be a problem."

But it was, and Alex knew that Peder knew it. All interviews had to be approved by Alex beforehand.

"Jakob Ahlbin only imposed one condition on Ronny," Peder went on. "That he immediately stopped any criminal activity he was involved in. And that was problematic, apparently."

"Oh?" said Alex, raising his eyebrows.

"The policy of the support group's very

straightforward," said Peder. "They're happy to help anybody at all get back on track with their lives again, but they insist the person stops *all* criminal activity they're involved in. That was what Tony Svensson meant when he said Jakob had asked Berg for something in return."

He took a breath and clicked onto the next picture.

"Ronny Berg, former burglar, had a major heist planned which would bring in lots of cash, and he wanted to keep his fellow members out of it. But the Sons of the People got wind of it and there was big trouble. That was when Berg decided he wanted to leave the organization, and he turned to the support group to help him, played repentant sinner, and pretended he didn't sympathize with the aims and ideologies of the organization anymore."

"Did they swallow it?" asked Fredrika.

"Hook, line, and sinker," said Peder. "To start with, at any rate. But then the Sons of the People tipped off the network that its new protégé wasn't that keen on abandoning crime, after all, and Jakob Ahlbin decided to drop him."

"So Berg went back to the SP?" said Alex.

"No, not at all," said Peder. "He staked everything on doing this dream heist and getting out of the country. But Jakob Ahlbin anticipated his move and tipped off one of the police officers in the support network, who passed it on to his police colleagues."

Peder looked pleased with himself.

"Where is he now, then?" Fredrika asked in confusion.

"He's here in Stockholm, in Kronoberg Prison," said Peder.

"And he told you the whole story?" Alex said in astonishment.

"He told me as much as he wanted to," said Peder. "I got the rest from the officers in the support group who had the tip-off from Jakob."

Alex drummed his fingers on the table.

"How does Berg feel about Jakob Ahlbin now?" he asked.

"Hates him," Peder said.

"Has he got an alibi for the night of the murder?"

"Yes, he was already under arrest. The armed robbery had already spectacularly misfired by then. That was last Thursday, I think."

"So several days before Jakob and his wife were found dead," Alex said thoughtfully. "Plenty of time to plan a double murder and give orders for it to be carried out."

Peder shook his head.

"In theory yes, I suppose," he said. "But in practice? No, I don't think so. Berg hasn't got that kind of network. Particularly not now he's without the backup and protection of the SP."

Fredrika was poring dark-eyed over her notebook and Joar did not move a muscle. But he looked as if he was gritting his teeth, Alex thought.

"I don't buy this," Fredrika said with an urgency in her voice that Alex had not heard from her for a long time.

"Don't buy what?" he asked.

"The right-wing extremist line," she said, with a new focus in her eyes. "It's like I was saying earlier, Alex, it all feels too advanced. Not the getting into a flat and shooting someone in the head, but the way it was done. And then there's the background of Jakob Ahlbin's condition. Whoever set up the murder must have known about it, that much is clear from the so-called suicide note."

She went on: "If we were to assume it was someone they knew, it would all seem less far-fetched. Then it wouldn't be at all strange that they'd been let into the flat or that there were no signs of a violent struggle."

"And it would explain the letter and the

insight into their private lives," Peder added.

"And what would the motive be, in that case?" Alex asked in frustration.

Fredrika observed him for a moment.

"I don't know. But I think we ought to take a closer look at the link between Jakob Ahlbin and the man who was run down in Frescativägen, Yusuf."

A man they could finally put a name to, with an indirect link to Ahlbin. Jakob had had contact with Muhammed, who in turn knew Yusuf.

"Has that link got anything to do with the right-wing angle?" asked Joar.

"Not as far as we know."

"But Muhammed was scared," Fredrika put in firmly. "His friend's son came to Sweden and died before he could even get to the Migration Agency."

"Having first dashed off to rob a bank," Peder supplied.

"Which gets us tangled up in all that messy bank robbery business," said Alex, pulling a face.

Fredrika held her ground and indicated that she had more to say.

Here we go, thought Alex. She's woken up again at last.

"There's one other thing," she said.

Alex noted that Joar was staring at Fredrika. He had not seen that side of her until now, Alex realized.

"The emails," said Fredrika. "I think Svensson was telling the truth when he said he didn't write them all."

The others looked at her expectantly.

"It came to me when I read them through again," she said. "Even the first time I'd felt it was slightly out of character for Svensson to make those references to Job. The emails that came from computers other than his home one have rather a different tone."

Alex looked dubious.

"Who would have access to his email account? The sender is clearly the same, whichever computer the emails came from."

"The emails sent from Svensson's own computer didn't come from his personal email account. They came from one that all the SP have access to," said Fredrika. "So that means plenty of people to give away passwords and user names and so on."

She leafed through the email printouts that she had brought with her.

"I'm positive," she said. "Whoever wrote these emails from other computers kind of tried to mimic the tone of the earlier ones, but didn't really pull it off. There are clear biblical references in all of them, but none in the ones from Tony's computer. The SP emails are much cruder and more direct."

"So what are you saying?" asked Alex, cupping his chin in one hand.

"I can't be totally sure," conceded Fredrika. "But maybe someone else knew about the threats Jakob had already had, and used them to flesh out the threat scenario against him. Maybe so we wouldn't look elsewhere, so they wouldn't be traced. But Jakob realized, I'm sure."

"Realized what?" asked Alex, sounding more irritated than he meant to.

"That the threats came from different sources. And were to do with different things. That would explain why Jakob decided not to say anything to Agne Nilsson about those last emails."

Fredrika pushed back some strands of hair that had flopped across her face.

"We could follow up the email that was sent from Farsta Library," she said. "You have to put your name on a list and show your ID card before you can go into the computer room there. They started doing that to clamp down on people coming in to surf porn sites."

"You check that out on Monday, then," said Alex to round off the meeting, adding: "And keep an eye on the case of the man run over at the university. I want to know what the national CID come up with on that."

Fredrika nodded and the rest got to their feet, since the meeting seemed to be over.

"Right, it's the weekend," Alex declared. "Let's go home."

Home. Anxiety gnawed at him as his thoughts turned to the two days off that lay ahead. Damn, he really had to come to some kind of decision. He left the Den without another word and trudged back to his room.

He wished his son would ring from South America.

Come home, he pleaded in his mind. Your mum hasn't been herself these last weeks.

He swallowed hard and touched the scar tissue on his hands. South America felt a bloody long way away.

Then he made up his mind. If Lena herself volunteered no explanation over the weekend, he would share his worries with her at the start of next week.

And in the shadow of his private anxiety, a work-related one was taking shape. If it was not Tony Svensson who had murdered Jakob and Marja Ahlbin, who the devil was it?

Darkness, cold, and a sky that was already as black as night met Fredrika as she left HQ to go home. Spencer would not be there until later; she had hours of solitude to kill.

I need a hobby, she thought as she walked from Kungsholmen to her flat by Vasa Park. And more friends.

Neither thing was really true. She had more friends than she had time for, and more leisure activities than she could ever fit in. But how did she end up with these voids of acute loneliness and inactivity? Fredrika had been wondering about this for several years and had concluded that the answer was actually quite simple: the problem was that she did not come first for anybody. There was no one for whom she took priority over everything else, and so from time to time she found herself feeling lonely and abandoned when all her friends'

288

diaries were full and they had no time to meet up with her, just when she needed their company most.

But was this evening really one of those times? It had been her own decision not to arrange anything with a friend while she was waiting for Spencer. On the other hand, no friends had rung, either.

The lonely, forlorn feeling had greatly intensified since she got pregnant. The exhaustion and nightmares played their part. And the wretched pains that sometimes made her want to scream.

She arrived home to a silent, empty flat. How she had loved this place when she found it. Big windows letting in huge amounts of light; polished pine floors. The original kitchen with a tiny maid's room opening off it that she could turn into a little library.

This was where I was reborn, thought Fredrika.

The lights glimmered into life as she went round the flat turning them on, one after another. She put her hand on a radiator and found it cool. Spencer always objected to how cold she liked to keep the flat.

Spencer. Always Spencer. *What does it mean, the fact that you and I were destined to meet?*

The sound of the phone ringing cut through the flat. Her mother clearly had something on her mind.

"Are you sleeping any better?" was her opening gambit.

"No," said Fredrika. "But I'm not in as much pain now. Haven't been today, at any rate."

"I had an idea," her mother ventured.

Silence.

"Perhaps you'd feel better if you started playing again?"

For a moment time stood still and Fredrika was drowning in memories from the time before the Accident.

"I don't mean lots," her mother quickly added. "Not lots, just a little bit, to help you feel more in harmony with yourself. You know I always play when I can't get to sleep."

There was a time when conversations like that would have been natural for Fredrika and her mother. Back then, they used to play music together and draw up guidelines for Fredrika's future. But that was then, before the Accident. Now Fredrika's mother no longer had a right to discuss Fredrika's playing with her, and sensed as much when her daughter did not respond.

She decided to change the subject.

"You've got to let us meet him, now."

Firm but with a note of entreaty. Asking to be part of her daughter's life again.

Fredrika felt shocked.

"Your dad and I are trying, trying really hard in fact, to reconcile ourselves to the situation you've faced us with. We're trying to understand the way you must have thought about this and planned it out. But we feel dreadfully excluded, Fredrika. Not only have you had a secret relationship with a man for over a decade, but now you're expecting his baby as well."

"I don't know what I can say," sighed Fredrika.

"No, but I do," her mother said briskly. "Bring him round. Tomorrow."

Fredrika weighed this in her mind and concluded that she could no longer keep Spencer and her family apart.

"I'll talk to Spencer when he gets here this evening," she promised. "I'll let you know."

Then she sat on the settee for a long time, brooding on the fateful question that had been haunting her for so long. What was the point, really, of falling in love with a man twenty years older than her who, married or not, would be leaving her long before she finished living her own life?

Alongside the darkness, fatigue, and

boredom came a soft call from a room she thought she had locked years before.

Play me, whispered a voice. Play.

She could not really explain afterward what impulse it was that finally prompted her to get up, go into the hall, and get out her violin for the first time since sentence was passed on her after the Accident. But suddenly there she was with the instrument, feeling the weight of it in her hands, so familiar and so infernally missed.

This was all I wanted to be.

By the time Spencer arrived a few hours later, the instrument lay in its case again. Newly tuned and played.

They came for him late in the evening. It was a procedure not unlike some he remembered from his past. Strangers arrived in the darkness with keys to a door only he should have been able to open. He lay stiffly between the sheets in the bed, with nowhere to go. Then he heard the man's voice, the Swedish one who spoke such good Arabic.

"Good evening, Ali," said the voice. "Are you awake?"

Of course he was awake. How much had he actually slept since he left Iraq? He guessed it did not amount to more than ten hours all told.

"I'm here," he said, climbing out of bed.

They came into the room, all of them at once. The woman was not with them this time, but the man had two other men with him, strangers to Ali. He felt embarrassed standing there in his underpants. And socks. His feet were always so cold. He had stopped worrying about the smoky smell in the flat. The fresh pungency of newly painted walls that had met him when he first stepped into it was long gone.

"Get your clothes on," said the man with a smile. "You're going to stay somewhere else until Sunday."

Relief spread through his body. He was going to get out of here — at last. Feel the coolness on his cheeks, breathe the fresh air. But the news also came as a surprise. No one had said anything about a change of accommodation.

He looked at his watch as he was pulling on his jeans and jersey; it was nearly midnight. The men moved around the flat like restless spirits. He could hear them in the kitchen, opening cupboards and the fridge. The food was all gone. He fervently hoped there would be more to eat at the new place.

They went down the stairs. The Arabic-speaking man went first, then Ali and the others brought up the rear. Out onto the pavement. Ali looked up and got snowflakes in his eyes. So much rain of that kind in this part of the world.

It was a bigger car this time, more like a minibus. Ali was to sit right at the back between the two strangers. The men put the bag he had been given in the boot. One man had a long overcoat on and reminded Ali of someone he had seen in a film. The other had a rather gruesome look. His face was strangely deformed. As if someone had slashed it down the middle with a knife and then sewed it back together. The man sensed Ali looking at him and turned his head slowly to meet his stare. Ali instinctively averted his eyes.

They drove through an estate where all the blocks of flats were the same. Then out onto a main road where the cars were going faster. Ali looked out to the right, then to the left. And suddenly, on the right. In the distance, but clearly visible. Something that looked like a gigantic golf ball, lit up like a temple.

"The Globe," said the man beside him.

Ali looked straight ahead instead. How often did you travel in a car and not know where you were going?

Night closed the car in its embrace. His eyelids felt heavy.

Sometime, he thought wearily. Sometime I shall reach the end of this never-ending journey.

Bangkok, Thailand

They could not force her to hand herself over to the police. But nor could they offer her any protection. Advising her to contact the local police straightaway, they threw her out into the street. She ran for her life, heading randomly down Sukhumvit. The exertion proved too much. With no food or drink inside her and the temperature nearing forty degrees Celsius, she only got a few blocks before she had to stop, trying to get her bearings. Her sense of direction had deserted her; she had no idea which direction she had run in.

Someone, she thought dully, someone — it did not matter who — should be able to vouch for who I am.

All her plans were in tatters. It was no longer a question of picking and choosing between friends and acquaintances and weighing up which of them she could confide in. Now she just needed all the help she could get.

Her knees gave way and she sank down onto the pavement. She tried to squeeze out one last drop of rational thought.

Think, think, think, she urged herself. What's my main problem right now?

Her lack of money was acute, but manageable. The lack of contact details for her nearest and dearest now that she had no access to her mobile phone or email was harder. But there were other ways of getting hold of telephone numbers, and she could open new email accounts.

The priority had to be getting hold of her father. There was a risk that he, too, might be in danger.

Her eyes misted as she thought of her father. Why wasn't he answering his phone? And her mother? Where had they both got to?

She counted her currency, and found she had enough baht for half an hour's Internet use and a couple of international calls.

Then that's it, I'll have nothing left, she thought, fighting to keep down the rising wave of panic that was threatening to overwhelm her.

The café owner was a kindly man who served coffee on the house once you were at your computer. She worked fast and efficiently. Found the telephone numbers of a handful of people she trusted and noted them down. Went to the Hotmail homepage and opened a new email account. On consideration she decided not to use her own name in her new email address and opted for a more cryptic pseudonym. Her fingers moved nimbly over the keyboard, writing a brief, concise email to her father. She sent it to both of his email addresses, the private one and the church one. She felt ambivalent about contacting the friend who had not got back to her. Was it a mistake to discount him at this point? The thoughts swarmed like eager wasps in her tired head. She wrote him a few words:

Need urgent help. Contact Swedish embassy in Bangkok and ask to fax them my personal ID and a printout of my passport record.

When she had finished her emails, she felt an impulse that she could not explain when she looked back. She went to the website of one of the Swedish evening papers. Maybe to feel closer to her own country for a moment, maybe to feel less like a fugitive.
But she felt neither of those things, because when the page came up it told her

that her parents had been found shot dead three days before, and that the police could not discount the theory that they had been killed by someone else. Mechanically, convinced that nothing she was reading could be true, she clicked her way through various articles. "Possible suicide," "history of mental problems," "devastated by daughter's death." Her brain stopped working. She quickly switched to the homepage of another newspaper. And then another. Ragnar Vinterman was quoted in several of the pieces. He was dismayed and upset, said the church had lost one of its leading figures.

The scream trying to find its way out got stuck somewhere in her throat, refused to leave her body. But she felt as if she were suffocating, and the headlines smashed into her like the front of a truck that had failed to stop at the lights and plowed across the carriageway to crash head-on into a much smaller vehicle. An all-pervading sense of horror made her shiver with cold despite the heat.

Look after me, she entreated in silent desperation. Deliver me from this nightmare.

Disconnected words came to her, forming prayers she had said with her parents as a child, making her want to get down on her knees by the computer.

"Don't cry," she whispered to herself, feeling her cheeks flaming and her eyes misting. "Oh God, don't start crying or you'll never stop."

Her acute need to breathe drove her out into the street to inhale the intolerable, overheated city air.

She was back in the café a minute later. Sat down at the computer. The café owner looked uneasy but did not say anything. She read two more articles. "Jakob Ahlbin is said to have been told of his daughter's death over the weekend . . ." She shook her head. Impossible. Things like this just didn't happen. Losing your entire family in one go.

On trembling legs she went over to the café owner and asked to borrow a telephone. At once. *Emergency. Please hurry.* He passed the receiver to her across the bar and insisted on helping her make the call.

She gave him the number, one digit at a time. The number she had not rung for so long but would still never forget.

Sister, sister dearest . . .

It rang and rang, and no one answered. Then the answering machine message cut in, the voice that reminded her of everything that felt so incredibly distant right now. And that was it. The tears flowed. Among all the thoughts swirling around in her head, there was only one that passed her by. The one that told her she had not read the newspaper properly, not grasped who was supposed to have died. When the beep went and she had to leave her message, she was sobbing:

"Oh please, please answer if you can hear this."

■ ■ ■ ■

SATURDAY,
MARCH 1, 2008

■ ■ ■ ■

STOCKHOLM

The realization that age was creeping up on him came with the night and woke him early. He had never been pursued by thoughts like that before, so he had no idea how to deal with them. It started when his wife pointed out that the lines on his brow had deepened into furrows. And that his gray hairs were getting whiter. A glance in the mirror confirmed her judgment. The aging process was accelerating. And aging was accompanied by fear.

He had always been very sure of himself. Sure about everything. First about where his studies were leading him. Then his choice of career. And then his choice of wife. Or had *she* chosen *him*? They still bickered about it good-naturedly when things were going well between them. But that was increasingly rarely.

Thinking about his wife temporarily banished his worry about getting old. Maybe that said something about the scale of his anxiety about their marital problems. They had met around midsummer, just before they both turned twenty. Two young, ambitious people with their lives ahead of them, imagining they shared everything. His interests were hers, and her values were his. They had a solid platform to stand on. He reminded himself of that over the years, when he could not think of a single rational reason for his choice of companion in life.

Although their relationship had hit the rocks, they still occasionally laughed out loud together. But the boundary between laughter and tears was a fragile one and sent them into silence again. And then they were back to square one.

The problems first started about the time he got to know his father-in-law. Or maybe it was only then that he really got to know his own wife properly. Either way, the conclusion was the same: he should never have accepted that blessed loan. Never.

For although in their youth they felt they had so much in common, there were naturally some things on which they could not agree. And very often, as in this case, it was to do with money. Or his lack of it, and his wife's demand to live in accordance with her station in life and be provided for by her husband, even though she planned to go out to work. Money was something he'd never had, or indeed missed. Not when he was a child growing up, nor as a young man. But then it seemed as though lack of money was going to be his misfortune and the woman he thought he loved would choose someone else.

Father-in-law, however, was well aware both of his daughter's sense of priorities and of his son-in-law's financial embarrassment and proposed a simple solution to a major dilemma: his son-in-law could borrow money to buy a house and that would sort everything out.

It sounded like a great idea. The money was discreetly transferred to his account, and, equally unobtrusively, a repayment schedule drawn up. Not a word was said to the bride. It turned out that in signing the promissory note, he was also mortgaging his whole life. The promissory note was accompanied by a strict prenuptial agreement. When love faded and the first crisis was a reality, his father-in-law had a very serious conversation with him. There could be no question of divorce. If there were, he would immediately have to repay his loan, and would also not be entitled to his share of the property afterward. When he said he was prepared to accept that, his father-in-law fired the salvo he turned out to have had ready from the outset.

"I know your secret," he said.

"I haven't any."

A single word:

"Josefine."

And that was the end of the discussion.

He gave a deep inward sigh. Why did all these wretched thoughts occur to him in the night? At the hour when any human creature had to let slip poorly hidden thoughts if they were to sleep soundly.

He looked at the woman asleep at his side, as if she were his wife. But she was not. Not while he still clung to his old fears. But she was carrying his child, and for that reason he would do everything right. Or at least as right as he could. Love was already there and it almost choked him to think of how much he loved her, and for how long he had done so, yet how rarely he had let her know it. As if he had been afraid it would all shatter if he expressed how much she meant to him. And if they had not met and things had not gone the way they did, he would never have endured it. That much was perfectly plain to him.

But the future? Impossible to say. Impossible.

Someone once said there was nothing so lonely as being in a couple with the wrong person. Few people knew that better than the man robbed of his nighttime repose. With his head and his soul burdened by the dark thoughts of the night, he lay by the side of the woman he saw as the great love of his life and delicately kissed her shoulder.

There was some light in Spencer Lagergren's life after all. And love. Her name was Fredrika Bergman.

A memory from another time and place found its way to the surface. The obligatory session with a psychologist when he applied to work abroad.

Psychologist: What's the very worst thing that could happen to you today?

Alex: Today?

Psychologist: Today.

Alex: [Silence.]

Psychologist: Don't think so much, give me something spontaneous.

Alex: Losing my wife, Lena, that would definitely be the worst thing.

Psychologist: I see from your form that you've got two children aged fourteen and twelve.

Alex: That's right, and I don't want to lose them, either.

Psychologist: But it wasn't them who came spontaneously to mind when I asked my question.

Alex: No, it wasn't. But that doesn't mean I don't love my kids. Just that I love them in a different way.

Psychologist: Try to explain.

Alex: Children are something you borrow. You know that from the word *go*. They're never intended to stay at home with you forever. The whole aim of my presence in their lives is to get them ready to manage on their own. But it's not like that with Lena. She's "mine" in an entirely different way. And I'm hers. We shall always be together.

Psychologist: Always? Is that the way you feel today?

Alex (forcefully): That's the way I've always felt. For as long as I've known her. We shall always be together.

Psychologist: Does the thought of that make you feel secure or stressed?

Alex: Secure. If I woke up tomorrow and she wasn't there, I wouldn't be able to go on. She's my best friend and the only woman I've loved unconditionally.

Alex swallowed hard. Why the hell was it so hard to work out what was wrong? It had been the same story yesterday. She turned away when he tried to look her in the eye, and flinched when he touched her. Gave that loud, joyless laugh and went to bed incomprehensibly early.

He hoped a few hours' work might distract his thoughts.

A deserted corridor met his eye as he stepped out of the lift on their floor. He plodded to his office and sank down in the desk chair. Riffled aimlessly through the piles of paper.

The case had popped up on the first newspaper website the day before, and he noted that the news had spread this morning to all the major daily papers. Damn all these leaks from within the force. It made no difference how closed a circle you worked in; there was always someone who happened to hear something not intended for his or her ears.

Matters were not helped by the prosecutor's decision the previous evening that they had to let Tony Svensson go, in view of what Ronny Berg had told Peder about the background to the Jakob Ahlbin affair.

"There's no technical evidence, no motive, and scarcely enough to prosecute him for unlawful menace either," summarized the weary prosecutor. "Unless you can come up with confirmation that he sent the messages from the other computers, too."

"Could it not just simply be that he sent them from different computers so he could claim they weren't from him? That he gave those last emails a different tone because he knew he would get away with it?"

"That may well be the case, but the onus is still on you to prove it. And you haven't done that."

Alex read the prosecutor's statement and felt frustrated. No, they had not been able to prove anything. But it made no difference, there was still something very fishy going on here. The only question was: what?

There's something about this right-wing extremist lead that takes us right into the Ahlbins' deaths, thought Alex. It's just that I don't know exactly what.

Dissatisfied, he plowed on. The murder weapon was a matter of interest. It was part of the collection of firearms Jakob Ahlbin kept in the holiday home that had been transferred into the ownership of his daughters some years before. There was no reason to suppose the hunting pistol had been separated from the rest of the collection, so it must have been fetched from the house at some juncture. Either by Jakob Ahlbin himself or by whoever shot him. Jakob was the only one in the Ahlbin family with a gun license. And the only gun cabinet was the one in the holiday house.

Perhaps Jakob had retrieved the weapon because he felt threatened? Alex did not think so. No one seemed to have taken Tony Svensson's threats very seriously. But there were still things that needed explaining. Alex pulled out a set of photographs they had taken outside the Ekerö house.

No damage to the property. No marks in the snow, either shoe prints or tire tracks.

Alex felt his pulse accelerate. *The pristine snow.* It was now almost two weeks since it started snowing. The snow had been lying on the ground ever since; it had stayed very cold. And when he and Joar were there on the Thursday, it was unmarked.

Admittedly there had been further falls of snow on the days in between, but not enough to hide shoe prints or tire tracks. So the weapon must have been fetched before Jakob Ahlbin heard the news of his daughter's death, before he had reason to take his own life. Which meant? Alex hesitated. If they assumed the hunting pistol had been brought from Ekerö to kill Jakob and his wife, was it not logical to conclude that it was not Jakob himself who went to get it?

But in that case, the person who did must have had access to a set of keys, since there

314

was nothing to indicate any kind of break-in. Or the person was so experienced a burglar that he had the sense to lock the doors when he left. Which took him back to Tony Svensson's associates.

And then there was the daughter Johanna. Who dumped tragic news on her father and then scarpered off abroad. Who vanished like a ghost from all the family photos in the Ekerö house. And who did not answer her emails or her phone.

Noises out in the corridor roused Alex from his musing. Peder suddenly appeared in the doorway.

"Hi," said Alex, surprised.

"Hi," said Peder. "I didn't think there would be anybody here."

"Nor did I," said Alex drily. "I'm just running through all the Ahlbin stuff again."

Peder sighed.

"I thought I might do the same thing," he said, avoiding Alex's eye. "Ylva's got the kids, so . . ."

Alex nodded. So many troubled people in this workplace. So often not enough energy for both family and work. And so often men and women chose to prioritize the latter.

He cleared his throat.

"I really think we need to see Ragnar Vinterman again," he said. "Want to come along?"

Peder gave an eager nod.

"Sure," he said. "And what about the Ljungs, who found the bodies on Tuesday?"

"What about them?"

"We should talk to them again, too. Ask about that difference of opinion that made them cool off toward each other."

Alex felt a sense of relief. There would be plenty to keep him busy for the whole of Saturday.

"Have we got hold of Jakob Ahlbin's doctor yet, by the way?" Peder asked as Alex got up to put his coat back on.

The question jogged Alex's memory: there had been a message the evening before and he had managed to forget about it.

"Heck, yes," he said. "He rang in yesterday, quite late. He'd been away and had just got back. But he was apparently going to have the medical records faxed over to us to start with."

Peder went to check the fax machine in Ellen's office. He came back with a small pile of paper.

Sorry I have not been available. Please contact me immediately on the mobile number below. I am keen to speak to

316

the police as soon as possible about this matter.

Sincerely, Erik Sundelius.

Peder was looking overheated in his outdoor things.

"Let's go down to the car," said Alex. "I'll ring him on the way."

Erik Sundelius picked up the phone at the second ring. For the sake of politeness, Alex apologized for ringing so early. It was scarcely ten and it was quite likely some people would not be up yet.

Sundelius sounded very relieved at being able to speak to the police.

"At last," he exclaimed. "I tried to get hold of you as soon as I got home and saw the headlines. I hope we can meet in person to discuss the things that need to be gone through. But there's one thing I want to tell you right now."

Alex waited.

"I have been in charge of Jakob Ahlbin's treatment for over twelve years," Erik Sundelius said, and took a deep breath. "And I can say in all honesty that there isn't a chance in hell he would have done what the papers say he did. He would never shoot himself or his wife. You have my word as a professional on that."

317

For the first time in months, Fredrika felt rested when she woke. The night had not brought a single bad dream. She woke early, around seven. Spencer was asleep at her side. And the violin lay in its case on the floor. It was in tune now. It was a morning that felt blessed in many ways.

He was very attractive, lying there. Even lying down, he looked unusually tall. The gray hair, usually combed into perfect style, was tousled.

She snuggled down under the quilt, pressing herself to his warm body. Her stomach knotted as she thought of the approaching dinner with her parents. Spencer had agreed to come along.

"It's going be a testing occasion," he mumbled just before he fell asleep.

As if it were Job's lot he had been asked to shoulder.

Fredrika's train of thought was interrupted as her thoughts involuntarily turned to work. To the Ahlbin case and the very last email Jakob had received before he died.

Don't forget how it all ended for Job; there's always time to change your mind and do the right thing. Stop looking.

Glad that work-related matters had dispersed her misgivings about dinner with her parents, she slipped cautiously out of bed. Heavily pregnant or not, she had litheness in her blood.

The baby stretched, a silent protest at its mother's unanticipated movements.

The Bible was in the middle of the bookshelf, easy to spot with its red spine and gold lettering. Surprised at how heavily it weighed in her hand, she sat down and began to leaf through it. Job, the man with his very own book of the Bible.

The text proved quite demanding. Long, and written in a style that called for constant interpretation of what the words actually meant. The story was simple enough. The devil had challenged God, who considered Job to be the most upright person in the world. Hardly surprising that Job was upright, said the devil, when God gave him such an easy time. God gave the devil the right to rob Job of his riches, his health, and all ten of his children, so he could show that Job would still be loyal.

Good grief. The Old Testament was full of unaccountably sadistic stories.

Job came through his tribulations pretty well, it turned out. He did allow himself to feel the merest hint of doubt about the reason for God's ill deeds, but he apologized afterward. And was paid back handsomely. God gave him twice as many cattle as he had had to start with, and a total of twenty new children to replace the ten He had let the devil take from him.

All's well that ends well, Fredrika thought caustically.

And once again repeated to herself the message Jakob had received.

. . . there's always time to change your mind and do the right thing.

She racked her brains as to what that could mean in terms of what she had just learned of Job's fate.

Jakob Ahlbin wasn't like me, she thought. He didn't need to look in the Bible to understand what the sender was trying to say. And the sender knew that, too.

She stood up and started pacing the room. The question was how familiar the sender was with the Bible. If you read the email carefully enough, you could interpret it as an offer to negotiate. A chance to change his mind. To do the right thing. Job doubted, but then he said sorry. And was repaid.

Fredrika stopped in midstep.

They were leaving the option of a settlement open even in that very last message. And Jakob Ahlbin turned them down. He refused to heed their warning to stop looking.

But what had he been looking for? And how had they known that he did not want to bargain? Investigations had shown that Jakob Ahlbin had not answered any of those emails he received.

They must have contacted him by some other means as well.

Fredrika thought hard. And remembered that they had found Tony Svensson's fingerprints on the front door.

Alex decided they would go and see Erik Sundelius first and then go on to Ragnar Vinterman's.

Erik, senior psychiatric consultant at Danderyd Hospital in Stockholm, saw them in his office. It was a small room but arranged so as to maximize space. Compact shelves along one wall were packed tight with books. On the wall behind the desk there was an enlarged photograph in brownish shades of dense traffic at a crossroads, cars queuing at a red light.

"Mexico City," clarified the consultant, following Alex's gaze. "Took it myself, a few years ago."

"Very nice," said Alex with an appreciative nod.

He wondered if this was the room where Sundelius saw his patients.

"This is my office. My consulting room's on the other side of the corridor," the doctor said, answering his unspoken question.

He sank into a chair.

"But I have to admit my level of patient contact has been limited in recent years. Unfortunately."

Alex took a look at him. His own experience of psychologists and psychiatrists was sporadic, and his perceptions of the way such a person should look were largely the result of his own bias, but in many respects Erik Sundelius did not look at all as he had expected. He looked more like a GP, with neatly combed hair and a side parting.

"Jakob Ahlbin," Alex said gravely. "What can you tell us about him?"

The face of the man on the other side of the desk fell, and he looked first at Alex, then at Peder.

"That he was the healthiest ill person I've ever met."

Sundelius leaned forward and clasped his hands on his desk, apparently wondering how to continue.

"He did have his bad spells," he said. "Very bad, in fact. Severe enough for him to be admitted for ECT treatment."

Peder squirmed at the mention of the electric shock treatment, but to Alex's relief he made no comment.

"Over the past three years I thought I could detect a change," the consultant went on. "A weight seemed to have been taken off him, somehow. He was always very concerned about the plight of refugees, but I think the increasing demand for his lectures gave him a new way of doing his bit for the cause that meant so much to him. I went to hear him speak once. He was brilliant. He chose his battles carefully, and won those he had to."

A slight smile crept over Alex's face beneath that creased forehead.

"Could you give me an example of one of those battles? I'm afraid this is an area in which we're very short of information in the case."

Sundelius sighed.

"Well, where shall I start? It goes without

saying that his radical stance on migrant issues got him on the wrong side of some factions in society. But it also had repercussions for his family and professional relationships."

Peder, who was making notes, raised his eyes from his pad.

Sven Ljung, Alex thought automatically. The man who found Jakob shot in the head.

"The most worrying aspect, of course, was the impact his work had on his relationship with his younger daughter," said Erik Sundelius.

"Johanna?" Alex asked, surprised.

A tired nod from the psychiatrist.

"Jakob took it very badly, not being able to get that relationship back on track."

The photos in the Ekerö house. The younger daughter disappearing from the sequence of family pictures.

"Johanna Ahlbin turned her back on her father when he took those refugees into his church?" Alex asked.

"No, before that, as I understand it. She didn't share her father's opinions on the subject at all, which inevitably led to conflict."

"Our information also indicates that Johanna distanced herself from her family because she wasn't religious like they were," said Peder.

"Yes, that was another problem," Sundelius confirmed. "It made Jakob all the more glad that his elder daughter, Karolina, was a wholehearted supporter of the campaign to help refugees, and shared her parents' faith, even if she wasn't quite such a devotee as they were. Jakob often mentioned it in our sessions, the pleasure he took in how Karolina had turned out."

Alex raised his eyebrows and was aware of Peder tensing up.

"But I assume relations with Karolina must still have been rather a burden to someone with Jakob Ahlbin's condition?" he said.

The consultant frowned.

"How do you mean?"

"I mean her serious drug addiction."

For a moment Sundelius looked as though he were about to burst out laughing, but then his face darkened.

"Drug addict? Karolina?"

He shook his head.

"Impossible."

"Unfortunately not," said Alex. "We've seen the autopsy report and the death certificate. The body bore all the signs of long-term narcotic abuse."

Sundelius looked from Alex to Peder, staring.

"Sorry, do you mean she's dead?"

The consultant clearly had not read the newspaper articles very thoroughly. Alex decided to take him through the case. He told him how the couple had been found, and about the suicide note supposedly written by Jakob Ahlbin, and the news of his daughter's death that had apparently pushed him to kill his wife and himself.

Sundelius listened in silence. When he did speak, his voice was strained, as though from anger or grief. Once again he looked as if he were about to burst out laughing.

"Okay," he said, putting his hands on the desk. "Let me go through this bit by bit. First of all, can you let me see a copy of the note Jakob left?"

Alex nodded, taking the sheet of paper out of his bag.

Sundelius read the typewritten message and looked at the handwritten signature. Then he pushed the note away as though it had burned him.

"The signature's Jakob's. But as for the rest . . ."

Alex opened his mouth to say something, but the consultant held up his hand.

"Let me finish," he said. "Jakob was my

patient for many years. Believe me — this letter was *not* written by him. Nothing about it is right, neither the tone nor the content. Even if he took it into his head to do what the letter indicates, he wouldn't express it like this. Who is it intended for? It's not addressed to anyone. Johanna, say, or a good friend. Just empty words directed at anyone and everyone."

He paused for breath.

"As I said before, you have to believe me when I say this is not something Jakob has done. You're making a terrible mistake to think so."

"You don't think he could have done it even after hearing his daughter had died?"

Then Sundelius could contain himself no longer. The laughter that had been showing itself in his face came bursting out.

"Absurd," he guffawed. "The whole thing."

He grabbed the letter again, and appeared to be trying to control himself.

"If, and I mean *if,* Jakob had had news of Karolina's death broken to him, there's no way he would have kept it from his wife. And he would have come to me — he always did when anything happened to disturb his mental state. Always. I'd go so far as to say that his trust in me was infinite in that respect."

"You're talking as though there's every reason to question whether he heard the news of the death at all," commented Alex.

The consultant tossed the sheet of paper onto the desk.

"That's exactly what I'm doing," he said. "Karolina was here sometimes, with her father. And so was her mother."

"As a patient?" said Alex, nonplussed.

"No, no, no," said Erik Sundelius, glaring at him. "Absolutely not. Simply to support her father. She always kept herself informed about how he was and what treatment he was currently having. It seems unthinkable to me that I could have missed the fact she was on drugs over a period of ten years."

Alex and Peder exchanged looks.

"But," said Peder, "we're afraid to say there aren't really any grounds for disputing it. I mean, the girl's verifiably dead. And there's the autopsy report, signed by a doctor who one of our colleagues has been in contact with."

"Who identified her?" asked Sundelius, screwing up his eyes.

"Her sister, Johanna," replied Alex. "She found Karolina unconscious and rang for an ambulance. We really need to get hold of her, incidentally."

Sundelius was shaking his head again.

"The whole thing's baffling," he said. "You're saying Johanna went round to Karolina's . . . ?"

He shook his head some more.

"In all the years Jakob was seeing me here, Johanna only ever came with him once. And she was so young then that she had no choice, so to speak. She was here because she had to be. I could see it in her, straightaway. And to go by what Jakob said, the sisters weren't very close to each other, either. Which was also a source of great sadness to him."

He hesitated.

"I don't know what sort of picture you've formed of Johanna, but the impression I got from what Jakob told me was that things weren't quite right with her."

There was a pause. Alex's brain was working overtime on processing all this new information.

"Did she suffer from depression, too?"

Sundelius compressed his lips and looked as though the question had put him on the spot.

"No," he said. "Not depression. But I must stress that I only ever met Johanna once or twice in person. She wasn't just standoffish, according to Jakob. She was full of anger and contempt that she openly showed to her family. The things he told me made her sound sick, disturbed."

"Maybe she had good reason for it?" said Alex. "Her anger, I mean."

Sundelius shrugged.

"Well, if she did, then that reason wasn't clear, even to Jakob. Anyway, the only thing I can say for sure is that his daughter's lack of peace of mind troubled him deeply."

Alex decided it was time to wind up the interview.

"So to summarize, what you're saying is . . ."

"That I don't for a moment subscribe to the theory that Jakob Ahlbin murdered his wife and then shot himself. Of course I can't claim a person who is dead is really alive, but I can tell you straight off that she was not a drug addict."

"You sound very sure of all that," said Alex.

"I am," Sundelius said deliberately. "The question is, how sure are you of *your* conclusions?"

As he spoke, he turned his head and looked out of the window. Almost as if expecting to see Jakob Ahlbin coming along through the slushy snow.

Winter had chosen to arrive in several bursts. When the first snow came, early in the new year, he had assumed that was that. But it never was, of course.

He sighed, suddenly feeling very tired.

It was a matter of concern that Jakob had not understood the full extent of his problem until it was too late, but it was to some degree typical of him. He had sometimes felt the man had made a positive choice to live his life according to the meaning of his Christian name: Jakob, a controversial name of Hebrew origin, which some claimed to mean "may He protect." It was an irony of fate that when he himself really needed help, nobody came to his rescue.

They had always hoped a solution could be found before the situation got out of hand. They had relied on him acting rationally, but he had not. Jakob was an emotional, impulsive person, and once he realized he was onto something, he refused to deviate from his chosen course. As if by the Lord's blessing they had found out about the threats directed at him by the organization Sons of the People and had decided to build on that, to scare him off. But Jakob had scented out his quarry and would not be put off.

So then it ended the way it had to, he told himself afterward. With a disaster that would have been all the greater if Jakob had been allowed to delve more deeply into what had come to his attention, which had initially pleased him so much.

"This is a turning point. I've heard fantastic news!" he had said, convinced he was talking to a friend.

But the friend was shaken and demanded to know more. Unfortunately Jakob had clammed up, possibly starting to sense that his friend was double-dealing. So the identity of his original source remained unknown to the circle. The only problem still left to deal with.

Then the telephone rang.

"I've got a name," said the voice.

"At last," he said, feeling a greater sense of relief than he cared to admit.

The voice at the other end said nothing for a few moments.

"There's a man in Skärholmen the police have been to see. He could be the one we're looking for."

He made a careful note of the few details the voice was able to supply. Said thank you and hung up.

So the wheels were rolling, most of them. The next day, another daisy would make his payment, and on Monday the main protagonist in the unfolding drama was expected back. Her arrival was warmly anticipated.

He shook his head. Sometimes the very thought of her generated naked fear. What sort of person was she? Someone who was willing to sacrifice so much — and so many — for a single aim needed careful handling. Normal people did not do what she had done. And then the anguish gripped him again, his sense that everything could have been different returned. If only things had not happened so damned quickly. If only everyone had obeyed the rules.

If only they had been able to rely on each other.

Peder Rydh rang Ragnar Vinterman to let him know they were on their way, just as Fredrika rang Alex on his mobile.

"I'm in the office," she said with an eagerness in her voice that Alex had not heard for months.

"Why, for heaven's sake?" was all he could think of saying, concerned as he was for her health.

"Something occurred to me, so I came in to do some thinking in peace. It's those threats Jakob received."

Alex listened attentively to Fredrika's conclusions about the emails and their content.

"So you're convinced it wasn't Tony Svensson that sent the ones from other computers?" Alex said doubtfully.

"Yes, definitely" replied Fredrika. "On the other hand, I'm not so sure he didn't know there were other people trying to put pres-

sure on Ahlbin. I think we ought to interview him again, get to the bottom of why he
went round to Jakob's flat, looking for him.
He could have been a messenger, willing or
unwilling."

"Messenger sent by someone who didn't
want to reveal himself, you mean?"

"Exactly. And that might also explain why
Tony Svensson paid his visit to Jakob Ahlbin when Ronny Berg was already in custody. We missed it at the meeting yesterday
— Tony Svensson must have been lying
about his reason for going round there."

Alex swallowed. Almost from the outset,
Fredrika had proved how swiftly she could
switch between theories and draw reliable
conclusions. If she had been a trained police
officer, Alex would have said she had a feeling for the job. But she wasn't, so he did
not really have a term for her, or her gift.
Intuition, maybe?

His silence left her the space to go on.

"So I checked Svensson's phone lists
again to see if anything odd showed up. And
found he'd rung Viggo Tuvesson twice."

"Uhuh?" Alex said quizzically, seeing with
relief that Peder was finally off his mobile.
"And who's he?"

"A police colleague of ours."

Alex braked sharply at a red light.

"And how do we know that? I mean, are you sure?"

"I'm sure," said Fredrika, and Alex could hear that she was smiling. "Tony rang his work mobile, you see. I came across the number in our internal phone directory."

A car honked its horn behind them and Peder gave Alex a startled look.

"It's green," he said, as if he thought the fact might have passed his superior by.

Alex hastily shifted his foot from the brake to the accelerator. Automatics were a gift to the human race, even if they weren't good for the environment.

"Well, I'll be damned," he muttered. "But there could be a logical reason for the contact, you know. I mean it hasn't necessarily got anything to do with our case. I've never heard of this Viggo Tuvesson."

Peder raised an eyebrow and followed Alex's side of the conversation with interest.

"He's with the Norrmalm district," Fredrika told him. "He and another officer were the first on the scene after the Ljungs found the bodies and called emergency services."

Alex felt his mouth go dry, and he glanced at Peder, who looked as though he was dying to know what information Fredrika had just imparted.

"Okay," he said into the phone. "We'll get to work on this first thing on Monday. Before you go home, would you mind writing a summary of all this crap — if you'll forgive a tired DCI his choice of words — and putting it on my desk?"

In case you're not in on Monday, he thought of saying.

"Done," said Fredrika. "In case I'm not in on Monday."

He gave a smile.

As they drove on toward Bromma, Alex put Peder in the picture.

"She's as sharp as a knife sometimes," Peder said spontaneously.

"She certainly is," Alex concurred.

As if he had never called her competence into question, though in fact he had done little else in her first few months with the group.

This time Ragnar Vinterman was not standing on the front steps to welcome his guests. They had to knock loud and long at the front door of the vicarage before he finally opened up.

They had discussed how they would conduct the interview in the car on the way. Of all the people they had spoken to, Vinterman stood out as the only one who still thought it likely that Jakob Ahlbin had killed himself. He was also the one most convinced that Karolina Ahlbin had a drug problem. This was causing them some concern, because he had been too close to Jakob for his impressions and opinions to be ignored.

"I'm afraid I won't be able to spare you very long this time," he said, the moment he showed his guests into the library, where the interview was apparently to take place. "I've had a call from a parishioner whose husband has been ill for a long time, and he's just died. She's expecting me shortly."

Alex nodded.

"We hope we won't need to take up too much of your time," he assured the clergyman. "But some new questions have come up and I'd just like to try them out on you."

It was Vinterman's turn to nod.

Alex observed him. Straight-backed, with his hands resting on the arms of his chair. A hunter, ready for action. Armed to the teeth. The situation felt familiar, like something out of a film Alex had seen.

The Godfather, he thought, and almost laughed out loud. As if this were some Italian sit-down where the first thing you all do is put your gats on the negotiating table.

Alex was baffled by the clergyman's change of attitude. But he was in no mood for compromise, either; he wanted proper answers to his questions. He was sure that Peder, a silent presence at his side, sensed the mood as well.

"Last time we met we were talking about Karolina Ahlbin's drug habit," Alex began, leaning back on the sofa. "Could you hazard a guess as to when she got into all that?"

Ragnar leaned back, too. He had an almost impudent look.

"As I think I made plain to you last time," he said, "virtually everything I know, I heard from Jakob. So it's hard for me to be precise on that."

He looked at Alex to make sure he was listening and understanding. Which he was.

"But at a cautious estimate I'd say her problems started in her late teens."

"She went straight onto hard drugs?"

"That I can't say."

He's backing off, thought Alex. Realizes what he told us has been contradicted.

"So did Jakob talk to you about this on a regular basis?" he asked.

"Yes," Ragnar said firmly. "He did."

"How many years did Jakob spend hiding illegal migrants out at Ekerö?" asked Alex, as if it were a natural extension of the conversation about his daughter's drug use.

"I'm afraid I don't know that either," the

clergyman said, crossing his legs.

"But you know he did it?"

"*Everybody* knew that," he said drily.

"But you decided not to mention it last time we were here?"

"I assumed it wasn't relevant to the case as a whole. And I really didn't want to blacken Jakob's memory in front of the police."

Alex smiled.

"How noble of you," he said before he could stop himself.

Vinterman's face darkened, and Alex went on.

"Were you involved in his activities yourself?"

"Never."

"Was anyone else in the parish?"

"I honestly don't know."

Alex felt his frustration growing. He glanced at Peder.

"Now you've had a few days to think about it," said Peder, "are you still convinced Jakob took his own life?"

The clergyman went very quiet. His bearing and expression changed, as though a sudden shadow had passed over him.

"Yes," he said clearly. "Yes, I am."

With ill-concealed eagerness, Alex leaned forward.

"Tell us how you see it."

Vinterman, mimicking Alex's body language again, leaned forward, too.

"I can't say Jakob and I had a particularly close personal relationship. But as colleagues, we were as close as it was possible to be. We exchanged confidences on a daily basis and had the same views on a great many questions of faith. So I think I can say I really did *know* Jakob. And believe me — he wasn't in good shape. Not at all."

"His psychiatrist thinks otherwise," Alex said matter-of-factly.

Ragnar gave a snort.

"Erik Sundelius? I lost confidence in him at a pretty early stage. Marja and I both begged Jakob to change doctors. But he was so damned stubborn, you know."

"And why did the two of you want him to change doctors?"

"He was irresponsible," replied the clergyman. "He would never adapt his methods, even though Jakob wasn't responding to the treatment. I freely admit I was so concerned that I decided to check up on him."

That's all we need, a vicar playing private investigator, Alex thought wearily.

"What did you find out?" asked Peder.

"That my judgment was correct. He's had two misconduct warnings from the Medical

Council for — how shall I put it — 'hazardous methods' used on high-risk patients; in each case, the patient ended up committing suicide. And he was prosecuted for the murder of his wife's lover."

Seeing the expressions of surprise on Peder and Alex's faces, he leaned back in his seat with an air of great satisfaction.

"But the police already knew all about that, of course," he said mildly.

No, Alex thought, his jaw set doggedly. We didn't.

"Damn," Alex said in exasperation once he had started the car and backed rather too fast out of the vicar's drive. "How the hell could we have missed that?"

"We didn't have any particular reason to check it out, did we?" Peder said, and was interrupted by the ring of his mobile.

Ylva. It was rarely good news when she rang.

"Peder, Isak's running a really high temperature," she said anxiously. "And he's got a rash on his tummy. I'm taking him to the hospital, but I wanted to ask if you could look after David while we're gone."

Fear caught Peder unawares. His son was ill and he wasn't there. His permanently guilty conscience reared its head again.

"I'll be right there," he said gruffly. "I'm in the car with Alex. He can drop me off on the way back to HQ."

Alex looked at him as he rang off.

"One of the boys is ill," he said. "Can you let me off at Ylva's? If Fredrika's in after all, maybe she could go to the Ljungs' with you?"

Alex nodded.

"Fine by me."

In the short drive to what had once been Ylva and Peder's shared home, Peder reviewed his situation in life for the hundredth time. The news that Pia Nordh was moving in with the repulsive Joar paled into insignificance. "Can you let me off at Ylva's?" he had said to Alex. As if it was an address like any other.

There had been a time when he felt as if his heart was about to blow to smithereens in his chest. It was a bloody long time since he'd loved anybody like that.

His mobile rang again. His brother this time.

"Hiii," said Jimmy in his usual, rather slow way.

"Hi," said Peder, and heard his brother laugh.

It was sometimes a real blessing that Jimmy was so easy to entertain, so easy to make happy.

"Something's happened," Jimmy said excitedly.

Peder laughed. "Something happening" could mean anything from a royal visit to a new lamp shade in his room.

"I've got a girlfriend."

The words struck Peder dumb.

"What?" he said dopily.

"A girlfriend. A proper one."

Peder gave an involuntary guffaw.

"Are you glad?" Jimmy asked expectantly.

A warm feeling spread inside him and smoothed out some of the knots that had multiplied there.

"Yes," said Peder. "What do you know, I am glad, in spite of everything."

A short time later, Fredrika and Alex parked outside the Ljungs' flat on Vanadisplan. The Vasastan area had always appealed to him, Alex told Fredrika in an unusual moment of candor. He and Lena had agreed that the day they grew old they would get themselves a pied-à-terre in just this part of town, for overnight stays, to avoid simply moldering away in their house out at Vaxholm. Fredrika felt uneasy as Alex's expression shifted from open to pained in the course of talking about himself and his wife.

That's what it is, she thought. He's worried about his wife.

Alex took the lead as they went up the same staircase Fredrika and Joar had taken a few days before.

They found the Ljungs' door ajar when they got to the floor where their flat was.

Alex gave an authoritative knock and Elsie Ljung came out to greet them.

"We left the door open so we'd hear you coming," she said.

They went with her into the living room, where her husband was waiting. They both looked tired and unhappy.

"Let me assure you we won't stay any longer than strictly necessary," said Alex, taking a seat in one of the armchairs round the coffee table.

"We do want to help," sighed Sven Ljung, dramatically flinging his arms wide. "And it's all over the media now, as well. Have you found Johanna?"

"I'm afraid not," said Alex. "But we have to hope she'll get in touch when she sees the news."

The elderly couple looked at each other and nodded. Yes, she was bound to get in touch, they seemed to be saying.

"We've got a few more questions about your relationship with the Ahlbins," Alex said in a voice that was soft but unmistakably firm. "So we'd like to ask you those. Separately."

Neither Elsie nor Sven replied, so Alex went on:

"If I talk to Sven here, then maybe Fredrika can talk to Elsie in one of the other rooms. Then we won't have to bother messing around at the police station."

He was smiling, but the message was crystal clear. The couple looked confused and anxious, and he tried to reassure them by saying it was perfectly routine in the circumstances.

Fredrika went with Elsie into the kitchen, closing the door behind them, and sat down at the little dining table. The baby was lying still, for now.

You must be asleep, she thought, trying and failing to suppress a smile.

"Your first?" asked Elsie, nodding in the direction of Fredrika's stomach.

The smile turned to a grimace. She preferred not to talk about the baby to strangers at all.

But she answered with a yes to avoid seeming rude.

For a minute she feared the older woman was going to start talking about when she was pregnant herself, but luckily she did not have to listen to any stories of that kind.

"Jakob and Marja Ahlbin," Fredrika said in a more demanding voice than she intended, to show that further inquiries about her unborn child were not welcome.

Her interviewee looked tense and doubtful.

"So how *were* things between the four of you recently?"

Elsie seemed at a loss.

"Much as they'd been for quite a while, I suppose," she said eventually. "Not as good as they had been, but still good enough for us to get together now and then."

"And why was that?" asked Fredrika. "Things not being as warm between you, I mean."

Elsie looked uncomfortable.

"Sven can really tell you more about that than I can," she said. "He and Jakob were the ones who had the disagreement."

"What did they disagree about?"

The older woman said nothing.

Fredrika softened.

"You needn't be afraid of telling me things that seem sensitive," she said, putting a hand on Elsie's arm. "I promise to be as discreet as I possibly can."

Elsie still did not speak. The kitchen tap was dripping into the sink. Fredrika had to stop herself getting up and turning it off properly.

"They fell out, some years ago," Elsie said in a feeble voice. "It was over Jakob's . . . activities."

Fredrika waited.

"The fact that he was hiding refugees," Elsie clarified. "Or planning to."

"And Sven objected to that?"

"Hmm, it wasn't that simple. It was more that Sven . . . well, he's quite practical in his way of thinking, and I think he reckoned Jakob was taking far too great a risk. And not getting anything in return."

Fredrika frowned.

"Surely there's never been any money in hiding illegal migrants?"

"No, and that was exactly what Sven felt was so unfair," Elsie said, her voice stronger now. "That Jakob intended opening house and home to people on the run without earning a penny for it himself. Sven reckoned a lot of the people who ended up here had significant resources. After all, it costs a fortune to escape to Sweden these days. And so Sven thought that if they had that much, they probably had a little bit more. Jakob was livid. He called Sven selfish, and a fool."

With every justification, thought Fredrika.

But she kept her mouth shut.

"Then it was a year before we spoke to each other again," Elsie said, and had to clear her throat. "But we live so close and, I mean, you can't help bumping into each other occasionally. Once we'd met like that a few times, we gradually started seeing each other again. It all felt fine. Not like before, but fine."

The kitchen was cold and a shiver ran through Fredrika's body. She looked through her notes and one thing leaped out at her.

"You said Jakob 'intended opening house and home?' " she inquired.

"Yes."

"But that was surely something he was already doing, not intending to do?"

Elsie looked nonplussed for a moment, but then shook her head firmly.

"No," she said. "Neither of those things. It was something he had done in the past, and was thinking of starting again."

"I don't quite follow."

"Jakob and Marja had a lot to do with refugee groups in the seventies and eighties, and were involved in a network that gave refuge to people in need. One of the things they did was to hide people in the basement of their house out in Ekerö. They carried on with that into the nineties, until 1992, I think. Then they decided to take a more hands-off approach. Until Jakob started thinking along new lines a few years ago. But it never came to anything."

Fredrika wondered if Elsie knew more than she was letting on. It was a bit suspicious that she kept saying "I think," only to deliver some very concrete bit of information like a date.

But curiosity got the upper hand and she pushed away the idea that something might be wrong.

"Why did nothing come of his plans?"

"I don't know," Elsie said evasively. "But I think his ideas caused some division in the family. Marja wasn't at all as committed to it as Jakob. And then we heard the Ekerö house had been transferred to their daughters' names. Neither of them were involved in their dad's activities as far as I know. Particularly not Johanna."

"No," said Fredrika. "We understand she didn't really share her father's view on the issue."

Elsie lowered her voice.

"Sven doesn't really want me to say anything about this, he thinks things like that should be kept within the family, but I'll tell you anyway, since the Ahlbin family

350

scarcely exists anymore. We were round at Jakob and Marja's for dinner once, at about the time Jakob was talking about getting back into his old activities, and their daughters were there. You could have cut the atmosphere with a knife when we started talking about asylum seekers and their plight."

"How do you mean?"

"Johanna got very, very worked up. I don't remember exactly what sparked it off, probably a combination of things. She started crying and left the table. Jakob seemed shaken, too, but he was better at keeping things inside."

"And you got no sense of what the conflict was really about?"

"No, not at all. It sounded like something from years before; I mean, Johanna only saw the family on rare occasions. I remember she shouted something like, "So you're going to destroy everything again?" but I've no idea what she meant by it. How could I?"

Elsie gave a strained laugh.

"Anyway, that was when Sven fell out with Jakob," she said in conclusion.

Fredrika crossed her legs, shifting her weight on the chair. It was going to be so nice the day the baby was born and her

351

body was her own again.

Then her eyes fell on Elsie's hand, which was gripping a water glass. The hand was shaking and Elsie's eye was twitching.

She wants to tell me something, Fredrika realized, and decided to bide her time.

Elsie did not speak, however, so Fredrika decided to help things along.

"Are you sure you don't know any more?" she asked under her breath.

Elsie pursed her lips and shook her head. Her hand stopped trembling.

"What about their other daughter, Karolina?" Fredrika asked, resigning herself.

Elsie's eyes were swimming.

"I still say what we said before. It's impossible that she died of an overdose."

And yet she did, Fredrika thought. What the hell are we overlooking about her death?

"But you weren't that close in recent years," she ventured. "Maybe you missed the signs."

Elsie shook her head.

"No," she said quietly. "We didn't. You see, Karolina was going out with our younger son, Måns, for some years."

"But . . ."

"I know," Elsie said, "we didn't tell you last time you were here. Mainly because it's such a sensitive subject, and because we both had such high hopes of the relation-ship. And everything was so topsy-turvy that day you were here . . ."

"I understand," said Fredrika, trying not to sound annoyed.

The urge people had to be the ones to decide what was worth telling the police or not often caused far more havoc than they ever realized.

"They weren't together anymore, your son and Karolina?"

Elsie shook her head and began to weep.

"No, I'm afraid not," she said. "Karolina found it too much in the end, what with all his problems, and we could understand that only too well. But it was our dearest wish that she would turn out to be the solution for him. That she would be able to give him the strength to break free."

"Free from what?"

"His addiction," Elsie sobbed. "That's how I know Karolina wasn't going through the same thing. But she carried all Måns' problems like a cross through her life. Until the day it all got too much. Then she left him, moved out, and got a flat of her own. I miss her as if she were my own child. We both do."

"And Måns?"

"When it started getting serious between

him and Karolina, he was much better, started work and stuck to the straight and narrow. But . . . once a man's had that damned poison in his blood, it's as if he can never really be rid of it. He went downhill again, and today he's just a shadow of who he was in those early days with Karolina. Unrecognizable."

Fredrika thought carefully, weighing her words.

"Elsie," she said finally. "Whichever way we look at it, Karolina's dead. Her own sister identified her."

"Well, in that case you'd better think of her as Lazarus in the Bible, the one Jesus brought back to life," Elsie declared, fishing a handkerchief out of her pocket. "Because I know in my heart and soul that that girl can't have died of an overdose."

Fredrika looked mistrustfully at Elsie. Felt doubtful, and tried to muster her thoughts. Elsie was keeping something else back, she felt it in every fiber of her being. And as if Job were not enough, the police now had a Lazarus to contend with.

The little white tablet was disturbing him as badly as a fly in the night. He glared at it angrily and almost wished it would dissolve before his eyes.

"You must take it tonight before you go to sleep," the man who spoke Arabic had said before he left. "Otherwise you'll be too tired to carry out your task tomorrow."

They had left him in the new flat the evening before and then come back this afternoon to go through the next day's schedule one more time. Somewhere in the midst of all his misery, he felt a great sense of relief. His journey was nearing its end and he would soon be a man without debts who could be reunited with his wife and even get in touch with the rest of his family to tell them he was all right. And with his friend, waiting for him in Uppsala.

The knowledge that his friend was out there somewhere, worrying about where he had got to, made him uneasy. They had said he was not on any account to inform any friends or family members where he was going. And he had broken their rule. Made a promise and not kept it. Please let his friend not start trying to find him. It would be a disaster if someone suddenly started asking questions and gave away his hidden presence in the country. The punishment would be severe if they found out he had let them down, he knew that.

His heart was pounding, keeping time with his growing anxiety. It was still only late afternoon; how would he hold out until tomorrow? He would have much preferred the project to be over and done with today, so tonight would be a night of liberation. But thoughts of that kind were unrealistic, he knew that now.

They would come and drag him out at nine the next morning. He would be introduced to his accomplice, who would drive the getaway car. The two of them would go to the place where the robbery was to be committed. He read the note they had left on the coffee table. It said Västerås, which meant nothing at all in Arabic. He wondered what it meant in Swedish.

Once he had done the robbery, he and the driver would come back to Stockholm and meet up with the others not far from the giant golf ball he had seen from the other car. The Globe. Once he had handed over his haul, he would be a free man.

"You're doing this for your countrymen's sake," they had told him. "Without this money, we wouldn't be able to finance our work. The Swedish state doesn't want to pay for our activities, so we take money from people who already have lots of it."

It was familiar, well-worn logic. You took from the rich and gave to the poor. When he was growing up he had kept hearing stories like that. Most of all from his grandfather, the only one in the family who had ever been to the USA . He told them incredible stories of how much money people had there and what they did with it. He told them about cars as wide as the Tigris and houses the size of Saddam's palace, where ordinary people lived. About the university, which was open to all but cost a vast amount of money. And about huge oil fields not owned by the state.

Grandfather should have seen me now, thought Ali. In a land almost as rich as America. Just a bit colder.

He shivered and huddled up on the sofa. Not that he had seen any huge cars or palaces. But that made no difference, because like everybody else he knew, he was totally convinced: Sweden was the best possible country for making a new start.

He glowered at the tablet and knew he would have to take it. He would never get to sleep otherwise. A good night's sleep was a prerequisite for performing well the next day.

For the sake of his wife and children. And his father and grandfather.

As they left the flat to go to her parents', Fredrika seriously considered canceling the whole arrangement. But Spencer, well aware of her reluctance, took her gently by the arm and led her out onto the pavement and over to his car.

And with that, their relationship entered a new phase.

It had always been just the two of them. Alone in a glass bubble with no dinner parties or family lunches. Their mutual breathing space where they recharged themselves and refreshed their appetite for life. A breathing space that now had to accommodate both an unborn child and some parents-in-law. The latter was bizarre, of course, since Spencer, unlike Fredrika, already had a set of parents-in-law.

"So when do I get to meet *your* parents, then?" she asked as Spencer pulled up outside her childhood home.

"Preferably never, if that's all right with you," he replied casually, opening the car door.

His arrogance made Fredrika roar with laughter.

"You're not getting hysterical now, are you?" Spencer said anxiously.

He walked round to open the door on her side. Fredrika beat him to it and pushed the door open just as he was coming round the bonnet.

"Look," she said in mock triumph. "I can get out of the car all by myself."

"That's hardly the point," muttered Spencer, who saw it as a matter of principle for a man to open the door for his female companion.

Let him open the door for his other woman, Fredrika thought waspishly, but kept her mouth shut.

She could see her mother through the kitchen window, which looked out on the road. The two of them were often told they were very alike. Fredrika waved. Her mother waved back, but to judge by her expression she was — despite having doubtless prepared herself — shocked to see her heavily pregnant daughter with a man the age of her own husband.

"Okay?" asked Fredrika, slipping her hand

into Spencer's.

"I suppose so," he answered, holding her hand in a warm clasp. "Can hardly be any worse than other things I've experienced in this context."

Fredrika had no idea what he meant.

Things got off to a bad start when she made the mistake of accepting a glass of wine she had not been offered.

"Fredrika," her mother exclaimed in dismay. "You're not drinking while you're pregnant?"

"Good grief, Mum," said Fredrika. "On the continent, pregnant women have been drinking for millennia. The public health body in Britain has just changed its recommendations and says they can drink two glasses a week with no ill effects."

This did nothing to reassure her mother, who had little time for the British findings and looked at her daughter as if she were insane when she raised the glass to her lips and took a gulp.

"Mmm," she said, with an appreciative smile at her father, who also looked extremely quizzical.

"Being in the police hasn't turned you into an alcoholic, has it, Fredrika?" he asked with a troubled look.

"Oh, for goodness' sake," she cried, not knowing whether to laugh or weep.

Her parents gave her long stares, but said no more.

The seating arrangement reminded Fredrika of the way she used to set out her dolls when she was playing with her dollhouse as a child. Mummy and Daddy on one side of the table and Guests on the other.

I'm a guest, she thought with fascination. In my own parents' home.

She tried to think when she had last introduced anyone to her parents. A long time ago, she realized. Ten years, to be precise. And the man in question had been called Elvis, which had amused her mother no end.

"I understand you work at Uppsala University," she heard her father say.

"That's right," said Spencer. "It sounds absurd to admit it, but I've been teaching there for thirty-five years now."

He laughed loudly, not noticing the way Fredrika's parents stiffened.

They ought to have lots in common, really, thought Fredrika. Spencer's only five years younger than Dad, after all.

Again she felt the same desire to burst out laughing that had come over her in the car. She coughed discreetly. She asked her mother if she could pass the gravy, which went so well with this delicious roast. Complimented her father on his choice of wine, but then realized it was a mistake to draw attention back to the fact that she was drinking at all. Her father asked how work was going and she said it was all right. Her mother wanted to know if she was sleeping any better now and she said sometimes, but mostly not.

"I hope you don't have to sleep alone every night," her mother said with a meaningful glance at Spencer.

"Sometimes I do," Fredrika said noncommittally.

"Oh?" said her mother.

"Ah," said her father.

And then they lapsed into silence. Absence of sound can be a blessing, or a curse, depending on the context. In this case there was absolutely no doubt: this wordless dinner was going to be a disaster.

Fredrika could not help feeling exasperated. What had her parents expected? They knew Spencer was married, knew she often slept alone, knew she would be bringing up the child at least partially as a single mother. An unorthodox arrangement, admittedly, but hardly the only lapse from orthodoxy in their family history. Fredrika's uncle, for example, had been bold enough to come out as a homosexual back in the sixties. And the family had always welcomed him on the same terms as everybody else.

Then Spencer asked a few polite questions about Fredrika's mother's interest in music, and the mood round the table grew a bit more cordial. Her father went to the kitchen for more potatoes and her mother put on an LP she had picked up in a secondhand shop a few days before.

"Vinyl," she said. "You can't beat it."

"I agree with you there," said Spencer, and snorted. "You wouldn't catch me buying a CD."

Fredrika's mother smiled, and this time the smile even reached her eyes. Fredrika started to relax a little. They had broken the ice and the temperature was rising. Her father, seemingly still a bit wary of this son-in-law of his own age, cleared his throat and said: "More wine, anybody?"

It sounded almost like a plea.

They carried on chatting, the words coming more easily for everyone at the table, even her father.

Fredrika wished she could have drunk more wine. Somewhere out there, a murderer was on the loose. And they had no sense at all of whether he thought he had finished the job now, or whether the murders of Jakob and Marja Ahlbin were part of something bigger.

Her thoughts went to their daughter Johanna, who must have found out about their deaths on the Internet by now. And then to Karolina, the one Elsie Ljung called Lazarus.

A day of rest tomorrow, thought Fredrika. But on Monday that's the very first thing I shall tackle. If Karolina Ahlbin *is* alive, why on earth hasn't she been in touch?

A thought flashed through her mind. Two sisters. One certifies the other's death and then leaves the country. But neither has actually died.

A bloody good alibi for both of them.

Could the simple, woeful case be that Karolina and Johanna were the murderers the police were looking for? Was it the daughters pulling all the strings and choreographing developments with such precision?

The thought made Fredrika feel light-headed and it hit her that drastic measures would be required if there was to be any hope of getting off to sleep that night and not lying awake thinking about those murders.

Maybe she should get her violin out again? Playing for a while ought to bring some peace of mind. Just for a while. Any more than that would be a waste of time.

She quietly drained her wineglass.

Time's running out for us, she thought. We need a new line of investigation. And we've got to find Johanna, double quick.

■ ■ ■ ■

Sunday,
March 2, 2008

■ ■ ■ ■

BANGKOK, THAILAND

The flat was tiny and hot. The sun was kept out by thick curtains intended as a shield against prying eyes. As if anybody would be able to see into a flat on the fourth floor.

She paced restlessly to and fro between the little living room and kitchen. She had drunk all the water but did not dare to go out for more, or to drink the tap water. Dehydration and lack of sleep were taking their toll, trying to force her over the edge which she knew all too well she was balanced on. Below gaped a yawning chasm that threatened to swallow her alive. She tried to think constantly about where she was putting her feet, almost as if she did not trust the floor of the flat to bear her weight.

It was two days since she had learned from the online press that her family had died, probably the victims of murder. She could scarcely remember the first hours after she found out. Seeing her collapse into tears, the café owner resolutely closed his premises for the evening and took her home with him. He and his wife put her to bed on their settee and took turns to sit with her all night. Her weeping had been wild and uncontrolled, her grief insupportable.

It was the terror that was her salvation in the end. The news of what had happened to her family put her own situation in a different light. Someone was trying methodically, systematically, to dismantle her life and her past, and wipe out her family. Wondering what could possibly be the motive for such actions, she was suddenly horror-struck. And the horror and fear brought new, rational insight, forcing her to take action on her own behalf. As the sun rose over Bangkok that Sunday morning, she was calm and collected. She knew exactly what she had to do.

She did not know the background to the tragedy she was now being forced to live through. But she knew this much: her own disappearance was a vital part of the operation. People did not stage nightmare scenarios involving murder and conspiracy without a good reason. She sensed that it was all directed more at her and her father than at her mother or sister. Presumably because they were both so actively involved with migrant issues. Possibly prompted by the information-gathering trip she had just undertaken. Information that was now gone.

It was all pointless, she thought. The whole thing.

Her lack of personal documents and possessions frightened the trafficker to whom she turned for help.

"Are you a criminal?" he asked anxiously. "I can't help you, if so."

She had met him when she first came to Bangkok. She had been following the refugee trail, mapping out how things worked in Thailand. It seemed absurd and incomprehensible that people from the Middle East traveled to Europe via Thailand. It took her several days to win his trust, to convince him that she was nothing to do with the police, but had come to the country on her own initiative.

"Why would a vicar's daughter get involved in this sort of thing?" he demanded scornfully.

"Because she's part of the reception system in Sweden," she answered, eyes lowered. "Because her father spent years hiding illegal migrants and now she's following in his footsteps."

"So how do you view me, then?" he asked,

his voice full of doubt. "Unlike you, I'm not in it for anything but the money."

"Which could be seen as reasonable," she replied, though she was far from convinced. "Since you're also taking enormous risks and could face a long prison sentence. So it seems reasonable for you to be paid in line with that."

That was how she had won his confidence and trust. He let her shadow him, meeting passport forgers and travel document providers, individuals engaged in subversive activities at airports and key figures in the provision of safe houses. The network was unobtrusive but extensive, and constantly pursued by a corrupt police force, halfheartedly trying to clamp down. And at the core of it all were the people the entire operation revolved round. The people in flight, delivered up to a network that was criminal at heart, with hopeless, empty eyes and years of chaos and disintegration behind them.

She had taken photographs and documented. Borrowed an interpreter and talked to a number of the people involved. Explained that her aim was to present a fair picture of all parties, that there was great public ignorance on the subject in Sweden, and that it would be to the benefit of everyone for this misery to be more widely known. To those earning money from the trafficking she promised complete anonymity and offered the carrot of indirect publicity and rising demand for their services. As if they could be more in demand than they already were; as if people had anyone else to turn to.

Bangkok had been her final destination. The journey had started in Greece, one of Europe's major transit countries, where she had documented the treatment of asylum seekers and how they reached mainland Europe. She had moved on to Turkey and then to Damascus and Amman. There were over two million Iraqi refugees currently parked in Syria and Jordan. Their options were exceedingly few; if they returned home they would in many cases become what were known as internal migrants — still without a home or any sound basis for a life. Out of two and a half million migrants, a very small proportion went on to Europe. There seemed to be innumerable ways of doing it, but most took the land route through Turkey. She went back to Turkey herself, accompanying one particular family to observe things at close quarters.

It was when they told her of their expectations of their new life in Sweden that her tears came. They had dreams of a bright new future, of jobs, and good schools for their children. Of houses and gardens and a society that would welcome them in a way best described as unrealistic.

"They need labor in Sweden," the man told her with conviction. "So we know everything will work out once we get there."

But she, like all those with inside knowledge, was all too aware that few of the family's expectations would be met and that it was only a question of time before they found themselves rendered passive and apathetic, and stuck in a cramped flat on some estate, waiting for a Migration Agency decision that could take an eternity and still be a no. And then the real running away would start. Running away from deportation.

She had rung her father at home and cried down the phone line. Said she understood now what it was that had utterly broken his heart when he got involved in this desperate struggle for human redress.

And now here she was in one of the safe flats in Bangkok herself, fleeing an enemy she did not even have a name for. The only thing that consoled her even the slightest was that she had made that phone call to her father.

When she thought back over her trip, she

began to suspect it was the final stage that had been the problem and perhaps triggered the catastrophe that had now befallen her. There had been talk of a new way of getting to Sweden from Iraq, Syria, and Jordan. Disconnected little hints, nobody could confirm anything. But what she heard fitted with what had come to her father's notice in Sweden. That there was a new operator on the scene, whose method involved a different set of values and smaller sums of money. Someone who was offering a simple way of getting to Europe, if you promised not to reveal anything about the arrangement before you left. But of course people occasionally let things slip anyway, which was how the secret had started circulating.

The new way used established travel routes, always via Bangkok or Istanbul. And always by air, never the overland route. That had given her pause for thought, because smuggling people in on flights was much more risky. But on the other hand, the new network only seemed to be taking on a very small number of clients. None of the people she approached had personal knowledge of anyone who had gone that way, it was all just hearsay. She had already been to Istanbul twice, and Bangkok had seemed a good place to round off the trip. So in one last attempt to contact someone working for the new operator, she went there. Made an extensive search, but without results. Or at least, without any results she had been aware of. But that might well be the answer to the riddle: she had gotten too close without knowing it.

She was weak with fatigue, paralyzed by grief. She took her pen and paper with her and lay down in the little bedroom. The air was still and heavy, and outside it was almost unbearably hot. But her body seemed to have switched off and refused to react. She curled into a ball on the bed and shut her eyes. When she was little, that had always been her best trick for shutting out all the bad things.

Her protector, the people trafficker, had been surprised to see her again so soon.

"I need your help," she said, and that made him listen.

She would pay when she got back to Sweden. When she tried to get at her bank details and have money transferred to Bangkok, she was informed that her accounts were closed and she could not possibly be the person she said she was. So payment would have to wait, and her protector accepted that. Maybe he saw her as a part of an exciting project, because he seemed positively elated at the prospect of helping her.

And as for her, she had only one thought in her head — getting home. At any price. Because although she believed the catastrophe that had befallen her was related to her own investigations, she was beginning to suspect that the full picture was less simple than that. The truth might lie closer to her and her family and be much more personal.

She dropped off, and did not wake again until it was dark outside.

STOCKHOLM

He waited for them at the agreed place, a few hundred meters from the Globe. The giant golf ball was fabulously illuminated in the darkness. He was one big smile; his heart was pumping wildly and the adrenaline made him see everything so vividly that evening. He had reached his goal at last, his journey was over, and now he could make his final payment. He stared up into the clear, starlit night, his head aching with the relief. Happiness hurt when it was this big.

A black car of a type he did not recognize pulled up alongside the pavement where he was standing. A window slid down and the person inside gestured to him to put his haul in the boot and get into the back, right-hand seat. He immediately complied. Opening the car door, he found the woman who had met him at the station sitting in the other backseat. Her face was impassive as he climbed in.

They drove through a cold, wintry Stockholm bathed in moonlight. He was virtually sure they were driving north this time. The spoils lay in their protective black sack in the boot. They must really trust him, since they hadn't even bothered to check he wasn't trying to swindle them.

The trust was mutual by this stage, so he felt no unease as they made the short journey. They took a turn off the main road into what looked like some kind of park. Despite the gleam of the moonlight, the night was too dark for him to be able to see properly. They indicated to him to get out, and he did so. The passenger who was sitting beside the driver did so, too. It was the man with the disfigured face. They kept the engine running.

The man's instructions were wordless; he merely pointed down toward the darkness of the park. Ali followed the pointing finger with his eyes and thought he could see someone standing there, down among the trees. Someone waving. The person stepped forward from the shadows. It was the man who spoke Arabic.

He wondered why the meeting had to take place in a deserted park in the middle of the night. Perhaps because their agreement was too sensitive to be dealt with when other people were around. He set off resolutely toward the Arabic speaker. The disfigured man was two steps behind him.

"I gather it went well today," the Arabic speaker said when he reached him.

He smiled at Ali, who beamed back at him.

"It all went fantastically well," he confirmed with the eagerness of a five-year-old keen to impress.

"You're a good shot," the man said. "Lots of other people would have missed a target that was moving so fast."

Ali could not help feeling proud.

"I have many years of training behind me, I'm afraid."

The man gave a satisfied nod.

"Yes, we know, and that was why we chose you."

He seemed to be wondering what to say next.

"Come with me," he went on, bowing his head in the direction of the woods, where a lake could be seen glittering though the mass of tree trunks.

Ali felt a sudden stab of doubt.

"Come along," said the man. "There's just one more little detail to be taken care of."

He gave such a warm smile that Ali's mind was immediately put at rest.

"When can I see my family again?" he

asked as he went after the man into a clearing.

"Very, very soon," said the man, and turned round.

A second later, a shot rang out. And Ali's journey was over.

■ ■ ■ ■

Monday,
March 3, 2008

■ ■ ■ ■

STOCKHOLM

The corridor was full of bustling activity when Bergman got in to work on the Monday. Ellen Lind gave her a wide grin as they met, just outside her room.

"You look radiant! Are you sleeping better now?"

Fredrika nodded and returned the smile happily, feeling almost embarrassed without knowing why. She did not really know why she was sleeping better, either. Perhaps the effect of Saturday's family dinner had been more positive than she had predicted. And perhaps playing her violin was helping. Now that she had started, she could not stop. The memory was in her fingers, and although she made some mistakes, she found she could play piece after piece.

Alex, by contrast, looked as though he had not slept particularly well as he opened the meeting in the Den a short time later and ran through what had come to light over the weekend.

He's sinking, Fredrika thought anxiously. And we're not lifting a finger to help him.

Peder and Joar had chosen seats as far away from each other as they could and were both staring fixedly straight ahead. The group had gone from tight-knit to unraveling in just a few days. Fredrika noted with some relief that for once the conflict did not center on her.

"I've checked out what Ragnar Vinterman told us about Erik Sundelius: the official warnings from his professional body and the prosecution for manslaughter. And it's all correct," said Peder. "The question is how it's significant, in the context."

"Need it be significant at all?" Fredrika asked. "Need it be significant in this particular case that Jakob Ahlbin's psychiatrist treated two *other* patients negligently, resulting in their suicide? We still don't think Jakob killed either himself, or his wife."

"No," said Alex deliberately. "No, we don't. On the other hand, we don't know exactly what we think *did* happen, either."

Fredrika looked doubtful.

"I've been thinking a bit about the Ahlbin sisters," she said. "And I'm starting to wonder if we've made a mistake in separating the two oddities, so to speak."

The others looked blank, and Fredrika made haste to explain.

"We keep talking as though the obscure elements in the case have nothing to do with each other. Jakob Ahlbin seems to have shot his wife and then himself, but we still don't believe it. Johanna Ahlbin seems to have vanished from the face of the earth, but we don't know for sure. And there are various reasons for suspecting irregularities in the matter of Karolina Ahlbin's death, but there, too, we don't know exactly what may have gone wrong."

Fredrika paused for breath.

"What if they're all interconnected? That's all I wanted to say."

With his chin propped in one hand, Alex looked ten years older than he really was.

"Well," he began, "I'm pretty sure nobody here has been imagining things *aren't* interconnected; the problem is that we can't quite see how. What thoughts did you have?"

"I thought it might not have been Karolina who died," said Fredrika, squirming a little. "I know it sounds mad, of course."

"But she was identified by her own sister," said Peder, frowning. "And she had her driving license on her."

"But how hard is it to get hold of a fake driving license if you need to?" asked Fredrika. "And what are the odds of a doctor finding out it isn't genuine? Karolina Ahlbin was identified by a sister whom we haven't seen hide or hair of since. And if Karolina's still alive, we know we haven't seen her either. And that's the crucial problem, as I see it. Why aren't they getting in touch, even though the story's all over the media?"

No one said anything. They had all seen that morning's papers — full of whole-page articles telling the Ahlbin family's story. This time the journalists had managed to find pictures of the two girls, too.

WHERE IS JOHANNA AHLBIN? shrieked one of the headlines, suggesting something could have happened to her, too.

"I hear what you're saying," Alex said to Fredrika, "and of course — you may be right. But there could be less dramatic explanations for the oddities. Karolina Ahlbin hasn't been in touch for the simple reason that she's dead, and Johanna because she hasn't found out what's happened yet. But I agree — if she hasn't come forward by the middle of the week, we'll have to take other steps."

"You don't think anything could have happened to her, do you?" asked Joar.

"Either that or it's like Fredrika says, and

she's got reasons of her own to keep away from the police."

Alex turned to Fredrika.

"Over to something else," he said. "You made a very good point about the content of the emails and the fact that Tony Svensson could have been contacted by whoever wrote the emails that weren't sent from his own computer. I had a word with the prosecutor and we can bring him in again. I want Joar and Peder to interview him together."

He raised his eyes, and there was anger in them.

"Together," he said. "Understood?"

The two men nodded.

"Fredrika's tackling the library in Farsta," Alex went on. "And I want us to keep chipping away at the circumstances surrounding Karolina's death. See if anyone's shown an interest in the body; there'll have to be a funeral and so on. Maybe she had some bloke we haven't heard about yet. Get back in touch with the hospital and keep damn well digging."

Fredrika nodded and looked happy with that.

Alex looked around him distractedly.

"I think that's it for now," he said.

"But what about the officer?" Peder objected. "The one with the Norrmalm police, that Tony Svensson was in touch with?"

"I'll deal with that myself," said Alex. "We'll have another meeting here at four o'clock this afternoon."

They were interrupted by a vigorous knock, and a detective from the Stockholm CID put his head round the door.

"I've just got some information to pass on about Muhammed Abdullah, who you and Fredrika went to see in Skärholmen last week," he said, his eyes on Alex.

"Oh yes?" said Alex, none too pleased by the interruption.

"He's dead," the detective said. "He had to go out on some sort of business yesterday, and he didn't come back. His wife alerted the police last night but she didn't get any help until this morning. He was found shot in the head in a car park not far from where they live."

Fredrika felt dismay and sorrow. The man had been pleasant and cooperative, despite feeling under threat. And now he was gone.

Alex swallowed.

"Well, I'll be damned," he said quietly.

"And that's not all," said the visitor. "Yesterday evening, a jogger came across a dead body that had been dumped in the water at Brunnsviken, where the jogging track follows the shoreline. The man hasn't been identified, but initial indications are that he was shot with the same weapon as Muhammed Abdullah."

It had been a long and trying night for Alex, lying sleepless beside his wife, hour after hour. Thoughts of Lena seared him like fire. He had promised himself to try to talk to her over the weekend, but had not been up to it. Or had not dared.

What if she's ill, what if it's Alzheimer's? he thought dully. What the hell will I do then?"

The fear of it paralyzed him. He wished she would tell him what was wrong, since he was too weak to make the first move.

Fredrika came charging in, stomach first. She was back up to speed now, with only a month to go until her due date.

"I just wanted to tell you I'm off to the hospital now."

"Sounds like a good start," said Alex.

"I rang Farsta Library, too," she went on, "and they promised to get back to me. They haven't got the data stored on computer, so they were going to look it up in their log-book."

A man from the technical division knocked on the door behind Fredrika.

"Yes?" Alex demanded.

"We spotted something when we were checking out the Ahlbins' telephone subscription," said the technician.

"Uhuh?"

"Notice that they wanted to cancel their landline subscription was sent in writing to Telia a week before the murders, with a request for the subscription to end on Tuesday the twenty-sixth of February — that's to say, the day they died."

"Who signed the letter?" asked Alex.

"Jakob Ahlbin himself. And he also rang and canceled his mobile contract the day he died."

"And his wife's mobile?"

The technician cleared his throat.

"That was active until last Wednesday morning, and then the contract was terminated. We don't know who by."

"Has anyone rung it?" asked Alex.

The technician nodded.

"In the time since we've had it here, the mobile operator has only registered two incoming calls: one from an unidentified number in Bangkok and one from a parishioner who clearly didn't know she was dead."

"Bangkok?" Fredrika echoed in surprise.

"Yep."

"So he canceled his phone subscription," Alex said. "Why would he do that?"

"If it was him who did it," Fredrika put in.

"Just so, if it was him who did it . . ."

"Which it probably wasn't," Fredrika went on. "It seems more likely, doesn't it, that it was the same person who canceled Marja's, a bit later?"

"It's perfectly possible to cancel another person's telephone subscription," the technician put in. "The only information they ask for, to check it's the subscriber ringing, is basic stuff like national identity number and home address."

Alex nodded and knitted his brows.

"The question is," he said irascibly, "why the hell was that so important? Cutting off their phones?"

The technician withdrew and a cleaner passed by in the corridor. Fredrika nodded to him that it was fine to do her office.

Alex picked up the report of the two fatal shootings the night before. The man found in the water at Brunnsviken had probably died only an hour or so before the jogger found him. The murderer might very well not have thought anyone would be out jogging in Haga Park at midnight, and not expected the body to be found so soon. As for Muhammed Abdullah, he had died about two hours before the other man.

Same weapon, same perpetrator, Alex wondered. A peripatetic murderer, then.

As if reading his thoughts, Fredrika said, "I think we can assume it was the same perpetrator in both cases."

Alex waited a moment and then asked, "And the link to Jakob Ahlbin? If there is one?"

"Yes, I think there must be one," said Fredrika, looking thoughtful.

Then she said, "I think they both needed silencing, and that's the link."

Alex's eyes grew wide.

"But why?"

"That's what I don't get," Fredrika said frustratedly. "Muhammed Abdullah was open with us about being scared when we met him, and with hindsight we know he had reason to be. And Jakob Ahlbin seems to have had reason to be fearful, too, but the question is whether he was aware of it himself."

"Exactly," said Alex. "And why was Muhammed Abdullah so bloody petrified, in fact? Well, because he was convinced he'd had sensitive information entrusted to him, and because he was scared the police were going to start looking into his connections with the traffickers."

"And he had time to pass the sensitive information about the new migrant-smuggling network on to Jakob," Fredrika supplied.

"One of those emails told Jakob to stop looking. Does that mean he was actively seeking out information that he should have steered clear of?"

"Seems a fair assumption."

"But can that really be the link?" Alex said dubiously. "I mean, it sounded like something *positive* for the refugees that there might be this cheaper, better alternative that would mean not having to put themselves into the hands of corrupt gangsters."

"Yes, you're right," said Fredrika. "It really would be odd if people smuggling refugees on generous terms went in for killing vicars at the same time."

The cleaner had finished and gave Fredrika a little wave as he came back past Alex's room. Then something else occurred to her.

"The man who was killed by the car outside the university," she said.

"The murdered bank robber?" queried Alex.

"Yes, him," said Fredrika. "He had supposedly come into the country that 'new' way, according to Muhammed, so it seems quite likely that he had some insight into how it operated. And he was murdered, too."

Alex looked doubtful.

"And the man in Haga Park?" he asked.

"I don't know," said Fredrika, feeling her pulse rate rise. "But there's something about that story that feels terribly . . . close . . . I just can't put my finger on it."

Alex stood up and looked at his watch.

"I'm going to try and track down this officer in Norrmalm who had contact with Tony Svensson," he said determinedly. "And let's hope the national CID can come up with more detail on these other murders during the day. Meanwhile, you find out all you can about goings-on around Karolina's death."

"Right, I'll get straight on with it," Fredrika said with equal resolution, and leaped out of her seat with surprising agility.

Alex's face split into a grin. The original Fredrika Bergman was back.

For the second time in swift succession, Tony Svensson was brought in for police questioning. This time he was rather less cooperative, and stared mutinously at Peder Rydh and Joar Sahlin as they came into the interview room.

"I've said everything there is to say," he bellowed. "You hear? I'm not saying another word, I tell you!"

Then he planted himself on his seat, folded his arms, and glowered at them.

Behind that façade of strength and cockiness, Peder could see something else: fear. He hoped it would not pass the clueless Joar by.

Peder was quite happy with the way his week had started. He loved it when things started hotting up at work; it was a good distraction from all the painful private stuff. Recent developments on the case had also meant a postponement of his appointment with the workplace psychologist.

"We'll get going on that when there's time," Alex ruled, and promised he would personally ring Margareta Berlin, head of HR .

So Peder was able to focus exclusively on Svensson.

"We've just got a few follow-up questions," he said quietly.

Tony continued to look furious.

"I'm saying nothing," he hissed.

Not true, thought Peder sarcastically, you're talking nonstop.

"Is there any special reason for that?" asked Joar.

He's got it, thought Peder. The question is whether he's going to fritter our advantage away again.

"Is there any special reason for what?" snapped Tony.

He clearly had the will to communicate after all — he just wanted some guarantees.

"Is there any special reason why you're refusing to talk to us anymore?" Joar asked slowly.

No reaction. Svensson's mouth was clamped shut.

"I think it was like this," said Joar, leaning across the table. "You felt pretty calm last time you were here, because you knew we only wanted to talk about what you had against Jakob Ahlbin, and because you knew that would all sort itself out. It wasn't you who sent those last emails and you knew we'd find that out sooner or later."

Joar took his time, trying to read in Tony's face whether he was getting through.

"But this time you're scared, because we want to talk about something else all of a sudden, and you know as well as we do that there aren't that many subjects we'd want to ask you about."

He leaned back in his chair again, giving Tony his cue to speak by adjusting the balance of power at the table. But Tony said nothing and his face was hard to read.

"We think you went round to Jakob Ahlbin's because he was interfering in your affairs again, and we think somebody else *sent* you to do that," Peder said softly. "And the only thing we want and need to know is who your contact was and what you were supposed to do or say."

He tried to catch Svensson's eye, running one hand across the table as if to brush away some invisible speck of dirt.

"Jakob Ahlbin and his wife were shot in the head," he said in a businesslike tone, but keeping his voice low to encourage a feeling of mutual confidence. "My colleague and I will find it very hard not to tie you into this investigation on suspicion of being an accessory to murder, unless you can give us some good reasons not to."

Svensson still refused to speak, and his solicitor put a discreet hand on his lower arm. Tony pulled his arm away quickly.

Shit, thought Peder. They must have put the frighteners on him to a point where he's more scared of whoever he's working for than he is of going to jail for being an accessory to murder.

"What did they say they'd do to you if you blabbed to anyone?" asked Joar, as if he had read Peder's mind. "Did they threaten to shut you up for good? Or were they going to make do with a good beating?"

Still no answer, but Peder could see Svensson's jaws grinding.

"I saw in your paperwork that you've got a daughter," he ventured.

And provoked a tangible reaction.

"Don't you touch her!' roared Svensson, leaping up. "Don't you touch her!"

Joar and Peder stayed in their seats.

"Please sit back down," Joar said mildly.

Peder tried to get Tony to look him in the eye.

"Was it her they were going after?" he asked. "Was it her they were going to take if

400

you squealed?"

Svensson subsided onto his chair like a punctured balloon. He did not look at either of them, just put his elbows on the table and leaned his head in his hands.

"Was that it, Tony?" asked Joar.

And — finally — got a silent nod in reply. Peder breathed a sigh of relief.

"We can help her, Tony," he said. "We can help you both. If you'll just talk to us."

"Like hell you can," Tony said hoarsely. "Don't you fucking well say you can protect any of us from them. Not a bleeding chance."

Peder and Joar looked at each other for the first time in the interview.

"Oh, yes we can," Peder said assertively. "And we can do it well, what's more. Much better than you could do yourself."

Svensson gave a weary laugh.

"If you believe that, then you haven't got a fucking clue about all this," he said through clenched teeth. "My only protection, my only bloody hope of surviving this and getting my daughter through it unharmed, is to not talk to you. Have you got that? If you really want to save me, you fucking well let me out of here right now."

A chair scraped on the floor as the solicitor made a slight movement.

"All we need is a name," said Joar. "That's all — then we'll do the rest."

"If you get your fucking name, there won't be anything called 'the rest,'" bellowed Svensson. "I haven't got a name. I've just got a fucking ugly face."

"But that's enough," said Peder. "Then at least you can identify him. We can give you pictures to look at, and if you recognize him —"

Svensson's harsh laugh cut him off in mid-flow and bounced back off the bare walls.

"Look at pictures," he said dejectedly. "You lot are fucking floundering and you don't even know it. It's not somebody like me you're looking for, you fucking numb-skulls."

Peder leaned forward.

"What are we looking for, then?" he asked tensely.

Svensson clamped his mouth shut.

"I'm not saying another word," he growled.

Peder hesitated.

"Okay then, tell us something about what you had to do, instead."

Svensson was listening.

"If you don't want to tell us who your contact was, at least tell us what they wanted you to do."

There was silence while Tony thought over what Peder had just proposed.

"I had to stop sending emails," he said under his breath. "And it was no skin off my nose, because like I said, our problems were sorting themselves out. But then there was another thing."

He hesitated.

"I had to go round to the vicar's and ring at his door. And hand over an envelope."

"Do you know what was in it?"

Tony shook his head. He looked despondent now.

"No, but it was important that it was handed over on that particular day."

"And Jakob took it from you?"

"Yes. He looked surprised to see it was me, but then he realized it wasn't about Ronny Berg."

Joar drummed his fingers lightly on the table.

"Did he read the letter while you waited?"

Tony sneered.

"Yeah, he did, as it happens. He was fucking furious, and told me to tell the people who'd sent me that they ought to think twice before threatening him. He said he was going to burn the letter when I'd gone."

"What did you get for doing those things?" asked Peder.

Tony looked him squarely in the eye.

"I got to carry on living," he answered. "And if I'm lucky, and if I play my cards right, my daughter will as well."

"So they threatened to harm her if you didn't do it?" Peder said gently.

Svensson nodded, his eyes strangely watery. Joar seemed to be thinking hard; then he sat up straight and threw back his shoulders.

"They've got her," he said, sounding almost fascinated. "They took her as a guarantee that you'd carry out your part of the operation."

Peder stared from Joar to Svensson.

"Is that right?" he asked.

"That's right," he said darkly. "And I've no idea how they're fucking well going to react to me coming in here again."

When they had finished the interview with Svensson, Peder and Joar requested a few minutes to confer before they let him go home again.

"I don't think he's bluffing," said Peder as soon as the two of them were alone.

The intensity of the hatred he felt for his colleague was affecting his judgment. The only thing softening his feelings an iota was the events of the weekend, when his son was ill and he had spent Saturday evening and most of Sunday with Ylva.

"It's important for us to stick together when we need to," he told her when she got back from the hospital to find him in the kitchen, preparing dinner for them all.

As if they were a family. As if they actually belonged together.

Ylva agreed with him, and for the first time in ages they spent a peaceful evening together. He asked how things were going at work, and she said she was feeling much better now. He was glad to hear it, but could not bring himself to talk about his own situation. He had never been able to bear feeling inferior to her in any way, and this was no exception.

Joar's voice brought him back to the present with a bump.

"I don't think he's bluffing either, and I definitely think we need to take the threat scenario seriously, but . . ."

"But what?" demanded Peder.

"I'm just not sure they've got his daughter as he claims."

"I am," Peder asserted, without much thought about what he was saying.

Which gave Joar the upper hand again.

"Really? Think it through carefully, Peder. Why would they take such a risk — because it is, a huge one — as to grab his daughter at the start? They could scarcely let her go again afterward, she'd be able to identify every single one of them. Which would mean they'd have to kill her, and then they'd be child murderers. There are plenty of hard men and ruffians who'd go a bloody long way to avoid that."

"But damn it, this lot don't seem to be your normal ruffians."

"True. Which makes it all the more implausible. They're too intelligent to take it out on a small child. I don't doubt for a moment that they threatened to, though. But that's another matter."

"So you mean Tony Svensson's lying about his daughter being abducted so we'll back off a bit?"

"Exactly. And keep our distance from him in future."

Peder thought about this.

"Doesn't really feel like an option. Keeping our distance, I mean."

"You're right there," said Joar grimly. "So I suggest you go in and wind up the interview and get the paperwork out of the way while I go up to the department and get a snap decision out of them to have this guy followed when he walks out of here. I reckon he'll go straight home to his daughter

406

to check she's okay. And then it wouldn't surprise me if he rings some contact on the other side to let him know everything's fine and he hasn't given us any crucial information."

Just for the moment Peder felt quite serene. They already had Svensson's phone tapped. Perhaps by the end of the day they would have the names of some of the men who had been threatening him.

It happened more and more rarely these days, but just occasionally Spencer Lagergren and his wife, Eva, would both be at home in the middle of the day and would make lunch together. Spencer had no idea what had prompted Eva to suggest one of these lunches on this particular day, but he knew better than to go against her wishes.

He got back from work to be greeted by appetizing aromas the minute he opened the front door.

"You've already made a start," he remarked when he came out into the kitchen a few minutes later.

"Of course," said Eva. "Couldn't just hang around waiting for you."

Spencer knew very well that the relationship he had with his wife was a mystery to his lover, Fredrika Bergman, and sometimes he felt the same himself. The element of total absurdity that the relationship had

408

acquired now he was expecting a baby with another woman was getting harder and harder to handle. But it had been impossible, of course, not to tell Eva about the undertaking he had made and the changes this was going to make to his life. At quite an early stage they had both taken to having other relationships outside their marriage, but it was ultimately only Spencer who had decided to keep seeing the same person for years. He knew it disturbed his wife, who had never been able to make any of her adventures on the side last long. But then it disturbed *him* that her lovers had been so many in number. And sometimes so young. As if there were any legitimate reason for him to have objections to her choice of male acquaintances.

"We scarcely saw each other over the weekend," Eva said almost cheerfully, "so I thought it would be a good idea to have a bit of time to ourselves now, over lunch."

Oven-baked lamb and potato was sizzling away and there was a big bowl of salad on the kitchen table. A thought flashed through his mind. Dare he eat any of this? Wasn't she behaving rather strangely?

"You've gone to a lot of trouble, I see," he said, going to the fridge to get some drinks.

"Oh, one has to sometimes, my dear," Eva

said sternly. "Otherwise one might as well just bloody give up."

Spencer tensed. In thirty years of marriage he had only ever heard his wife swear five times. But he made no comment.

"Wouldn't you say?" she demanded.

"Yes, of course," he said, not sounding as though he believed — or even understood — what he was saying.

Her long fingers clasped the bottle of balsamic vinegar. Salad dressing was a must.

"And how was *your* weekend?" she asked, thumping the vinegar bottle down onto the table.

It was enough of a statement for him to grasp that something was wrong. He slowly shut the fridge door and turned round. And saw her on the other side of the table.

She had always been beautiful. Slim and elegant. There was still nothing wrong with her appearance. Her thick hair was swept back from her face and up into a simple but classic arrangement. As usual, a stray lock had escaped and fallen across her face. Her eyes were big and green, oceans in which the pupils were like desert islands. High cheekbones and full lips. In other words, she was a very attractive jailer.

Spencer suppressed a sigh. Because that was unfortunately exactly what she was, and had been these past twenty years. His jailer, the cross he had to bear.

He met her gaze and gave a start. His jailer was crying. Good grief, when had he last seen her cry? Five years ago when her father had his heart attack? Tough as old boots, he was over eighty-five now and still far too hale and hearty for Spencer to anticipate any brighter prospects. Though it was naïve, of course, to imagine that the old devil's demise would bring him any kind of salvation. Fathers-in-law from hell always had a way of coming back.

"You've got to keep me informed, Spencer," she said quietly. "You can't just leave me outside."

Spencer frowned and prepared to defend himself.

"I've never kept anything from you," he said. "I told you about Fredrika and I told you about the baby."

She gave a hollow laugh.

"Good God, Spencer, you were out almost the whole weekend without telling me where you'd got to."

I didn't know you cared, he thought wearily.

Out loud he said, "It may have seemed like that, but it wasn't how I meant it."

He cleared his throat.

411

"As I told you before, Fredrika hasn't been well during her pregnancy, so —"

"And how's it going to be later on?" Eva interrupted. "Have you thought about that? Are you going to have the baby alternate weekends or weeks, or what's the plan? Will you be bringing it along when we go out to dinner with our friends, and if so, how are you going to introduce it?"

She shook her head and went to check the food in the oven.

"I thought we'd talked about this," said Spencer, and could hear how feeble it sounded.

Eva slammed the oven door shut.

"*You* may have talked about it," she said. "*We* haven't."

She paused before she went on.

"If there is such a thing as *we* now."

As he opened his mouth to reply, she waved her index finger at him to tell him to be quiet.

"I've resigned myself to the fact that you and I have felt for a long time that we needed to have other partners for our own well-being," she said mutedly, and took a deep breath. "But for you to decide to go off and *start a family* with another woman . . ."

She clapped her hand to her mouth and

412

for the first time for several years he felt the urge to hold her.

"How could things turn out like this, Spencer?" she wept. "How could we get trapped in this relationship where neither of us is happy and we can't love each other?"

Her words hit home and his mouth went dry.

She clearly had no idea what her own father had done.

Do I need to care? thought Spencer. What could possibly be worse than this?

Fredrika Bergman wedged herself behind the steering wheel and set off for Danderyd Hospital. The case had been coming to the boil all weekend, and now it was Monday, it had positively exploded. Two more bodies, one directly linked to the deaths of the Reverend and Mrs. Ahlbin. A suspected perpetrator who in Joar and Peder's judgment was more to be seen as a star witness. A psychiatrist who was trying to convince the police his patient was incapable of taking his own life, though past experience showed how wrong his judgment had been on previous occasions. And two clergymen, Sven Ljung and Ragnar Vinterman, who both seemed to know Johanna Ahlbin but had presented them with entirely contradictory views of her.

Coming away from the Ljungs' flat during the weekend, Fredrika and Alex compared notes, and found that Elsie had been by far the more forthcoming of the two. Sven had not said a word, for example, about their own son's addiction and the fact that Karolina Ahlbin had been at his side for several years. Alex actually rang him later in the day to ask straight out why he had kept it from the police, and received the following reply: "Because I feel so ashamed of my failure as a parent. And now I feel even more ashamed because I've dragged Karolina's name through the mud by not saying anything."

Fredrika had found the name and contact details of their son, but had to lower her expectations when she saw that he was currently detained under the law in an institution for the treatment of addiction. According to Elsie, he was in a clinic outside Stockholm, where he refused to cooperate with staff and had no contact with the outside world. It seemed that his latest overdose might have caused some brain damage, but the doctors could not be sure. Fredrika was obliged to rule him out as a potential star witness.

Danderyd Hospital was where Fredrika herself was to give birth later that spring, and she felt a frisson of excitement as she went in through the main entrance. The hospital smell promptly brought her down to earth again. What was it about care institutions that always smelled so off-putting? Almost as if death itself had crept into the ventilation system and was breathing on everybody in turn as they came in or out through the doors.

Fredrika's mobile phone bleeped in her pocket, and she took it out. A message from her mother to say that she and Fredrika's father had enjoyed meeting Spencer over the weekend.

Shamefaced, she slipped the phone back into her jacket pocket. Her mother was under no obligation to understand or accept her daughter's lifestyle. But it was nice if she did, even so. Since the weekend everything had felt much simpler, but also infinitely more difficult. Her parents had not been wrong to question how she was actually going to manage on her own once the baby was born. Spencer would pull his weight financially, of course, but Fredrika knew she faced disappointment on the practical and emotional fronts. A man of almost sixty who had never been a father before was very likely not to be the stuff of which nests were built.

Fredrika had already spoken on the phone to Göran Ahlgren, the duty doctor when Karolina Ahlbin was admitted. Today he received her in his office. He was good-looking, Fredrika caught herself thinking, and found she was smiling a little too broadly. Unfortunately he returned a smile of the same sort and looked her up and down with his sharp, granite-blue eyes. She estimated him to be somewhere between fifty and fifty-five.

"Karolina Ahlbin," she said, trying to sound businesslike to hide her initial flirtation. "You were here when she came into A and E."

The doctor nodded.

"Yes, I was. But I'm afraid I have no information beyond what I told you on the phone."

"Some new facts have come to light which rather complicate matters," said Fredrika, frowning. "Far too many people who knew Karolina have been assuring us that she was never a drug addict in her whole life."

Ahlgren put up his hands.

"I can only base my opinion on what I saw and documented myself," he said magnanimously. "And the case I was presented with was a young woman's extremely ravaged body. Bearing all the wretched marks of long-term addiction."

"All right," said Fredrika, opening her handbag. "Just to be on the safe side."

She took out two photographs.

"Is this the woman who came in the ambulance and identified herself as Karolina Ahlbin's sister?"

The doctor took the picture and recoiled.

"Impossible," he mumbled.

"Sorry?" said Fredrika, trying not to show how expectant she felt.

Ahlgren shook his head.

"No," he said in bewilderment. "That is, I don't know."

"What is it you don't know?" Fredrika asked abruptly, taking the photo as the doctor passed it back.

"I mean I don't feel sure, suddenly. The woman in the picture is quite like the one who died here, but . . ."

The doctor gave a sigh of resignation.

"No, it's not the same person," he admitted.

Fredrika's grip on her notebook tightened.

"Are you sure?"

"No, I need to look into it in the course of the day. I've never experienced anything like it. We followed all the procedures that —"

Impatient and elated, Fredrika interrupted him.

"The woman had no other injuries?" she asked.

"How do you mean?"

"Any injuries that might point to an alternative cause of death?"

"No," said the doctor. "I've seen the autopsy report and there are no anomalies that didn't fit the normal pathology of this woman."

"Normal pathology." The phrase made Fredrika shudder. "But the concrete cause of death was a heroin overdose?"

"Yes, to put it in simple terms."

"And she had injected herself with it in her flat?"

Ahlgren stared at her.

"I don't know anything about that. All I know is that she arrived here by ambulance and that it was her sister who found her in the flat. Where she got the drugs wasn't relevant for her treatment here."

Fredrika knew that to be true, but the police officers who were called to the hospital should have taken an interest. It was their job, not the hospital's, to establish whether there were any grounds for suspecting a crime. She wondered how much effort had actually been put into investigating the circumstances of Karolina's death.

"Could anyone else have injected her with the drugs?" Fredrika asked mistrustfully.

"Yes, that's possible," Ahlgren replied.

"But why would anyone do that?"

Because she had to disappear.

Fredrika knew they had already lost far too much time.

"I want a DNA test done on Karolina Ahlbin's body. I want to be absolutely certain that she was the one who died here, ten days ago."

"I'll see to that, of course," the doctor said swiftly. "But we need some DNA to compare it with."

"You can start by comparing her DNA with her parents'. That ought not to be too difficult: they're all here under the same roof."

Alex Recht gloomily noted that the rotten weather was continuing as he looked out of the window on his way to Norrmalm police station. It had proved an easy matter to locate the officer from that district who figured in the investigation of Jakob and Marja Ahlbin's deaths. A few quick calls to the individual's superior and he knew the person he wanted was at the station, writing a report.

"Keep him there," said Alex. "I'm on my way."

It was just a few steps from group HQ to the Norrmalm police station. They were in adjoining buildings and the glassed-in walkway linking them enabled him to move swiftly between the two worlds without taking a step outside.

Lena rang to say she was on her way home from work and wasn't feeling well. Alex was worried, but also a bit irritated. Why was she making a habit these days of telling him some things and saying nothing at all about others? And what in heaven's name was up with him? Saying nothing, day after day.

With an effort he put aside all thoughts of Lena. Now was now, and now meant work.

He found Viggo Tuvesson in his office, bent over his computer keyboard. Alex cleared his throat loudly and knocked on the doorframe. It took the man a second to turn round, but when he did, and saw Alex, his face lit up into a smile as if he had just spotted a close friend he had not seen for a long time.

"Alex Recht," he said, so loudly that it made Alex jump, unused as he was to hearing his whole name trumpeted like that. "To what do I owe the honor?"

Alex couldn't help staring at the officer and wondering what crime his disfigurement was a punishment for. The scar ran through his top lip and up toward his nose, which was bent and buckled.

Good God, thought Alex. Why didn't someone make a better job of fixing that?

Alex warily took a seat in Tuvesson's visitor's chair. With his legs crossed and his chin in his hand, the younger man definitely had ownership of the meeting. That much was clear from the outset, even though Alex was senior in rank.

Alex coughed again, attempting a trial of strength with the joyless but energetic eyes observing him with such fascination. Like a monster's.

"You were there when they found Jakob and Marja Ahlbin last week," he said in an authoritative tone, keen for the discussion to be on his terms.

"Yes," said Tuvesson, looking expectant.

"Had you met either of them when they were alive?"

The question seemed to catch him off guard. The expectant look was replaced by one of surprise.

"No, not that I recall."

"You hadn't encountered either of them previously? In other contexts, I mean."

"Well, I'd read about the Reverend Ahlbin in the papers of course," he said slowly. "But as I say, I hadn't met him personally."

"No, so you said." Alex said, equally slowly.

Viggo shifted position in his seat and banged his knee into the desk. The pain made him grimace.

"I heard it was your group that got the case as a whole," he said.

"Yes," said Alex, "it did. And that's why I'm here."

"I'm very happy to help," said Viggo, smiling his weird smile again.

"We're very grateful," Alex said with an unnecessary nonchalance in his voice, and went on: "Tony Svensson, then. Do you know him?"

The policeman nodded.

"If you mean the Tony Svensson who's in Sons of the People, then yes, I know him."

"Can you tell me how?"

"Because he's done some of his business here on my patch. That was how our paths crossed."

"What sort of business?"

Tuvesson gave a laugh.

"We suspected him and his lads of selling alcohol to minors at Odenplan, but we could never prove anything."

Alex vaguely recalled having heard about the matter before.

"Did you bring him in for questioning?"

"Oh yes, but he kept his trap firmly shut. Seemed to be having a laugh with us. Very clever, actually. Impressively well up on all the legal stuff. Knows exactly what he can get away with, so to speak."

Like he did with the emails, thought Alex. Knew exactly how to word them so it would be hard to call them actual threats.

"When was this?" he asked.

Viggo shrugged.

"Hard to remember exactly, but I can check if you like. About a year ago, I'd say."

Alex gave a thoughtful nod. That fitted with what he already knew.

"And since then? Have you had any further contact with him, I mean?"

Again they looked at each other, searching for hidden facts in each other's eyes.

"Yes," said Viggo. "He rang me a couple of times at work."

"And what did he want, if you don't mind me asking?"

"Wanted to grass on a former member of his network, some guy who wanted to go solo on a heist. Good old Tony evidently found that hard to accept."

Tuvesson kept his hands in his lap.

"I gather Tony Svensson's cropped up in the Ahlbin investigation as well."

"That's right," said Alex. "That was why I wanted to check if you had anything in particular on him."

It was a clumsy, transparent excuse. It was obvious to anyone that Alex had sought out Tuvesson to try to find out what contact there had been between them. But Viggo let it pass.

"I promise to get back to you if anything turns up. Sorry to disappoint you, but that's all I've got for now."

"That's how it goes sometimes," said Alex, getting up. "Thanks for your time."

He shook hands with Tuvesson and headed for the lift that would take him back down to the walkway. It wasn't just that he was disappointed with what Viggo had had to say. According to Ronny Berg when Peder talked to him, it was Jakob Ahlbin and not Tony Svensson who tipped off the police about his plans for a coup. There had been no mention of a Viggo in that context.

Alex took out his mobile and rang Peder.

"How are you two getting on? Have you let Tony Svensson go yet, or am I in time to ask him one more thing?"

When Fredrika got back from the hospital. Alex decided the two of them ought to pay a visit to Muhammed Abdullah's widow out at Skärholmen.

"Do you think she'll want to see us?" Fredrika asked uneasily. "She might be blaming us for her husband's death."

"But it still feels like the right thing to do," said Alex. "And I'd be glad to have you with me, since you were there last time."

For the second time in a just few days, they set off to Skärholmen. Alex felt under pressure.

"Good idea to ask for that DNA sample," he said. "When do we get the preliminary result?"

"We should know by this evening whether the dead woman was related to the Ahlbin couple, and that should really be all we need. If not, we'll have to try to find some of Karolina's DNA in her flat, so they've got something to match to their test sample. But I think we can be pretty sure the tests will prove it wasn't Karolina who died."

"That'll put the cat among the pigeons," Alex muttered.

"I found the officers who went to the hospital at the time of Karolina's death. They didn't see any reason to mistrust her sister's statement, so all they did was speak to the nursing staff and the ambulance crew. Since the autopsy didn't show up anything odd, they didn't pursue the matter."

This was a highly questionable statement in many ways, as Alex and Fredrika both knew. It exasperated them that such a vital detail in the case had passed so many people by.

"We need to issue their descriptions, both of them," said Fredrika, meaning Karolina and Johanna Ahlbin. "We know it was Johanna who came with the woman in the ambulance, and if she deliberately misidentified a stranger as her dead sister, then she's got some explaining to do in this murder inquiry."

Alex smiled.

"And what's our justification for issuing Karolina's description?"

Fredrika laughed.

"We're worried about her?"

Alex found that he was laughing, too. For as long as there was such friction between Peder and Joar and for as long as Fredrika seemed stable and not desperately short of sleep, he preferred her company to the men's. Maybe he was imagining it, but her pregnancy seemed to have brought a degree of harmony with it. Or perhaps it was just that she had too many other things to think about to be quite as spiky in the office.

Alex's mobile rang. It was Peder.

"Tony Svensson got very worked up when I confronted him with that new information," he blurted out. "He said he hadn't fucking well rung any copper to grass up

Ronny Berg."

"And you believe him?" asked Alex, on tenterhooks.

"Oh yes," came Peder's reply. "But that doesn't rule out them being in contact for some other reason."

"They did have contact, that's for sure," said Alex. "Did you give him Viggo Tuvesson's name? Ask if he knew him?"

"No," said Peder. "I didn't see there was any need to give away the name at present, while we know somebody's threatening Tony, and don't know what this Viggo is up to. I just asked if he had any contacts in the city police and he said he didn't. Not in the Norrmalm district or anywhere else."

"Excellent," said Alex. "Excellent."

He ended the call and turned to Fredrika.

"Bother. It looks as if that cop is mixed up in something shady after all."

Fredrika had been right: Muhammed Abdullah's wife was not at all happy about their visit. This time there was no tea and biscuits, and the flat was full of people when they got there. It took Fredrika several minutes of diplomatic groundwork before the woman agreed to speak to them briefly in the kitchen, just the three of them.

Her body language signaled nothing but

mistrust and animosity as she sat down at the kitchen table. Fredrika could see she had been crying, but she remained composed throughout the interview.

"I told him to be careful, and not to talk to you," she said, her voice trembling. "But he wouldn't listen."

"What made you think he needed to be careful?" Fredrika cautiously asked.

"Yusuf never got here," she said, presumably referring to the man run over at the university. "We waited and waited but he never got in touch. Then I knew, I just knew there was something wrong with the so-called network that helped him get over here."

"Your husband had his own contacts for that sort of thing, didn't he?" Alex gently prompted.

"Contacts, yes, but he was never part of the organization himself," the widow said adamantly. "It would have been far too risky."

"Did he talk to any of his contacts about the new network?" Fredrika asked.

The widow shook her head.

"No," she said. "Never. Yusuf had told us it all had to be very secret. So when he went missing, we were really worried."

"Did you or your husband ever receive

threats of any kind?" asked Alex.

"No," the widow said quietly. "Not as far as I know, anyway."

Alex thought about this. Jakob Ahlbin was sent threats before he was murdered, and someone had perhaps even tried to bargain with him. But Muhammed Abdullah was shot practically on the open street, with no warning.

"I've been through my husband's emails and post," said the widow. "I didn't find anything there."

"And his mobile?"

She shook her head.

"He had it with him when he went out and I haven't seen it since."

This made Fredrika and Alex feel uneasy, because the police had not found a mobile on Muhammed Abdullah when they searched the body.

"What made him go out last night?" asked Fredrika.

"Muhammed got a phone call," the widow said. "When we were watching TV. It only lasted about thirty seconds and then he said he had to go out and see to something."

"Did he tell you who had rung?"

"No, but it wasn't unusual. Sometimes one of his contacts would ring and he'd have to go and see them at short notice. I never asked about it. For the children's sake, it seemed better for only one of us to be involved."

Fredrika could sympathize with that. But it did not bode well that the mobile had vanished. They could always look at the pattern of calls to and from that number, of course, but without the phone itself there was no way of telling if he had received messages or threats by text.

"And when did you realize something was wrong?"

"After a couple of hours. He wasn't usually gone that long when he went to see his contacts."

"And you rang the police?"

"Yes, but he hadn't been gone long enough for them to take any action, they said. So after ten, I went out to see if he'd taken the car when he went out, or gone on foot . . ."

Her voice fell away and she swallowed hard, several times.

"But you didn't find him?" Fredrika said gently.

The widow shook her head.

"But I must have been out there just about the time he died."

As she went on, hearing her words inflicted almost physical pain: "I was there when they found him this morning. He was lying facedown in the snow. The first thought that came into my head was that he'd catch cold if he stayed there like that."

The woman's dark eyes were glittering with tears but she did not cry. Grief had so many faces and expressed itself in so many different ways. Sometimes it even made people beautiful.

Peder Rydh went over and over his notes from his latest interview with Tony Svensson. Thoughts came and went like stray guests in his head.

It seemed incontrovertible that Tony Svensson and the Sons of the People had had a major clash with Jakob Ahlbin. It seemed equally clear that that conflict had been resolved, and that the person in dispute with Jakob Ahlbin when he died was Ronny Berg, now in Kronoberg Prison. But Ronny Berg had an alibi for the time of the double murder, which meant that if he was behind it, he must have hired someone to carry it out. And that did not sound very plausible.

In parallel, he had to consider the anomalies surrounding Karolina Ahlbin's death, the alleged trigger for an act of desperation on the part of her father. What the hell would their next step be if it turned out not to be Karolina who had died?

Peder racked his brain. The group had made certain basic assumptions. For example, the fact that the threats sent to Jakob Ahlbin not from the Sons of the People email account but from computers other than Tony Svensson's had a direct link to his subsequent murder.

But need that be the case? wondered Peder. Maybe it was a red herring.

The third one in a row, if so. It wasn't suicide and it wasn't Tony Svensson and the SP. And maybe it wasn't the mystery emailer, either.

But that couldn't be right. It must all hang together, even if for the time being it was impossible to see how.

Fredrika had drawn her colleagues' attention to the fact that the mystery emailer seemed to know his Bible, and well enough to use it to make allusions that would provoke the recipient.

So could there be a link to the church?

Peder had a strange feeling in the pit of his stomach. And what about the man run over outside the university who was now, via the murdered Muhammed Abdullah, tenuously linked to the Ahlbin murder case as well? How did he fit into the picture?

Alex had given Peder and Joar a quick account of Fredrika's latest idea. Her theory that the victims were being silenced so they would not reveal a highly sensitive secret. A classic motive, but Peder could not for the life of him see what secret could be so big that it was worth murdering several people for.

He decided to backtrack a little. He could hear Joar out in the corridor, talking in a warm voice to someone he was clearly on very close terms with. Peder pressed his fingers to his temples, trying to keep his thoughts in check. If he let himself think about Pia Nordh now, all would be lost. He stared intently at his notes from the last Tony Svensson interview.

One phrase leaped out at him.

It's not somebody like me you're looking for, you fucking numbskulls.

The words had been Tony's response to Peder and Joar's suggestion that he look at some police pictures to pick out the person who had forced him into the conspiracy against Jakob Ahlbin. What was he getting at? Peder's pulse started to race. Tony was intimating that the police would not have a picture of that person on file because he was not a known criminal, unlike Tony himself. The words *not somebody like me* took on a different significance if you let your imagination range more freely. Not somebody like me . . . but somebody like you. Was that what he was hinting at? So a police officer did figure in this investigation after all.

And various clergymen.

It was hard to think of categories of people who had less in common with Tony Svensson than those two.

Peder brought up the telephone lists on his computer screen. Tony Svensson had indeed rung Viggo Tuvesson, on three occasions, but had never been rung by him. Not on that phone, anyway. What was more, all three calls were made after Svensson stopped emailing Jakob Ahlbin and someone else took over. Peder brought up more lists, this time Svensson's overall call log. Had he been rung from some other number in the crucial period that they could link to Viggo?

The group's administrator had done sterling work and identified the most frequently occurring numbers. But there were also lots of calls from mobiles with unregistered pay-as-you-go accounts, and it was impossible to say who owned or was using them. Svensson had been contacted from fifteen such numbers in the past month. Maybe one of them belonged to the man —

or woman — who had approached him and forced him into the role of double-dealer? Maybe a policeman, or maybe a vicar. Someone who was not like Svensson.

Peder closed the Excel files of phone numbers. He would have to start all over again and take a fresh approach. Just then, Joar knocked at his door. Peder did not say a word, but glared as crossly as he could.

"Surveillance rang," Joar said curtly. "We were right: Tony Svensson's daughter's as free as a bird. He went straight round to her school."

"Good," said Peder, equally curtly.

"And he made two calls when he was with his daughter."

Peder was in suspense.

"One was to the girl's mother, his ex, and the other was to an unregistered mobile."

Peder sighed. What had he expected?

"But we were at least able to tell roughly where the owner of the phone was when he took the call, and the record of calls and connections to phone masts told us where he'd spent his day."

"And where was that?" asked Peder, on the edge of his seat.

"Here in Kungsholmen. In the area of, or indeed in, the Kronoberg block."

"In Norrmalm police station, for example?"

Joar smiled.

"Hard to say, but yes, maybe even there."

On the way back from Skärholmen, Fredrika Bergman had an idea.

"Could we go out to Ekerö and have a look at the daughters' house?"

"Why?" asked Alex with a look of surprise.

"Because I haven't had a chance to see it yet," was Fredrika's simple answer. "And I think it would help me to understand Karolina and Johanna better."

"So you feel sure both of them are implicated in the murder of their parents?" Alex asked curiously.

Fredrika put both hands on her stomach.

"Perhaps," was all she said.

Alex rang the prosecutor and got verbal permission to make a follow-up visit to the house, so they went via HQ to pick up the copy of the house key that the technical boys had made since the last visit. Half an hour later, they pulled up outside the house.

Alex frowned as they got out of the car.

"Somebody's been here," he said, pointing to parallel tire tracks in the snow, which was just beginning to thaw.

"Aren't they the ones you made last time you were here?" Fredrika asked.

"No, they're from a different car," said Alex, starting to take pictures of the tracks with the camera in his mobile phone.

Fredrika looked around her, breathing in the cool air and appreciating the silence.

"It's a lovely place," she said out loud.

"No doubt it was even nicer before," said Alex, putting his phone away. "There used to be a meadow here," he said, pointing to the neighboring property. "But the local council sold it off for development, of course."

"A meadow," repeated Fredrika, and a dreamy look came into her eyes. "Must have been pretty idyllic, growing up here."

Alex went ahead of her to the house. The snow was compacted under his feet. The lock grated when he turned the key and the door made a faint protest as he opened it.

"Well, here we are, do come in," he said to Fredrika, standing aside to let her go first.

It was always fascinating to go into someone else's home. Fredrika had been along on a number of house searches and often found herself starting to fantasize about the people who lived in the house or apartment. Whether they were happy or unhappy, poor or rich. Sadly enough, the reason for the police being there was often all too obvious to see. The home sent out signals of misery or social exclusion, and the dust lay thick on every surface.

The Ahlbin sisters' house was not one of those. It felt homely and welcoming, even though it was clearly only a holiday place. Alex seemed busy with something in the kitchen, so Fredrika took a tour of the rooms, first downstairs and then upstairs. All the beds were made up, but under the heavy bedspreads the sheets smelled of damp. The wardrobes were empty apart from a few items of casual wear, all in Jakob Ahlbin's size. The rooms were tastefully uncluttered but the furnishings still managed to be personal. Fredrika's eye came to rest on a pressed flower in a frame, hanging on the wall. She had to go closer to see it properly. A pressed daisy, so old and brittle that it looked as though it might disintegrate any moment. All alone on an otherwise bare wall.

I wonder why? thought Fredrika, moving on to the next room.

She looked at all the family photos hanging on the walls and standing on chests of drawers, and all the toys and children's shoes that must have belonged to the girls when they were little. Just as her male colleagues had done, she noted Johanna Ahlbin's disappearance from the pictures. She was in them, and then suddenly she wasn't.

Was it symbolic? she asked herself. Did Johanna come to be seen as a less important part of the family? And if so, why? Or was it she who broke with the rest of them?

Fredrika started going through the pictures systematically. First the upstairs ones and then those on the ground floor. She took down the frames, opened them, and checked the back of each photo for any dates or annotations. She was pleased to see that whoever framed the pictures had been very methodical, identifying virtually all of them.

Jakob, Marja, Karolina, and Johanna, autumn '85.

Jakob and Johanna laying up the boat for the winter, '89.

Marja and Karolina when the well froze, '86.

Fredrika was so engrossed in the operation that she did not hear Alex come up behind her.

"What are you doing?" he asked, making her jump.

"Look," she said, holding out one of the photos. "Someone's dated them all."

Alex followed her long, agile fingers with fascination as she silently opened up frame after frame. When she had finished, it was impossible to tell that every frame had been taken down, opened, and then put back together again.

"In 1992, something changes," she said with conviction, clapping her hands to get the dust off.

She pointed to one of the photos.

"Here," she said. "The family celebrating midsummer 1992. It seems to have been the last midsummer they were all here."

She waved a hand along the top row of pictures.

"They were here every year from the time Karolina was born. It seems to have been just them, nobody else. Just Jakob, Marja, and the girls."

Alex took down the 1992 picture with a thoughtful expression.

"According to Elsie and Sven Ljung, this was about the time Jakob stopped hiding the refugees," he said.

"Yes, you're right," said Fredrika. "But we weren't really told why."

"No," said Alex, hanging the picture back on the wall.

His pregnant colleague raised her magic finger again and pointed.

"This is the other time," she said. "The other one Elsie mentioned."

Alex looked at the picture.

"It's the last picture Johanna's in, taken in

2004, which just fits. A family barbecue in the garden."

"What happened in 2004?" asked Alex.

"That was when Jakob Ahlbin started talking about going back to hiding refugees. Which apparently upset Johanna a great deal. And then Sven and Jakob fell out after Sven suggested Jakob could make some money out of the operation."

"Christ," muttered Alex. "Capitalizing on human misery, what the hell made him think that was such a great idea?"

The pine floor creaked beneath their feet as they moved to and fro along the wall.

"This was where it started, with his refugees in the basement," Alex said. "I just can't get my head round how, though."

Fredrika shivered.

"We've simply got to find Johanna Ahlbin now," she said. "It feels to me as if time's running out."

"I feel the same," Alex said grimly. "As if we're heading for a bloody meltdown and can't lift a finger to save the situation."

Fredrika did up her jacket, which she had left undone while they were going round the house.

"But at least we know now when it all started," she said. "This was where the Ahlbin family fell apart and this was where someone came to get the murder weapon. It all started here, in 1992."

Daylight was fading by the time Alex and Fredrika got back to Kungsholmen. Alex often thought how senseless it was that it got dark in the middle of the afternoon for large parts of the year. And then never got dark in the summer. There was no balance at these latitudes, he thought.

He called his group together for a quick update before they all went home. Fredrika had to slip straight out again to take a call.

"If nobody has any objections, I'd like to start by declaring the rightwing extremist angle defunct, and dropping it," he began.

Nobody objected.

"The only thing of value we've learned about the extremists and the threats from Tony Svensson and Sons of the People is that they came to someone else's attention, and that person then exploited the dispute between SP and Jakob Ahlbin to conceal his own crime," Alex concluded.

He was about to go on when the door burst open and Fredrika came in with a look of triumph.

"Tell us, then," said Alex.

Peder pulled out a chair for Fredrika to sit on, keen to have her on his side of the table rather than Joar's. Joar pulled a face and Alex suppressed a sigh.

"A simple blood test proved that the woman, the drug addict, can't possibly be related to Marja and Jakob."

"Well, well . . ." began Peder.

"Which at least in theory rules out her being Karolina Ahlbin. I mean, she could be adopted or something. Not that it's likely, but the hospital wanted to make sure it had covered itself this time. So they did what they should have done from the word 'go': asked for copies of her dental records. And no — the woman *wasn't* Karolina Ahlbin."

"Bloody incredible," said Joar, tossing his pen onto the table.

Alex looked in his direction. He could not recall having heard him swear before. Peder sent him a look, too, but not a sharp one.

He's already seen that side of him, thought Alex. I'm the one not keeping up.

Peder's mobile rang and he hastily switched it off.

"My brother," he said. "He's been ringing all day, he just keeps on."

"If you want a word with him, do feel free to pop out," said Alex, who was aware of Jimmy's situation but kept it to himself.

Peder shook his head firmly.

"Then we know for sure that Karolina's sister deliberately identified another woman as her sister," Alex said. "But we haven't heard from Karolina despite the fact that the news of her parents' deaths is splashed all over the newspapers."

He paused.

"So what does that tell us?"

"Either she's dead, or for some reason she can't get in touch. Maybe she's being held somewhere, against her will?" said Peder.

"Or she's in on the conspiracy," said Joar.

Fredrika cleared her throat.

"There's got to be some reason for her to go along with being declared dead, as it were. We've been to her flat and it looks as if it's been standing empty for weeks."

"But wasn't she missed at work?" queried Ellen, who seldom said anything at the meetings.

"She's a freelance journalist," replied Fredrika. "Or trying to be. She wasn't doing very well out of it financially, if her latest tax return's anything to go by. Which ties in quite well with the profile of her as a drug addict, incidentally."

"Be that as it may, someone's gone to a lot of trouble — with or without her consent — to build up a story round her death," observed Joar. "But why?"

"To make the next death, that is, the Ahlbins' so-called suicide, more plausible," suggested Peder.

"Or to kill two birds with one stone?" said Fredrika, brainstorming. "If we go back to our working hypothesis that Jakob was murdered to keep him quiet, maybe there was good reason to keep Karolina quiet, too. Various informants have told us how close she was to her father."

Alex sighed and kneaded his face with his hands.

"But why Marja?"

Nobody responded.

"Why do you also kill the wife of the man you're trying to silence? And the argument that the murderer was taken by surprise to find her at home doesn't hold water, because he could just have taken care of Jakob some other time."

"Maybe it was urgent?" Peder said. "And if you want it to look like suicide, there aren't that many places besides the victim's own home to choose from."

"What about the suicide note?" asked Fredrika. "How did it look? Do we think it was written in advance, or what?"

"It was printed out from Jakob's computer," replied Joar. "The document had been saved onto the hard disk and it was dated the same day, and saved at about the time of the murder, according to the computer."

"Let's sketch ourselves a profile of the murderer," said Alex with a degree of excitement in his voice. "Someone stages the Karolina death on the Thursday. Someone goes out to Ekerö and gets into the house unnoticed to fetch the murder weapon. Someone goes round to Jakob and Marja's flat on the Tuesday with a plan all worked out, and shoots them both in the head after first forcing Jakob to sign his own suicide note. What conclusions can we draw from all that?"

Before anyone could say anything, he started answering his own question:

"One. The murderer knows the Ahlbin family extremely well. Two. The murderer has some level of access to the Ahlbins' flat and their daughters' house; he's patently been able to get into both without any visible damage to the front doors, and it's only in the latter case that someone could have let him or her in voluntarily. Three."

Alex paused.

"Three. The murderer must have known the family for some time, since he or she was able to play on both Jakob's state of health and the fact that Karolina was the daughter he was closest to."

He stopped.

"Four," said Fredrika. "The murderer thought — or at least had reason to think — that Karolina Ahlbin wouldn't come forward and reveal that she wasn't really dead."

The others looked at her.

"Quite right," Alex said slowly, with a nod of approval, but Peder just looked confused.

"Why didn't they just kill her?" queried Alex. "If it was vital for her to disappear, and I think we can assume it was, why not get her out of the way permanently?"

Fredrika went pale.

"Maybe they did. Maybe that's why we haven't heard from her."

Joar shook his head.

"No, that doesn't make sense. Why go to the bother of killing her twice? Why not do away with her straightaway and then use her actual death to explain why Jakob killed his wife and then himself? To my way of thinking, it seems much more plausible that

449

she was in on the plot."

"Because there was no opportunity, or because she's part of the setup," Alex declared. "Nothing else fits."

"In view of her good relations with her father," said Fredrika with her head on one side and a hand resting on her stomach, "perhaps the most likely answer is that they couldn't get hold of her when they needed to kill her."

"True," said Alex. "But that still leaves us with the question: Where was she then, and where is she now? Have we talked to many of her friends?"

"We haven't had time yet," said Peder, sounding tired. "We haven't been treating it as a priority, because we thought she was dead, plain and simple. And it's been quite hard to track them down; we haven't had access to her phone records or emails. And she's got no formal place of work, either, has she?"

"If we tell the media we're looking for her and issue a description, we're going to look like idiots," said Alex, thinking hard about what best to do next. "But I wouldn't mind betting it'll leak out anyway."

"Not if we keep a tight lid on things," objected Joar.

"If it doesn't leak out from here, it will

from the hospital," Alex said wryly. "There's not a chance it won't be out by the end of the evening."

Fredrika leaned forward.

"So let's preempt them," she said.

"How?"

"We hold a press conference," she said. "Then we're first with the news. Classic media logic. If you want ownership of how a story's presented and followed up, you have to be the one to break it."

Alex looked in Ellen's direction. It was going to be a long working day.

"Can you get together with the information department and write a press release? Meanwhile, I'll try to get some support for this among the higher echelons."

He looked at his watch again.

"Say we'll hold it two hours from now, at six. Until then let's all try to make sure nothing leaks out."

Media training was evidently increasingly popular these days, but any opportunities of that kind had unfortunately passed Alex Recht by. So he felt pretty lost when he took his place on the platform for the meeting with the press.

He made a short statement of which the gist was: The police had received new information to prove beyond doubt that it was not Jakob and Marja Ahlbin's daughter who had died the Thursday before they were found shot dead in their flat. It would therefore be appreciated if anyone with any information about the current whereabouts of either Karolina or Johanna Ahlbin could come forward. Neither of them was suspected of any crime; the police merely wanted their help in order to reach a better understanding of the circumstances surrounding their parents' deaths.

"But what about Johanna?" asked one of the reporters. "How can you not suspect her of any crime? She must have known it wasn't her sister that she came to hospital with and identified."

Alex took a sip of water even though he was not in the least thirsty.

"That's just the kind of point we need the opportunity to clarify," he said, trying to sound authoritative. "We need to know exactly what the circumstances were that led to an unknown woman being identified as Karolina Ahlbin a week ago."

Fredrika was standing right at the back, observing her boss throughout the short press conference. On the whole she thought he made a pretty good job of it.

Just as Alex was winding up the conference, her mobile vibrated in her jacket pocket. She quickly left the room so she could speak undisturbed.

A faint hope of it being Spencer crept over her from nowhere. They had not been in touch with each other that day and she was missing him.

To hell with that, she thought wearily. Missing Spencer was like wishing for a white Christmas. If it happens, it happens, but it's not worth getting your hopes up.

When she was able to answer the phone, it wasn't Spencer, of course, but a colleague from the national CID. He introduced himself as one of the investigators working on the series of security van robberies to which the man Yusuf, run over at the university, could be linked.

"We've found something that I thought you'd like to know about," he said.

Fredrika was all ears.

"When the case came to us, we did another scene-of-crime investigation," he said, "and we found a mobile phone with the dead man's prints on. It was almost twenty-five meters from the body, so it was probably flung out of his jacket pocket when the car initially rammed into him."

There was a crackle on the line; reception was not very good just where Fredrika happened to be standing.

"We took all the information off it and got hold of details of the calls made to and from it, from the phone company. It had only been used a few times, and in all cases the incoming calls were from unregistered pay-as-you-go accounts."

"Yes?"

There was a sound of paper rustling.

"Sven Ljung," he said eventually.

"Sven Ljung?" Fredrika echoed in astonishment.

"Yes, he's the listed subscriber to the phone which the hit-and-run victim's mobile had been in touch with. It was Ljung he rang; two short calls."

Fredrika was thinking furiously, trying to fathom how it all fitted together.

"When were these calls to Sven Ljung made?"

"Two days before the robbery was committed."

Fredrika took a deep breath. The circle appeared to be closing, but she still did not understand what she had in front of her.

"Oh, there's one other thing," said the detective. "We were able to secure traces of metallic silver paint on the victim's clothes, which also happens to be the color of Sven Ljung's Mercedes."

"Have you been able to match them?" asked Fredrika, suddenly unsure what was technically possible.

"We thought about that — it isn't necessarily significant, there are loads of cars that color, but when we discovered Sven Ljung had reported his car stolen the evening before the murder took place, we thought it was all getting more interesting."

Thoughts were whirring round in Fredrika's head and anything to do with Spencer found itself relegated to a kind of mental waiting room.

"Have you spoken to him? Sven Ljung, that is?" she asked, her voice husky with suspense.

"Not yet, but we're working on it," replied the detective.

They had a few more exchanges about the likelihood of Sven Ljung being an accessory to the hit-and-run murder, and thus possibly also the murder of Jakob and Marja. Then they ended the call and Fredrika pocketed her phone.

People came crowding out of the room she had just left. The press conference was clearly over. Then her phone rang again.

Spencer, thought Fredrika automatically.

She was wrong again.

"This is very peculiar," said her contact in

the technical division. "I checked Jakob Ahl-bin's emails again and he had one from his daughter, several days after she died. As if she was still alive."

Fredrika gripped her phone tightly.

"From which daughter?" she asked, quietly so none of the reporters would hear what she was saying.

"From Karolina," said the technician, sounding baffled. "But she's dead, isn't she?"

Fredrika ignored his objection.

"Can you read me out the email, please?" she said.

Dad, sorry to have to tell you this by email, but I get no answer when I try ringing your mobile. It's all a complete disaster here. Stuck in Bangkok in a terrible fix. Need help right away. Please answer as soon as you get this! Love, Karolina.

Bangkok. So it was Karolina who tried to ring her mother. Fredrika felt tears coming into her eyes.

"So she didn't know," she whispered, mainly to herself.

"Hello?" the technician broke in. "It can't have been Karolina who sent the email, can it? Because she's dead."

In Fredrika's head there was only one answer to his question:

"Lazarus."

BANGKOK, THAILAND

Still oblivious of her own death and resurrection, Karolina Ahlbin boarded a flight from Bangkok to Stockholm later that evening. Paralyzed by the belief that she was returning to her home city to bury her entire family, she was scarcely able to feel the pressure of the situation facing her. According to the smuggler, a nationwide alert had been issued and her picture had been in all the Thai newspapers. So she could not leave the flat and had to resign herself to being cut off from the flow of news about the murder of her parents and sister in Sweden.

Her ally, the people smuggler, had worked fast since she asked him for help. But he freely admitted that it was a tricky challenge. His usual modus operandi when helping migrants get from Bangkok to Sweden was to get hold of the passport of an individual as similar in appearance to the migrant as possible. If the migrant traveled in possession of a genuine passport indicating citizenship in an EU country, there was nothing to prevent them entering Europe.

The fact that there was a widespread trade in passports was not much help to Karolina's smuggler. The passports he was able to buy on the secondhand market were those not of Swedish citizens with blond hair and blue eyes but of people originally from other countries. So when Karolina sought him out in desperation and begged for a way of leaving Thailand "in the next few days," he was faced with a problem. After a few hours of brooding, the smuggler decided the only thing to do was to identify a Swedish tourist who looked vaguely like Karolina and then steal her passport.

She scrutinized the picture suspiciously when he handed her the passport.

"You can't leave the country except in disguise, anyway," the smuggler assured her when he saw how downcast she looked. "They'll be on the lookout at the airport for you and anyone else wanted by the police. Change your hairstyle and color, and get some new glasses. At least then you'll have a shadow of a chance."

As mechanically as if she were a clockwork

toy, she took the steps he suggested. Cut her hair short and dyed it. Then she sat apathetically on the edge of the bed for hours. Now she had even lost her own appearance. And she still did not know why.

An hour later she was at the airport with the stolen passport in her pocket, feeling her pulse rate rise as she approached security and passport control. The airport was crawling with uniformed police and Karolina had to make a real effort to avoid eye contact with any of them. When she was finally waiting at her gate, her pulse slowed a bit at last and sorrow washed over her again.

I've lost everything, she thought emptily. My identity and my life, my freedom. And above all — my family. I've nothing and nobody to go home to. May the devil take whoever did this.

Sinking into her airline seat half an hour later and fastening her seat belt, she felt too exhausted even to cry. Her escape had become cold and mute.

And she was beyond all salvation.

I have become a nonperson. I have become the sort of person who feels nothing.

She leaned her head on the backrest and thought one last thought before sleep claimed her: God help me when I find out who did this. Because I can't be answerable for what I might do.

At another airport in a different part of the world, considerably nearer to Sweden, Johanna Ahlbin prepared to board a plane home to Stockholm, unaware that her sister was heading to the same destination on a different plane.

Her yearning for home intensified when she shut her eyes and pictured her beloved. The one who was always at her side, the one who had sworn never to leave her. He thought he was the stronger of the two of them, but in fact he was exactly as inferior as he had to be.

Her love for him was strong and solid, in spite of everything.

The only man she had ever let near her, the only one scarred enough to keep her secret without being terrified by it.

My darling prince of peace, she thought.

And she reached a decision, just as she heard the loudspeakers announce that all passengers were to fasten their safety belts and switch off their mobile phones.

She would ring the police straightaway and tell them she was on her way home. Once through to the switchboard, she asked for the man who had spoken at the press conference she had seen on TV earlier in the day.

"Alex Recht," she said. "Can you put me through to him at once? My name is Johanna Ahlbin. I think he's been waiting for my call."

■ ■ ■ ■

Tuesday,
March 4, 2008

■ ■ ■ ■

Stockholm

It was almost as if Alex sensed the moment he woke up that this was the day he would later look back on as the one that changed his life. At least that was how he would remember it, when everything was over and he was left alone: the certainty he felt in his body and mind the moment he opened his eyes, ten minutes before the alarm clock rang.

He got up quietly and crept out to the kitchen to make the first cup of coffee of the day. He could not even bring himself to look at Lena as he left the room. The very sight of her unyielding back was painful to him. When he got back from work the day before, she had been so tired that she could scarcely say a word to him. She said her head ached and went to bed before eight, just a few minutes after he came through the door.

But now it was morning and work drew

him on like a mirage in the desert. The memory of the call from Johanna Ahlbin, put through by the exchange just after seven the previous evening, made his heart beat faster. She had been very brief, apologizing for not getting in touch. And he had had some apologies of his own. For the fact that she had heard the news of her parents' death via the media. For the fact that they had not got hold of her in time. She assured him that she knew they had done their best and that it was partly her own fault. Which had enabled him to resume a rather sterner tone when he informed her that the police wanted to interview her as soon as possible.

"I'll come in tomorrow," she promised.

And now it was tomorrow.

He had just put on his coat when he realized Lena was there behind him in the hall. He gave a start.

"You scared me," he muttered.

She smiled, but her eyes were as lifeless as a stretch of frozen water.

"Sorry," she said feebly.

Clearing her throat, she went on: "We've got to talk, Alexander."

Had he not already known there was something awfully wrong, he would have known it then. Lena had only ever called him Alexander once before, and that was the very first time they met.

He knew instinctively that he did not want to hear what she had to say.

"We'll do it this evening," he said, opened the front door, and went out onto the doorstep.

"This evening's fine," she said in a muffled voice.

He closed the door behind him without saying good-bye, and went to the car. And on the other side of the door, just as he turned the key in the ignition and revved the engine, Lena sank to the floor and started sobbing, and could not stop for a long time. In that moment at least, there was no justice for either of them.

Fredrika had started to worry something was wrong, and anxiety took up permanent residence inside her mind. She was still sleeping well at nights, but sleep was bringing her neither the harmony nor the rationality she had expected, just more energy for brooding. Spencer had answered when she phoned him the previous evening, but sounded distracted and said little, beyond the unexpected news that he was going away and would not be back until Wednesday evening. He would not be able to see her before then, or to talk on the telephone. He had scarcely touched on where he was going, and had ended the call rather abruptly by wishing her a good night, saying they would speak again soon.

Naturally her pregnancy was making her emotions more volatile than usual, but Spencer's change in behavior unsettled her for other reasons, too. Perhaps it had been a mistake to take him round to her parents' after all? He would hardly have suggested it himself. But on the other hand, the weekend dinner date had had a more or less miraculous effect on her mother, whose comments about the baby and its father were now exclusively positive whenever Fredrika spoke to her.

Was it perhaps the need to dampen down her anxiety that sent her off to work early that morning? At any rate, by half past seven she was already there. The team's corridor was deserted, but she could tell that both Peder and Joar were in. She decided to go and see Peder.

"Anything from the national CID on Sven Ljung yet?"

"No, they're waiting until they've got in some of the other information they're trying to assemble."

"What are they waiting for?"

Peder sighed.

"Bank account transactions, for example. It's always worth checking if there's money tied up in these things."

Fredrika went to her office, and Joar came in after her.

"Interesting email from our friend Lazarus yesterday," he said, meaning Karolina Ahlbin. "Particularly in the light of the fact that her sister finally made herself known later on in the evening."

"Certainly is," agreed Fredrika, taking off her coat and leaning forward to switch on her computer.

"Though it could be an attempt to put us off the track. Karolina trying to look innocent."

"The question is what she'd be trying to look innocent *of,* and to *whom,*" said Fredrika.

"Drug offenses," supplied Joar.

"What?"

"New information's come in by fax from the Swedish embassy in Bangkok after our press conference. They're six hours ahead of us over there."

Fredrika took the sheet of paper Joar held out to her and read it with growing surprise.

"Has anybody rung this Andreas Blom, who apparently interviewed her when she went to the embassy for help?" she asked.

"No," said Joar. "We left it until you got here."

"I'll ring straightaway," said Fredrika, reaching for the phone even as she spoke.

She glanced over the fax again as she waited for an answer. Karolina Ahlbin was evidently known to the Thai police as "Therese Björk."

Maybe she preferred Therese to Lazarus, Fredrika thought exasperatedly.

Peder was given a special dispensation to postpone his session with the psychologist for a few more days. He ended the call to HR boss Margareta Berlin with a feeling of relief. She sounded more reasonable now, but he had no time to stop and analyze whether it was because he sounded different himself.

Ylva texted to say that his son was much better. He felt another surge of relief and replied that he was glad to hear it. He had scarcely put down his mobile before it bleeped again.

Why not come over and eat with me and the boys tonight, if you've got time? The boys are asking for you. Ylva.

Without thinking he fired off a reply:

470

Good idea! Will try to be there by six latest!

He regretted sending the message the instant it had gone. How the hell could he promise to be anywhere by six — he hadn't the faintest idea how the Ahlbin case might develop in the course of the day.

Damn. His veneer of feigned cool cracked to reveal the disintegration underneath. And he thought those most forbidden of words: *Nothing's ever going to work in the long run. Not with any woman. I've got to make my mind up.*

It was unclear to him at that moment quite what it was he had to make up his mind about. But he knew it was not a healthy sign that he viewed dinner with his own family as an imposition, an inconvenient duty. As if work was the only soul mate he wanted in his life.

Furious for no reason, he grabbed the phone again and rang one of his contacts in the CID who was dealing with the double murder on Sunday night.

"Anything new on the Haga Park murder?" he asked.

"No, not a thing. So we thought we'd release the victim's picture to the media and hope somebody recognized him."

471

"No match for the prints either?"

"Not a whiff. But we might have something else. Or in fact — we *have* got something else."

Peder was listening.

"Sven Ljung's car was found just outside Märsta by a woman out for an early morning walk."

"Bingo!" cried Peder, with more enthusiasm in his voice than he had first intended.

"Don't get too bloody carried away," said the other detective. "The car was set on fire and it'd been burning a fair while by the time we got there."

Peder's spirits plummeted. A burned-out car would mean very few clues.

"Well, at least it means we know there must be some link to the case, or cases," he said determinedly. "Otherwise the person who took it would hardly have bothered to set fire to it."

"Probably not," his CID colleague agreed. "And there's another thing we've found out."

"What's that?" Peder asked.

"That it was very probably used as a getaway car after the security van jobs, not just the one in Uppsala but also the one the media reported in Västerås over the weekend. In the Uppsala case we've nothing more to go on than some witness statements that it was a silver metallic car, but in Västerås we got bits of the registration number, and they tallied with Ljung's."

Peder rang off with a lingering sense of achievement. Sven Ljung's car seemed to be implicated in robberies as well as murders. The net was closing and Peder smiled.

It was afternoon in Bangkok by the time Fredrika got hold of Andreas Blom. He sounded troubled, to say the least, and expressed great concern at the information on the desk in front of him.

"The really distressing thing," he said in his lilting Norrland accent, "is that she sat here insisting that her name was Karolina Mona Ahlbin. And that she needed a new passport because she'd been robbed in the street. But when I rang the Swedish tax authorities, it turned out to be impossible that she was who she claimed to be, because the woman with that name and that personal identity number was deceased."

"Didn't it strike you as odd that she was able to come out with another person's name and ID number, just like that?"

"Good Lord, I did what I could. And it's not that unusual for people in her situation to use double identities."

Fredrika's brain attempted to rearrange itself into accepting the idea of Karolina Ahlbin as a drug addict after all. In spite of the irregularities where her passport was concerned, the evidence was pretty overwhelming.

"What exactly — *exactly* — did she say her problem was?" she asked slowly.

"That she'd had all her valuables stolen, like money, passport, and plane tickets, and that she'd had a problem in the hotel where she'd been staying, and all her things had somehow vanished from her hotel room. Though she kept quiet about the hotel part to start with and didn't bring it up until I confronted her with our other information."

"Did you ring the hotel she claimed she'd been staying at? I don't mean the one where her luggage and the drugs were seized."

"Oh yes," said Andreas Blom. "But only after she'd left. And they weren't prepared to back up her story at all. They said she was lying and had come stumbling into their foyer saying she had been mugged and was a hotel guest. But none of the staff recognized her and she wasn't in their computer system."

"All right," Fredrika said in a measured tone. "All right, let's just see if we can tease this out . . ."

She broke off, realizing this was really a matter to discuss with a colleague rather than a diplomat in Thailand. She took a breath and carried on anyway.

"Why call the police if she was only hours from being declared wanted by them for drug offenses?"

"Pardon?" said Andreas Blom.

"The raid on the hotel where she was supposedly staying happened only hours after she left it. The time of her report of the mugging, according to what you faxed over, was more or less the same. Why would she contact the police and draw all that unnecessary attention to herself at such a critical juncture?"

"But if she really was robbed," began Andreas Blom, "then she needed a new passport to get home on . . ."

"Exactly. And she needed a copy of an official police report of a stolen passport before the Swedish embassy could help her get a new one. But why go to the police just then and not earlier?"

Andreas Blom went quiet.

"Yes, one might well ask," he conceded. When Fredrika did not respond he went on: "It isn't the embassy's business to take a view on the question of guilt; all we can do is offer a person in Karolina Ahlbin's position good advice."

"I do realize that," Fredrika said quickly, though she suspected that Karolina Ahlbin had not received the support she deserved.

She ended the conversation courteously and went back to her notes. She shuffled through the papers faxed over from Bangkok. A copy of the passport found in the hotel room that was said to be Karolina Ahlbin's. Therese Björk's. With Karolina's photograph in it. But how . . . ?

Fredrika rang Andreas Blom a second time.

"Sorry to bother you again. I just wanted to ask whether you've had a chance since then to take a closer look at the passport which you at the embassy thought was Karolina's, the one that was supposedly a Therese Björk's?"

"The Thai police have got it," replied Andreas Blom. "But we've been in contact with them since she disappeared and they've decided it's a forgery."

Fredrika thought about this. A young woman falsely declared dead in Stockholm who then turned up in Bangkok with a false passport, belonging to a person who had an officially registered ID in Sweden. Who would dare undertake such a plan?

Someone who knew Therese Björk was

not going to notice or have any objections to her identity being used to muddy some drug dealing in Thailand.

A suspicion had been born and was growing stronger with every passing second. It took her less than two minutes to get Therese Björk's personal details from the police address register. She learned that Therese was a year younger than Karolina Ahlbin and registered as living at her mother's address.

Following a hunch, Fredrika tapped Therese's personal identity number into the police database. She featured in a number of cases and had convictions for several minor crimes and misdemeanours. Fredrika moved on to the register of suspects. She came up there, too, suspected of assaulting a man she claimed was trying to rape her.

After a moment's hesitation she lifted the receiver and rang the number. She would just have time before the morning meeting in the Den. Someone picked up after the fifth ring.

"My name's Fredrika Bergman," said Fredrika. "I wonder if I could ask a few questions about your daughter Therese?"

For the first time in decades, he felt he was acting decisively and proactively in the issue that had come to color his entire adult life. Too many years had gone by already and his idea would probably turn out to have come far too late. But that was not the most important thing; Spencer Lagergren had made up his mind. And the journey he was now embarking on could only be made alone.

No one must know, he decided. At least, not until afterward.

He drove from Uppsala toward Stockholm and on to Jönköping. It looked as though the clouds might break and let a bit of sun through. A beautiful winter's day in early March. With some irony he noted that he had chosen a very attractive backdrop for his project.

His thoughts went involuntarily back to those early days with Eva. The sense of solidarity they had shared, the life's work they had decided to make a reality, these had no counterpart in his later life. There had been occasions when he had almost wondered if he ever loved her, but they were very few in number. Of course he had loved her, and it would be absurd to maintain anything different. The problem was that it was a love built on the unhealthiest of foundations. He had confused passion and attraction in a way that could be described as unsuccessful at best and disastrous at worst. As if you could build lifelong love on physical desire. As if you could retain physical desire when the party was over and the daily grind set in, when the body that had been a land of exploration and adventure became the most familiar domestic territory.

He found it impossible to remember which of them had relaxed their hold on the other first. There was so much of their past that he had chosen to lock into that basement room marked FORGOTTEN.

How could we do this to ourselves?

Most of the guilt indisputably lay at his father-in-law's door. Father-in-law knew Spencer's darkest secret, the secret so shameful that he had never admitted it to his parents or friends. The fact that he had discovered just before he got engaged that he had fathered the child another woman was expecting. That he had chosen to buy a house in another university town in another part of the country and shift his career from Lund to Uppsala. That he had let down the other woman even though there was still time to do the right thing, in favor of something that seemed more desirable.

The baby had never been born. Because of Spencer's weakness, its mother, Josefine, decided to abort it, which was still considered a sin in those days. By some irony of fate, or was it as a punishment, Spencer and his wife never had any children of their own. Three miscarriages were followed by years of fruitless trying. Until at last they had to face the fact that there would be no children. Perhaps it was even a kind of blessing, for by that stage they had long since stopped wanting any.

Then Fredrika came into his life. And he had actually let her down, too.

Spencer felt a lump come into his throat at the thought of her. That beautiful and intelligent woman who could have had who the hell she liked — if she had only believed in herself a bit more — but who had always come back to him.

Every time. Every time she came back to me.

Perhaps he should have said no. But then she should, too. And she could definitely have refrained from coming back.

We just couldn't, he thought. We just couldn't bring ourselves to say no to something that was so much better than what we already had. Loneliness.

"It's some years now since I stopped missing my daughter," Therese Björk's mother said simply.

As if it was the most natural thing in the world. As if there was some dividing line where parenthood ends and something else takes its place. Estrangement and discord.

"I do still love her," she said matter-of-factly. "And I cry in the evenings because she isn't with me any longer. But I don't miss her. She's made that impossible, you see."

Fredrika would really have preferred to go round and see Ingrid Björk personally. On reflection it felt like the wrong choice to have yielded to her impulse and picked up the phone. But Ingrid Björk's tone indicated that she did not mind. She could cope with a conversation about the most important person in her life over the phone.

I'm damn sure I couldn't, Fredrika

thought wearily. I don't seem to be able to cope with anything much at the moment.

"When did things start to go wrong?"

Ingrid Björk thought about it.

"Oh, early on, when she was in lower secondary school," she said confidently.

"That early?"

"Yes, I think so. Therese was such a restless spirit; there were things that seemed to leave her no peace. Her dad and I did our best to support her. But I'm sure it wasn't enough."

She went on talking about her daughter. About the little girl who grew up into an irresponsible teenager, out of control, and the body invaded by a disturbed mind. About her first boyfriend, who led her astray, and her first visit to the child psychiatrist. Years with a succession of psychologists and therapists, none of them ultimately able to save either the daughter, or her parents' marriage. She tried to describe how she had struggled to save her daughter from going under irrevocably, but was finally forced to admit that the project was doomed and she would never get her daughter back.

"That's the way I see it," she said gravely. "As if she's not mine any longer, because she belongs to her addiction."

"But she's registered as living with you,

isn't she?" Fredrika queried.

"I'm sure she is, but it makes no difference. I haven't seen her for ages. She stopped getting in touch when she realized she'd be getting no more money."

The words tore at Fredrika. Words intimating that children could be lost to you even if they were still alive were something alien in the world she knew.

"Why have you rung to ask me all these questions?"

Ingrid's question broke into her thoughts.

With agile fingers, Fredrika extracted the file from the bottom of the heap on her desk. The copy of the autopsy report on the person initially believed to be Karolina Ahlbin.

"Because I'm afraid I know exactly where your daughter is at this moment," she said in a subdued tone.

There was a rather febrile atmosphere in the Den when Fredrika came in at the last minute and took a seat at the table.

"Before this interview with Johanna Ahlbin, I want us all to try to identify the gaps and question marks in what we know, the ones we think she can help to clarify," said Alex. "I also want us all, as a team, to establish if there's anything we need to be aware of in the interview, any advantages we don't want to fritter away."

"I've been able to identify the woman we initially took to be Karolina Ahlbin," Fredrika announced, afraid Alex was going to race ahead at the same pace at which he had started, leaving her no opening.

The others looked up in surprise.

"The woman who died of an overdose almost two weeks ago was called Therese Björk. I've just been talking to her mother on the phone."

"Therese Björk?" echoed Joar. "The name Karolina Ahlbin was using in Thailand?"

"Yes."

Peder shook his head as if trying to make everything fall into place.

"What the hell does this mean?"

"Maybe that Karolina and Johanna staged the whole drama together," suggested Alex. "She'd hardly have given the Thai authorities that particular name otherwise."

"But she didn't," Fredrika snapped.

"Didn't what?"

"She didn't give that name herself; it was the embassy staff who confronted her with the details, which they got from the Thai authorities who'd seized the false passport."

"But why would she have a false passport with those details in it if she didn't know

485

who Therese Björk was?" asked Peder, looking lost.

"I don't know," Fredrika said with a look of exasperation. "Karolina flatly denied to the embassy people that she had ever stayed at the hotel the police raided."

"So you reckon she wasn't part of the conspiracy against Jakob Ahlbin, but more of a victim?" Joar said.

"Something like that," Fredrika said. "We'd already considered the possibility, hadn't we? That someone wanted to get her out of the way, I mean, but failed. That the intention all along was for her to die, but the murderer wasn't able to do the job, for some reason."

"So you're saying someone killed Therese Björk specifically in order to have Karolina Ahlbin declared dead in Sweden, while Karolina was put out of action where she was, in Thailand?" said Alex, sounding unconvinced.

Fredrika drank some water and nodded slowly.

"But why?" thundered Alex. *"Why?"*

"That's just what I think you should ask Johanna," said Fredrika. "She's the one who made the misidentification that set all this in motion, after all."

Peder shook his head again.

"What about Sven Ljung, then?" he said. "How do he and his car fit into all this?"

"Do they need to?" Fredrika persisted. "Maybe it's as just as we first thought, and these are two entirely unrelated cases."

"No way," said Joar. "There are just too many connections."

"But are there, really?" asked a skeptical Fredrika.

Her voice died away at the sound of Alex's fingers drumming on the table.

"There don't need to be that many for us to find them hard to ignore," he said, his eyes on Fredrika. "We're pretty sure Sven Ljung's car was involved in the Yusuf murder up at the university, and in the security van robberies in Uppsala and Västerås. And we know Yusuf was a friend of the man Muhammed in Skärholmen, and *he* had been in touch with Jakob Ahlbin."

"Who was found dead in his own flat by none other than Sven Ljung," finished Fredrika with a sigh. "I know, I know. He must have something to do with all this, I just don't get what."

"What have the national CID had to say about Sven Ljung?" Joar asked Peder with a frown. "How long are they thinking of waiting before they apply for an arrest warrant?"

Peder's face darkened as Joar addressed him.

Hmm, thought Fredrika. They still can't stand each other.

"They rang back just before the meeting," said Peder. "They reckon they'll have everything ready by the end of the morning, then they'll bring him in for a first interview this afternoon."

"From now on I want feedback on every move the CID make on this," Alex said doggedly, adding: "Peder, I want you to ask to sit in on the interview."

With the enthusiasm of a ragamuffin who has been tossed a large coin for opening a gate, Peder said he would ring them the minute the meeting was over.

"As far as interviewing Johanna Ahlbin goes," Alex went on, "I'd like Fredrika to come with me and take the lead on that."

Everything went quiet.

Just like it's always been, thought Fredrika. Stony silence whenever I get given some especially juicy task.

She knew what Alex would have to add for equilibrium to be restored, and sure enough, it was only a matter of seconds before he went on: "The primary reason for that, of course, is that it seems important to have a female colleague present when interviewing a young woman like Johanna."

Fredrika kept her eyes on Peder and Joar, awaiting their reaction. None came. It was only when Alex started speaking again that she thought she saw Peder's face twitch.

"But on top of that, Fredrika is as competent an interviewer as anyone else in this room. Just in case there's anybody here who misunderstood what I said to begin with."

Fredrika turned to Alex in astonishment, and he gave her a crooked grin.

Things are looking up, she thought, and the prospect made her feel quite dizzy.

Automatically, as in any other situation that made her feel happy or sad, she put her hand to her stomach. Only to realize that it was a long time since she had last felt the baby move.

Everything's fine, she thought quickly to stem the surging tide of worry she had just unleashed. It's just asleep.

So she forced herself to smile at Alex, despite her rising sense of apprehension and her continuing concern about why Spencer had gone off at such short notice.

The phone in her pocket vibrated silently, forcing her to pull herself together. She went briskly out of the room to take the call. It was the librarian in Farsta, ringing back.

"Sorry it took so long," the lady apologized.

"No problem," Fredrika forced herself to say.

"I've been through the lists for the time in question," the woman went on, and cleared her throat.

Fredrika waited tensely.

"Though I'm not sure this can be the person you want," the librarian said doubtfully. "It seems to have been a middle-aged lady at the computer you asked about."

"Oh," Fredrika said hesitantly. "Have you got a name or date of birth?"

"I've got both," the librarian said, with evident satisfaction. "The woman was born in January 1947 and her name is Marja. Marja Ahlbin."

Fredrika rushed back into the Den and stopped Alex, who was the last person leaving the room.

"It was Marja Ahlbin who'd booked the computer in Farsta that the email was sent from."

"Good God," exclaimed Alex.

Fredrika looked him straight in the eye.

"What if we've misjudged the whole wretched thing," she said. "What if Jakob really did shoot his wife, but in self-defense, and then couldn't live with what he'd done and wrote the suicide note?"

"And where would Karolina's death fit into that scenario?"

"I don't know," Fredrika admitted, starting a mental count of the number of times she had said those words in the past few days.

"We don't know a goddamn thing," snarled Alex. "And I'm getting mighty fed up with always being one step behind in this mess."

"And Marja's possible involvement in the threats to Jakob?"

"I haven't the least bloody idea at the moment," Alex muttered.

Fredrika frowned.

"I'll check that out, too," she said, sounding as determined as Alex had done.

"What?" he asked, confused.

"We know where the other emails that weren't from Tony Svensson's home computer were sent from," Fredrika replied. "A 7-Eleven convenience store. I'll check with Marja's phone provider to see if her mobile was in use in or near either of those locations at the appropriate times."

"You do that," said Alex. "And try to come up with the answers double quick. We need plenty of data to back us up when we confront Johanna Ahlbin."

"I know," said Fredrika. "Because she's the only one who can solve this case for us, that's for sure. Or her sister."

You seldom got a breakthrough early in an investigation, Peder Rydh had learned that over the years. But there was something very special about some of the cases he had worked on since he joined Alex's group. Something that made them develop very quickly, and then explode into an orgy of loose threads and leftover pieces of puzzle.

I like it, he thought reflexively. Hell, I don't think I could live without it.

He made sure he didn't even glance in Joar's direction as he went into his room and shut the door. Following Alex's instructions, he rang his contact in the national CID to ask how close they were to an arrest, and said he would like to be present at the interviews when they took place.

"We're bringing him in after lunch," said his contact. "We've had surveillance on him since last night; he and his wife seem to be lurking in their flat."

"Neither of them been out since yesterday?"

"Nope, doesn't look like it."

"Well, at least he's not trying to flee the country."

The CID man changed tack.

"We've had the information on Sven Ljung's private finances that we were waiting for," he said in a voice indicating there was more news to come.

Peder waited.

"It looks as if our friend Sven had real problems in the financial department in recent years. The flat's mortgaged up to the hilt — he remortgaged in December, in fact — and on top of all that he owes various loan companies a fair whack. He and his wife sold a holiday house two years ago and managed to make quite a packet, but that money seems to have disappeared."

Peder listened attentively. *Debts, Money. Always bloody money.* Was it that simple this time, too?

"But what do they live on, he and his wife?"

"Their pensions, basically."

"Nothing to splash about, in other words," observed Peder.

"That's putting it mildly," said the other investigator. "And his wife's got no assets to speak of, of course."

"But they did have that house," Peder reminded him.

"They certainly did." The other man chuckled. "And they made a decent profit there, a million kronor. And that money's all gone, too."

That's not all, Peder was thinking. We know where all the money's gone, we just can't remember at the moment.

"We're working on the hypothesis that Sven got into this whole robbery thing because his finances needed a boost and for no other reason," his colleague said.

"And what about the murder of that Yusuf, up at the university?"

"I suppose they wanted to get rid of their robber so they could brush it all under the carpet," came the simple answer.

Too simple.

"Which "they" would that be?" Peder asked dubiously.

The other man was starting to lose patience.

"Well, of course we don't think Sven Ljung set all this up on his own," he said in a slow, exaggerated way, as if talking to a child and not a trusted colleague.

"Have you come up with names for any of the other people involved yet?"

"We're working on it," said the other man. "We'll get back to you when we've got something."

Peder was about to hang up when he remembered another thing Alex had asked him to do:

"Keep an eye out for Marja Ahlbin in the investigation."

"But she's dead, isn't she?"

"Yes, but it's not impossible you'll find some earlier contact between them."

His mouth went dry as he said the words. Alex had told him that Marja was behind some of the threats to Jakob.

Marja and Sven, he thought. Was it your fault your families fell out?

As a little girl, Fredrika loved jigsaw puzzles. She had done her first thousand-piece jigsaw at the age of ten. As her grandfather put it, she had one heck of an eye for detail and a memory like an elephant.

"Magic," her mother called it, and stroked her hair.

Alex gave Fredrika fifteen minutes to engage in a bit of magic before they went down to meet Johanna Ahlbin. The new information from the CID was duly incorporated into the investigation, which had now been in progress for a week and seemed to be approaching some kind of resolution.

"It's gone quickly," said Alex.

Fredrika could not contradict him. It *had* gone quickly, and it brought a sense of relief to have got as far as an interview with the elusive Johanna Ahlbin.

Why did you leave them in the lurch? Fredrika wondered. And what the hell did your mother have to do with it all?

This last point took her breath away. To the extent that she had felt obliged to ring the library again and ask what their procedures were. The librarian was adamant. Anybody borrowing a computer for Internet use had to provide ID. That made it very improbable that it could have been anyone other than Marja who sent the email.

The technical division went through Marja's phone lists again and found that at one of the two other critical times she had been in the vicinity of the 7-Eleven store in question. Fredrika rang the store, but they had no way of checking who had been on a specific computer at any given time.

Circumstantial evidence, thought Fredrika. Sometimes that's as good as it gets.

If she excluded Marja's potential involvement in all that had happened, Johanna emerged as the most likely perpetrator. Her parents would have no hesitation in letting her into their home, and several of their informants had mentioned her problematic relationship with her father. And he somehow seemed to be the one all this was directed against. According to the supposed suicide note, it was Jakob and not Marja who fired the fatal shots. And it was Jakob who had been threatened, not Marja, though she might possibly have been the one issuing the threats.

A movement from the baby she was carrying interrupted her deliberations.

"God, how you scared me," whispered Fredrika, running both hands over her stomach.

Her eyes filled and it was hard to breathe. There was too much happening all at once. The baby, work, Spencer. She took a gulp of water and felt her body absorb the liquid. Permanently stressed and worried. Never satisfied for more than the occasional day.

The baby obviously had to be her priority. Spencer could be, if he tried a bit harder. She scrunched up a bit of paper fiercely and threw it into the bin. But the blessed man never did, did he? And now he was off on some sudden mission he refused to let her in on.

So I shan't give a damn about him for now, Fredrika decided, and went back to her notes.

She stared at the short list of questions she had drawn up for Johanna Ahlbin.

We were looking for her for several days, Fredrika thought, but we should have been looking for Karolina at the same time — or in fact even more urgently.

Where was Karolina now? Was she still in Thailand? And how did Thailand fit into the picture, anyway? At the embassy, Karolina had said that she was the victim of some kind of plot, that she most definitely was not Therese Björk, and that she had never set foot in the hotel where her possessions had been found in the raid.

Fredrika gathered up her papers and prepared to go down to Johanna Ahlbin. Another thought flashed through her mind as she closed the door of her room behind her.

Why had nobody else known Karolina was away, and reacted to the news of her death in Stockholm? Elsie and Sven had not questioned the fact that she was apparently still in the country. Nor had Ragnar Vinterman, nor Jakob Ahlbin's psychiatrist. Admittedly the police had not interviewed all that many of Karolina's own friends and acquaintances. But even once her name and fate were all over the media, no one came forward and told the police that Karolina was in fact abroad and could not possibly be lying dead at the hospital.

Why had she left the country on the quiet? Fredrika wondered. And when, if ever, would she be back?

Sudden insight made the ground sway beneath her feet for a moment. There was one person, someone they had discounted, who might just be able to answer those questions. Someone the police had never contacted because it had been dismissed as fruitless, but that person had been very close to Karolina.

She pushed open the door of her room again and thudded back down into her desk chair. It only took her a minute to find the number she was looking for. She waited patiently for an answer as it rang, and rang.

The snow started to fall a few hours before lunch. With tired eyes she watched the heavens through the window. The heavens, the place where the God who had failed her so often was said to be.

I got nothing out of loving You, she thought sullenly, feeling not a shred of fear.

Few people thought of her as old, but judgments of that kind could not have been more wrong. She *was* old, tired and unhappy after years of difficulties and complications. In those first times of trial she had turned to the church, and to the Lord who watched over them all, but in the end she had got so dreadfully tired of her prayers never being heard, so she stopped putting her hands together when it was time to pray in the services at church.

"He never listens," she whispered in response to her husband, when he discreetly tried to correct her.

At first they had argued about it, because her husband refused to accept the hard words she directed at their Lord.

"That's blasphemy," he hissed in her ear. "And in church, what's more!"

But what else could she do? The two sons she had borne, and initially seen as a blessing, had developed into a curse like a great bruise on her soul. She had expected them to grow up strong and be each other's closest friends, but they had turned out as different as Cain and Abel. And she scarcely saw either of them these days. She scarcely missed the elder, who had done his younger brother such harm. But the younger one. He had always been a bit weaker, a bit more lost, and a much kinder, better person than anyone else in the family; he had never really been able to cope with being perpetually in second place, overshadowed by his more successful brother.

I saw it too late, she thought as she watched the snowflakes fall from the gray sky. And now there's nothing I can do.

She was so deep in thought that she did not register his steps behind her.

"What are you looking at?"

"The devil himself," she said.

He gave a faint cough. His blue eyes sought out something else to look at, down in the street. They came to rest on a single car, parked by the pavement.

"They've been parked there since yesterday," he said, so quietly that she could not initially make out what he had said.

"Who?" she eventually asked, puzzled.

A tired finger was pointing at her.

"There's something we need to talk about," he said. "It's only a matter of time before the whole thing goes to hell."

She looked at him for a long time.

"I know," she said, feeling the tears welling up inside her. "I already know it all."

The first thing that struck Alex and Fredrika was that Johanna looked quite unlike her pictures in the Ekerö house. They were both taken aback to see the tall, attractive woman with long, fair hair waiting for them at the appointed time in the big lobby of the police building. Above all they were surprised by how calm and collected she seemed, these being qualities rarely revealed in photographs.

Not exactly the image of a woman who has just lost her entire family, thought Fredrika.

The moment Johanna took their hands and said hello seemed almost unreal. So many days' silence and suddenly here she was in front of them.

"I'm truly sorry to have been so hard to get hold of," she said as they went to the interview room Fredrika had booked. "But believe me, I've had my reasons for not

503

coming forward."

"And we'd very much like to hear them," said Alex, with a politeness in his voice that Fredrika could not remember hearing before.

They sat down at the table in the middle of the room. Fredrika and Alex on one side, Johanna Ahlbin on the other. Fredrika observed her with fascination. The high cheekbones, the large, enviably shapely mouth, the steely gray eyes. The beige top she was wearing was simply cut to fall straight from her broad shoulders. She had no jewelry except for a pair of plain pearl earrings.

Fredrika tried to interpret the young woman's expression. All she was feeling and having to bear must have left some kind of mark. But however hard she scrutinized Johanna Ahlbin's countenance, there was nothing to draw from it. Fredrika started to find the other woman's composure unsettling.

There was something terribly wrong, she sensed it instinctively.

To her relief, Alex made a brusque start.

"As you realize, we were very keen to get hold of you. So I suggest we start with that: where have you been these last . . ."

Alex frowned and stopped.

". . . nine days," he went on. "Where have you been since Monday the twenty-fifth of February?"

Good, thought Fredrika. Now she'll have to tell us where she was on the night of the murder.

But Johanna's reply was so swift and short that it took them both unawares.

"I've been in Spain."

Alex couldn't help staring.

"In Spain?" he echoed.

"In Spain," Johanna confirmed. "I've got the travel documents to prove it."

A moment's silence.

"And what were you doing there?" asked Fredrika.

Silence fell again. Johanna seemed to be considering how to answer, and for the first time she seemed to be showing the effects of what had happened.

A façade, Fredrika suspected. She had been so focused on keeping up a façade that she had become utterly disconnected from her emotions.

"The original plan was for me to go there on private business," she said hesitantly. "I'd already arranged the time off work and . . ."

She broke off and looked down at her hands. Long, narrow fingers with unpainted nails. No wedding or engagement ring.

"I'm sure you're aware of my father's involvement in refugee issues?" she said.

"Yes," said Alex.

Johanna picked up the glass of water she had been given and took a few sips.

"For years I felt very ambivalent about all that," she began her story. "But then something happened last autumn to change everything."

She took a deep breath.

"I went on a trip to Greece; we were going to seal a deal with an important client. I stayed on for a few days to make the most of the warm weather there before going back to the Swedish cold. And that was when I saw them."

Fredrika and Alex waited in suspense.

"The refugees would arrive by boat in the night," Johanna went on in a low voice. "I wasn't sleeping very well just then, it happens sometimes when I'm stressed. One morning I thought I'd take a walk to the harbor in the village where I was staying, and I saw them."

She blinked several times and attempted a smile before her face fell.

"It was all so undignified, so degrading. And I thought — no, not thought — I *felt* how wrong I'd been all those years. How unfair I'd been on Dad."

A dry laugh escaped her lips and she looked almost as if she might cry.

"But you know how it is. Our parents are the last people we give in to, so I chose not to tell my father about my change of heart. I wanted to surprise him, show him I was in earnest. And I planned to show him that by doing some voluntary legal work for a migrant organization based mainly in Spain. I was going to be there for five weeks in February and March."

Five weeks, the period of time for which she had leave of absence from work.

Since she seemed to have come to a halt, Alex took up the thread.

"But it didn't work out," he said.

Johanna Ahlbin shook her head.

"No, it didn't. I got dragged into Karolina's plans."

Fredrika shifted uneasily in her seat, still with an overwhelming sense that they had not been given the full story.

"So what happened, Johanna?" she asked softly.

"Everything was completely blown apart," she said, suddenly looking very tired. "Karolina . . ."

She broke off again, but composed herself to go on.

"Karolina had very cleverly sold herself as

the good, loyal daughter. The one who always took such an interest in what Dad was doing, but it was all totally fake, so I found I couldn't even pretend to be interested in all that stuff."

"In what sense do you mean it was fake?" asked Fredrika, remembering all the statements they had had about Karolina sharing her father's outlook.

"She put it on, year after year," Johanna replied with a dark look fixed on Fredrika. "Claimed she felt passionately about Dad's campaigns and shared his underlying values. But none of it was true. In actual fact, the so-called help she gave Dad and his friends was simply that she gave the police anonymous tip-offs about where to find the migrants and how the smugglers operated. To get them here."

The room suddenly felt very cold. Fredrika's brain was racing as it tried to take in the picture being painted for her. Was this where police officer Viggo Tuvesson came into the investigation?

"I tried, countless times, to tell Father that Karolina wasn't a scrap better than me. That she was actually a worse person, because she engaged in lies and deception. But he wouldn't listen to what I told him. As usual."

Johanna looked grimly resolute. Fredrika almost felt like asking why she wasn't crying, but refrained. Perhaps the grief was all too private.

"What about your mother, then?" asked Alex, and instantly had Fredrika's full attention.

"She was somewhere in the middle," Johanna said rather evasively.

"How do you mean?"

"In the middle, between me and Dad."

"In terms of her views, you mean?"

"Yes."

"What did Karolina have against refugees?" Fredrika put in, and then corrected herself: "I mean what *does* Karolina have against refugees?"

It was plain to see the effect on Johanna of this revelation, already released to the media, that Karolina was now definitely known to be alive.

She said nothing for a minute, and the words when they did come had all the more impact.

"Because she was raped by one of the refugees Dad was hiding in the basement of our house at Ekerö."

"Raped?" Alex repeated in a slightly skeptical tone. "We haven't found any reports of a rape in our records."

Johanna shook her head.

"It was never reported. It couldn't be, Mum and Dad said. It would have exposed their whole operation."

"So what *did* they do?" Fredrika asked tentatively, not really sure she wanted to know.

"They dealt with it the way they dealt with everything else," Johanna said sharply. "Within the family. And then Dad wound up his operation at the speed of light, you could say."

Fredrika thought back to her visit to Ekerö, and could see that Alex was doing the same. The photographs on the walls, dated up to a certain midsummer in the early nineties. Johanna fading from the pictures like a ghost. Why Johanna and not Karolina?

"Can you put a date on the event you've just told us about?" Alex asked, though he already knew what the answer would be.

"Midsummer, 1992."

They both nodded, each jotting down a note. The picture was getting clearer, but it was still not in focus.

"And what happened after that?" asked Fredrika.

Slightly less weighed down by the burden of all she had to tell, Johanna appeared to relax a little.

"The Ekerö house was anathema to us after that; none of us liked being there. It wasn't just Dad's hiding of fugitives that stopped, it was as if the whole family died. We were never there to celebrate midsummer again; we would just go for the odd week or weekend. Mum and Dad talked about selling it, but in the end they didn't."

"And how was Karolina?"

For the first time in the interview, an angry look came into Johanna's face.

"She must have been feeling absolutely awful, as you'd expect, but it was as if she was pretending it hadn't happened. Before all that, it was actually the other way round: *I* was the favorite and she was the one who always wanted not to be part of our family. After the rape I took her side, because I didn't think any good that Dad's activities did could ever outweigh what happened to her. So you can imagine how astonished I was to find that Karolina seemed to think it was all okay."

"You must have been terribly bitter," Alex prompted cautiously.

"Dreadfully. And lonely. Suddenly it was as though it was my fault the family had split apart, mine and not Dad's or Mum's. Or Karolina's, for that matter."

"What felt most frustrating?" Fredrika asked.

"What I was telling you before," Johanna said mutedly. "That although Karolina was changed by what happened, and openly admitted to me that she despised the migrants who came to Sweden, she pretended something else to Dad and Mum."

And not just to them, Fredrika thought to herself, but to family, friends, and acquaintances as well.

"So you distanced yourself from the family, so to speak?"

Johanna nodded.

"Yes, that was the way it went. I couldn't bear the hypocrisy. And I didn't miss any of them, either. Not much, anyway. And definitely not after Dad started talking about taking in refugees again, and I was the only one in the family who seemed to mind."

Fredrika and Alex exchanged looks, unsure how to proceed. Their impression of Karolina had changed radically in the course of less than an hour. But they were still far from through with this, they both knew that.

It was at that point Fredrika registered the tattoo on Johanna's wrist, almost hidden by her watch. A flower. Or to be more precise, a daisy. Where had that motif featured recently? Then she recalled the dried flower, the sole ornament on one of the bedroom walls.

Johanna tracked Fredrika's gaze and tried to conceal the tattoo by moving her watch strap. But Fredrika's curiosity was already aroused.

"What does the daisy mean?" she asked bluntly.

"It's a reminder."

Johanna's voice was thick as she said it, her expression ambiguous.

"Karolina's got one, too," she added.

"A reminder of what?"

"Of our sisterhood."

A sisterhood so charged that its symbol had to be hidden under a wristwatch, Fredrika reflected.

It was Alex who broke the silence.

"Johanna, you've got to tell us the rest now. You said you were taking five weeks off work to go to Spain, but Karolina's plans got in the way. What happened?"

As lithely as a ballet dancer, Johanna straightened her back.

"You want to know why I identified a dead person as my sister although I knew it wasn't her?"

"We certainly do."

"I can give you a simple answer: because

she asked me to."

"Who asked you to?"

"Karolina."

Another silence.

"Why?"

Tears came into Johanna's eyes for the first time in the encounter. Fredrika felt something akin to relief when she saw them.

"Because she'd gotten herself into such a hellishly difficult situation that she literally needed to disappear off the face of the earth. That was how she put it, anyway."

"Did she give you any more details?"

"No, but God knows I kept asking her to. Over and over again. But she wouldn't answer, just said her past was catching up with her and she'd realized what she had to do. She explained her plan, the idea that she'd die without really dying. My job was to ring for an ambulance and then identify that druggie as my sister. And leave the country. So then I went to Spain."

"How did you know she was a drug addict, the woman who died in place of your sister?"

"Karolina told me. And you could tell by the look of her. That she'd put herself through it."

"Was she still alive when you got to the flat?"

"It didn't look like it, but she must have been. The ambulance crew tried to save her."

"That must have scared you stiff."

Johanna made no reply.

"Why did you help her with such a spectacular stunt as staging her own death if she wasn't prepared to tell you why?" asked Alex.

A faint smile crept across Johanna's impassive face.

"The bond between sisters can be stretched to any length without breaking. It never occurred to me she could be referring to that midsummer episode when she said the past was catching up with the family. But once I realized it was, I stayed on longer in Spain."

Uncertainty made Fredrika grip her pen even harder.

"How do you mean?"

As if Fredrika had said something completely insane, Johanna leaned across the table.

"But how else could it all fit together? Why else would she have done what she did?"

The line between Alex's eyebrows deepened to a crater.

"What is it you think she did?"

"I think she had Mum and Dad murdered.

And now she's going to come for me, as well. To punish us for not being there when her life was destroyed in the meadow outside our holiday house."

"Do you think she needs protection?" asked Fredrika as the lift doors parted and they emerged into the team corridor.

"Hard to say," muttered Alex. "Bloody hard to say."

"At least we know now that we were right, you and I," Fredrika said, almost gaily.

Alex looked at her.

"About it all starting in the holiday house at Ekerö, like we said."

Alex glanced at his watch. Time had flown, as usual. It was well past lunch and Peder would be off to the national CID to take part in the interview of Sven Ljung. From where he stood, Alex shouted to everyone to come to the Den and make it snappy. Nobody dared drag their feet at the sound of his order, though Fredrika headed for the staff room at a semi-jog to grab a sandwich on the way.

Of course, thought Alex. The woman's

about to have a baby, of course she's got to eat.

"What have we got, to corroborate her story?" asked Joar once Alex had filled them in on what Johanna had said.

"Not much," admitted Alex. "On the other hand, we haven't got much to contradict her version, either."

"Are we remanding her in custody?" asked Peder. "I mean for obstructing the course of our inquiries, or for her part in Therese Björk's death, however minor it was?"

Alex sighed.

"We're not sure enough of our facts yet," he answered. "As for the obstruction, she can explain that by saying she was too scared of what her sister might do once she found out her parents had been killed. And as far as the misidentification's concerned, we haven't enough to go on as things stand. Johanna couldn't even tell us how Therese Björk died; she claims Therese was already there when she got to her sister's flat."

"And that's precisely where we ought to be able to make progress," Fredrika interrupted. "An individual who as far as we know had nothing at all to do with either Karolina or Johanna was picked up by ambulance from Karolina's flat and later died in hospital. That makes Karolina's flat a potential crime scene. How soon can we get access to it?"

Joar gave Fredrika a cautious smile.

"Quick thinking," he said. "But unfortunately I don't think a CSI in Karolina's flat's going to yield much. We've already been there and trampled all over any potential evidence when we were looking for a key to the Ekerö house."

"More to the point, Johanna followed her sister's instructions to go back to the flat and clean up after she'd wrongly identified Therese Björk," Alex added, reminding Fredrika of the latter stages of their interview with Johanna.

"Did Johanna know Karolina was in Thailand?" asked Joar.

Alex nodded.

"Yes, but she didn't know why. When we told her that her sister was wanted for drug offenses, her guess was that Karolina needed the money to pay whoever she hired to kill her parents."

The room went quiet.

"It really feels as if we should be interviewing Karolina Ahlbin as well," said Peder.

"Yes," said Alex, and took a deep breath. "I'd go so far as to say that until we can find out what Karolina's been up to these past few weeks, we're stuck."

Fredrika looked as though she had something to say, but she refrained.

"Was she able to tell you anything about her mother's role in all this?" Joar was curious to know.

"Not a word," Alex said.

"Well then, we wait eagerly to hear what the Sven Ljung interview produces," said Joar, squinting at Peder. "Maybe that's going to shed some light on Marja's role."

Fredrika overcame her indecision and said:

"Erik Sundelius. Jakob's doctor."

"Yes?" said Alex.

"He implied Johanna was mentally disturbed."

"So he did," said Alex. "But there we have a man who forgot to impart various bits of information about himself, as we know. So I'm not sure how much weight we should give to what emerged from our interview with him."

"I agree," said Fredrika. "But several people told us Johanna wasn't well, so we can't be entirely sure."

"Of what?"

"Of whether either Karolina or Johanna is sick enough to have her own parents murdered."

■ ■ ■ ■

When she was younger, Fredrika had often asked herself if she would have preferred having a sister to the brother she had grown up with. As a child, she had sobbed out loud when she read Astrid Lindgren's story *My Sister Dearest,* and in adult life she had often wished she had a sister to exchange thoughts and ideas with. Poring over her notes from the interview with Johanna brought to mind all the myths surrounding the special bond that was said to exist between any pair of sisters.

We didn't know anything about Johanna, thought Fredrika, feeling a rising sense of fascination. And just as our focus was shifting onto her, she sought us out by herself.

She returned briefly to one of her earlier theories, namely that the sisters had collaborated in the murder of their parents.

Motives. Separately, each sister had a motive, but if they were jointly guilty, the police lacked any clear idea of a motive.

Karolina's motive, as Johanna had described it, was not hard to understand. What a broken person must you be after an experience like that. Undoubtedly broken enough to manipulate those around you the way Johanna had described.

But Fredrika was still dubious: surely someone would have seen through her? The Ljungs, the Reverend Vinterman, or the psychiatrist. Or her own parents, for that matter. Hadn't anyone ever questioned her loyalty to her father?

She gave an involuntary shudder. There was no limit to people's imagination when it came to hurting other people. A new picture of Karolina Ahlbin was emerging. A picture that encompassed a set of problems quite different from the one Fredrika initially had in mind. Johanna being slowly erased from the family picture, and finally losing everything and everyone. A young woman who might be in desperate need of protection.

She thumbed the latest fax from Bangkok. There was nothing to indicate that Karolina Ahlbin had left Thailand, which was reassuring. But if she was the one behind the double murder of Jakob and Marja, she clearly had the capacity to contract killers from a distance.

Either she is as disturbed as her sister, Johanna, made her out to be, thought Fredrika. Or else . . .

She put down the sheet of paper and let her eyes stray to the window and the snow falling outside.

Or else Karolina, too, was a victim of the conspiracy that led to the murder of her father.

And her mother.

But why?

Fredrika anxiously checked the clock. It was nearly two, and Spencer had still not been in touch.

She felt she was being assailed by difficulties from all sides. She was aware of a fleeting sense of impending danger.

We're missing something here, she thought, trying not to let the all-too-familiar feeling of fatigue get the better of her. And it's something big, I'm damned sure of it.

She swallowed hard, feeling anxiety contract her windpipe. She ought to go home and leave the case to people with the proper stamina and tempo in their bodies. Go home, go to bed and sleep. Or play some music.

As her thoughts went to her violin, her arm felt numb and tender. She knew there was not a single part of her body that she was not prepared to defy.

When the phone on her desk rang, she virtually sprang to attention.

"Fredrika Bergman."

Silence, then a wheezing intake of breath.

Then Fredrika knew who it was.

"Måns Ljung?" she asked, trying not to sound too eager.

More chesty breathing, someone saying something disjointed. Then suddenly much clearer.

"You rang about Lina?"

"That's right, and I'm very glad you were able to ring me back."

A strained laugh at the other end.

"Did Mum tell you I wouldn't be up to talking on the phone?"

Yes, thought Fredrika. And I was so stupid that I bought it, without further ado.

It was Elsie's comments that had made the police decide against interviewing her and Sven's son Måns, even though he had been Karolina's boyfriend for several years.

"I'm an in-patient at a so-called rehabilitation clinic, but if it's to do with Lina, I've always got time to talk. Sorry if I sound a bit ropy . . . I've got some sort of infection."

Fredrika could not have cared less about his state of health. The important thing was that he was capable of holding a conversation.

"That's all right," she said, and tried to sound professional. "What I really need to know is whether Karolina's tried to contact you in the past week."

Silence.

"Why are you asking?"

With one hand round the telephone receiver and the other on her stomach, Fredrika took a deep breath.

"Because I'm afraid she's in trouble."

Another hesitation.

"She rang and asked me for help last week."

"Did she say what the matter was?"

"Said she couldn't get hold of Jakob or Marja and it was going to be difficult to get home because someone seemed to have closed down her email and canceled her flight home from Thailand."

She must have realized, thought Fredrika. And been scared.

"Did you know she was there? In Thailand, I mean?"

There was a short fit of coughing, and it sounded almost as if Måns had put down the receiver.

"No," he said eventually. "We're not in touch very often these days . . ."

But she trusted you, Måns.

"What did she want help with?"

"Getting hold of Jakob. And sorting out her trip home."

She could hear him snuffling.

"But I wasn't, like, in a fit state to help

her with anything like that."

"Is that what you told her?"

A sigh.

"No. And I didn't tell her that her dad was dead. Couldn't bloody well bring myself to. Not on the phone."

"So what did you do, then?" asked Fredrika, feeling exasperated on Karolina's behalf.

"I rang my brother, he's good at getting things done," Måns said in a feeble voice. "And asked Karolina to wait. But by the time I rang back, something must have happened, because she wasn't answering her mobile any longer."

"Did she send any emails?"

"She might have — I don't check them all that often."

Fredrika found herself breathing in the same, strained way as Måns.

"And what about your brother?" she said, almost whispering, and unaccountably afraid of bursting into tears. "What did he do?"

"He just rang back and told me there wasn't much he could do, and she'd have to buy a new air ticket home. He advised me not to tell her about Jakob over the phone."

Sensible, thought Fredrika. Sensible brother.

And she asked one last question.

"What does your brother do?"

Her follow-up question remained hanging in the air, unsaid. *Is he a druggie in rehab, too?*

"You might know him," said Måns. "He's a policeman."

Fredrika had to grin at her own unwarranted prejudice. But the grin froze into a grimace as Måns went on: "His name's Viggo. Viggo Tuvesson."

Feeling as if he was moving with the same force as a goods train on a straight stretch of track, a determined Peder strode the last few meters to the interview room where Sven Ljung was waiting. His CID colleague Stefan Westin, who was taking the formal lead in the interview, told him the arrest had all gone very quietly. Elsie and Sven were sitting having coffee when the police rang at the door, almost as if they were expecting someone to come and fetch them. Elsie looked tearful as they took her husband out of the flat, but had not protested out loud.

"She seemed pretty bloody resigned," was the way Stefan Westin put it.

Expectations of the impending interview were running high. Peder felt a distinct tightening of his chest as he entered the room and shook Sven Ljung's hand.

He felt enormous relief that he and not

Joar had been entrusted with this interview by Alex. He had to regain some of the ground he had recently lost. He also knew that within the organization he needed people to have more confidence in him. As things stood, it was too easy to despise him and discount him. *Must, must, must do better.*

Stefan Westin took charge as they began the interview with Sven Ljung. Having never met Sven before, Peder was struck by how tired and old the man looked. He took a surreptitious glance at his paperwork. According to his notes, Sven was not yet even sixty-five. Still relatively young, in Peder's eyes. But there was something about the older man. He looked sad and distressed.

As if in mourning, after some heavy, secret loss.

Stefan Westin's voice broke into his thoughts.

"You reported your car stolen ten days ago, Sven. Have you any idea who could have taken it?"

Sven said nothing.

Peder raised an eyebrow. He had seen that sort of silence before, during the interview with Tony Svensson. If they had gone and brought in yet another person scared into silence by God knows who, it was going to be a tough and not particularly fruitful interview.

Sven started to talk.

"No, none at all."

The room fell silent again.

"But are you sure it was stolen?" asked Stefan.

Sven nodded slowly.

"Yes."

"How did you come to discover it was missing?"

"I needed it on the Friday morning, nearly two weeks ago. And it wasn't there in the street where I'd left it the day before."

He suddenly looked much smaller. Deflated.

"We've got compelling evidence that your car was involved in two aggravated robberies of security vans, and a murder, during the time you say it was stolen," announced Stefan Westin, and Sven turned pale. "Would you like to tell me where you were at the following times?"

Sven had to think about it when he was confronted with the various dates. He said that on each of them he had been at home in the flat with his wife. Just the two of them.

Stefan pretended to be digesting what Sven had just said.

"Yusuf, do you know him?" he asked,

referring to the man run over at the university.

Sven shook his head.

"No."

The chair legs scraped across the floor as Stefan Westin pulled himself up to the table and leaned across it.

"But we know he rang you," he said patiently. "Several times."

"Perhaps he was just somebody you knew and that's all there is to it?" Peder prompted when Sven said nothing.

"That's right," said Stefan. "Someone you knew, who just happened to get run over by your car outside the university. I mean, these things do happen, don't they?"

He looked at Peder and put up his hands.

Then Sven could not hold back his tears.

Silent, rather dignified tears.

Time stood still and Peder scarcely dared to move.

"I swear I haven't seen the car since it went missing," Sven said finally.

"We believe you, Sven," said Stefan. "But we don't buy your story that you don't know who took it. We scarcely even buy that it was stolen at all; we think you lent it. More or less voluntarily."

"And reported it stolen to rule yourself out as a suspect," Peder went on mildly.

A voice and tone that he had previously reserved for his sons. And Jimmy.

The thought of Jimmy hit him like a bolt from the blue. Christ, how many days since they last spoke? Jimmy had been trying to get through, hadn't he? And Peder hadn't taken the call, or several calls in fact.

The elderly man on the other side of the table wiped the tears from his cheeks and a resolute look came over him.

"I truly don't know who took the car, or what for."

"Or you do know, but daren't tell," Stefan said bluntly.

Or don't want to, thought Peder. Out of loyalty.

"But you ought to be able to tell us how you knew this Yusuf," he said out loud.

Sven considered this.

"He got my number from some, er, mutual acquaintances. But it was a mistake. I wasn't the one he wanted."

Stefan and Peder pricked up their ears. Mutual acquaintances?

"And what are their names?"

Another hesitation.

"Jakob Ahlbin."

His eyes were shifty, but his voice was steady.

He's lying so well he's convinced himself,

thought Peder.

"Never on your life," said Stefan in such a hard voice that Sven blanched again.

And as Sven continued to sit there in silence, Stefan said, "You'll gain nothing but the odd hour or minute from stalling the interview like this," he said quietly. "Wouldn't it be a relief just to tell us the whole story straight out?"

Sven's eyes filled up again.

"It would take a damned long time," he said under his breath.

Peder and Stefan leaned back ostentatiously in their chairs.

"We've got all the time in the world, Sven."

"It began when Jakob Ahlbin talked of starting to offer refuge to illegal migrants again. Johanna went through the roof and Jakob and I fell out badly after I suggested he could make a lot of money out of it. Jakob called me a selfish fool and I retorted by calling Jakob cowardly and self-effacing. I needed money," admitted Sven.

"I always have, at least ever since Måns' addiction got out of hand. His antisocial habits have cost us vast sums. His stealing and embezzlement have driven us to distraction, but we never had the heart to shut our door to him. Once he even managed to convince himself, and me, that he was getting better and needed some money to start a business. But that all fell apart, of course, and his mother and I didn't know which way to turn after we lost several hundred thousand."

He went on wearily: "It had never occurred to me before that there was money to be made from Jakob's activities, from hiding refugees. But I came to realize it must be possible, since the people who came over had paid so much for the trip itself, and I thought they must surely have assets with them when they got here. So I put the idea to a good friend . . . and we started up."

He turned his head away to cough.

"We hid the refugees in remote holiday cottages that we could rent at a cheaper price than they paid us."

"Did it bring in a lot of money?" asked Peder.

"Yes, but still not enough," Sven said sadly.

"Who were you in partnership with?" asked Stefan.

Another bit of information Sven was reluctant to reveal. And when the answer finally came, it was one they should have expected, but Peder realized he was still shocked.

"Ragnar Vinterman."

Stefan and Peder sat dumbfounded and wide-eyed as Sven stumbled on through his story.

"Ragnar wanted to expand the operation because he needed even more money. He'd lost a lot on bad investments and property speculation abroad. But I felt, well, I felt I couldn't support his new idea. So I said I was pulling out. It wasn't just that I felt it was morally wrong, it was a damn risky proposition calling for a lot more people to be involved. Smugglers, reliable interpreters, document forgers."

Sven lapsed into silence.

Peder sensed they were nearing a point in the story at which it was going to be harder to get any more out of Sven.

"And how did Ragnar react when you said you wanted out?"

"Very angrily."

"What was the expanded operation that he was suggesting and you didn't want to be in on?"

Anxiety and stress were taking over Sven's body.

"Refugee smuggling," he said.

Peder held his breath.

"In a new way."

"What does that mean, 'a new way'?" Stefan demanded, but Peder kept his cool.

Here it comes, he was hoping. The last bit of our jigsaw puzzle.

And now Sven had started to talk, it was as if he could not stop, though he did navigate very skillfully round all the points where he should have provided more detail. Names, for example.

"Ragnar thought it cost an appalling amount for a refugee to get from, say, Iraq or Somalia to Sweden, and that one ought to be able to lure in selected individuals by offering them an easier way of getting to Sweden."

"And the aim of that would be what?" asked Stefan, looking skeptical. "It all sounds remarkably generous."

A joyless laugh from Sven echoed round the interview room.

"Generous," he repeated, looking irate. "Believe me, for a man of the cloth Ragnar Vinterman shows exceptionally poor understanding of what that word means. No, Ragnar's plan was to entice individual refugees over here, who would get in on false documents and then commit crimes to order. Special, handpicked individuals with a background in the military forces. Then they'd be sent home again, and no one would ever be able to catch the perpetrators of the crimes or trace their link to us."

"The security van robberies that have been keeping us busy in recent months," began Stefan, and Sven nodded eagerly.

Peder was familiar with the robberies. Minutely planned, and accompanied by violence that was in an entirely different league from the kind generally used in robberies like that.

"I refused to be part of that hateful business, but when I saw the news reports of the robberies, I realized it was up and running anyway."

A new line creased Stefan's brow.

"You said the plan was to send the refugees home again?"

Sven nodded.

"So why, in at least two cases, have they been found dead in the Stockholm area?"

"I've no idea," said Sven, looking scared stiff.

"You must have had contact with Ragnar Vinterman about this since," Peder persisted.

Sven nodded again.

"But only when Ragnar sought me out to make sure I was going to keep my mouth shut. And when Yusuf rang me. He got my number from someone in the network who thought I was still part of it. Ragnar saw to all that."

Something must have gone horribly wrong, Peder thought to himself as he totted up the grand total, the crescendo of violence and death that Ragnar Vinterman's business had generated in the past two weeks.

"What about Jakob Ahlbin, then?" he asked. "Did he know any of this was going on?"

Sven met his gaze with a pained expression.

"No, we didn't tell him what we were starting. But I think . . ."

They waited.

"I'm afraid he sniffed out the truth even so. And that naïve good-for-nothing evidently went to Ragnar and said he'd heard rumors that a new smuggling network had established itself in Sweden."

"A network supposedly much more generous than the rest," said Peder.

"Exactly," said Sven.

"And that set everything in motion," Stefan summarized.

"I think that must be what happened," said Sven. "But I don't know anything definitely."

Stefan waited a moment and then tried

again: "Who the heck was it that took your car, Sven?"

"Don't know."

"There's not a cat in hell's chance Ragnar did the whole thing on his own. Who else was with him?" asked Peder.

But Sven's mouth was sealed now, and the two interviewers realized they were coming to the end of the road.

"If anybody's threatened you . . ." Peder began.

Sven closed up like a clam.

Peder decided to try a new tack.

"According to the police report that was made at the time you and Elsie found Jakob and Marja's bodies, an officer called Viggo Tuvesson was first on the scene. Why didn't you tell us he was your son?"

"It didn't seem necessary," said Sven.

"According to information we've recently received, Viggo went to Marja and Jakob's after a call that you and Elsie made direct to his mobile. Why didn't you ring the usual emergency number?"

Sven sighed.

"It was so much easier to ring Viggo direct."

"Is he part of Ragnar Vinterman's network?" Peder asked bluntly, and Sven turned pale again.

"I can't imagine he would be," Sven said quietly, but both Peder and Stefan could see he was prevaricating.

Peder decided to pile on the pressure with another question.

"Johanna or Karolina Ahlbin, then? Were either of them part of it?"

Sven shrank even further and turned even paler.

"Another question I can't answer," he said in a muted voice.

"And Marja," persisted Peder as it dawned on him what a ghastly situation must have confronted Jakob in the last hours of his life. "Was she in on it, too?"

Sven merely shook his head.

"Who was it, then, Sven?" Peder said exasperatedly. "Who was it that murdered Marja and Jakob, or had them murdered?"

Silence.

With some effort, Peder found a gentler way of expressing himself, "Are you scared, Sven?"

The older man nodded mutely.

Then he sat back in his chair, saying nothing.

There were ways of getting information even without the cooperation of Sven Ljung. Going back over the analysis of telephone data the police had been working on throughout the investigation, new contacts could be established now that more telephone numbers had been identified. Marja had rung Ragnar Vinterman a number of times, even quite late at night when it seemed unlikely they were discussing work-related matters. And when new lists of traffic to and from Vinterman's number finally came in after an urgent request to his phone company, it was possible to link Vinterman both to the man killed outside the university and to Muhammed in Skärholmen, victim of the Sunday evening shooting.

Two telephone numbers to unregistered pay-as-you-go accounts recurred in all the telephone lists, and this, combined with the fact that neither Johanna nor Karolina Ahlbin featured among the contacts, was a source of frustration to the team.

"That bloody Viggo Tuvesson from the Norrmalm force isn't here either," thundered Alex Recht when they were all assembled in the Den with cups of coffee in their hands at about half past five that evening. "We've nothing on him beyond the fact that he's been in touch with Tony Svensson now and then. And the fact that he's Sven and Elsie's son."

"He couldn't give any plausible explanation for his contact with Tony Svensson, though, could he?" Fredrika added.

Alex muttered something inaudible and fastened his eyes on her.

"Shouldn't you go home now?"

She shook her head.

"No, I'm fine. I'll stay a bit longer."

Peder was fiddling with his watch and looking worried.

"Do you need to get home?" Alex asked him.

Peder looked dejected.

"Well, I was supposed to be eating with Ylva and the boys tonight, but —"

"Go!" Alex bellowed, making his younger colleague jump. "Go home and eat. I'll ring if I need you back."

Light feet bore Peder out of the room and he shut the door behind him.

Two seconds later he opened it again: "Thanks."

"Do we think we can now say for certain why Jakob Ahlbin died?" Joar asked rhetorically.

"No," said Fredrika, just as Alex said "Yes."

They looked at each other in surprise.

"He was murdered to keep him quiet, just as you thought," Alex said irritably, and glared, but Fredrika shook her head. "The only question is who did it."

"But what about Marja?" she objected. "Why did she have to die as well? I mean, we're also working on the hypothesis that she was part of Vinterman's network."

Alex looked bedraggled. In conjunction with the CID, he had had to apply for immediate surveillance of Ragnar Vinterman, to make sure he did not try to get away if and when he found out Sven Ljung had been arrested.

"Maybe Marja's death wasn't intentional," Alex said sternly.

Fredrika pursed her lips and said nothing.

"Okay, let's go back over this," Joar suggested firmly. "Who do we think had a motive for murdering Jakob, or Jakob and Marja?"

"Either the Vinterman network or one of the daughters," said Fredrika.

"You mean Karolina?" said Alex.

"No, I mean either of them. I'm keeping an open mind until we've heard the other version."

"All right —" began Alex, but was interrupted by Ellen's knock at the door.

"Sorry to interrupt," she said, "but there's an urgent fax from the Thai police."

Alex read it with a look of concern.

"Damn. The Thai authorities are pretty sure Karolina Ahlbin left Bangkok yesterday evening on a direct flight to Stockholm. She was traveling on someone else's passport. They got some information when they raided a known people smuggler who operates out of Bangkok."

Anxiety spread through the room.

"What does that mean for us?" Fredrika asked quietly.

"That if they're right, she's already back in Sweden," Alex said dully. "And that whatever her role in all this has been, she's no doubt extremely worked up. Heaven help Johanna when she finds her."

"Bloody hell," said Joar under his breath.

"But where will she go?" Fredrika asked

agitatedly. "She's more or less on the run, wanted for serious crimes."

Alex gave her a long look.

"We've no choice now, we'll have to sound the alert and issue her description. For her own sake, if nothing else."

Time had finally caught up with them, and that was all there was to it. And she knew Sven would try until the very last minute to avoid shouldering the responsibility he would have to take. So Elsie stood up resolutely from the kitchen table where she had been sitting since the police took Sven away, and went into the hall.

I should have done the right thing ages ago, she thought grimly. But they say it's never too late to put right what you once did wrong.

As she struggled into her heavy winter coat, her eye fell on one of the family photos hanging on the wall. It had amazed her that the police had been in their flat three times and failed to recognize Viggo in the picture. But then, Viggo had been a different man then, a man with an undamaged face.

Elsie felt like weeping.

His role must be clear to them now, she realized as she pulled on her woolly hat. Even if they didn't know precisely what he did, they must know that he had a part in all these horrors.

She stroked the picture with trembling fingers. Once upon a time, they'd been a proper family, a unit in which everyone cared about everyone else and wanted what was best for them. But it seemed so long ago, now. They had long since lost Måns to his addiction, and as for Viggo . . . She let out a heavy sigh. He had always chosen the more difficult path. It had surprised them that he wanted to join the police, but they were also baffled by his reluctance to let the doctors try to do something about the scar that so disfigured his face.

"It's my trademark," he told them when the matter first came up between them.

"Says who?" Elsie asked doubtfully.

"The one I love," he replied, and then turned away and got on with something else.

It had been hopeless trying to get any more out of him. He refused to say whom he had met, and was adamant that he had no intention of letting his parents meet her. Months went by and became years. They heard no more about her, and assumed it had ended.

But Elsie knew her son and over time a suspicion started to take root. With a pounding heart she had posted herself near the front entrance to his block of flats last summer, and her suspicions were confirmed when he emerged hand in hand with a woman Elsie would have recognized from half a mile away.

"Nothing ever comes free with that woman," she had tried telling her son. "Don't go thinking she's who she pretends to be. Her mind is sick, Viggo. As sick as they come."

But he refused to listen and said he had a right to go his own way. What was a modern-day mother supposed to say to that?

Elsie resolutely put her keys in her handbag and opened the front door. She hoped the police hadn't all gone home for the day. Above all she hoped that the woman detective, the pregnant one, would still be there. She seemed to understand things even without Elsie saying them.

I thought I was looking after them, sparing them from the worst, she thought wearily. When in fact I was just paving the way for our downfall.

She stepped onto the landing and raised her eyes.

She heard herself gasp to see who was standing there.

"You?" she just had time to say before

surprisingly strong arms bundled her back
into the flat.

The snow that had fallen in the course of the afternoon made the road surface slippery, and if he had given it a thought, he might have pulled over and spent the night at a hotel. But his thoughts were locked on to the one thing that felt worth dwelling on just then — the fact that he was going to seek out his father-in-law, thump his fist on the table, and be rid of that tyranny at last — and he kept driving. He knew the country roads of Småland; they changed little over the years. He passed through villages and small towns and felt tears come to his eyes as memories he had thought gone forever forced their way to the surface, punching through his soul.

I've been a fool.

He had made two important calls before setting off from Uppsala. The first was to his employer, saying he would not be in for a few days. The other was to Eva, to tell her that he would be leaving her when he got back from his trip. He had been surprised by her silence, and her closing remark had stunned him:

"Aren't you going to miss me at all, Spencer?"

Miss.

The word made his heart almost break.

I've missed more in these past years than you could ever imagine, he thought as he hung up.

But in the warm bubble of the car he was missing nothing and no one.

"You're at a crossroads and have to decide which way to go," his father said, when he moved from Lund all those years ago. "I can't really make out what it looks like from where you're standing and you don't seem to want to tell me, but there's one thing I want you to know — the day you need somebody to talk to, I'm here to listen."

A whole lifetime had gone by since Spencer rebuffed his father, and he had still to discover the full extent of the damage it had done.

I was greedy, he admitted to himself. I wanted everything and my reward was less than half. Because I deserved no more.

At one point in the slow hours of the drive, his thoughts went to Fredrika Bergman. She pretended she did not like him opening the car door for her, though it was a damn lie that she would accept anything else. What would everyday life with her be like? Did they really want to become fixtures in each other's life, or would they discover what so many other people in their situation do when they finally get the chance to move in together? That living with each other was only an attractive proposition as long as it remained unattainable? People were good at fooling themselves that way. They never missed what they already had, which meant they didn't appreciate it, either.

Spencer felt slightly nervous at the thought. Maybe Fredrika, being so honest, would declare that she didn't want him near her in the way he was now planning.

What the devil will I do then? Spencer wondered listlessly. Where the hell do I go then?

Perhaps it was the weight of all his brooding that made him careless, and he lost control of the car. It took him a few seconds to realize it had lost traction on the snowy, icy road surface, and the skid took him onto the other side of the carriageway. A moment later, the crunching shriek of colliding vehicles resounded along the forest road beneath a black night sky from which the snow just kept on falling. Witnesses saw them meet, buckle, and be thrown off the road, where they crashed into the hard trunks of trees that had been standing along the roadside for many, many years.

Then came silence.

When it got to six o'clock, Fredrika went to the staff room to heat up a pasty. Alex came in after her and it struck her that he seemed reluctant to go home.

"We can't get hold of Johanna Ahlbin," he complained exasperatedly.

"Not even on that new mobile number she gave us?"

"No."

The microwave pinged and Fredrika took out her dinner.

"Might be just as well to send a radio car to her flat to check everything's okay," suggested Fredrika.

"I'd already thought of that," said Alex. "They just reported back that there was no answer when they rang the doorbell and the place seemed to be in darkness. They rang at a few neighbors' doors, but no one had seen or heard anything."

Alex took a seat opposite Fredrika as she

sat down to eat.

"Why wouldn't Sven Ljung give us the names of the other people in the Vinterman circle?" he said, thinking aloud.

Fredrika chewed and swallowed. The pasty had gone rubbery in the microwave and tasted disgusting.

"Either because he's scared, or for reasons of personal loyalty."

"That's what I thought," said Alex. "It could easily be that he's trying to protect someone, and hasn't been scared into keeping his mouth shut at all."

"His son Viggo, for example," said Fredrika. "A father shielding his son, that's pretty classic."

Alex nodded, his head seeming heavy.

"Quite right," he said. "You know, I talked to that Viggo and he didn't breathe a word about being the Ljungs' son or growing up virtually next door to Jakob and Marja Ahlbin and playing with their daughters. He even claimed he'd never met them."

Fredrika quietly set down her knife and fork.

"We definitely know Karolina "played" a great deal with their son Måns," she began.

"Yes?" said Alex.

"Do we know how much the girls had to do with Viggo?"

Alex was slow to answer.

"Not sure," he eventually responded. "I don't think technical has managed to get through his phone lists today; they didn't come in until later."

Another bit of pasty was forced down Fredrika's throat.

"I think we're going to find something there," she said. "I reckon this whole thing is a lot better thought through and structured than we can see as yet. I checked when Viggo changed his surname, for example, and he did it the year he went to police training college."

"Good grief," exclaimed Alex. "Could he have been in on it from the word 'go,' when they started taking money for hiding illegal migrants in 2004?"

"Of course he could," said Fredrika. "And to avoid attracting attention if his father got caught, he made sure to keep his distance from the family by changing his name."

"Which clearly worked pretty well," Alex muttered.

"Not at all," Fredrika contradicted him. "We're sitting here now, knowing it failed."

Alex gave a lopsided smile.

"But we couldn't be any further from arresting the damned man if we tried."

"Can we put surveillance on him?"

Her boss's smile grew broader.

"They've been on him for the past hour," he said. "He's sitting tight in his flat, apparently."

"Awaiting instructions, perhaps?"

"Could well be," Alex agreed.

He answered after the second ring.

"I'm setting off now," she said.

"Okay. You want me to come with you?"

She went quiet.

"Not yet," she said eventually, but with such hesitation in her voice that he knew straightaway he wouldn't be able to stop himself going after her.

He felt frightened for her, the way he always did when she was reckless.

"It could be dangerous," he said.

"I know that," she said in the same muted tone.

"Take care of yourself."

"Always."

They lapsed into silence and the stress of it all made him grind his teeth. He had to ask.

"Did you go round to Mum's?"

He heard her stop in midstep.

"Yes."

"And?"

Another pause.

"She wasn't in."

"Damn. So she's one step ahead after all —"

She interrupted him, and said firmly, "We'll just have to hope for the best."

"And prepare for the worst," he finished.

He sat looking out of the window for a long time after she rang off. His jaws were clenched as he came to his decision. He was much better equipped for physical combat than she could ever be, that was what made them such a successful team. She was the strategist, drawing up the guidelines for their work, while he made sure any problems that arose were dealt with and got out of the way. Time after time.

He took the decision on pure impulse. He was not just going to stay in his flat while the one he loved fought for her life in the theater of war, where she had suffered such injury all that time ago and learned to view every stranger with the greatest caution and suspicion.

Fredrika was just putting things away and finishing for the day when the call came through from the switchboard. An Elsie Ljung was down at reception looking for her. She was very agitated and said it was urgent.

Fredrika had decided that it really was time to go home and devote some time to herself and her unborn child. She had started feeling that something was not quite right when she and Alex were chatting in the staff room. The baby seemed to be keeping still in a new way, as if summoning up the strength for something imminent.

"You're not thinking of coming out now, are you?" she murmured to herself.

But her uneasiness about the baby was still overshadowed by her worry at not being able to reach Spencer. The phone just rang unanswered whenever she tried. The exhaustion in her body and mind were inhibiting her efforts to come up with a logical explanation. He had been so terribly secretive before he left, not like himself at all.

The receiver weighed heavily in her hand as she spoke to the switchboard operator. Elsie Ljung had taken it upon herself to come to the police out of working hours. Was there something she wanted to get off her chest?

She pulled herself together and went in to tell Alex.

"Shall we go down together?" he asked. "I'm okay to stay a bit longer."

"Don't know," Fredrika said dubiously.

"She apparently asked to speak to me on my own. I've got a feeling she might have something important to tell me."

"I'll wait here, then."

With a slight nod, Fredrika came out of his room to go down and meet Elsie. A glance out of the window as she left showed thick snow coming down. The regal capital was clothed in white again. And a thought came into Fredrika's mind: Nice not to be out on the roads tonight. They could be really treacherous.

Karolina felt she was only keeping the car on the road by pure strength of will. She had driven this route so many times, longing to get there and be enfolded in the warm walls of the house and all its memories. They were mixed memories, of course, some of them terrible ones that she would gladly have written out of history if she could. Her father had said it was impossible to try to change the past, but you could always improve your own way of relating to it. Bruises were an indication of where you'd been, not where you were going.

The memory of her father stung and smarted, bringing tears to her eyes. *How had it all gone so wrong? How had they been forced to pay such a high price?*

She thought she knew. Not precisely, but more or less. As her plane landed at Arlanda that morning, she suddenly knew that the disaster that had befallen her parents could not possibly be anything to do with her trip or her father's special interest in migrant issues. The insight pulsed through her body as the wheels of the plane bounced along the tarmac.

This is personal, she thought.

The moment she understood that to be the case, she also realized who she was up against. Nothing is more of an asset in battle than knowing your opponent. And of all the opponents it could have been, there was none she felt she knew better.

Once again she rang the number from which she had tried, in blind panic and as ultimate proof of her utter naïveté, to get help in Bangkok. And again it rang and rang until it switched over to voicemail. But she knew — *she sensed* — her enemy at the other end, knew she was sitting there with her hand on the phone and not answering. Her voice was cold when she finally spoke:

"I'll meet you where it all started. Come alone."

For the first time in his adult life, Alex did not want to go home. His chest tightened and he thought of his father, who had survived a heart attack a few years before.

"It's inherited, you know," he had warned his son. "Look after yourself, Alex, and listen to your body when it tries to tell you something."

But work had to take priority in his mind over worries about his health. There had been a quick call from Lena, wondering when he would be home.

"Later," muttered Alex, hanging up with that nagging feeling of things being all wrong, but still putting off the moment of truth.

The surveillance officers keeping watch on Viggo Tuvesson rang in straight afterward. Tuvesson had left the flat and was on his way to Kungsholmen by car.

"Maybe he's coming into work," Alex said doubtfully, looking at the time, which was just after seven. "But don't let him out of sight."

A few minutes later they rang again. Tuvesson seemed to have no plans to come to HQ; he was heading out of town on Drottningholmsvägen.

Alex's first thought was of Ragnar Vinterman.

"He's on his way to Bromma," he said excitedly. "Keep in touch with the team in

Bromma and see if Vinterman's on his way out, too."

But Vinterman was still safely ensconced in his vicarage and the surveillance team there had nothing new to report.

It was worrying Alex that Johanna Ahlbin seemed to have disappeared off the police radar again. It might mean she had run into trouble herself, but Alex felt in his bones that something else lay behind it.

He looked at the piles of reports strewn around his desk like a broken-up jigsaw puzzle. A vicar who wanted to do everything right, but who had got on the wrong side of virtually his whole family. Two more men of the cloth who had found themselves with such severe financial problems that nothing was holy to them anymore. A policeman so deep in the shit that it was hard to understand how he had been able to stay within the system for so long. And two sisters who both appeared to have lost everything one midsummer's eve, fifteen years ago.

Alex found himself thinking back to his visit to the Ekerö house with Fredrika. The dated pictures, young Johanna choosing a different path, away from the family. Maybe along with her mother. Karolina, staying on in the happy family circle despite the violent attack she had suffered.

Or could it have been the other way round, Alex wondered, with Johanna as the rape victim, turning her back on the family as a result? And Karolina becoming her father's favorite.

His pulse started to race. But who had carried out the actual murder? The crime scene investigation had given them not a single lead; all the prints and other traces led back to the couple themselves, to Elsie and Sven Ljung or to police officers and ambulance crew at the scene. And at the time of the murder, both Johanna and Karolina were verifiably out of the country.

Alex glanced through the crime-scene report again, his brain revving fast. Could it simply be the case, after all, that Sven Ljung had let himself into the flat and murdered Jakob and Marja? Alex knew that was wrong before he even finished thinking it. His brain locked instead on to the most obvious name. The man who could have got away with the whole thing if only he had not been so careless as to use his work telephone when he was drawing up the plans for the appalling crimes he was prepared to commit.

The telephone on Alex's desk rang so loudly that he almost cried out.

"He's not going to Bromma, either,"

surveillance reported.

"Where is he heading, then?"

"To Ekerö."

And that gave Alex the last thread he needed, and he realized with horror where the Ahlbin sisters must be.

As if in a trance, he ended the call and rang the central command unit. He asked them to send all available radio cars to the Ahlbin family's holiday home at Ekerö.

Looking back, there was no clear dividing line that evening between the time when Fredrika felt secure in her existence and the time when her whole life began to disintegrate. It was an irony of fate that she actually postponed the moment herself by not taking the first call that came through from Spencer's home number.

I've been waiting all day, so now he can jolly well wait while I talk to Elsie Ljung, she decided angrily.

Alex rang her on her mobile just as she was getting a glass of water for herself and the visitor she had escorted to an interview room. He updated her on the situation in a few brisk sentences, warning her that they could be in for a very nasty end to the evening. There was no need for him to say it; Fredrika could imagine all too well how a confrontation between the two sisters might end.

"Are you going out there?" she asked.

"I'm in the garage with Joar and a couple of CID officers," Alex replied. "We're going with the flying squad. You concentrate on teasing out of Elsie how Viggo fits into all this. And try to get a handle on which sister it is we need to be most wary of."

"They both seem equally disturbed," mumbled Fredrika, sounding more casual than she meant to.

"I don't think so," said Alex, his breathing sounding rather shallow. "I think Johanna was lying about which of them was raped that summer, and I think she may have hated her family ever since."

They were about to end the call when Alex added:

"If I haven't made it clear before now, I just want you to know I'm going to miss you in the team when you go off on maternity leave."

As if it was something he felt he needed to say before he got into the flying squad minibus and left HQ. For some reason it reduced Fredrika almost to tears, and she had to compose herself for a moment before going back to Elsie.

The last thing she did before she opened the door of the interview room was to turn off her mobile phone.

"So," she said to Elsie as she put the water down on the table. "What brings you to see us this evening?"

Like many good storytellers, Elsie had a wonderful memory for detail to fall back on as she told her tale to Fredrika.

"We went out to Ekerö to surprise them that midsummer's eve," she said in a low voice. "Marja and Jakob had told us, you know, about the way it was usually just them, just the family, but our plans fell through that year and the boys got on so well with their girls, so we thought we were bound to be welcome if we just turned up."

They had been surprised all right. Elsie's memories of that evening were vivid.

"Driving back later that night, we knew things we could never have imagined about the way Jakob and Marja lived. We didn't have a clue that he hid refugees like that, and we didn't know about his medical condition, either. It was Marja's decision not to ring a doctor or the police; she said as long as the girls got away from the holiday house, it would only be a matter of time before wounds healed and memories faded. It was complete madness."

Elsie looked furious and Fredrika felt a sense of exasperation coming over her, too.

But she had learned not to judge people too hastily or too harshly. Who knew what experiences from her own past life had made Marja act as she did?

"But surely it was only one of the girls who was . . . injured?" Fredrika began, hearing Elsie talk about them in the plural.

"That depends how you look at it," Elsie said tersely. "Karolina was a physical mess, of course, but Johanna was beside herself. It was as if her whole world had fallen to pieces when she realized her parents weren't thinking of any more drastic measures than just getting the refugees out of the house as soon as possible and clearing off back into town."

Fredrika swallowed.

"So it *was* Karolina who was raped, after all?"

"Oh yes," said Elsie, "and later, when she was grown up and fell in love with our Måns, he and she had a lot of private chats about what happened that evening."

A look of great sadness came over her as she described the time when Karolina was coming and going as a daughter-in-law in their home.

"Karolina was awfully good at expressing things in words," Elsie said, the tears coming into her eyes. "When she was a child, she clearly didn't know what to make of the "guests in the basement," as her parents called them. And in those first years after the rape she very naturally felt a burning hatred of every immigrant she saw. But then something happened which changed all that."

Elsie looked unsure of herself.

"You must say if I'm telling you things you already know."

"I'm more than happy to listen," Fredrika said, working out in her head how many minutes away from Ekerö Alex must be by now.

"Karolina was involved in a car accident just after she took her driving test," Elsie said. "She was visiting relations in Skåne and the car skidded on black ice when she was going across a bridge. The car went straight through the side of the bridge and fell into the river. She'd never have got out if it hadn't been for a young man who saw it happen. He threw himself in after her and fought like a tiger to get the car door open and get her out."

"And this young man was an immigrant?"

Elsie smiled through her tears.

"From Palestine. After that, Karolina couldn't let herself carry on feeling the way she had done. She accepted what had happened that summer and came over to her father's side. Maybe because she'd done everything she could for several years to show how much she hated him and blamed him. And believe me, Jakob paid a high price."

"It made him ill?"

"Extremely. It was the first time he was so bad that he had to be admitted for treatment. Marja was the only one who went to visit him."

A suspicion began to take shape in Fredrika's mind.

"And Johanna?"

Elsie took a slow, deep breath.

"Well, her story's really far more tragic than Karolina's. You see, she was Daddy's girl all the time she was growing up. And when Jakob let Karolina down so grotesquely after the rape — because however we choose to look at it, it was a sort of betrayal — Johanna fought her sister's corner. Year after year. Until Karolina's car accident and conversion. That left Johanna with nowhere to go. Her relationship with Jakob was in tatters, and suddenly her sister was Daddy's favorite. I think Johanna felt cruelly let down."

The photos in the Ekerö house came into Fredrika's mind.

"So she turned her back on the family," she murmured.

"Yes, or at least, she only saw them sporadically. And it was when Jakob started talking about hiding refugees at the holiday house again that she decided to cross the line and become her family's worst enemy."

Fredrika frowned.

"Like I told you last time we met, she went through the roof and said she never wanted to hear such a tasteless proposal again. And Marja agreed with her."

Marja. The woman who sneaked into the library and sent threats to her own husband.

"Jakob's idea caused a huge amount of friction in the family," sighed Elsie. "Jakob and Marja made a last desperate attempt to put things right by giving the girls the Ekerö house as a present. But it was already too late by then."

"How do you mean?" asked Fredrika, unconsciously holding her breath.

Elsie looked at her hands and gave a little twist to her wedding ring.

"He'd already lost Marja by then," she whispered. "She'd changed sides and started working with Ragnar Vinterman when he set up the new operation. But Jakob didn't find that out until much later. And by then he was already staring into the abyss that

Johanna and Viggo had spent so long getting ready for him."

The clock seemed to stop. And Fredrika waited.

"Viggo?" she echoed out loud.

"Johanna and our Viggo found each other on the quiet at about the same time as Jakob came up with the idea of restarting his old project. And that's why I'm here," said Elsie. "Because Sven would never be capable of giving Viggo away to you lot, in spite of all he's done to us and his brother."

But there were other reasons, too, and Fredrika knew it.

"And I came for Lina's sake," Elsie confirmed in a husky voice. "Because I think something dreadful's about to happen to that girl. You see, Viggo didn't get interested in Johanna until later. It was Karolina he really wanted. And he couldn't take it when she turned him down."

"She chose Måns in preference to Viggo?"

"Yes, and they both paid for it. Viggo did all he could to push Måns even further into addiction and break up the relationship. And he won, in the end. Viggo told tales to Måns' employer and he lost his job and had nothing to do but hang around at home all day. Viggo spread rumors about Måns, too, presenting him to his friends in a bad light.

Måns went downhill fast. Johanna had a hand in that, as well. Though her motive was really to get at Karolina rather than Måns."

"And then Viggo got together with Johanna, instead?"

"Yes, once it was all over between Karolina and Måns. But they kept the relationship very discreet. They presumably thought it best to, considering all they were planning together. Even Marja didn't know, although she was working with them on the refugee operation. They'd been together for several years before I realized they were a couple. And I didn't say a word to anyone except Sven. We decided their relationship wasn't really any of our business, and we'd just have to wait and see. I regret that now."

Fredrika hesitated over what had to come next.

"How would you describe the state of Johanna's mental health?"

"She's sick," said Elsie. "Utterly sick. Definitely not the sort of woman I'd want as a daughter-in-law."

"Have you had any contact with Karolina over the past few days?"

It was Elsie's turn to hesitate.

"She came to find me," she said. "Today. She was worried about Måns and wanted to make sure he was all right. I tried to get her to see reason and hand herself over to the police, but she said she had something important to do first. She said she had to face the person who had destroyed her before she could move on. I think I know where they might be."

"So do we," said Fredrika, and thought to herself: They deceived Jakob and Marja and lots of other people. The murder of Jakob and Marja was never a matter of dangerous secrets and people needing to be silenced. It was just a clever front for the real motive: personal vengeance.

The house lay dark and deserted as Karolina parked the hired car in the driveway. Without the slightest hesitation, she opened the car door and got out into the snow. She tramped as quickly as she could round the house and in through the basement door. A few moments later she was back out again and unlocked the front door on the other side of the house. A wave of memories overcame her as she stepped inside and closed the door behind her, still in the dark.

This was where the story had started, and this was where it would reach its conclusion.

First they had destroyed everything for her and Måns. Weakened him to a point where he could no longer be counted on, so any relationship with him became impossible. After that, they had carried on working through their plan, so methodically and purposefully that it had scared her witless.

She moved toward the living room. She stretched out an arm and ran her fingertips along all those dear photographs as she passed them. She was the one who had once helped her mother put them up.

Everything had started falling apart right back when she was a child; she realized that now.

But there were other things she could not make head or tail of, and she would demand answers from her sister about those, as soon as she turned up. Karolina crouched down by one of the big windows and scanned the darkness in front of the house. With all the lights off, she would be invisible to anybody trying to look in, but have a better view of the garden herself.

She kept a tight hold on the shotgun she had loaded in the basement, which was now resting in her lap. She was ready to meet her sister, any second now.

The flying squad minibus was having trouble gripping the slippery road surface, but the driver accelerated even so. Fredrika's call came through to Alex when they were about ten minutes from the house.

"Elsie's confirmed almost everything we thought, and told me more besides," she reported. "Hiding the migrants was a joint project of Viggo and Sven's from the word "go," but unlike Sven, Viggo carried on in Ragnar Vinterman's expanded operation. It was Viggo who took the Ljungs' car and reported it stolen so they'd be in the clear if there were suspicions it had been used to commit a crime."

"Well, I'll be —" began Alex.

"There's more," Fredrika broke in. "Elsie's sure that Viggo killed Jakob and Marja and that he and Johanna staged the whole thing. They've been together for several years, but they didn't let on to anybody. Oh, and it turns out it was Karolina who was raped at the holiday house, not Johanna."

Fredrika paused for breath as Alex tried to slot all this new information into the tragic framework. Two brothers, two sisters. Two disintegrating families, and strong individuals who broke loose and demanded redress.

"Could she tell you anything about Viggo's reasons for murdering his girlfriend's parents?" he asked briskly.

"Revenge," Fredrika said. "Viggo and Måns were with their parents on a surprise visit to Ekerö the evening Karolina was raped and heard all about it from Johanna. What nobody realized was that both boys were in love with the same girl, Karolina. To start with, it wasn't a problem because she didn't want either of them. But later on, when she'd left home to study, she got interested in Måns. In a crazy attempt to outdo the competition, Viggo located the man who raped Karolina, who turned out still to be in the country."

A gust of wind caught the minibus and tried to knock it off the road. Alex had to concentrate hard to hear what Fredrika was saying.

"His confrontation with the rapist ended very violently: Viggo was knifed in the face and fled. He's apparently had a terrible scar ever since."

"I thought it was a cleft-palate operation that had gone wrong," Alex said, bitterly recalling what Tony Svensson had said to Peder and Joar:

It's not somebody like me you're looking for . . . I haven't got a name . . . just a fucking ugly face.

"That was what everybody who met him later thought," Fredrika said eagerly. "And the family let them think it, because they were ashamed of the real reason for the scar. The incident was never reported to the police; Karolina's rapist had too many motives for keeping out of judicial hands."

"I don't suppose Karolina was very impressed by Viggo's bit of bravado?" Alex guessed.

"No, she wasn't, and that seems to have been one of the things that pushed him into helping Johanna with her plan. He never forgave Karolina's family, or his own, for condemning what he'd done. Johanna was part of the Vinterman network as well, and she got her mother to join, too, because Marja had strong objections to her husband's idea of starting up his voluntary work again. She felt the refugees had cost her so much personally that she never wanted to help them for free again. Ragnar tempted her with money and I'm sure Johanna had some strong arguments, too."

Fredrika swallowed.

"Lots of people were damaged for life that midsummer eve."

"And Elsie and Sven knew this all along," Alex said dully.

"We have to understand them," Fredrika said. "They've been fearing for their own lives since they found Jakob and Marja. The only thing they dared give us was their conviction that Jakob hadn't done it himself. They hoped we'd find out the rest."

Alex paused.

"Good God, what a betrayal on Marja's part," he said in a voice that Fredrika had never heard him use before.

"I don't think so, Alex," she said. "I'm sure Johanna convinced her mother there was no risk in the project. Maybe she played on her feelings of guilt about the past, too."

"And when she realized the full ghastliness of it . . ."

". . . it was too late. But she tried anyway. We know she sent those threats to Jakob, and I think we can assume she sent them with the best of intentions. She was trying to save what could still be saved."

Alex stared out of the minibus window at the whirling snow. He thought ahead to the Ekerö house, where the sisters must be gearing up for their final battle.

"She could have done more," he said sternly. "Then maybe she and Jakob would still be alive today."

"But they might not. She was a pawn in Johanna's game, and *she* presumably wanted nothing better than to see her parents dead. She was just waiting for the right opportunity."

Initially Karolina could not be sure if it was her sister walking up the road toward the house. She leaned up against the window, pressing her forehead to the cold glass to try to see better. When the figure turned in at the driveway, Karolina's heart missed a beat. It really was her sister.

She did not slow her steps as she walked — almost strode — very upright, with her long hair hanging loose down the back of her coat, across the garden and up the steps to the front door. Then Karolina heard her pause, and saw the door handle slowly press down. The door opened and Johanna stepped inside, tall and slender and covered in snow. As if she had known all along that Karolina was crouched on the floor by the big window, she slowly turned toward her.

The bright ceiling light went on as Johanna flicked the switch on the wall.

"Sitting here in the dark?" she said, observing her sister and the gun.

Karolina leaped to her feet, raising the weapon.

"I need to know why," she said grimly, clutching the gun in her chilled hands.

Not once on all those hunting trips with her father had she ever dreamed she would have to use her skills to defend her own life one day. Against her own sister.

"Betrayal."

Karolina shook her head.

"You're sick. You've had your whole family wiped out and you have the gall to say you're the one who feels betrayed."

Her sister's face twitched.

"I did everything for you after that god-damn midsummer's eve," she hissed. "*Everything.* I even had the daisy tattoo done as an everlasting reminder of what you'd been through. And what did you do? Turned your back on me and turned Dad against me."

Karolina felt the tears prick her eyes.

"You've never done anything for anyone but yourself, Johanna. And you turned Dad against you yourself."

"You're lying," Johanna yelled with such force that Karolina flinched. "Just like the lie that you didn't care about Måns or Viggo."

"We were so young," whispered Karolina impotently. "How can you still be blaming me for that?"

"Viggo tried to take revenge for your sake," Johanna went on loudly. "And you thanked him by choosing his brother instead."

Mention of Viggo frightened Karolina. She had not realized he was mixed up in all that happened, but of course he must be. Bit by bit the truth dawned on her, and she felt her strength draining away as the picture became clear.

"So now you understand," Johanna said gently. "I must say you impress me, Lina.

You not only extricated yourself from that unpleasant state of affairs in Thailand, you also managed to get back to Sweden and find out the truth."

"Måns," whispered Karolina.

"Quite right." Johanna smiled. "It was stupid of you — very stupid, in fact — not to realize who Måns would turn to when you rang and asked him for help. We were one step ahead of you the whole way. I wanted you for once in your life to experience what it was like for me, invisible to everything and everyone."

"But you never were invisible," protested Karolina. "You were the one everybody could see. Good grief, I spent half my childhood hearing that I ought to be more like you."

The air inside the house felt thick in the throat. Johanna was standing stock-still, but for a repeated clenching and opening of her fists. She was seething with rage.

"That's exactly it. *Half* your childhood. Then things got better, didn't they? But not for me. Nor for Viggo."

Fear and fatigue made Karolina start to cry.

"I thought this was all about that wretched new network of smugglers," she said through her tears, the gun shaking in her hands. "Drawing Mum into all this. How could you?"

Johanna's face darkened still further at the sight of her sister's tears.

"I never intended forgiving any of you. *Not ever.* Believe me, everything that's happened was going to happen sooner or later anyway. But when our fool of a father kept on sticking his nose in things that were none of his business, I have to admit it got more urgent than we'd originally planned. And it was so easy to pull the wool over Mum's eyes, it was almost pathetic. She was completely convinced that only Dad was in danger."

The room closed in as Johanna spoke. Johanna, who had both her parents murdered without feeling the slightest remorse. Karolina still could not quite accept how deranged her sister must be. Her desire for explanation was still not satisfied.

"I read all about it in the papers," Karolina said. "And talked to Elsie. Between you all, you've murdered so many people."

Johanna put her head on one side.

"I do admit that more lives have been lost than we first calculated, but when people can't stick to the simple rules of the game, it's hard to be accountable for their actions. We expressly told them they weren't to let on to anyone that they were going to Sweden, yet several of them still did precisely that. So we couldn't send them home again."

"We? You and Viggo, you mean?"

Johanna sneered, but said nothing.

"What were you thinking?" said Karolina. "That Mum and Dad would die and I'd rot in jail in Thailand?"

"I think you deserve a confession after putting us to such trouble," Johanna said in a businesslike tone. "We had hoped you'd be back home before we tackled Mum and Dad's activities. But then we realized you'd sniffed out one of our most vital collaborators in Bangkok, and we had to take action."

"Just so you know, I didn't realize how close I'd got."

"No, but that doesn't really change anything, does it? You had to be dealt with on the spot, we decided that straightaway. A challenge for us all, but a bit of imagination finds a solution to most things here in life. It was a piece of cake to shut down your email accounts, since you'd usefully provided Dad with your password and user name. Just think, he kept them in a notebook on his desk. So easy I was almost disappointed. And we had all the contacts we needed to make stuff happen in

Bangkok. The mugging, shifting your gear to another hotel, putting the drugs in your room, tipping off the police so they mounted the raid."

Johanna stopped for a moment.

"Everything has its price," she said. "No one can do what you lot did to me without paying for it."

Its price. Words piled up in Karolina's head, but in the wrong order. She thought about Viggo again. Viggo, who had got into her parents' flat, raised a gun, and shot them in the head. At what point had they realized they were going to die? Did they ever get time to realize why?

"Why didn't you tell us you were a couple?" Karolina asked feebly. "You and Viggo."

A hollow laugh echoed round the room.

"What was there to tell, Lina? That I'd picked up the pieces you didn't want? You and I have scarcely seen each other for years, so why should I confide in you?"

There was nothing to say, nothing to add. It was all over, and this was the end. *Everything has its price.* So Karolina abandoned the topic, and asked, "Where is he now? Is he waiting for you somewhere?"

"He's in the garden," Johanna answered in such a cool voice that Karolina had to take her eyes off her and turn her head to the big window at the front of the house.

And she saw his outline, out there in the falling snow. The man who had once loved her so much that he had committed a crime to take revenge for an injustice she had long since put behind her.

"You're never going to get away with this, the pair of you. You've deceived too many people, forced them into a chain of murders I refuse to believe they wanted to be part of."

"It's very touching that the last thing you do in your life is to worry about how I'm going to get out of this awkward situation," Johanna said.

If the light had not been on in the room, she would have seen what he had in his hands and possibly been the first to shoot. But in the event it was Viggo, surrounded by swirling snow and standing a few meters from the house with one of her father's shotguns raised to his shoulder, who fired the first shot. The weight of her sorrow was the last thing she felt.

The police were very close to the house when the shot rang out. It reverberated dully among the snow-laden trees and sent the adrenaline pumping round the officers' blood.

Damn, thought Alex, sensing Joar's eyes on him.

The vehicles braked to a halt in the snow, the doors were wrenched open, and the cold air streamed in. The squad left the minibus first and took up their positions round the house. Over the radio the detectives heard one of them say there appeared to be two people standing talking inside the house. Neither of them came out when the police ordered them to do so.

Alex peered up toward the house with a growing sense of anticipation. That horrendous holiday home, cradle of so much unhappiness and tragedy. Unspoken tensions mingled with the cold evening air. Alex blinked and knew everyone else was thinking the same thing. If there were two people visible through the window, was there a third, the victim of the shot they had all heard?

Johanna looked at her sister's limp body. A pool of blood was slowly spreading out beneath her. Johanna reached out a hand and switched off the light.

"Thank you," she said to Viggo, stroking his arm.

He stood numbly beside her.

"It was the only right thing to do," Johanna said in a low voice. "And you know it."

She followed his look out of the window, to the flashing lights of the police vehicles and dark figures moving across the snow.

"We won't get anywhere," he said.

She looked unsure, but not for long.

"Well, we've nowhere to go, anyway."

Slowly he turned toward her.

"So what shall we do?"

"We'll do what has to be done."

She slowly bent down and picked up the gun that Viggo had put aside. Blinded by his own naïveté and the belief that in Johanna he had found a woman who loved him, he did not react when she pointed the barrel of the gun in his direction.

"You never loved me as much as you did her," Johanna said in an empty voice as she pulled the trigger and shot him in the chest.

For a single second she stood still, staring at the wounded body. She did not care what happened now; she had achieved her goal. Wearily she tossed down the weapon and made herself run out onto the front steps in full view of the silent police officers:

"Help me," she screamed. "Please help me! He shot my sister!"

■ ■ ■ ■

Ragnar Vinterman realized the game was up several hours before the police rang at his door. He felt nothing but relief when it came down to it. So much had gone so completely and utterly wrong. People had had to pay with their lives for his, and other people's, greed.

The truth of the matter was that at heart, Ragnar shared Jakob Ahlbin's innocent view of the group of people known as refugees, who found their way to Sweden. He had most certainly not felt he was exploiting people in real need when he first provided them with food and lodging for payment, or when he got the idea of expanding his venture into people smuggling. Initially, nothing could have been further from his mind. Everybody could pay the price he was asking, after all. It ought not to be a problem for any of the parties involved.

But then Sven put his foot down and refused to continue the collaboration. At that point, Ragnar started to feel the first hint of doubt. Unlike Jakob, Sven could not be dismissed as emotional or irrational. Sven was a solid sort of person, but forced into criminal activity so he could provide the huge sums of money being milked out of him by his son. But he did not lack a sense of basic judgment, and that was what made Ragnar so unsure when Sven openly declared he had had enough.

The problem was Marja and Johanna. Ragnar had wondered, certainly, how two women in Jakob's own family had come to move so far from the fundamental values the family had once all shared. But if *they* saw nothing to object to in the operation, why should Ragnar?

Just once, he had tried to discuss the matter with Marja, but she seemed troubled and embarrassed by his overture and evaded his questions. Her only proviso was that Jakob must not on any account find out what was going on. And he did not, until one of the handpicked refugees Johanna called daisies broke the cardinal rule, and told a friend how he got to Sweden.

That was when we lost our grip, Ragnar thought hopelessly. That was when we turned into murderers.

The scheme was only in action for six months. It had been easy to create a network for generating money from hiding refugees, but harder to build up structures for bringing people to Sweden illegally, making them commit complex crimes, and then sending them home again. In actual fact they only sent three people back before they came to the conclusion they would have to dispose of the daisies some other way. People talked too much, it was as simple as that. And talk generated rumors, and that was not acceptable.

He would never forget that evening when, about to retire to bed, he heard on the radio that a couple had been shot in their home at Odenplan. He had carried on hoping to the very last that it would not need to go that far. That Jakob would see reason. But as usual, Jakob did not allow himself to be frightened into silence, and then there was only one way it could end. And Marja . . . Johanna insisted she had to be taken out of the equation, too, because she would never keep quiet if they had Jakob killed.

It would never fade, the memory of Johanna's impassive face as she informed him they could leave the silencing of her parents to her. Nor did Ragnar think he would get an answer to the question that was causing his clergyman's heart such torment: what must be missing from a person for them to be capable of killing their own maker?

Then the bell rang and Ragnar went to open the door. The police would demand the names of the others involved in his operation. The woman who knew the document forger, the man who spoke Arabic, all those people making a living smuggling refugees.

I shall give them everything, Ragnar decided. Because I have nothing more to hide.

He opened the door without saying a word and handed himself over to the police without demur. And the parish had lost yet another of its faithful servants.

The next call came just as Fredrika was about to go home. It was past nine o'clock, and Alex had rung in a final report that sounded so crazy she could hardly take it in. Johanna Ahlbin had handed herself over to the police, claiming to have shot Viggo in self-defense after he murdered Karolina. According to the doctors, Viggo was dead but Karolina would probably pull through.

"We're eagerly awaiting her statement," Alex said sarcastically, and urged Fredrika to go home.

But Fredrika didn't. First she sorted and filed away all her paperwork, then she realized someone ought to ring Peder and let him know how events had played out. He seemed cheerful.

"We're just having dinner," he said. "My

brother's here, too."

She thought he sounded in good spirits. Or possibly a touch embarrassed. Either way, she was glad for him. It would be a good thing for all concerned if Peder got his priorities in life sorted out.

The wind had dropped and it had briefly stopped snowing as she pulled on her coat to walk home. Her mobile rang and she saw it was another call from Spencer's home number, which she answered as she put on her hat with the other hand.

Strange he's not using his mobile, she thought.

"Is that Fredrika Bergman?" said an unfamiliar female voice.

Taken aback at the realization of who she must be talking to, Fredrika stopped dead in the deserted corridor.

"Yes," she said finally.

"This is Eva Lagergren. I'm Spencer's wife."

Fredrika had worked that out already, but somehow it was still such a shock that she had to sit down. She sank slowly to the floor. Then Eva Lagergren said the words that nobody wants to hear: "I'm afraid I've got bad news."

Fredrika held her breath.

"Spencer's been involved in a car crash.

He's in hospital in Lund."

No, no, no. Anything but this.

Misery hit her like a punch in the stomach, and she had to lean forward and clutch her belly.

Deep breaths. In, out.

"How is he?"

Her voice was scarcely a whisper.

She heard the other woman's intake of breath.

"They say he's critical but stable."

Eva seemed to be hesitating, and it sounded as if she was crying when she went on: "It would be good if you could get there this evening. He's sure to want you there when he wakes up."

Alex had a strangely festive feeling as he drove back into the city. His body felt far too wired for him to want to go straight home from Ekerö, so he went to HQ to write his report and wind down. Fredrika must have called it a night; her light was off and her coat had gone.

Alex was still feeling quite upbeat as he turned into the drive of his house in Vaxholm. Then it struck him that he and Lena were meant to be having a talk that evening, and he hadn't even rung to tell her he would be very late.

He glanced at his watch. It was after one in the morning. The chances of Lena still being awake were minimal.

So he was very surprised to find her sitting in an armchair in the living room. He could see she had been crying, and it also struck him that she had lost weight. A great deal of weight, what was more. Then fear washed through him like physical pain. It was as if he was seeing his wife properly for the first time in several weeks. Thin, pale, and without luster.

I've missed something crucial, something dreadful.

"Sorry," he mumbled, and sat down on the sofa, facing her.

She shook her head.

"I rang the switchboard and they told me what was happening. Did it go all right?"

The question made him want to laugh.

"Depends what you mean by all right," he muttered. "But basically no, it didn't go all right. Not at any level, in fact. The special group's future looks shaky, to say the least."

Lena shifted uneasily in her seat, grimacing as if it hurt to move.

"There's something I've got to tell you," she said in a choked voice. "Something I've known for a while, but . . . I just couldn't say anything. Not until I knew for sure."

He frowned, feeling his anxiety turn to panic.

"Knew what for sure?"

What was it that she couldn't even tell her very best friend? Because he knew he was, just as she was his. That was what lay at the core of their long, secure marriage. Their relationship was founded on friendship.

Guilt cut his soul like a knife. She wasn't the one who had forgotten it; he was.

I've spent so bloody long chasing ghosts that I lost my senses, he thought hopelessly.

And even before she started speaking, he knew that what she was going to say would change everything and rob him of any chance of making up for his grotesque mistake.

"I'm going to have to leave you," she sobbed. "You and the children. I'm ill, Alex. They say there's nothing they can do."

Alex stared at her, blank-eyed. As the consequences of what she had just said sank in, he knew with utter clarity that for the first time he was facing a situation he would never be able to accept. Still less learn to live with.

They fell asleep with their arms around each other. It was late. The house was dark and silent, and outside, the snow had stopped falling. That was the last of that winter's snow, except for a few showers in April.

And by the time autumn came, it was all over.

■ ■ ■ ■

Autumn 2008

■ ■ ■ ■

The compassionate detective inspector

"Did you have a good summer, Peder?"

Peder Rydh reflected.

"Yes, thanks. It was great, actually."

"Do anything in particular?"

Peder's face lit up.

"We had a motoring holiday in Italy. With our little boys and my brother, Jimmy. Totally crazy, but unforgettable."

"So you and Ylva are together again now?"

"Yes. I've sold my flat and moved back home."

"And that feels good?"

"Very good."

There was a pause.

"We met a couple of times before your summer break, and I seem to recall you were a bit negative about our sessions to start with."

Peder squirmed.

"My experience of psychologists has been pretty mixed. I didn't know what to expect."

"Ah, I see. And now what do you think?"

Peder hesitated for a moment, but then decided there was no reason to lie.

"It's been good for me," he said simply. "I've realized a few things."

"Things you weren't aware of before, you mean?"

He nodded.

"There was a lot of friction last winter between you and one of your colleagues, Joar. How are things now?"

"Under control. I couldn't care less about him."

"Really? But you have to work together, don't you?"

"No, he was transferred back to the Environmental Crime Agency. Or maybe he asked to go, I don't know."

"So that only leaves you and Alex Recht?"

Sadness made Peder's eyes fill up.

"Er, it's just me and a temporary substitute at the moment. Nothing's been decided for definite, you could say. Alex is on leave for a few weeks."

His voice petered out.

"I wanted to see you to follow up on how you were, Peder. And to ask you a few last questions."

Peder waited.

"What's the very worst thing that could

happen to you today?"

"Today?"

"Today."

Peder pondered.

"Don't think so much, say something spontaneous."

"Losing Ylva, that would definitely be the worst thing."

"And the boys?"

"I don't want to lose them, either."

"But it wasn't them who came spontaneously to mind when I asked."

"No, it wasn't. But that doesn't mean I don't love them. Just that I love them in a different way."

"Try to explain."

Peder took a deep breath.

"I can't. I just know that's how it is. If I woke up tomorrow and Ylva wasn't there, I wouldn't be able to carry on. I just wouldn't be able to cope with what Alex is going through at the moment."

Peder ran out of words. Ylva had given him a fresh chance. Now it was up to him to make the most of it.

BAGHDAD, IRAQ

Farah Hajib had already accepted that the man she loved was dead and would never come back, when a gray-haired, Western-looking man turned up at her front door.

He spoke no Arabic at all, and the English she had learned at school was not enough for her to make out what he was saying. So she signed to him to go with her to the house next door where her cousin lived, because he was good at English and had worked as an interpreter for the American forces.

Guests from the West were still a rarity in Baghdad. Those who did come were nearly all journalists or from one of the diplomatic missions bold enough to maintain a permanent presence in the area. But Farah could see straightaway that her guest was of another kind. He had a different sort of physical fitness and his eyes were constantly scouring his surroundings for danger or things worth observing.

Police, she guessed. Or the military. Not American, but perhaps German.

But it was not the man's behavior Farah would remember. It was the boundless sorrow and pain she thought she could see in his eyes. A sorrow so deep she could hardly look at him. She decided her guest was too strange to be bringing any sort of good news. It would be a short visit to her cousin.

"There's something he wants to give you," her cousin said after a few minutes' conversation with the man.

"Me?" she echoed in astonishment.

Her cousin nodded.

"But I don't know him."

"He says he comes from Sweden and works for the police. But he's on leave at the moment. He says he investigated your fiancé's death last spring."

The words took Farah's breath away and she looked at the older man's grief-stricken face.

"He says he's afraid he can't stay long because there's someone else he has to see before he goes home. Another woman who lost her husband last spring. His name was Ali."

Just then, her cousin's wife came out of the kitchen, curious to see who this guest in their house was.

The stranger gave her a cautious nod and said something to Farah's cousin.

"He congratulates you on the baby you're expecting," the cousin said to his very pregnant wife. "One of his close colleagues had a baby a few weeks ago and he's going to be a grandfather by Christmas himself."

Farah gave a melancholy smile, still at a loss as to why this man had come to see her out of the blue.

The he quietly put his hand in his pocket and took out a tiny object.

Her fiancé's engagement ring.

Without even thanking him, she took the ring and looked at it until the memories that it evoked overwhelmed her and her tears began to flow. When she looked up at the man who said he was a Swedish police officer, she saw he was crying, too.

"It was his wife's suggestion that he should come here and give you the ring," the cousin explained in a mumble, troubled by the guest's tears.

"You must thank her and send my greetings," Farah said stiffly.

She could almost have sworn that the stranger was smiling through his tears.

ACKNOWLEDGMENTS

Daring to say thank you is important. At least it is for me. In thanking someone, you are acknowledging that they had a hand in your work. That you did not do it all by yourself. And should — in fact — not try to do it all by yourself.

Writing a book is really like baking a very complicated kind of cake. As you struggle with the mixture and the meringue and the icing, you need extra pairs of hands. And you need time and energy, motivation and patience.

I find it easy to write. The words come of their own accord; there's no need to force or coax them out. But sadly that is no guarantee that they will be perfect. I see it the minute I print the text out from the computer; I can tell where the story isn't holding together. And I wrestle with all those letters and words, trying to force them to lie in the right way. Sometimes it works.

But sometimes it doesn't work at all.

First of all, a warm thank you to everyone at my Swedish publishing house, the fantastic Piratförlaget! *Sofi, Anna, Jenny, Cherie, Madeleine, Ann-Marie, Lasse, Mattias, Lottis, Anna Carin,* and *Jonna* — where would I be without your energy and constant encouragement? Particular thanks to my publisher, *Sofia,* who carries on constructing a framework to keep the way ahead open, and makes me believe I can write any number of books. And to my editor, *Anna,* who always, always (and that repetition was deliberate, Anna) has the stamina to go on even when I don't, and is the raising agent in the part of the cake mixture that's called editing.

Many thanks, too, to everyone at the ultracompetent Salomonsson Agency — *Niclas, Leyla, Tor, Catherine,* and *Szilvia* — who have secured enormous success abroad since the start of our collaboration in May 2009. I'm proud to be represented by you!

Thanks to all the friends and colleagues who are following my journey through the book world step by step, almost as if I were a rock star and not a writer. It's wonderful the way you don't just read my books but even get me to sign them when you've bought them as presents for other people.

Thanks to *Malena* and *Mats,* who provide me with time.

Thanks to *Sven-Ake,* who continues to support me when my own knowledge of police work runs dry.

Thanks to the sales staff at Walter Borgs Jaktbutik, who helped me select the perfect murder weapon.

Thanks to designer *Nina Leino,* who makes my books look so incredibly smart.

Thanks to *Sofia Ekholm,* who continues to occupy a special place in my writing. There's soon going to be a new typescript to read through — I hope you have the time and the appetite!

And thanks to my family, who take such unconditional delight in my successes and travel the length and breadth of the country to be there when I'm talking about my book or kicking my heels behind the signing desk in some bookshop or other.

Thank you.

Kristina Ohlsson
Baghdad, Spring 2010

ABOUT THE AUTHOR

Kristina Ohlsson is originally from Kristianstad in southern Sweden. She is a Counter-Terrorism Officer at OSCE (the Organization for Security and Co-operation in Europe). *Unwanted* and *The Daisy* are the first two installments in her crime series featuring Fredrika Bergman. She currently lives in Vienna, Austria.

The employees of Thorndike Press hope you have enjoyed this Large Print book. All our Thorndike, Wheeler, and Kennebec Large Print titles are designed for easy reading, and all our books are made to last. Other Thorndike Press Large Print books are available at your library, through selected bookstores, or directly from us.

For information about titles, please call:
  (800) 223-1244

or visit our Web site at:
  http://gale.cengage.com/thorndike

To share your comments, please write:
  Publisher
  Thorndike Press
  10 Water St., Suite 310
  Waterville, ME 04901